ZED ESSENTIAL FEMINISTS

Zed Essential Feminists is an ambitious series of readers presenting the major work of some of the world's most significant feminist thinkers in individual volumes. Oriented around the understanding that feminist voices continue to make some of the most important critical interventions in progressive political debates around the world, the series celebrates the power of these voices and gathers together important work often unavailable elsewhere.

Zed Essential Feminists sets itself against the common assertion that we are living in a post-feminist era in which the major battles of the late-twentieth-century women's movement have ceased to be relevant. Each volume offers the reader a comprehensive selection of writings that will both introduce and provide a complete and essential reference to an essential feminist voice.

ABOUT THE EDITOR

Adele Newson-Horst is a professor of English at Missouri State University. She earned her B.A. degree at Spelman College, an M.A. at Eastern Michigan University, and a Ph.D. at Michigan State University. Her most recent publications and research focus on Nawal El Saadawi; *The Dramatic Literature of Nawal El Saadawi* was published by Saqi Books in 2009.

The Essential Nawal El Saadawi

A Reader

EDITED BY ADELE NEWSON-HORST

Zed Books

LONDON & NEW YORK

The Essential Nawal El Saadawi: A Reader was first published in 2010 by
Zed Books Ltd, 7 Cynthia Street, London N1 9JF, UK and
Room 400, 175 Fifth Avenue, New York, NY 10010, USA

www.zedbooks.co.uk

Editorial Copyright © Adele Newson-Horst
Copyright in this Collection © Nawal El Saadawi

The right of Adele Newson-Horst to be identified as editor
of this work has been asserted by her in accordance with
the Copyright, Designs and Patents Act 1988.

FSC
www.fsc.org
MIX
Paper from
responsible sources
FSC® C013604

Typeset in Monotype Bulmer by illuminati, Grosmont
Cover designed by Lucy Morton at illuminati
Index by John Barker
Printed and bound in Great Britain by
CPI Antony Rowe, Chippenham and Eastbourne

Distributed in the USA exclusively by Palgrave Macmillan, a division of
St Martin's Press, LLC, 175 Fifth Avenue, New York, NY 10010, USA

A catalogue record for this book is available from the British Library
Library of Congress Cataloging in Publication Data available

ISBN 978 1 84813 334 1 Hb
ISBN 978 1 84813 335 8 Pb
ISBN 978 1 84813 336 5 Eb

Contents

About Nawal El Saadawi

NAWAL EL SAADAWI is a renowned Egyptian writer, novelist and fighter for the rights of women and the working poor. She started writing in 1944 when she was 13 years old. She has published over forty books, reprinted and reissued in Arabic, and is widely read in her country and all Arab countries. She has achieved widespread international recognition after the translation of her work into over thirty languages. *The Hidden Face of Eve* was her first book to be translated to English by her husband Sherif Hetata, and was published by Zed Books in 1980.

Nawal El Saadawi was born in Kafr Tahla, a small village by the Nile north of Cairo. She graduated from the University of Cairo Medical College in 1955, specializing in psychiatry. She practised as a medical doctor, both at the university and in Kafr Tahla.

From 1963 until 1972, Saadawi worked as director general for public health education in the Ministry of Health. In 1972 she lost her job in the Egyptian government because of her book *Women and Sex* (1972), which was subsequently banned. In this book she linked health to economics, to politics, to religion, to history, to sexuality and to culture. She was the first medical doctor to fight against the cutting of children under religious–cultural slogans. Her books were censored in Egypt and she had to publish in Lebanon. Her most famous novel, *Woman at Point Zero*, was published in Beirut in 1973. It was followed in 1976 by *God Dies by the Nile* and in 1977 by *The Hidden Face of Eve: Women in the Arab World.*

In 1981 Nawal El Saadawi publicly criticized President Anwar Sadat's policies and was arrested and imprisoned. She was released one month after his assassination. In 1982, she established the Arab Women's Solidarity Association (AWSA). The Egyptian Branch of AWSA was outlawed in 1991 by the government. Her name appeared on a fundamentalist death list, after she published her novel *The Fall of the Iman* in Cairo in 1987. She was obliged to leave her country, teaching at Duke University in Durham, and Washington State University in Seattle. She returned to Egypt in 1997 to continue writing and organizing women. In 2004 she stood as a candidate in the presidential elections in Egypt, but was forced to withdraw her candidacy in the face of government persecution. She declared that her move was symbolic, to expose the lack of democracy.

In 2001 a court case was raised against Saadawi, accusing her of apostasy and demanding her divorce by force from her husband. She won the case with the support of human rights organizations in Egypt and internationally. She won other court cases against her and her daughter Dr Mona Helmy, a poet and a writer living in Egypt, through increasing support inside and outside of their country, the last of which, in 2008, demanded the withdrawal of her Egyptian nationality after her play *God Resigns at the Summit Meeting* was published by Madbouli in Cairo in 2007.

Nawal El Saadawi holds more than ten honorary doctorates. Her many awards include the Great Minds of the Twentieth Century Prize awarded by the American Biographical Institute in 2003, the North–South Prize from the Council of Europe and the Premi Internacional Catalunya in 2004. Most recently she was the 2007 recipient in the USA of the African Literature Association's Fonlon–Nichols Award, which is given annually to an African writer for excellence in creative writing and for contributions to the struggles for human rights and freedom of expression. Her books are taught in universities across the world.

Nawal El Saadawi now works as a writer, psychiatrist and activist. Her most recent novel is *Zina, The Stolen Novel* (2008).

Timeline

1931   Born in Kafr Tahla, Egypt, on 27 October

1937   Forced to undergo a traditional clitoridectomy

1946   Demonstrated against the British occupation of Egypt

1955   Graduated from the University of Cairo with a degree in Psychiatry

1955   Married fellow physician Ahmed Helmy

1955   Daughter Mona Helmy born

1956   Divorced Ahmed Helmy

1957   Earliest writings published: *I Learned Love*, a collection of short stories

1958–72   Worked as director general of public health in the Ministry of Health

1958   *Memories of a Woman Doctor* first published, her debut as a novelist

1964   Married Sherif Hetata, a physician and novelist

1964   Son Atef Hetata born

1966   Received Master of Public Health degree from Columbia University

1968–72   Editor of *Medical Association Magazine*

1968–73   Co-founder, Arab Association for Human Rights

1972   Published her first work of non-fiction, *Women and Sex*

1972   Dismissed from her post as director general of public Health for writing *Women and Sex*

1973–78   Served as writer at the High Institute of Literature and Science

1973–76   Worked on researching women and neurosis in the Ain Shams University's Faculty of Medicine

1974   Received the High Council for Literature Award

1979–80   Served as the United Nations Adviser for the Women's Program in Africa and the Middle East

1981   Founded the Arab Women's Solidarity Association (AWSA)

1981   Imprisoned for two months in Qanatir Women's Prison after she criticized President Anwar Sadat's one-party rule

1982   Founder of *Noon Magazine*

1982   Received the Literary Franco-Arab Friendship Award

1983–87   Founder vice-president, African Association for Women on Research Development, Dakar, Senegal

1988   Received the Literary Award of Gubran

1988–93   Name appeared on death lists issued by fanatical organizations

1989   Received the First Degree Decoration of the Republic of Libya

1989–91   Editor of *Health Magazine*

1991   AWSA banned after criticizing US involvement in the first Gulf War

2001   Sued by a fundamentalist Islamic group to annul her marriage to Hetata on the grounds that her heresy was causing harm to his soul

2004   Received the North–South Prize from the Council of Europe

2004   Presented her name as a candidate for the presidential election

2007   Received the Fonlon–Nichols Award from the African Literature Association

Preface

WE ARE IN 2008.

I am walking in a strange street in a strange place, maybe any city I lived in for a few days or for many years, in different continents, different countries and different times. Time is changing like place, a day may look like a year, and a year may pass like a day; the past may be the present or the future, and the present may be all that we have. Time may go backward, and I am a child of seven in my little village by the Nile. I hear people in my village say, 'I am seven years old and should stop playing with children. I am a wise old woman at the age of ten, ready for marriage.'

Today, I hear people say I am seventy-seven years old. The words 'seventy-seven' sound like nothing, like thin air in a dream. They say I am from Egypt. I cannot remember the place or the time. Place and time are inseparable and can be demolished and reconstructed like a monument of stone, like life and death, God and the Devil, dreams and reality.

The word 'Egypt' sounds so strange, so familiar, like my face in the mirror. People say my mother gave birth to me in Egypt. My mother was called Zaynab. Her name shakes me, makes me cry; my whole being aches. Was it the womb of my mother or the womb of my dead grandfather? Or the womb of The Male God who gave birth to Adam? I saw the face of my mother last night in a dream.

She was sad, so sad, so remote, far away. I could not touch her; I could not remember her name. I said to myself in the dream, she has been dead since 1958. Half a century has passed since she disappeared; she was only forty-five years old when she died. I am seventy-seven? Thirty-two years older than my dead mother, yet I am still alive? Amazing.

I decided after I was born, when I saw the sad face of my mother, that I would never live her life. I never dreamt of El Saadawi, the father of my father. El Saadawi is the strange name of a strange man who died more than ten years before I was born. He died of sexual exhaustion, they said. Nobody knew how many women he fertilized; this was his right, given to him by his God as a man born from a sacred male womb. I did not see a picture of El Saadawi. He died before his village knew anything about photographs. I cannot imagine his face in my dreams except as a little male organ. My grandmother, his wife, told people that his organ was very small relative to other men. How did she know about other men? I heard her saying that he compensated for his inferiority complex by penetrating any hole in a body or in a wall.

I cannot imagine that the name of this hyper-sexual man is printed on all my books, all my papers, including my Egyptian passport. They call it my ID. Wherever I travel they ask me about my ID. In May 2008 I won the case in Cairo Court of Maglis Al Dawla, and my ID was not withdrawn from me. I was accused of criticizing the Divine in my play *God Resigns at the Summit Meeting.* To criticize God is equal to criticizing His Majesty the President of the State or the Pharaoh. The punishment ranges from death to being deprived of Egyptian ID or nationality. No country allows me to move on its soil without seeing my ID. This little piece of paper is more important to the whole world than to me, and yet who am I without this paper carrying the dead name of El Saadawi and the face of the sacred Eagle, the stamp of the state?

I hate my name El Saadawi. I am happy to shed it after death, since dead people carry the name of their mothers in the hereafter. God is the only one who knows the truth, or the real father. All or most people live with their fake fathers until death. But women, after being mothers, should be virgins again like the Virgin Mary. In paradise, my hymen will be repaired to become a virgin again. Male believers living in paradise will rape me every night but God will repair my hymen the next day. This will go on for eternity since I live in paradise. Maybe hell is better. My grandfather El Saadawi will not be my real grandfather after I die. He will not be the father of my father. The mother of my father Sitti El Hajja, Mabrouka, my peasant grandmother, was not so stupid as to be faithful to the unfaithful...

Place and time change with age and more knowledge. A home may become prison or exile or grave. I am more free when I am homeless, familyless, identityless, nameless, creedless, classless, raceless and genderless. To gain knowledge is to gain my real ID, but knowledge has become a sin since the appearance of the Old Testament. The God of Ibrahim cannot dominate people unless they are ignorant.

What is your home? Is it a place and time and regime that betray you? Does it make you a slave to God and King or President? Separation between religion and state did not happen in any part of our world: West or East. In a recent interview with Barack Obama and John McCain, the first question asked concerned their faith. The USA is a Christian state, no less religious than the Jewish state in Israel, or the Islamic state in Iran or Saudi Arabia. The mask of secularism may differ in thickness, may be less visible, but religion is always there, hidden under hallowed big beautiful words.

No one can be elected president in the USA unless he declares his Christianity, unless he flatters the American Church and the Jewish state in Israel. And this is called Democracy or Free Elections, like the Free Market, the freedom of deception and exploitation. When the American president betrays his wife he goes to church to cleanse his sexual sin. His God forgives him and the American Constitution does not punish him. But if he betrays his country he is punished by his God and his Constitution. God and state are inseparable. Neither cares about the rights of the wife. To betray your wife is not a sin in the American Constitution or in any other constitution, West or East. You can be a sexual traitor but faithful to your state or party. You have to distinguish between your political activities and the activities of your male organ.

The American president can hold the Bible in one hand and declare war against Iraq or any country in the other hand. He can say 'God Bless America' while bombing peaceful civilians just to get their oil or diamonds. God wins the war for the USA and Israel all the time. Because He is their God, not the God of the terrorist Muslims. He is the God of the Bible who gave the Promised Land to His Chosen People. You can kill a whole nation in the name of your God then win the Nobel Prize for Peace.

Item Two in the Egyptian Constitution says that the only source of the constitution is the Divine Law (Shari'a Law). Under this law men have sexual and social freedoms, not given to their wives. No law in Egypt follows Shari'a Law except the Marriage Law. Women should be always under the control of God and the state. I was considered a traitor to the state because I wrote a play exposing divine and state contradictions. In fact, it was the state which betrayed me by hiding these contradictions from me, by giving me false knowledge in schools, and brainwashing me with the immoral marriage code derived from Divine Law. God gives men the right to betray their wives. Women should be faithful to their husbands or God will burn them in hellfire.

Time is slow in this place; I walk slowly in time and space. Without me walking in time and space, there is no time. There is no home, just a dead memory of the past. Now I remember the name of this city, Atlanta, in the south of North America. I came here to teach the unteachable: Creativity and Dissidence. In fact, I hate teachers. All I can do for my students is to undo what teachers did to them. I tell them that how we think is more important that what we think. I tell them to write about the most shameful moment in their childhood, the most fearful moment. When shame is no longer shame and fear is no longer fear, creativity starts. Creativity transcends the artist's or the creator's identity, herself or himself. It transcends religion, nationality, history, family, sex, gender, class, race and all.

Creativity is the unity of the unconscious and the conscious mind, what we might call the super-conscious, the knowledgeable whole self. Creativity is not a divine gift, it is the long, hard work of undoing the divine split between the body and the mind or the so-called spirit; to undo the Freudian psychoanalytical split between the unconscious and the conscious, between the id, ego, and superego, between the self and the other. People speak of the magic of art, but there is no magic in creativity. It is so simple that it appears complex. It is so true that it appears to be fiction. It is common sense, like a child asking her mother or father, 'Who created the stars?' The answer comes automatically, 'God created the stars', and then the child asks spontaneously, 'And who created God?'

The child is born cleverer than her parents. We lose our natural intelligence, our spontaneity, through education at home, in school and in church or in the mosque. Creativity opens the doorway to another kind of pleasure, one more enjoyable than sex or food or money or fame or political heroism or literary glory or winning the highest international prizes. The creative person precedes the academic scientist in knowing the unknown. Science and the Arts are separated in universities. Therefore most creative people do not belong to the academy. A creative work communicates more than the sexual instinct and more than the death instinct. Creative people do not die; they live after death in their creative work.

I stop walking. I sit by a small lake in a park. The full moon is reflected on the water. The air smells of jasmine and my mother's hair when I was a child. Memories of childhood shake me; I shiver with the recollections, the pleasure and pain, the happiness and sadness. I swallow my tears with my memories. I met the wrong men most of the time. I was deceived by words like *love, freedom, justice, equality, family, motherhood, faith, faithfulness, honesty, high human values, truthfulness* and by dreams of a classless, genderless, and raceless society. I lived in this utopia. I am not cured of it yet. I am seventy-seven years old and still believe in justice, freedom and love. I have not changed much since I was seven years old.

On a bench I see two old people sitting together, a husband and wife, smiling at each other in tenderness. I smile at them with tears in my eyes. Tenderness makes me cry. Love to me means tenderness.

Tenderness means fairness. I have not yet met my love. Is my love not yet born? Not created by God from the earth? Not yet evolved out of natural selection? Maybe my love is there, elsewhere, nowhere, in a different place and time, and for a different me. We need a new human evolution, a new kind of men and women who are able to know. Love in our world is blind. Blind love means: to give something you do not know to somebody who does not know it; to give something you do not have (yourself) to somebody who cannot have it. Love cannot exist in a world based on divisions between masters and slaves, men and women, rich and poor, West and East, those who have military power and those who do not.

I have not known sexual pleasure in my life. My loving state and my loving family amputated my only sexual organ when I was a child. They said it was the order of our loving God. His majesty created this part of my body then gave orders to cut it. This is His Wisdom. Fanatics accuse me of not loving Him for His fairness and kindness. According to His order, I should wear a veil so that men do not look at my face and be seduced by my beauty. If I were God I would order men to cover their eyes, or, better, I would have created them without eyes, rather than veil women. This is in the name of justice or common sense. Religious fanatics shout obscenities at women for not wearing the veil. On the other hand, postmodern neoliberal fanatics shout obscenities at women for wearing the veil. Young women resolved the paradox by covering their heads to please God, and uncovering their bellies wearing tight jeans to please the free market. I have felt homeless in my home and in all countries and places in this patriarchal capitalist military world, so writing became my home. Nobody can take this home from me. It is not an ID or a nationality to be taken away.

Home means feeling safe, happy, free, loving and lovable. Home is not a place; it is a feeling. It is movement in time and place that gives me the feeling of beauty and love. Exile to me is to stop writing. I studied medicine but I hate doctors and their profession. They are part of the free market, which is freedom of the powerful to exploit the less powerful. But I love science as I love art. They are inseparable like place and time, like body, spirit and mind. Facts and fiction are inseparable like dreams and reality. I move naturally from prose to poetry, from fiction to nonfiction, from dreams to reality, from childhood to old age, from science to art, from my body to my mind and spirit. They are one. They are inseparable.

In our time science and the arts are joining hands and reinforcing each other. In good medical schools music, poetry, literature, history, economics and politics are taught to students to produce better doctors. In good art schools anatomy, biology, physics, philosophy and politics are taught to students to produce better artists. In good academies spirituality and materialism are inseparable, like science and the arts.

This will lead to new movements that emphasize justice, freedom, beauty, love, rather than divine law or sacred holy books. This new cognitive revolution will end the postmodern false debate about faith or about the existence or nonexistence of God, about identity and the spurious postmodern question: Who are you? And then there is the issue of covering or uncovering women, to be naked or to be covered. It is false because nakedness and veiling are the two faces of the same coin – as are religious fundamentalism and postmodern neocolonialism. They work together underground, on the ground or in heaven, for the sake of the free market.

We need to end this unjustified faith in democracy, the free market, free elections, and Western or Eastern civilization. The words *democracy* and *freedom* have become the most violent in our postmodern era as they are based on deception and the power of the global media and telecommunications industry. Deception is a violent war against the mind. I never lose hope, because hope is power, and because human progress is eternal. It is an ever-changing constant. I have hope because we are learning how to fight back, how to globalize from below, locally and across the world, through the Internet and telecommunications, in face-to-face meetings and through writing. These reflections are but a drop in this new ocean.

Atlanta, 2008

The World of Nawal El Saadawi
or Nawal Zaynab (*the name she would prefer to take*)

AT THE FIRST Writers' and Literary Translators' International Congress, held in Stockholm in the summer of 2008, one of the few men in the audience posed a series of questions to Egyptian novelist, physician and activist Nawal El Saadawi, who was seated on stage with Antiguan author Jamaica Kincaid. In the Great Hall of the Stockholm City centre, El Saadawi stood up and directed the man to come closer 'so I can see you'. The man complied, moving from the rear of the auditorium to the foot of the stage, whereupon she stooped slightly and peered directly into the man's eyes as he spoke.

A hallmark of her persona, this steady gaze has continued over more than fifty years of public life. There is about the work of Nawal El Saadawi an unflinching and unequivocal gaze. This gaze — which manifests itself in the eyes of her various fictional characters and is vicariously present in the accounts of 'atrocities' related by the narrators of her works — is an awareness of the realities of the place of women the world. Politically, socially and economically, she has insisted on 'unveiling' and keeping at the forefront the realities of inequality. In a recent interview El Saadawi forcefully asserted: 'If I don't tell the truth … I don't deserve to be called a writer' (*World Literature Today*, January–February 2008). And what truth is it that she insists upon? In the 1979 preface to the English edition of *The Hidden Face of Eve* she wrote:

The oppression of women, the exploitation and social pressures to which they are exposed, are not characteristic of Arab or Middle Eastern societies, or countries of the 'Third World' alone. They constitute an integral part of the political, economic and cultural system, preponderant in most of the world — whether that system is backward and feudal in nature, or a modern industrial society that has been submitted to the far-reaching influence of a scientific and technological revolution.

Her stories, no matter how tragic and difficult to hear, are told by a narrator who is unrelenting in uncovering the paradoxes of human behaviour and the resultant injustices. Are there 'heroes' in her work? Yes, but not by Western standards. Her characters, male and female, are drawn with the complexity that governs human nature. Her peasants, her characters of status — religiously or socio-economically privileged — and her authority figures are steeped in the cultural paradoxes of their world. And her women defy victimization.

Zed Books published the first *Nawal El Saadawi Reader* in 1997, and it has since been twice reissued. In the introduction, Nawal El Saadawi wrote that the work explains, in non-fictional terms, the ideas and themes contained in her novel *Love in the Kingdom of Oil*. She was very much affected by the first Gulf War.

> My novel *Love in the Kingdom of Oil* is about ... suffering. And it describes what happens when its heroine tries to escape her oppression — in all its forms. It deals, that is, in fictional terms with the ideas and themes contained in the non-fiction writings in this anthology. (7–8)

Her concerns continue. The *Reader* covered the gamut of modern-day global phenomena as they affect women and the poor most especially. Its hallmark is the irony with which El Saadawi connects seemingly contradicting truths. She has a gift for connecting issues and making comparisons in her works that at once startles and illuminates. The selections were based on 'my feelings of what I like best about my writings'.

Our decision to compile a new reader stems from the need to examine these issues afresh, and to explore the new issues El

Saadawi has placed on the literary and social radar over the past decade.

El Saadawi merges the lines between fiction and nonfiction, between poetry and drama, between biography and other imagined worlds. She granted herself literary licence to do so in a process during which she struggled over the years to reunify the body, the mind and the spirit. For her utopia does not exist; instead she favours 'multiples'. She explained to me,

> I am for multiples: poly gods, poly ideas, poly topia; therefore I am more in favour of polytopia and not utopia. In ancient Egypt polytheism (many gods, females and males) was more democratic than one god, one idea.

When she is distracted by unsubstantiated criticism or not credited for her contribution to the advancement of Arab women's rights, her husband tells her, 'Fifty years from now you will evaluated and elevated to your proper place' in Arab feminist studies. She reasons that she cannot write a prescription for an ideal world.

> I am a medical doctor, a psychiatrist, but I hate writing prescriptions for people. I just help them to write their own, and to cure their problems (physical or mental) by their own willpower and new awareness. Our world will change for the better by the power of collective will of united people fighting together to end all types of inequalities (based on gender, religion, class, race, nationality, etc.). We together, globally and locally, men and women, can change this unjust capitalist patriarchal racist religious world to a better one. To do this we need to: Unveil our mind and Unite glocally (globally and locally).

The Essential Nawal El Saadawi is divided into four parts. Part One includes recent and important articles and essays, running the gamut of topics from why El Saadawi writes, to her reaction to President Barack Obama's speech in Cairo in June 2009. El Saadawi does not address problems in isolation. Her nonfiction reveals truths about self and society. In the essay 'Why I Write', she explains: 'Writing slows us down, makes us think, contemplate, connect different disconnected ideas.' And as always in her poetics, 'facts and fiction are inseparable like body and mind ... I write fiction to tell the truth.'

Part Two comprises fiction and poetry. El Saadawi's fiction is haunting, provocative and laced with taboo subjects. The veracity of her tales is often established by a narrator with an account of a conversation or a letter. This hallmark ambiguity, seminal place of mothers, and ever-piercing eyes recur throughout.

Part Three offers a sample of her drama — *Twelve Women in a Cell*. Most recently, El Saadawi has published two plays: *Isis* and *God Resigns at the Summit Meeting*. The latter was published to charges of heresy and apostasy.

Part Four comprises interviews which help to round out the persona of Nawal El Saadawi, seeking to tie together her love of the land and her love of freedom.

Adele S. Newson-Horst, August 2009

PART ONE

Articles, Essays and Nonfictional Prose

1

How to Write and Why

It was my mother, Zaynab, who taught me how to speak, then how to put words on paper or how to write. The first word I uttered was *Mama*, my mother. The first word I put on paper was *Nawal*, my name. When I went to school the teacher asked me to write my name on my notebook. I wrote the word *Nawal*. The teacher said I should write my full name, not just my first name. So I wrote *Nawal Zaynab*. The teacher was angry; he erased my mother's name and ordered me to write my last name, El Saadawi. El Saadawi was a foreign name to me, the name of a grandfather who died before I was born.

I never liked the name El Saadawi; it was like a foreign body attached to me, but I had to write it all the time, on all my papers and books, until I was known as El Saadawi by everybody who knows me. However, deep inside me I never felt it was me or my real name.

From childhood I kept a secret diary on which I wrote my real name: Nawal Zaynab. I felt a strong urge to write. I wanted to erase the false name imposed on me. Writing is a human cultural activity to express the hidden truth, the hidden true self, the hidden language. Speaking and writing are similar and different. Both help self-expression and communication with others, but speaking is more ancient than writing. Speech is a human instinct wired into our brains by many thousands of years of evolutionary selection. But writing is a recent cultural acquisition. Oral language evolved more than 100,000 years ago. Writing evolved less than 6,000 years ago.

Writing slows us down, makes us think, rethink, contemplate, connect different disconnected ideas. While we write we are not silent. We read silently what we write. An orator moves us more viscerally than our own silent reading. The music of speech is drained out of silent reading. While I write I add my imaginary inflections to the text. Reading silently is a relatively recent invention. Writing is a second language to be learned. It can be a visual language, a sign language.

Most often ideas come to me when I am alone, in complete silence. I hear ideas in my head moving. I love being alone to grasp my inner voice. This tendency has caused me trouble with people around me. My second husband became suspicious if I left our bed to be alone. When he saw me writing he wanted to read what I wrote. I had to hide my writing in a secret place. He thought I was in love with another man. I tried to convince him that I was writing fiction but he could not understand. At last he came to me and said, 'Me or your writing, you have to choose.'

I chose my writing and left him. The pleasure of writing to me is more than sexual pleasure, more than any pleasure. Writing is essential to my life, like breathing. I can live without a husband but I cannot live without writing. By writing I become one with the world and with myself. Writing is a physical and mental activity. Languages end up in the left hemisphere of the brain. In most people the left hemisphere is specialized for rapid sequence recognition, which it does better than the right hemisphere. Both coordinate creative thinking. In music perception the left hemisphere is better than the right hemisphere at recognizing rhythm, whereas the right hemisphere is better at recognizing melody.

Everywhere I go journalists ask me this question: 'How can you write fiction when you are a medical doctor?' Studying medicine helped me to write better fiction. To my mind, facts and fiction are inseparable, like body and mind. Through creative writing we undo the false opposition between emotion and reason, between the irrational and rational, between the scientific and the literary or fictional. I write fiction to tell the truth. We grasp reality better through the imagination. To write we have to depend on technology, from the Gutenberg Press to the Internet. Creative writing of fiction and nonfiction has allowed us to achieve things our brain cells can hardly comprehend. I write to emerge from the dark to the light of knowledge, from the chaos of the unjust world to a new world of justice, freedom and love. I write to challenge the superpowers on earth and in heaven. Both are living on war, exploitation and deception. Both discriminate between people according to race, gender, class, religion and other traits. I write to change myself and the world for the better.

February 2009

2

How to Fight against the
Postmodern Slave System

About my dreams

FROM MY DEEP SLEEP I was awakened by a terrible sound, like a sudden explosion coming from under my pillow. It was the television of my neighbour who cannot live without it. A very thin wall separates her television from my bed. I have slept since childhood embracing my pillow, pressing it to my head or my chest — a habit inherited from my mother or grandmother. In fact, I can sleep without a husband but I cannot sleep without a pillow. It may be due to an inherited gene (not just a habit) because it runs in my maternal family. This gene has evolved perhaps through a biological revolution against the patriarchal, feudal, racist values embedded in divine books since slavery. I think this gene is more sophisticated, more aware of social injustice, than previous undeveloped genes that I think revolted only against sexual deprivation.

I opened my eyes to a horrible feeling that something had exploded in my brain — a living cell, a pulsing artery, a malignant tumour. It was 7 a.m. on Thursday, 11 September 2008, seven years after what they call 9/11 in the USA. Since I came to the USA, I have never stopped worrying about my physical and mental health or dying by a terrorist bomb. In Egypt, under the local oppressive religious regime, I suffered political, social and economic pressures and oppressions, but I did not worry about my health. In fact I felt very healthy, full of energy to fight back. Since I came to the USA I have been bombarded day and night with frightening words of terror and images about breast cancer, life or death insurance, heart attacks, blood clotting or thrombosis, angina pectoris, Alzheimer's, psychosis, neurosis, depression and other mental illnesses. I hate sickness, doctors and the smell of hospitals. I became a medical doctor just to please my father before he died during the 1950s. I think that most working creative people live healthy and die healthy. My illiterate peasant grandmother, who worked in her field under the sun, lived and died healthy. She never went to a doctor. She was an energetic happy woman struggling with the men and women in her village against the oppressive mayor, King Farouk and British colonizers. I still remember her jokes against the mayor and her ringing laugh. She was a creative agricultural worker and a clever storyteller with a wide imagination. I think that creativity brings happiness, and happiness brings physical and mental health. When I am absorbed writing a novel I feel healthy and happy. I never feel sick when I am struggling with others against the global or local oppressive powers.

I stretched my hand and switched on the electric light. I discovered that my head and chest were not bleeding. I could walk to the living room. I could even open the fridge and drink water. I felt happy, being alive again after temporary death. I started thinking about my future plans, what I want to do from now until I die in a terrorist attack or from breast cancer. I may live another ten or even twenty years. Yesterday while walking in the park I met a woman walking fast. She smiled at me. We started talking. She looked my age but she was over ninety, twenty years older than me. I felt refreshed. I will live at least twenty more years.

Of course I will continue to write fiction and nonfiction. But I have a new dream, to make films, or at least one film based on one of my novels. I have already written the scenario; in fact I have written two, but they are the prisoners of my computer. I have no access to this formidable world called cinema or moving pictures.

Another dream is pending in my head: to establish a place or an institute for creative dissident men and women, where they are able to find the freedom and energy to do their work. This place or institute will be like a haven for those people in need of a place to work and develop their creativity within a supportive group or community, for those who are forced to leave their native homes because of their creativity and free thoughts.

Under this postmodern, capitalist, religious, military system more and more creative women and men are forced to live in exile. Exile can be outside your country or within your native home. I experienced both types of exile. Here in the USA I have to carry the title Alien Non-resident. It is more oppressive than all names given to me by my oppressive regime in Egypt.

The increasing power of the capitalist military system is accompanied by the increasing power of religious fundamentalist political groups. Today, religion plays an increasing role in politics all over the world. The capitalist, patriarchal, postmodern false democracy, based on the false free market, needs God to justify its injustices, to cover up the increasing dictatorship, the growing gap between the rich and the poor, between men and women, and between the so-called First and Third World; to conceal its military economic and political wars with a sacred mission, to disguise its state terrorism under cover of a loving benevolent merciful God. But His Majesty is also cruel and violent with the Devils who do not obey and submit to Him. He is thirsty for blood, loving disasters, destroying nations that are at variance with His Prophet or Messenger, instilling fear of the Others, the infidels, those who do not believe in His holy books, instilling hate, resentment, racism, sexism, deception, contradictions, double standards, war and hypocrisy. All these unethical, inhuman values are to be found in the three divine books of monotheism and other religious books.

Why are more people going back to religion?

Many people are deceived by the media and the political–religious educational systems sponsored by the state. The state in any country cannot survive without controlling and veiling people's minds with the fear of God. 'God-fearing' is the highest ethical description of good citizens globally and locally, in the West and in the East. Churches and cathedrals are the most glorious holy buildings in Christian countries, no less than mosques in Islamic countries. Even in the so-called secular countries the separation between state and religion never really happened, even in Europe, which is relatively more secular than the USA. Fanatical religious political leaders became stars in the so-called free democratic elections and in the big media all over the world. Religion is a political ideology; you cannot distinguish between politics, religion, economics, ethics, morality, sexuality, culture, history, science, art, body, mind and spirit.

Some sophisticated postmodern men and women are not religious (they do not believe in divine books or even the existence of a God), but they refer to what they call spirituality. They believe in the split between the body and the spirit, which is the core of religion. They are not aware of the paradox, nor do they want to be aware of it. They enjoy their hunger for both spiritual and material gratification. They believe in human ethics and social justice but they support the war in Iraq, in Palestine and in other parts of the world. They believe in equality between the sexes or even classes but they support unequal global trade and the capitalist free market.

Some less sophisticated people need their God to cure their incurable diseases, or postpone their death, or forgive their sins, or save them from disasters, or fight with them in their wars, like G.W. Bush and other heads of big states or superpowers. Most people believe in the Bible or the Qur'an or their chosen divine book without ever reading them. They defend the Book of God without knowing it, or studying it, or discovering its contradictions, biases and defects.

The fanatical religious groups in Egypt who have had my name on a death list since 1988 following the publication of my novel *The Fall of the Imam* have never read this book or any of my books. They tell the media: 'We do not read heretical books.' How do they know a book is heretical without reading it? This is the same as worshipping a divine book without reading it. Blind faith leads to blind fundamentalism, blind fanaticism, blind racism, blind sexism, blind hate and blind love. The person who killed the writer Farag

Foda in Cairo on 8 June 1992 was a poor illiterate fisherman who had never read a book written by the author he killed. Religious crimes or so-called honour crimes are political, economic, cultural, social, moral and historical crimes. Like religious wars, they hide behind the invisible God to rob, colonize, loot, plunder, rape, exploit and satisfy their greed and insatiable physical and material appetites. Jewish fundamentalism, Islamic fundamentalism, Christian fundamentalism and other religions are spreading widely during this 21st-century postmodern era for inhuman political-economic reasons and not for moral or ethical or human reasons.

Barack Obama, during his presidential campaign in the summer of 2008, praised and supported the state of Israel. To gain votes and funds he ignored the fact that the state of Israel was established by military violence, killing and displacing a whole nation, the Palestinian nation. G.W. Bush in the USA and his Republican Party are part of the Judeo-Christian fundamentalist powers that play a major role in US politics today. The Republican vice-presidential candidate Sarah Palin told ministry students, during the summer of 2008, at her former evangelical church, that the USA sent troops to Iraq on a mission from God. She used her God to justify killings in Iraq and to cover up her neocolonial economic oil war with spiritual slogans. She asked the students to pray for a plan to build a $30 billion natural gas pipeline in her state, Alaska, calling it God's will. Sarah Palin said she would work to implement God's will from the governor's office, but that she could not do anything if the hearts of the Alaskan people are not with God. A few women and men opposed her and said that the job of the president is to unify American people around policy goals and not divide them by religion. But those genuine voices were ignored by the big US media funded by capitalist money. Many ordinary people in the USA do not believe in the capitalist, terrorist God of Sarah Palin and Republicans. They are fed up with the deception of Judeo-Christian fundamentalist increasing powers in the USA but they are silent. They constitute the silent majority; they have common sense but they do not have access to the media or political-economic power.

Where is the American feminist movement?

I wonder, where is the feminist movement which had an effective voice in the USA during the 1960s and 1970s? Why are women disconnected, disillusioned, depoliticized, not only in the USA but all over the world, as has happened to the socialist and other progressive movements everywhere?

US media and cultural life are full of religion. Feminists are going back to the church or to spirituality, unaware of the fact that the core of patriarchy, of women's oppression, lies in this split between the body and the spirit. Many feminists supported Hillary Clinton and Sarah Palin because they are women. Simply being a woman does not make one a feminist. Sarah Palin's policy, declared in her own words, is against real feminism, real democracy and real civilization. She covers her violent, military, capitalist, patriarchal policies under labels such as loving God, pure spirituality, good motherhood, humanism and family values. She sounds more brutal than the likes of G.W. Bush, John McCain, Margaret Thatcher, Angela Merkel and Condoleezza Rice.

I expected that feminists in the USA would not sleep the night of that speach and would organize demonstrations against Sarah Palin, but nothing happened until the day I sat down to write this article. I wanted to send the article to the feminist movement in the USA, but I did not know where it was or who its leaders are. I felt the danger of McCain–Palin and Republican policy inside the USA and all over the world, including my country Egypt in North Africa. We live in one world, not three or four. We live in a neocolonial era, not the so-called postcolonial era.

The USA is a superpower with nuclear and other weapons of mass destruction. If no power can stop its aggression, many nations will be in danger, especially those with oil or diamonds or other precious natural resources. Iraq, Palestine, Afghanistan, Darfur–Sudan, Somalia, Rwanda and other countries are being destroyed before the eyes of the entire world. The United Nations and the International Criminal Court did nothing to stop the destruction of those countries. Why? Because our postmodern world is still a slave system governed by military power, patriarchy and dictatorship and not by justice or democracy. Women like Sarah Palin who reach high office in this world are more patriarchal and more militaristic than their husbands, bosses or fathers. I still remember the thrill in the voice of Sarah Palin speaking about war and guns. Perhaps she dreams of blood flowing in Iraq more than oil; perhaps, embracing her hunting rifle in her bed, she dreams about shooting hundreds of Iraqis, Palestinians, Afghans and wild animals from the air.

Everything Sarah Palin says and practises is against the liberation of American women. Her conception of motherhood reminds me of my poor peasant neighbour in my village during 1937. I was six years old. My illiterate neighbour spoke about God, like Sarah Palin, believing that children come from God and they are all part of God's plan. My neighbour had five children, like Sarah Palin, and was pregnant with the sixth. She was against abortion, like Sarah Palin, and thought that abortion is against God's will. But Sarah Palin is more dangerous than my neighbour, who died giving birth to her sixth child, because if Sarah Palin becomes US president or vice president she will destroy more nations. She thinks that Iraq and other countries are there to be invaded and plundered. This is the plan of God, not the plan of the Republican Party, in the USA.

How to fight back?

Despite my disagreement with some of the policies of Barack Obama and the Democratic Party (especially those related to Israeli state aggression and the capitalist, neocolonial so-called free market) I believe the feminist movement in the USA should unite and fight to get Obama elected as president in November 2008. If the McCain–Palin party wins through he American nation will live more fearful years than those of G.W. Bush. The whole world will also live another nightmare. The postmodern slave system will be more destructive, more uncivilized, more brutal, more terroristic, more deceiving and more religious or 'spiritual'. The feminist movement should unite with other progressive and socialist movements struggling to free the USA from religion.

One of the lessons of the horrible events of 11 September 2001 is that they opened the eyes of many people to some real facts; one of which is that all religions — not only Islam — are a great source of war, bloodshed, political strife, social divisions and terrorism. Terrorism within the USA has become more dangerous than that coming from the outside. Jewish fundamentalism is no less dangerous than Christian fundamentalism, and neither is less dangerous than Islamic or other fundamentalisms.

I have witnessed here in the USA the relentless war against women and the poor, against secular values, abortion rights, stem-cell research and the teaching of evolution in state schools. The faith-based initiative, the new union of religion and state (now endorsed by most political leaders, Republicans and Democrats), threatens the core of human rights, women's rights, the rights of the poor classes and other races, and the rights of people believing in gods other than that of the Bible. Feminists and progressive people should unite to keep State and Church separate, to retain a godless constitution that treats all people equal regardless of their religion, gender, class, race, nationality or so-called identity. The word *identity* is a postmodern term that divides people, like culture, ethnicity, nationality, language, colour and religion. Real democracy means real freedom based on free thinking, creativity and dissidence. Democracy means the freedom to be dissident and to speak your own mind and not the mind of priests and sheikhs or gods or presidents or other authorities on earth or in heaven. People all over the world should unite and struggle globally and locally to achieve these goals in our societies, to get rid of our local dictators who work hand in hand with global dictators.

Atlanta, Georgia, 11 September 2008

3

First Trip outside the Homeland

IN CHILDHOOD, the homeland was love. My mother's warm breast.
The smell of milk. My father's hand on a cold night covering me. My
grandmother's voice on summer evenings telling tales of monsters
and sea sprites. The aroma of bread and cress and prickly pear.
The jug on my cousin Fatima's head, brimful with water of the Nile.
The waves of the sea at Alexandria. And the roar of students in the
streets shouting: 'Down with the King!'

In my youth, the homeland became revolution, and revolution
was love. Now love was forbidden, revolution too became forbidden,
leading me to prison rather than to freedom.

My life's dream was flight and escape from prison. In my childhood, I had a recurrent dream: my father was dead and I started
going out without permission. In my youth, I had another but similar
dream: my husband was dead and I came of age.

My father was the greatest love of my life, and yet I envied
children who had no fathers. The first revolution in my life was
against my father — he wanted to marry me to a man I did not
love. With the fantasy of adolescence, I lived in daydreams. In
fantasy, I loved a hero who bore arms, smote enemies and freed the
homeland, then held me in his arms and kissed me till I swooned
and forgot father, mother, sisters, brothers and grandmother, and
all my pain.

But when he *did* hold and kiss me, I did not swoon. Neither did I forget anything, not even my grandmother's tales of monsters, genies and spirits. I discovered the first facts of life: that first love is an illusion, heroism is fantasy, and the homeland is not liberated.

In the middle of the night, I crept out of bed. The sound of snoring was loud; his mouth open, over his top lip a thick black moustache. On tiptoe I opened the door and went out. I walked rapidly, almost running. I had only one goal: for my mother to wrap her arms around me. I stopped suddenly, when I remembered that my mother was dead and that she had never once in her life embraced me. My father too was dead, without ever having embraced me; neither me nor any of my brothers and sisters.

I'd be away at boarding school for the whole academic year. Then I'd come home, but no one would embrace me or kiss me. In our house, kisses did not mean love. Love was just deep feelings, deeply buried. Not words or embraces or kisses but silent love, expressionless and motionless, except in fantasy.

It was the tragedy of my life; reality is always less than fantasy. My life became one continuous attempt to realize fantasy and dreams. And what was the dream of my life?

I saw myself on a white stallion, flying through the air, in my hand a sword with which I felled the enemy and liberated the homeland. I had been born in a country ruled by foreigners. My grandmother gasped when I told her about my dream:

—That's no dream for girls.

—What do girls dream of then, grandmother?

—Of bridegrooms and wedding dresses.

But I dreamed neither of bridegrooms nor of wedding dresses. Still, my grandmother bought me a wedding dress ten years before the bridegroom came.

Every holiday, my father bought me a new dress and my brother a gun and small aeroplane with a spring which you wound up to make it fly. In the yellow cardboard box lay my present: a silky white dress with ruffles on the bodice and lace on the sleeves. I shouted angrily:

—I want a plane and a gun like my brother.

—You'll be beautiful in the new dress, my mother said.

—I don't like dresses, I yelled.

—That girl should have been a boy, my grandmother shouted.

Despite my grandmother, I would look up at the sky with the eyes of a ten-year-old. Would a day come when I'd fly in an aeroplane? Could I fly through the air like a bird, far away from this prison into which I had been born?

In dreams, I would fly without an aeroplane. My body lifted into the air and I circled above the rooftops and trees and seas. Then, suddenly, my body would plummet earthwards and plunge to the bottom of the sea.

—Flying in dreams means success. You'll marry a king or the son of a king, my grandmother said.

—I hate the king, I hate marriage, I would shout at her.

—As crazy as your mother, she would say, flapping her hand angrily.

My mother hated King Farouq, but my grandmother hated only the English and used to sing along with the radio:

> King of the country, oh so wise,
>
> King Farouq, apple of my eyes.

I can hear the sound of my new black shoes on the floor of the airport as if it were yesterday. Twenty years have passed since I first saw an aeroplane on the ground. It looked bigger than I'd imagined. In the sky, it looked as small as my brother's, the one with the spring.

I stood in the queue, before and behind me foreign men and women, expensive leather cases in their hands, woollen coats over their arms, heads held high, backs stiff, tall in stature.

I raised my head and straightened my back. I was as tall as any one of these men, and the women were shorter than me, their skin chalky white, their eyes yellow discs, their mouths lipless lines moving rapidly when they talk, like taut instrument strings or whips.

In the washroom mirror, I saw myself wearing the black raincoat I bought from Omar Effendi shop after getting my exit permit from the passport office in Tahrir Square. I was holding a new black bag with a shoulder strap, and sticking from its outer pocket was the tip of a green passport, a long red ticket and a square yellow immunization card.

Through the wide glass window I could see the planes on the tarmac, like huge hunting birds or mythical reptiles. The roaring of take-off and landing rang in my ears, ran through my body like a shiver, a mixture of terror and joy and courage and fear and obscure sadness. It reminded me of my wedding night and of the night my father died.

In the mirror, my eyes sparkled with an intense black light, my skin brown and flushed with enthusiasm. The door of the aeroplane before me opened onto the wide world.

The policeman sitting at the entrance to the airport stopped me and asked for my papers. I handed him the yellow paper with the stamp of the eagle, the symbol of the state. The policeman examined the yellow paper, making sure the eagle stamp was real and not forged, that the state agreed to the transfer of my body beyond the borders of the homeland.

What has the state got to do with the movement of my body?

The policeman moved his eyes from the yellow paper to my face; then slowly from my face to my photograph glued onto a bit of cardboard. My face did not look like the photo. He did not see the momentary sparkle of hatred that glinted in my eyes as I looked at him. He did not know that between policemen and myself there existed a 3,000-year-old enmity, stemming from the time the god Amoun dominated and destroyed the civilization of Isis and slavery came into existence.

He stared into my face with narrow eyes, the thick moustache on his upper lip quivered, reminding me of the snoring that came from beneath another large black moustache.

—This is the authorization of the state. But where's her husband? I heard him say.

I stared at him in surprise. Dictatorship may mean that the state controls my whereabouts. But husband? Does he, too, govern the movement of my body? What's the dividing line between being state property and husband's property? My eyes clouded but then I suddenly realized I was not married. The mist cleared and my voice rang through the airport hall like a silver bell:

—I have full jurisdiction. Nobody governs me other than the state.

—I'm asking for your husband's authorization, the policeman snorted gruffly.

—And I'm telling you that according to the law, I can travel without a husband's authorization because I'm a free woman, without a husband.

—Have you got anything to prove you're not married? he shouted angrily.

I snatched out of my bag a long piece of paper that looked like a birth or graduation certificate. I held it over my head like a flag or lifebuoy. With another quick movement, I placed it in his hands.

He brought it up to a police magnifying glass and examined it closely. He checked the stamp, the authorized signatures and the witnesses, then snorted:

—Why didn't you tell me from the start that you've been divorced?

—I haven't *been* divorced, I replied angrily. I *am* divorced.

Although twenty years have passed since that first trip abroad, my voice still rings in my ears as I stress the word *am*. The policeman sitting in front of me behind a metal enclosure stares at me with narrow, half-closed eyes, like those of an imprisoned animal. I can still recall the movement of his hand as he raised it and brought down the black stamp like an iron hammer on my passport and let me pass.

At first, I could not believe he had let me pass. Slowly I walked ahead, thinking that he'd stop me. But he didn't. I took some more steps, a little less cautiously, and still he did not stop me. Joy and surprise overcame me: I leapt across the borders of the homeland as though reborn, clapped my hands like a child and moved across the ground as if about to soar off into the air, my face skyward, and my back towards the homeland. On the aeroplane steps, I looked back, imagining a policeman was following me and that at the last moment he'd stop me. Then the doors closed and the steps were removed. Through the round glass window, I saw the observation balcony; hands were raised and waving. Not one of them waved to me. Many faces, but not one of them that I knew.

I turned my head with the plane as it taxied away from the airport buildings and my eyes clouded over. Through the mist, my daughter's face appeared, her small hand waving, tears in her honey-coloured eyes. I went up to her to kiss her and take her hand firmly in mine.

Pain just under the ribs, deep, and heavy as lead. A piece of myself was still there, in that small apartment — her skin was the same colour as mine, her fingers looked like mine. I imagine her crawling on hands and knees; she looks wide-eyed towards my bedroom and does not find me. I tensed my body as if to get up and go back, as a sudden surge of maternal feeling in the form of passionate longing swamped my joy at travelling. The homeland waved to me from afar, like a child's round face, eyes filled with tears; five delicate fingers which wrap themselves around mine on contact, like a stake fixing me to the homeland, like a root burrowing into the earth; I had become like a mother tree when I had not yet outlived my own childhood. My motherhood and my childhood both lived within me in mutual contradiction. My longing for my daughter was as contradictory as my longing for the homeland, the desire to belong only equalled by the desire to escape.

My fingertips trembled as I felt the seatbelt, the aeroplane roared as it began to take off; then suddenly I was separated from the ground, lifting into the air, the beat of my heart rising and rising. The plane shook as if about to fall. Then the beating under my ribs subsided. Beside me, a man was reading a foreign newspaper as if he were sitting at home. He had a long curved nose, reddish-white skin, and was wearing a multicoloured tie; his fingers holding the newspaper were white, the nails carefully manicured.

Through the round glass window, the yellow sands stretched on and on. Houses receded and shrank and the River Nile was a thin white thread, its banks two black ribbons; then the desert like a sea of sand, sprawling on the horizon.

For the first time, I saw my homeland from afar. It had grown small, a mere line twisting like a narrow snake in an expanse of desert. Everything in my life receded: my joy and my longing, my motherhood and my childhood, my hopes and my dreams. Everything had shrunk. Even Abdel Nasser and his thundering voice and the rows of statesmen quaking before him had become a mere line at the bottom of the page of a foreign newspaper held by the fingers of a foreign man.

I had believed that my homeland was the whole world, just as when I was a child I believed that our street was the whole homeland. As I grew up so the street grew smaller. But when my being reached out beyond the homeland, the earth shrank and new feelings, that I was larger than before, filled me.

Through the window, the wings of the plane kept their shape and size, fixed, motionless and suspended in space above waves of steady white clouds. Nothing in the universe moved, not the clouds, not the plane, not even the tea in the cup placed on the white plastic table hanging on the back of the seat in front of me.

I stared fixedly hour after hour; it is then I discovered that travelling by train was more enjoyable, if only for the movement I would see from the train window. Telegraph poles and trees would run backward so fast the eye couldn't catch them, filling me with the movement of life as I sped towards my goal, the blood racing in my veins at the same speed, emotions flooding with happiness. Since childhood, travel had all the joy of a feast day. For it, I'd put on new clothes and new shoes. I'd not sleep from happiness and get up before the dawn call to prayer or the cock's crow. Travel then was by car or train and within the homeland, from Cairo to our village of Kufr Tahla or to Manouf or Alexandria or al-Giza or to wherever the Ministry of Education wanted to transfer my father.

My brothers and I would race to sit by the window. My brother was a year older than me but I'd beat him to it. My little brother, though, would cry and cling to the window, so I'd leave him the seat. My sisters were younger than me and the youngest one sat on my mother's lap.

I knew nothing about aeroplanes other than the distant hum I heard in the sky and a small body that glinted on the horizon, the size of a dove, whose movement was as slow as a cloud. My imagination was unable to conceive of its true size or speed. I could not imagine how normal-sized human beings could fit inside it, looking down on us like gods from above the clouds. My imagination did not extend to picturing myself inside an aeroplane in the sky looking down on the universe from a tremendous height. My imagination extended horizontally with the movement of the car or the train on the tracks, or my feet, and the reach of the Nile at ground level.

When I raised my head vertically towards the sky, the eyes of those around me became alarmed, particularly my grandmother's. From the time I was born, she looked anxiously at my raised head. Should I have been born without a head? If I stretched my neck, her anxiety increased and she'd shout: Don't lift your head like that! Can't you see how proper girls walk?

Proper girls walked with their heads bowed. Till the day she died, my grandmother kept on saying that I wasn't proper. That was my grandmother Amna, my mother's mother. But grandmother Mabrouka, my father's mother, would place a tall clay jar on my head and say: Don't bend your neck like that! See how the village girls walk with heads high. But she believed that girls' heads were only held upright like that in order to carry clay jars on them.

I loved grandmother Mabrouka more than grandmother Amna and I preferred to travel to her mud house with its wooden veranda and drink from the water jug and bathe from the water of the Nile, although my mother preferred going to her own mother's house in Cairo. My father, like me, loved to spend the summer holiday in his mother's house in the village. My parents argued about it at the start of every summer holiday but it was never a bitter argument and it ended with neither of them winning. There was a sort of balance between the great powers in the house: one time my mother would pack the bags and we'd travel to her family, another time to my father's family, and so on.

A few days before travelling, I'd take all my clothes out of the wardrobe and pack them into a large suitcase. My mother would come and empty the suitcase into the wardrobe, shouting: Don't take all your clothes. Anyway, it's not time to go yet!

She would stand on a high wooden chair and on tiptoe reach up to put the case on top of the wardrobe. From where I stood looking up, I could see her fat, white and hairless calves stretching up under her silky robe to even fatter and whiter thighs, then coming together at the end in one deep dark line. A strange thought would come to me: that I had dropped into the world from this dark line. This was immediately followed by an even stranger thought: that my father too had a connection with this dark line. Here my thoughts stopped completely, as if I'd reached the end of the world. I returned to earth, then clambered onto the high wooden chair and reached up to the top of the cupboard, but I could not get to the suitcase.

Every night, from the start of the summer holidays, I would dream that my arm grew longer and longer and grasped the suitcase, that all my clothes were moved from the cupboard to the case, that my mother was waking me at dawn to put on my new clothes — my father made sure the windows and doors were locked, the taxi waited outside. The sound of the engine buzzed strangely in my ears and the smell of petrol in my nose intoxicated.

At the train station, everything seemed amazing: the high platform, the tracks running endlessly in a deep trench, the sounds of bells and the whistles of trains, the thick smoke billowing from black funnels, the people running with cases in their hands, the *samit* seller calling out loud, the steep steps of the train. I would grasp the metal rail and put one foot on the step, imagining that the train would move off while my other foot was still on the ground. But the train did not move and I would run to my seat and look out of the window. The station and the houses stayed still and I was just thinking that the train would never move when suddenly my head was thrown violently backwards then forwards, the houses began retreating, followed by the telegraph poles that started running after each other, one by one.

I put my head out of the window, sobbing for joy. The wind made my hair fly, my wide-open mouth gulped in the air and the smoke as I felt my father's hand pulling me back. His voice rings in my ear, mixed with the noise of the train wheels: Put your head in!

I pull my head back from the window. But I'm inside an aeroplane, not a train, and the window is small and round and made of sealed double glass. The sky is a constant blue, the clouds a constant white. There are no moving trees or telegraph poles and I can't put my head out of the window. Neither can my body feel any movement. It's as if I'm in a closed tin can. The seat belt around my body ends in a metal lock. Its touch on my chest is like a doctor's stethoscope dangling on rubber tubes round my neck. Behind me, an old man is coughing. His cough is dry, from smoking, not from tuberculosis. My ears are attuned to identifying diseases from the type of cough.

Every day, from eight in the morning until two in the afternoon, I would listen to the coughing of the long queue. I put a metal earpiece between jutting ribs and listen to the whistle of air, to the rush of blood and pus. I bring the X-ray machine down onto the chest, saying to the patient: hold still. And instead of holding still, he coughs into my face, showering me with spittle. I step back quickly and press a bottle of medication into the veined hand, saying: One tablet, three times a day, after every meal.

The voice, weak with wheezing, repeats: After every meal?

—Yes, I say, after every meal. Three tablets per day, after three meals!

The question comes in gasps: Three meals?

—Yes, three meals, I repeat.

One day, at the end of the queue was a woman, one child in her hand, another on her shoulder: Would I be sick with tuberculosis if I ate three meals a day? she raged.

Every day, staring out of my window onto the brackish pool, I would look up at the small patch of sky between the walls and address God: Who is responsible for such misery on earth? You or the head of state?

I held the head of state responsible and not God, for I still believed in divine justice.

One day the telephone rang suddenly, making me jump. I imagined that the security department in the ministry had picked up my deep-seated doubts in the justice of state as a voice with a cultured accent came through: A ministerial decision about your travelling in the doctors' delegation to Algeria has been made.

With every trip abroad, I thought, I will not return. But I did, every time. My longing for my daughter drew me home, together with my longing for the land, the smell of the earth and the soil and the air, the familiar faces and features. My ears craved the language and the accent of home, a craving which was a sharp pain in my ears, in the heart under my ribs, in the movement of blood in my veins; like the craving of an addict for the pain of poison.

I stared from the window at the earth of the homeland. The face of the security official was still before me, his bald head shining like that of a turtle, his eyes two white lenses without lids or lashes. He had examined me from head to toe and my whole being turned into a shrimp glued under the lens of a microscope, an apparatus like an X-ray machine revealing what was inside me. I hid the hatred deep within and drew over my face saintly features full of love and fear, for nothing threatens security like hatred or love without fear.

It was the first time that I had stood for examination before a security official, to get that small rectangular booklet called 'a passport'. It was the first time in my life that I had owned a passport. With the passport safely in my handbag, I walked along the street, head held high in pride, as though with this booklet I had climbed up a rung. But the pride soon dissipated, as the huge administrative building of Mugama' Tahrir swallowed me up and my body fell into a pit crammed with panting, sweaty bodies. I too began panting as I ran from office to office, in my hand papers stuck with stamps of green and yellow and signatures of red, black and blue. Finally, I ended up in the security office. The clerk looked like any other clerk — bald head and soft voice. He looked me up and down, stared at the photo of my face, then asked me: Why are you travelling to Algeria?

—To attend the Arab Doctors' Conference, I said.

—Are you a doctor? he asked, as though surprised.

—Yes, I replied.

Looking into my face, he said:

—What do you think of the revolution?

—Which revolution? I asked.

But understanding the question, I then said: Yes.

—Yes? he said.

I started to think.

—What are you thinking about? the man scolded angrily.

—About the answer, I said.

—Does the question need thinking about? he asked, surprised.

At that moment, thinking seemed to me to be something shameful. The meeting ended quickly. I spent a month waiting to get an exit visa, but the visa did not appear.

Tuesday came. The following day, Wednesday, was the travel date. I went to the security clerk and asked:

—Why is my visa late?

—It's always late, he replied.

- Isn't there a way to speed it up? I have to travel tomorrow.

—No way to speed anything up, he answered.

I returned home. The walls of the apartment were closing around me. I put out my hand to the telephone as the ringing of the bell echoed in my ears. No one in the world, I am completely alone. I went to the window to look out at the people in the street. A smell like the overflow of a sewer filled the air and the wind carried dust and heat. People moved in the street like dead ghosts from another world. A police wagon with a piercing siren towed a car behind it. Violet feelings of alienation surged through my body.

A red bus pulled up. My daughter jumped from it, wearing a blue tunic with a white collar, satchel in hand. She looked up at the window and saw me. She smiled, her eyes glowing with joy. I ran to the door and waited till she'd come out of the lift, then took her in my arms. She buried her head in my chest. The smell of childhood in her hair awakened my maternalism and dispelled my alienation.

I prepared food for her and sat watching her eat with relish. My whole being focused on that plate towards which she put out her small hand, which she raised to her mouth, the movement of her small jaws as she chewed the food with pleasure.

That night I slept with my arms around her, as if embracing the whole world. Nothing in the world afforded me such gratification — no man or work or travel. My imagination that night was still. One picture dominated my mind: that the plane had fallen into the sea with me in it. My disillusion with travel turned into joy at being saved from death and I fell into a deep sleep.

In the morning when I opened my eyes all my desire for travel had completely vanished. I went to the hospital like any other day, but the telephone rang beside me and the cultured voice said: Your visa has arrived.

I put the phone back on the hook. Security permits, it seems, do not come when people want them, but when they stop wanting them, they suddenly come from who knows where, like fate and divine decree.

I awoke to a voice coming from the ceiling of the plane announcing that we were circling over Libya. My body was slumped into the seat, a delicious torpor running through my being. I had crossed the borders of the homeland. I rested my head against the back of the seat, closed my eyes, then opened them. There was music in my ears and a pair of blue eyes looking at me, smiling. A woman was sitting in the seat next to mine, holding a large plastic doll in her arms, rocking it as if it were a living child.

—Have you got any children? she asked me.

—Yes, I said.

—I can't have children, she said sadly.

—There are things in life other than children, I said.

—Like what? she asked.

—Work, travel, love... I replied.

—Have you ever been in love? she asked.

The question surprised me. Nobody had ever asked me such a thing before. But her question seemed normal. I had a desire to open my heart to this woman who did not know me; we would part and not meet after today.

—Do you want to know the truth? I said.

—Yes, she replied.

—I've had the illusion of love, but I haven't loved yet, I said.

She laughed, throwing back her thick blonde hair. I noticed a gold tooth in her upper jaw. Her nails were long, manicured and painted red. She took a lock of her hair between her fingers, licked her top lip with the tip of her tongue and said:

—There's no such thing as love.

—Where are you from? I asked her.

—I'm Italian. I work in Benghazi.

—What do you do? I asked.

—I'm a dancer, she said, lighting up a cigarette.

Then, her voice lowered, she continued:

—And a prostitute.

With an almost instinctive movement I recoiled from her. It was the first time I'd met a prostitute. I'd only read about them in novels and seen them in movies. From the corner of my eye, I studied her features, her arms, her legs. Everything about her was normal, unremarkable. I had thought that prostitutes must be remarkable in some way. I stared at the five fingers of her hand in surprise, as though expecting her to have six or seven. Suddenly I came to with a violent shake, as if the plane had fallen into the sea and my stomach with it. Clutching the seat with both hands, I shouted: What's happening?

The Italian woman said: We're landing at Benghazi.

A rectangular panel of light lit up above my head. English lettering read: *Fasten seat belts. Extinguish cigarettes.* A female voice announced over the intercom that the plane was landing; I didn't hear the rest because the microphone swallowed up half the words and the deafening roar the other half. The walls of my ears stuck together and closed up under a sudden pressure. All I could hear was a piercing whine. Then suddenly my ears opened with a pop, the pressure vanished completely and I heard what sounded like the roar of a waterfall. My body was shaken with the thump of the wheels of the plane as they touched the ground.

My face must have been ashen because my heart was pounding and my throat completely dry.

Through the window, I saw her on the tarmac of Benghazi Airport, walking in line, one slender white arm carrying the plastic doll as if it were her only daughter, her other hand holding a yellow leather case.

A gust of sand blew, making her blonde hair fly and I saw her cover her white shoulders with the edge of her shawl. But the

Benghazi wind defeated her and lifted the shawl off her shoulders. Brown faces ravished her, hungry eyes devoured her.

I saw her stop, then turn towards my window. She waved to me from the distance with a small white handkerchief and I waved to her with my hand, a curious apprehension running through my being.

When we landed in Algeria the warm late afternoon sun shone above the towering green mountains and trees. For the first time in my life, I saw a mountain rising towards the disc of the sun. In Egypt, I have seen only flat land. Jabal al-Mugattam is not a real mountain, and the green in Egypt is not this deep, intense colour.

Behind me a voice said *hamdillah ala as-Sallama* — thank God for your safe arrival. I turned to see a long brown face, a neat, decorative moustache on its upper lip. His name was Dr Jamil Yasser, and he was a professor of mine at college.

—Are you alone? he asked.

—Yes, I said.

—Come with us, he said. We'll take a taxi to the hotel.

His wife was with him, a large woman tottering on spiky high heels. The Algerian driver spoke in French. My wristwatch showed 8.30 but the sun was still in the sky.

Dr Jamil Yasser said: Haven't you changed your watch? It's 5.30 p.m.

I turned the hands of my watch back three whole turns.

Despite my numerous trips around the world during the last twenty years and although I have turned the hands of my watch backwards or forwards many times, I still remember that first time I changed time with my own hands. I had thought that the movement of my watch was inviolable, untouchable, unchangeable. Those hands governed my waking and my sleeping, my work time and my pleasure time. They ruled the days of my life, during my youth or my adulthood. Not I myself, nor anyone else, not even the person who had made them and shaped them into hands, could move them backwards or forwards by one minute. But these two inviolate hands I could now move back three whole turns.

Surprise changed to joy, as if I had pilfered three hours from the gods and added them to my life... or as if I had gone around the globe three times while standing in the same place.

As I walked on Algerian soil, the sun still in the sky, I said to myself: The sun has set for people in Egypt, but it's still in *my* eyes. Is it the same sun or another one?

The Algerian accent seemed to me like a new language, the Algerian features strong, sharp and as lofty as a mountain. The people's national anthem, when I heard it played for the first time, reminded me that I was on Algerian land, the land of a million martyrs; the war of liberation and *fedayeen*; prisons of torture and *Jamila Buhareed*; French soldiers and the atrocities of colonialism; Frantz Fanon and his book *The Wretched of the Earth*; Ben Bella with his round face and tall stature, like that of Abdel Nasser.

Ben Bella opened the medical conference. The Ibn Khaldoun hall was full of Arab doctors. They talked of the Algerian revolution, of sacrificial work, of liberation from colonialism. But soon they divided into specialized committees and began talking about diseases of the heart, stomach and spleen.

In the evening there was music, song and Algerian dancing. Words and tunes on the piano mixed with the beat of tambourine and *'oud* (lute), French words with Arabic; I saw eyes in which were revolution and anger; eyes in which were resignation and satisfaction; elegant, semi-naked women; women with heads and faces covered under heavy veils, their cloaks wide and white.

In the Arab *qasba* quarter the beating of the tambourine and the *'oud* dominated the piano and the words, Arabic dominated French. The humid alleyways, the old dilapidated houses, the eyes of women from under their white *hijab*, the wan faces of the children. A woman came towards me, her face and body hidden under a cloak, a child on one arm, the other one stretched out to me, palm up:

—Give me a piastre, she said in French.

It was the first time I had heard anyone begging in French. I thought beggars knew only Arabic.

I returned to my hotel room before midnight, to find a piece of paper — neat decorative words like the neat decorative moustache, one letter lying beside the next, like one hair lying beside the next, so neat, it's like a notice: *I invite you to dine with me tomorrow. Jamil Ali.*

I hardly recognized the name. Was it Dr Jamil Yasser? I had attended some of his lectures in the Ali Ibrahim auditorium in the medical faculty of Qasr al-'Ain. He had delivered a talk at the conference the previous day on a new method of removing brain tumours. He was of medium height and stocky, especially round the middle and thighs. In conference halls I had seen him walking with his wife, a few steps in front of her.

In the morning, the telephone in my room rang:

—This is Jamil, a voice said.

—Jamil who?

—Dr Jamil Yasser.

—But on the note you wrote 'Jamil Ali'.

—My names are Jamil Ali Yasser.

—Then why didn't you write Jamil Yasser?

—I was worried in case someone else found the note.

—Do you mean that 'Jamil Ali' is a pseudonym?

—Something like that.

—And why disguise yourself?

—Traditions make us, wherever we travel.

—Are you against traditions?

—When I travel, yes.

—Is your wife coming with you?

He was silent for a moment, then said: No. She prefers staying in the hotel. Shall I pick you up at 6.30?

—No, I said.

—Are you turning down my invitation?

—No, I'm turning down the invitation of Jamil Ali.

—Why?

—Because I don't know him.

—And Jamil Yasser's invitation? he asked. Would you accept it?

—No.

—Why?

—Because I *do* know him!

From Algeria I took the plane to Paris. Flying no longer held its initial magic. Through the double window I saw the Straits of Gibraltar, the strip of sea between the continents and Europe.

The word *Europe* filled my head with fantasies. The first time I had heard it was from my father. I was still a child when I heard him say that outstanding students went to Europe to do their research. I thought my father was better than any man in the world, that nobody could be more outstanding than he. When I grew up a little, I discovered that King Farouq was more renowned than my father. I asked my grandmother why my father had not become king. As I grew up still more, my father decreased further in stature. Then I learned that there were men who had travelled to Europe to do their research and he had not. My father died at sixty-one years of age without having seen Europe, without having taken a plane.

We were circling over Spain. I stared out of the window as if I would see Andalusia, green lands and bullrings. As I focused on the abyss beneath the wings of the plane, the earth looked red under the glare of the sun, the buildings the size of pinheads. Beside me, a man was reading a newspaper. I noticed the word *morning* in French. I had learned French in primary and secondary school, but I hadn't spoken it in over ten years. The man smiled and asked me in French where I came from. Egypt, I said in English, my voice sounding strange in my ears. The English word was clear but it was not *Misr*, the Arabic word.

The man repeated 'Egypt?' in surprise, as though Egypt were the other end of the earth. His features looked strange: he had reddish skin, a long pointed nose and thin tight lips, and large hands covered with dark spots. I was overcome by feelings of alienation as I heard the man say: Is it your first time in Paris?

Swallowing hard, I replied: Yes.

At that moment, I wished the plane would take me back home. My daughter's eyes, filled with tears, beckoned to me. On the window were droplets of water like rain. The clouds changed colour and became heavy, dark and frightening. Between the gaps in the cloud, the ground appeared even stranger and further away. The man beside me abandoned his newspaper and closed his eyes; an air hostess was laughing with one of the passengers; a woman was reading a magazine and next to her a child played with small coloured blocks. Everything in the plane was safe and cosy.

The air hostess passed along with jugs of tea and coffee; the aroma of coffee was strong and my normal sensations returned, together with the sudden realization that I was on the way to Paris.

Paris. The word is magic. None of the men in my family had ever visited Paris — in my childhood I had read of Egyptian men who had travelled there but the only two I remember now are Saad Zaghloul and Taha Hussein.

In my fantasy about Paris, beautiful blonde women dance on the banks of the Seine, their eyes blue, their legs smooth and pink, and the sound of music fills the universe.

The airport was huge and had many passages. I tried to follow the signs to reach the exit. The ground was shiny clean and sparkling and the faces of the people were fresh and pink, their bodies slim and fast-moving. The high stiletto heels of the women rang on the ground briskly; the men's heels, too, were purposeful and brisk. Elegant bodies surged before me in quick and orderly succession, like the waves of a graceful river.

The streets of Paris were broad, the trees very green, the houses trim, their balconies hung with flowers. On no balcony did I see clothes spread out on a washing line.

I went down the steps to the Metro. It was very crowded and fast-moving, but no one bumped into anyone else. In the seat facing me in the train, a girl and boy embraced each other, engrossed in a long kiss — although the train was packed, nobody looked at them. I tried to take my eyes off them. When the train stopped at the Champs-Elysées, I rushed out and climbed the stairs to the street. Before me, I saw the great Arc de Triomphe and the wide street bordered by shops with huge glass windows. The faces around me looked radiant, their footsteps lively, their clothes chic, of various colours and styles, trousers glove-tight, dresses short.

Freedom was embodied before me, and it was contagious. I straightened my back, raised my head and strode with firm strides, swinging my arms. I bought a huge red apple, took a bite out of it and, with a group of young people, headed for a pleasure boat on the River Seine. Along both banks were buildings with wonderful domes and stone figures on top, like deities of old before a heavenly god appeared. The Eiffel Tower was an iron giant that sent a tremor through my body. A cold wind brushed my face and my heart was heavy, my chest filled with terror. I was unfamiliar with the sky above the towering walls of this city and this unfamiliarity stripped away pleasure and beauty.

In the Louvre, I wanted to throw my arms around him, his familiar features and huge head, his wide solid shoulders. As my fingers explored his shiny bronze body, the smell of the desert and the pyramids came back to me. Foreign tourists gazed at him with inquisitive blue eyes. The word *Sphinx* sounded strange; for me, his name is Abu al-Houl. His resting place in the Giza Desert was more beautiful than his place here in the Louvre museum. His eyes picked me out from among all the strange eyes — like me, he felt foreign and longed to return. I drew nearer and put my arms around him as if to lift him and return.

I spent a day wandering around the Louvre, passing among the various statues and paintings, then returning to Abu al-Houl. Beside him I felt soothed.

In one of the halls, I saw people gathered around Venus where she stood in all her splendour, goddess of beauty as they call her. She had one arm. I stared at her face to discover the secret of her beauty. Her features were quite ordinary. Beside her stood Athena, goddess of wisdom. People didn't look at her, even though she was more graceful than Venus, and more beautiful. Is wisdom in a woman undesirable and therefore unattractive?

At the picture of *La Gioconda* or *Mona Lisa*, I stopped for a while. It was the only painting behind glass. As the light reflected off it, I saw my own image inside the frame and not that of *Gioconda*. I moved my head to the left and to the right, but to no avail. Rows of people stood before the *Gioconda* in awe, each waiting their turn to see her close up. But as soon as they approached, the light reflected from the glass and they saw their own faces and not that of the *Mona*

Lisa. Yet they turned away to leave their place to others, whispering: Wonderful! Wonderful!

An hour passed as I stood and gazed at the *Gioconda*, and saw my mother's face. Rationally, I knew that she was dead and buried in the overcrowded graveyard near Jabal al-Muqattam and that the face in front of me was that of the *Mona Lisa*, but all distinction between past and present had disappeared and scenes of my life from childhood unfolded one by one before my eyes. When I was a child, I had loved my father more than my mother. He was out of the house for half the day, did not scold me as my mother did when I went out without permission, and paid my school fees. But as I got older, I grew to love my mother more than my father. She would not go to sleep before I came home, prepared supper for me, and sat with me so that I ate. At night, I would sense her walking in on tiptoe to cover me up.

I stared at the faces of the people standing in homage before the *Gioconda*. What dazzled them in da Vinci's lines? What moved deep inside them? Was it deep-down pleasure in the forbidden? Or was it the hidden hatred of the holy?

From the corner of my eye, I delved into people. No one looked at me; they were all held in the sway of art, or so it seemed to me. A priest stood in homage in his holy attire: even his eyes were filled with the magic of the *Gioconda* and her sinful attraction.

I walked along the banks of the Seine exposing my hot face to the cool refreshing wind. The sun was setting and the wooden kiosks displayed paintings and old books, reminding me of al-Izbekiah. Fruit was carefully laid out on shelves, flowers were multicoloured, people sat in cafés, in front of them gleaming trays, glasses and cups sparkling in the sunlight.

I noticed the towers of Notre-Dame Cathedral, its ancient engravings and the sculptures standing under the light. In front of the huge door, a man sold dried, sweet-smelling plants in cloth bags, and beside him a man was selling coloured balloons. Tourists from different countries filled the place; some sat on the ground, eating and drinking beer from iced cans.

The wide vestibule inside the cathedral was damp and dark. The candlelight created a mysterious and unearthly atmosphere with a smell of smoke or burning candles. When I was a child, damp and dark were associated with holy places, veined hands, lined faces, black robes, weak, wrinkled eyes swimming with sadness. The majority were poor women. Why do women and the poor fear divine punishment more than others?

I looked up at the altar. A man and a woman were on their knees before the holy deity. Both displayed humility, but the woman's was greater. Her head was bowed, both eyes closed, but the man had one eye open and glanced at me, standing to the side.

Candlelight filled the hall with ghosts — a strange smell, like death. An old man with a long white beard muttered, a book in his hand, his eyes small and sunken beneath a pair of glasses, his drooping eyelids opening and closing with a fast regular movement, like those of my uncle Sheikh Abd al-Hamid. He was the youngest of my grandmother Mabrouk's thirteen stepbrothers from her father's four wives, and used to sit in the courtyard, a Qur'an on his lap, murmuring faintly. His drooping eyelids opened and closed rapidly with the movement of his head, yellow prayer beads between his fingers. The patter of his three wives' sandals never stopped, their high-pitched voices squabbling until sunset, when each would go to bed in her own room. He would go to his first wife's room on Saturday night, rest for one night, then enter the room of his second wife on Monday night. The third wife was the youngest and was graced by Tuesday and Wednesday nights. On Thursday nights he rested.

His first wife once whispered in my ear: Your uncle will go to hell. He doesn't share out his nights fairly.

I did not understand what she meant. I was still a child and only knew that the week had seven nights. My uncle gave his wives four nights and rested on two. So where was the seventh night?

I asked him one day as he was sitting in the courtyard reading the Qur'an.

Friday night, he said, I give to Allah, for it is a blessed night.

In my small room on Saint-Germain I lay on the bed, closed my eyes then opened them. I moved my head and saw the suitcase on the table. Hanging from its handle was a small red and white label with *Paris* written on it. I remembered with surprise where I was. It seemed strange to me, almost impossible. The room was not very different from any other room; a wardrobe, bed, closed window. My eyes remained fixed on the case, with its red and white label, to confirm that I really had come to Paris.

I got dressed and went out into the street. I sat on the pavement of a café facing the Luxembourg Gardens and the whole world passed before my eyes like a gushing river: faces from all four corners of the earth, all languages and accents. I stretched out my legs relaxedly, slowly sipping my coffee. Since that first visit to Paris, I have loved sitting in pavement cafés. On other visits, that seat in that café remained my favourite place. The Latin Quarter is the most beautiful area. My room in that small, elegant hotel on Boulevard Saint-Germain, the bookshops and theatres and small cinemas where I sat on a warm, comfortable seat, stretched out my legs, and followed the scenes of authors from Shakespeare and Ibsen and Bernard Shaw and Chekhov to Molière and Sartre and Jean Genet.

I was still sitting in the café at three o'clock — I had two hours left before going to the airport to leave Paris. I ordered a large glass of beer and some long thin chips. The smell of the beer and its icy touch inside me was refreshing. I let my body sink further into the seat, closed my eyes, felt the warm rays of the sun on my eyelids. I never enjoyed sitting in cafés at home. Cafés in our country are for men. They sit on chairs, ogling the women passing by, from the front and from the back, from head to chest, then turn to examine the back of the legs and backside.

The sun vanished behind a grey cloud and the wind blew cold. I still had an hour left. I could walk to the Metro station. I had a small suitcase which I towed along behind me on wheels. I don't take many clothes with me on journeys. I wash my clothes by hand, hang them up in the bathroom and find them dry in the morning.

I walked alongside the railings of the Luxembourg Gardens and decided not to go down into the Metro station. I wanted to go on walking. I could walk to Place Albert Mayo and take a bus from there to the airport. Walking in the streets of Paris was so pleasant. But was there enough time? I looked at my watch. It had stopped.

I asked a woman passing by what time it was. She was walking quickly, some books and files sticking out of the leather bag over her shoulder. Tall and slim, she was wearing sneakers, black trousers and a white wool jacket. She stopped walking, glanced at her watch and said:

—It's a quarter to four.

—Thank you, I said.

She looked up at me and I saw the shining blue in her eyes. I watched her smile and look at me, then heard her say, before quickly continuing on her way: *Vous êtes belle, madame.* Her voice rang in my ears: *You are beautiful, Madame.*

Before her words had sunk in, she disappeared. I spun round but saw only her back as she briskly walked away, a straight back inside a white wool jacket, a slender body and light, rapid strides.

It remained with me in the bus to the airport. Her image came back to me, the blue of her eyes as she smiled, her straight back and sprightly footsteps.

In the plane I stood looking out over Paris from the rear window. The lights were like clusters of pearls on red squares. I looked at my face in the mirror hanging above the washbasin, as if a new face were looking at me. The features resembled mine, but they seemed new. The skin glowed browner than ever, the eyes were larger, the black pupils more glittering. I whispered to the mirror: You are beautiful, Madame. I used to whisper it silently so that no one should hear. Besides, there was no one at home who saw me as beautiful. I did not know why, but standards of beauty did not apply to me. In my heart of hearts I had other standards which I knew *did* apply to me. It was an instinctive knowledge that arose from deep inside myself with no confirmation from the outside world. And yet it was an absolute and certain knowledge — certainty itself.

However, no one around me told me I was beautiful. Not my father, not my mother. And grandmother Amna would purse her lips in distress, telling me I had inherited my father's brown skin.

Grandmother Mabrouka would stare at my front teeth and pull a face saying: You've inherited fangs from your mother.

At school, when the girls were angry with me, they would tell me I was as tall and thin as a telegraph pole.

My mother did not regard my tallness as shameful, but she thought my little sister more beautiful than me because she had inherited her own white skin and soft hair.

My hair was not coarse, but it was not soft either and it had natural waves. But my aunt thought it coarse and she'd take me with her to the hairdresser to get it straightened out with fire-heated metal tongs. I can still smell burning hair and remember choking on the singeing and the smoke. I would pull my head away from between the hairdresser's hands and the tongs would scorch my ear or the tip of my nose.

When my maternal aunt had differences with my paternal aunt, my maternal aunt would accuse me of having frizzy hair and dark skin like my father's ancestors, and my paternal aunt would say that I got my 'fangs' from my mother's ancestors. My maternal aunt bought me a box of powder with which to hide my brown skin and my paternal aunt advised me not to open my mouth when I laughed. Her only remedy for my height was that I should walk with a hunched back.

I straightened my back and neck until my head touched the low ceiling of the aeroplane. I washed my face with *Eau de Cologne* to open up the pores of the skin and clear it of traces of powder.

My face always looks more beautiful in aeroplane mirrors than it does in the mirror at home or in any other mirror in the country. I don't know: do my features change simply by crossing borders, or are aeroplane mirrors of better quality?

2👄 *My Travels Around the World* was first published in Arabic in 1982, and translated by Shirley Eber in 1985.

4

Preface to
The Hidden Face of Eve

THE OPPRESSION OF WOMEN, the exploitation and social pressures to which they are exposed, are not characteristic of Arab or Middle Eastern societies, or countries of the 'Third World' alone. They constitute an integral part of the political, economic and cultural system, preponderant in most of the world — whether that system is backward and feudal in nature, or a modern industrial society that has been submitted to the far-reaching influence of a scientific and technological revolution.

The situation and problems of women in contemporary human society are born of developments in history that made one class rule over another, and men dominate over women. They are the product of class and sex.

But there are still many thinkers — men of science, writers and social or political leaders — who close their eyes to this fact. They wish to separate the arduous struggles of women for self-emancipation from the revolt of people everywhere, men and women, against the present structure of society. Yet it is only this radical change that can end foreign and national class exploitation for all time and abolish the ascendancy of men over women not only in society, but also within the family unit which constitutes the core of patriarchal class relations. This core of relations remains the origin of the values and sanctified beliefs which throughout the ages have

cemented, reinforced and perpetuated a system of class and patriarchal oppression, despite all the changes which society has known
since the first human communities were constituted on earth.

Influential circles, particularly in the Western imperialist world,
depict the problems of Arab women as stemming from the substance
and values of Islam, and simultaneously depict the retarded development of Arab countries in many important areas as largely the result
of religious and cultural factors, or even inherent characteristics in
the mental and psychic constitution of the Arab peoples. For them
underdevelopment is not related to economic and political factors,
at the root of which lie foreign exploitation of resources and the
plunder to which national riches are exposed. For them there is no
link between political and economic emancipation and the processes
related to growth, development and progress.

Development in such circles is visualized as a process of cultural change, of modernization along the lines of Western life, of
technological advance which would permit better utilization of the
resources, quicker and bigger profits, and more effective and efficient
ways of pumping out oil from under the shifting desert sands or
the depths of ocean beds. All this under one condition, and one
condition only: such resources must continue to serve the interests
of international capitalism and the multinational giants that still rule
over a large part of the world. Development must be submitted to
the laws of unequal exchange and ruthless exploitation.

Some Arab and Islamic countries have been the theatre of such
modernization processes at the hands of national governments and
rulers largely controlled by Western interests. The result has been
nothing more than a form of pseudo-development, a dual system
composed of a small modern sector linked to the interests of multinationals and a large traditional agricultural sector producing for
export, a population where a restricted minority shares in some of
the gains while the vast majority sink from poverty to ever deeper
destitution, a ruling class fed on opulence and wealth and the masses
fed on deprivation and a loaf of bread or a bowl of rice. The income
and profits generated from this form of development stream into the
strongrooms of Western banks and the coffers of international corpo-

rations, while the gap between the 'developed' and the 'developing' grows ever wider and deeper. In the United States of America, the $360 billion-a-year oil industry's 'official' profits for the five sister oil corporations increased in 1978 by as much as 343 per cent over the previous year, while in the Arab countries a million children still die annually before reaching one year of age, as a result of poverty, sickness and malnutrition. Their intake of essential food items such as proteins and vitamins is only one-tenth of that fed to dogs and cats in the United States of America.

With the ever growing chasm which separates a minority of rich people who own the wealth and control the power of nations, and the vast majority worn out by exhaustion, toil, sickness and hunger, problems are daily growing more acute, conflicts are becoming more sharp and bitter, popular explosions more frequent, and everywhere the struggle of developing peoples for freedom, independence and social equality is a widespread phenomenon which is shaking the foundations of an imperialist system built on social, racial and sexual discrimination. In almost every country of the 'Third World' the conflict between classes in its open and clandestine, legal and illegal manifestations is growing with each passing day.

The Iranian Revolution of 1978-79, which swept before it the Pahlavi dynasty, is an indication that people in the underdeveloped countries are no longer able to stand the growing pressures of an economic crisis that is affecting wider and wider sections of the urban and rural workers, the middle classes, the intellectuals and the national bourgeoisie, and burdening the life of millions, both men and women, whose existence is already one long trail of suffering from birth to death. Yet in Iran the Shah was the self-proclaimed leader of a modernization process which, it was said, had brought increasing prosperity to the country, but which in fact had only engendered incalculable riches for a handful of corrupt, degenerate and sanguinary despots, and a train of misery and death for those who worked the fields, operated the machines, ran the schools and colleges, and turned the wheels of everyday administration and business in a country where oil revenues had attained $9 billion a year.

The Revolution in Iran, therefore, is in its essence political and economic. It is a popular explosion which seeks to emancipate the people of Iran, both men and women, and not to send women back to the prison of the veil, the kitchen and the bedroom. The Iranian Revolution has lifted the banners of Islam overhead, as banners of freedom from imperialist oppression in the economic, social and cultural life of more than 37 million people. For Islam in its essence, in its fundamental teachings, in its birth and development under the leadership of Muhammad, was a call to liberate the slave, a call to social equality and public ownership of wealth in its earliest form, that of a 'House' or 'Bank' in which all surplus wealth was to be deposited and used for feeding and clothing and housing the poor. Early Islam laid the first foundations of what might be called a primitive socialism, for the money deposited in the 'House of Wealth' belonged to all Muslims equally, irrespective of their tribe or class. But primitive socialism in Islam did not last long. It was soon buried under the growing prosperity of the new classes that arose and thrived after Muhammad's death, and that increased their influence when the Muslim warriors burst beyond the narrow frontiers of the Arab desert and flowed out from the burning sands into the green valleys of Syria, Iraq and Egypt. Primitive socialism received its first blows at the hands of Osman Ibn Affan, the Fourth Caliph of the Muslims and head of the Ommayad dynasty in Damascus.

Thus arose in Islam the struggle that began, and was never to end, between those who hoped or believed or fought for social justice, freedom and equality, and those who stood for class privilege, feudal oppression and whose descendants were later to side with the Turkish domination, with French, British, Italian and German colonialism and later with international imperialism headed by the United States of America.

Thus it came about that, from the time of Osman Ibn Affan in the eighth century AD, history was to plunge the Arab Islamic peoples into a long night of feudal oppression and foreign domination, reaching its darkest depths under the Turkish Empire, which, ever since it conquered and ruled, has symbolized what is most corrupt, degenerate, obscurantist, inhuman and reactionary in the annals of the Arab peoples.

Thus it was also that women were condemned to toil, to hide behind the veil, to quiver in the prison of a harem fenced in by high walls, iron bars, windowless rooms, and the ever present eunuchs on guard with their swords.

In their quest for liberation from the injustices and oppression exercised against them by foreign invaders and internal feudal rulers, the Arab peoples could see no hope except in the application of those principles of social equality, freedom and justice which constituted the essence of Islamic teachings. This explains why the great majority of revolutionary Arab leaders who fought against feudal despotism in its various forms, internal or external, and later against colonialism, as well as the pioneers and thinkers who played a role in the cultural and intellectual development of the Arab peoples particularly during the reawakening of the nineteenth and early twentieth centuries were also leaders and pioneers in Islam. We can cite as eminent examples Gamal El Dine El Afghani, Abdel Rahman El Kawakbi, Abdallah Nadeem and Sheikh Mohammed Abdou. It is both interesting and significant to note that their thought and action not only aimed at the liberation of Arab peoples from the rapid expansion of colonialism in its economic, political and military forms, and from the oppression of feudal regimes, but also dealt with problems related to women's status and the need to draw them into the mainstream of life and of the struggle for emancipation.

The Iranian Revolution of today, therefore, is a natural heritage of the historical struggle for freedom and social equality among Arab peoples, who have continued to fight under the banner of Islam and to draw their inspiration from the teachings of the Qur'an and the Prophet Muhammad. Thus it is that Islam, a religion characterized not only by its philosophical and theological content, but also by the fact that since the early days it penetrated into the arena of politics and also embraced the economic and social aspects of everyday life, has been and still is the banner and inspiration for conflicting forces — for feudalism, oppression and reaction on the one hand, and for the freedom fighters and martyrs in the cause of Arab liberation on the other.

The past years have witnessed a growing conflict which is being fought out on the basis of Islam, between the forces of progress and those of imperialism and reaction. As the contradictions in the world of today grow deeper and more acute, the battle for people's minds and convictions is expanding in scope and complexity. This battle is being fought in all areas. Islam is one of the essential arenas because it spreads its influence over crucial regions of the world, rich in resources and human potential. The conflicts within Islam are directly related to the struggle for control of the oil fields.

Since Islam still exercises a profound influence over the 80 million people who constitute the Arab world, both the forces of reaction and those who stand for freedom and progress are waging a battle to win the support of the vast majority who still base their attitudes and behaviour towards many of the problems of society and of everyday life on the teachings of Islam.

As a result, the last two decades have seen a vigorous revival in the political and social movements of Islamic inspiration. These movements consider that Islam can be an effective weapon in the hands of the Arab peoples against oppression and exploitation. Parallel to this development, and related to it, increasing efforts are being made to spread the effective utilization of Arabic as the national language. The Algerian Revolution, which fought French colonialism by mobilizing Islamic potential, has also carried out a vigorous Arabization campaign. This is characteristic also of other countries in North Africa where French had replaced Arabic as the official language under the colonial regime.

The movements aiming at cultural emancipation, independence and identity run parallel to and intertwine with the political and economic struggles waged by the peoples of underdeveloped countries. They are growing in depth and maturity both in North Africa and in Sub-Saharan Africa. Peoples everywhere are not only breaking the bonds of political and economic dependence, but also the cultural chains that imprison the mind. They are probing into their past, rediscovering their origins, their roots, their history;

they are searching for a cultural identity, learning anew about their own civilization, moulding a personality genuine enough and strong enough and resolute enough to resist the onslaught of Western interests and to take back what was plundered over the centuries: natural resources, labour producing value, goods and profits, and the creations of intellect and culture ... and to restore the roots that take their sustenance in the past and their nourishment in cultural heritage. For without these roots the life of a people dries up, becomes weak and futile like a tree cut off from the depths of the soil, and loses both its physical and moral force.

This vast, deep and sweeping movement for liberation is, nevertheless, exposed to serious reverses as a result of the blows directed against it from both external and internal enemies. Imperialism continues to fight back viciously and often effectively in defence of its interests in the Islamic and Arab world. In this conflict any and all weapons can be used to contain the rising movement of peoples fighting for their rights.

Among these weapons is the use of religion, the 'sword and the words of Islam'. Any ambiguity in Islamic teachings, any mistake by an Islamic leader, any misinterpretation of Islamic principles, any reactionary measure or policy by Islamic rulers can be grist to the mill of imperialist conspiracy, can be inspired by CIA provocations, can be blown up and emphasized by Western propaganda, and can be manipulated or born of intent in order to be used in fighting back against the forces of progress. Only a short while ago, the Western press orchestrated a campaign against the Iranian Revolution accusing it of being reactionary, of imposing on women the veil and the chador, of attempting to deprive them of the civil rights they had enjoyed under the rule of the Shah. It tried to depict what was happening in Iran as a social change geared towards the past, traditionalist, and fanatical, rather than as a political and economic movement advancing under the pressure of a militant popular uprising surprising in its depth and resoluteness. Such counter-revolutionary machinations are characterized by their variety, subtlety, and the thought given to understanding the complexity of each situation and to ways of playing skilfully on the various contradictions. Even revolutionary and leftist movements can be utilized in this 'game of nations' and become unwitting instruments in the hands of reactionary forces posing under the guises of democracy, liberalism, humanism, modernism and human rights. The Western press suddenly discovered that 'human rights' had to be defended in Iran. Progressive feminist movements intervened on behalf of Iranian women, not realizing that sometimes the form and even the content of their intervention was being used to discredit the Iranian people's struggle against American intervention. At the same time Western interests and agents are in fact encouraging the most conservative and orthodox forces of Islam so as to build up a rampart against the progressive wings of the Revolution by opposing Islam to the socialists and communists, who are described as no more than atheistic tendencies in a society of believers.

Capitalist circles today are facing a dilemma. They are in need of Islam and utilize it as a buttress against progressive and socialist movements. But at the same time they realize that Islam has been an important force for people's liberation at various stages of its history, including contemporary Arab societies, and that once again it can play an important role in the struggle against exploitation and oppression. This explains why the United States of America has adopted such an ambiguous stance with regard to the Islamic movements in the Arab world and the Middle East, a two-faced stand characterized by an attempt to preserve and reinforce them at times, while criticizing, attacking and weakening them at others. The essence of American policy in this regard is to strengthen the reactionary, obscurantist and fanatical wings of Islam, and to divide, weaken and distort those movements that mobilize the masses in the Arab world to take an anti-imperialist, anti-feudalist or socialist position. Let us not forget that, at the very time of writing (mid-1979), Islamic movements in the Arab countries have opposed the Israeli/Egyptian 'Peace Treaty' which has been conceived, engineered and almost negotiated by the USA — a treaty which, instead of bringing peace, has divided the Arabs, strengthened Zionism, turned the Middle East into a theatre for American military bases and intervention, and led Egypt further down the path to capitulation and a deepening political and economic crisis.

In this double-dealing game with Islam, the Western powers are supported by those Islamic regimes and those political and religious leaders following in the path previously paved by their predecessors for Turkish domination, and later French and British colonialism, those who utilized Islam as an instrument of oppression against the people, and who maintained that religion believed in and defended class privileges and was opposed to disobedience against the ruler, the father and the male, those who depicted revolt, revolution and the struggle for freedom as the greatest of all crimes, and who considered dissatisfaction of the ordinary person with poverty, destitution and disease as heresy. For was it not God Almighty who bestowed the good things of life on people in the way which he saw fit, depriving some of the bare necessities and bestowing upon others riches and pleasure without end? He who is a believer, therefore, must perforce accept the will of God with peace, calm and a deep satisfaction!

Religious teachings and campaigns have played, and continue to play, an important role in maintaining and reinforcing reactionary regimes. Religious obscurantism, superstition and fanaticism have been and still are dangerous instruments in the hands of those rulers or classes that wish to disarm and divide the Arab peoples, instilling in their minds and hearts the conviction that destiny is all-powerful and that fatalism and resignation are the highest of virtues.

Yet all through the centuries that followed Muhammad's first establishment of Islamic rule in the Arab Peninsula, there have been religious thinkers and leaders who have insisted that Islam cannot be understood properly if it is taken simply as a conglomeration of unrelated precepts and statements. These brave people have opposed the isolation of sayings like 'and we have made you to be of different levels' or 'one above the other' or 'men are responsible for women' from their general context and from the essential principles of Islam in order that they might be used to support backward interpretations of Islam.

The broad character of the Iranian Revolution today means that it has drawn into its ranks a wide spectrum of Islamic leaders and religious thinkers. Some of them are enlightened and progressive. Others are not and tend to cling to traditionalist Islamic beliefs. These latter are the source of the pressures being exerted on women, of interpretations that require the body and head to be covered by a chador, or the emancipated working woman to be isolated once more within the precincts of the house. These slogans are either upheld out of ignorance of the real principles of Islam or are part of a connected plan aimed at holding back change, dividing the ranks of the Iranian people, and facilitating the success of the numerous conspiracies that are being hatched against the Revolution behind the scenes.

There are rulers in certain Arab countries who continue to use religion against the interests of their peoples. The Sadat regime in Egypt did everything in its power to help in the revival and strengthening of conservative Islamic movements since 1970, in order that they might be used against progressive and socialist tendencies within the country. The government not only abstained from interfering in any way with their activities, but also helped them by opening up channels for financial and political support. Women were encouraged to wear the veil, and female students wearing modernized forms of Islamic dress were a familiar sight in the streets of Egyptian cities and on the university campus. Long articles extolling the virtues of motherhood and the dangers of female participation in paid employment appeared in the news-papers, and special radio programmes talked incessantly about woman's role in the home.

The Egyptian ruling class, however, retreated rapidly from this position and evinced serious alarm bordering on panic when the same Islamic movements started to attack the peace treaty with Israel and to defend the rights of Palestinians. This alarm was magnified a hundredfold by the sweeping march of the Iranian people battling to destroy the heritage of a tyrannical dynasty that had ruled the country over fifty-seven years. Since large sectors of the revolutionary forces were drawing their inspiration from Islam, it now became necessary to attack what had been defended with such remarkable ardour before.

At the same time, the Western press once again started to attack the 'fanaticism' of Islamic movements. An enthusiastic campaign was launched in defence of Iranian women condemned to the dark walls of the chador. Iran overnight became peopled by hundreds of thousands of women, impressive yet chilling as they stood clothed in their long black robes, while the incessant click of Western cameras carried this medieval sight to millions of readers all over the world. Yet this enthusiasm for women's rights, or even human rights, was sadly lacking when thousands of Iranian men and women were being shot dead by army guns, or assassinated or tortured in the underground cells of the Savak, or when a whole people — men, women and children — was forced to flee its land to settle in the tents of refugee camps, or when peaceful populations were being burnt to death with napalm or torn to pieces by cluster bombs.

No doubt, any attempt to force women back into the chador or the home is a reactionary policy, unworthy of any revolution that wishes to emancipate people and abolish exploitation and misery. It is necessary that women unite everywhere to strengthen and broaden their movement towards liberation. Solidarity between women can be a powerful force of change, and can influence future development in ways favourable not only to women but also to men. But such solidarity must be exercised on the basis of a clear understanding of what is going on in the underdeveloped countries, lest it be used to serve other purposes diametrically opposed to the cause of equality and freedom for all peoples. It is necessary at all times to see the close links between women's struggles for emancipation and the battles for national and social liberation waged by people in all parts of the 'Third World' against foreign domination and the exploitation exercised by international capitalism over human and natural resources. If this link is forgotten, feminist movements in the West may be used not to further the cause of women's liberation but instead to participate in holding back the forces of freedom and progress in the countries of Asia, Africa and Latin America.

Of course, I oppose the desire of certain religious leaders in Iran to see women covered in the chador or deprived of the civil rights they have gained over the years. Such religious leaders either do not understand Islam correctly or have accepted to serve a dubious cause. A religious leader is not a God; he is human and therefore liable to go wrong and to make mistakes. It is necessary that his words and actions be submitted to democratic control and critical appraisal by the people whose life he wishes to influence and even direct. He should be questioned and appraised by the women and men he is trying to lead. Iranian women have shown that they are capable of standing steadfastly against attempts to throw them back into the past. Supported by enlightened religious leaders and progressive men, they have succeeded in throwing back retrograde attempts against the status of women and their rights in society.

The religious movement of Iran is a concrete example on a higher and more advanced level of the age-long struggle that has continued in Islam between progressive political leaders and religious thinkers and those whose values and attitudes towards society are inspired by narrow class privileges and an orthodox traditionalist interpretation of Islam. An eminent leader may himself be the subject of inner contradictions so that his vision of certain aspects in the political and social struggle is enlightened, whereas his horizons in other areas remain limited and rigid. He may fight vigorously for the liberation of his country from foreign domination and yet look upon women as inferior creatures who should be subject to the will and fantasies of men. In this world of ours is it not true to say that very few are the men who not only intellectually believe in equality between men and women, but also are capable of practising it in everyday life? And is it not also correct to say that, even within the socialist movement itself, a backward position so far as women is concerned still remains characteristic and indicates that in many spheres socialist and Marxist thought and practice have still a long way to go?

Time and time again, life has proved that, whereas political and economic change can take place rapidly, social and cultural progress tends to lag behind because it is linked to the deep inner emotive and psychic processes of the human mind and heart. Men are very often the victims of such contradictions in their attitude towards women. The role of women's organizations, and of the political struggle of women, therefore continues to be a crucial factor in any changes which will ultimately lead to the complete emancipation of women and to real equality between the sexes. Only through the influence exerted by political action and effective organization will this social and cultural change be possible. Such is the law of progress, and the status of women is no exception. Men must come to understand, and even be compelled to make, the changes within themselves which are so necessary for human progress and which they seem so reluctant to embrace.

The feminist movements in the West which are devoting great efforts to the cause of women everywhere are beginning to understand the specific aspects of the situation in underdeveloped countries which have to be taken into account by women's liberation movements. For although there are certain characteristics common to these movements all over the world, fundamental differences are inevitable when we are dealing with different stages of economic, social and political development. In underdeveloped countries, liberation from foreign domination often still remains *the* crucial issue and influences the content and forms of struggle in other areas, including that of women's status and role in society. Cultural differences between the Western capitalist societies and Arab Islamic countries are also of importance. If all this is not taken into account and studied with care, enthusiasm and the spirit of solidarity on its own may lead feminist movements to take a stand that is against the interests of the liberation movements in the East and therefore also harmful to the struggle for women's emancipation. This perhaps explains the fact that progressive circles among Iranian women adopted a somewhat neutral attitude to some American feminist figures who rushed to Iran in defence of their sisters against the reactionary male chauvinist regime 'that was threatening to imprison women behind the black folds of the chador'.

It is necessary to understand that the most important struggle that faces women in Arab Islamic countries is not that of 'free thought' versus 'belief in religion', nor 'feminist rights' (as understood sometimes in the West) in opposition to 'male chauvinism'; nor does it aim at some of the superficial aspects of modernization characteristic of the developed world and the affluent society. In its essence, the struggle which is now being fought seeks to ensure that the Arab peoples take possession of their economic potential and resources, and of their scientific and cultural heritage, so that they can develop whatever they have to the maximum and rid themselves once and for all of the control and domination exercised by foreign capitalist interests. They seek to build a free society with equal rights for all and to abolish the injustices and oppression of systems based on class and patriarchal privilege.

It is worth noting in this connection that it is precisely the current reactionary regime in Egypt, after having linked its fate to that of American and Zionist interests in the Middle East and abandoned the struggle of Arab peoples for a just and lasting peace, that started to attack the Iranian Revolution as opposed to the values of a modern civilization and the rights of women.

Our past experience has always shown that any strengthening of the links that bind the Arab peoples to Western interests inevitably leads to a retreat in all spheres of thought and action. Social progress is arrested and the most reactionary and traditionalist circles in society begin to clamour for a return to orthodoxy and dogma. The social and economic rights of the vast majority are subjected to attack, and women become the first victims of the general assault against freedom and progress. Radical social change is replaced by superficial modernization processes that favour the elitist and privileged groups in society, and the women belonging to these groups are transformed into a distorted version of the Western woman, while the vast majority of toiling women in industry, agriculture, government administration, commerce and trade, or in the teaching and liberal professions, find themselves victims of increasing oppression and a sharp decline in their standards of living. Superficial processes of modernization, whether in the West or in the East, will never lead to true equality between women and men in the economic, social, political and sexual aspects of life. Sexual rights as practised in many Western societies do not lead to the emancipation of women, but to an accentuated oppression where women are transformed into commercialized bodies and a source of increasing capitalist profits.

In addition, modernization processes in the West sometimes bestow 'equal rights' on that small minority of women belonging to the middle or upper classes. These find their way into business or the liberal professions and may even become members of parliament or ministers. But usually such women are as conservative as the men to whose class they belong, if not more so. The positions they enjoy do not serve to liberate women from the inferior position which is characteristic of such societies. On the contrary, they perpetuate inequality between men and women by masking the real situation and affording a pretence of change, whereas in fact no real change has taken place.

When Margaret Thatcher, leader of the Conservative Party, became the first woman prime minister of Britain in May 1979, the Western press acclaimed this event as a significant development. And yet many people might feel that Margaret Thatcher's policies will probably lead to a deterioration in the situation of women, for it is not the mere fact of her being a woman which is important, but the class and policies she represents. A Conservative government will necessarily be antagonistic to the rights of working people, democratic liberties and socialism, and this inevitably leads to a similar position with regard to movements for women's emancipation. This will not only affect policies as regards women in England. Britain still exercises considerable influence in world affairs and particularly over a certain number of the countries in Africa and to a smaller extent in Asia.

The struggle of women in underdeveloped countries is not a narrow fanatical movement prejudiced in favour of the female sex and rising to its defence at any cost. We know that progress for women, and an improvement of their status, can never be attained unless the whole of society moves forward. We believe that fanaticism of any form should be opposed, whether religious, political, or social. Victory in the long and difficult struggle for women's emancipation requires that women adopt a flexible attitude and be prepared to ally their efforts with all those who stand for progress. Women should be ready to cooperate with democratic and nationalist forces, progressive religious movements, as well as with socialist and Marxist-oriented trends and organizations. It is the unified efforts of all these forces that permitted the Iranian people to carry through a successful revolution against the fifty-seven-year-old rule of the Pahlavi dynasty, and it is this unified effort that remains the main guarantee for its future development. This explains why the enemies of the Iranian people are concentrating on attempts to divide these forces, to play one off against the other. In these divisive attempts, any slogan and any force can be utilized as long as it serves the main purpose — no matter whether that force be progressive or retrograde, capitalist or socialist, democratic or rigid and fanatical, chauvinistic and racialist or internationalist. The women's liberation movement is no exception.

Women have always been an integral part of the national liberation movement in the countries of Asia, Africa, the Middle East and Latin America. They fought side by side with the men in Algeria against French colonialism, and as part of the Palestine Liberation Organization's struggle against Zionist and imperialist aggressive policies aimed at depriving the Palestinian people of their national right to self-determination. And women fought too in Yemen against the British occupation and Arab reactionary intrigues, in Mozambique against Portuguese colonialism and Rhodesian punitive expeditions, in Vietnam against successive armed invasions of their country by the French, the Japanese, the Americans and now the Chinese.

Through their participation in the struggle for national liberation and for economic and social reconstruction they have gained many rights. Nevertheless, once the new systems of government are in place, whether national democratic or socialist, they very often cease to advance in a significant manner so far as women's status in society is concerned. This is noticeable in the socialist regimes of Eastern Europe, in Algeria after independence, and in other countries like North Korea, China and even Vietnam. This is due mainly to the fact that women have not succeeded in becoming a well-organized political force capable of ensuring adequate representation for themselves at all levels of government and administration, as well as in the political institutions and structures built up after the national or social revolution in society. Despite the crucial role they play in all fields of economic and social endeavour in the factories, fields, social services, different professions and at home, and the fact that they represent half the population in each country, their representation within the political power structure is always limited to a minority, and sometimes even a very restricted minority.

The new ruling classes and governments are composed of men, and have a tendency quickly to forget the problems faced by women, or at least not to give them the attention and effort that are required. Instead of attempting to sweep away patriarchal class relations within the family, these are maintained in one form or another, and the values related to them continue to hold sway.

The changes that have taken place in the Arab countries are characterized by a shift from feudalistic structures to capitalism, and sometimes even to early stages of socialist orientation. These changes are usually accompanied by an accelerated industrialization which requires a rapid expansion of labour outside the home and which draws hundreds of thousands of both men and women into the production process and the numerous services and organizations that grow up. Families migrate in large numbers from the rural areas to the cities, which tend to swell at a phenomenal rate (anything from a 4 per cent to 13 per cent annual increase in the population). Working women not only grow in numbers but they face a whole range of new problems resulting from the social changes to which they are exposed. They are deprived of the support, assistance and numerous functions that were previously afforded by the extended family system. Their children used to be cared for and looked after by members of the extended family whenever work called their mothers to the fields or elsewhere. Social, psychological and even financial support was forthcoming and numerous tasks were undertaken in common so as to alleviate the burdens of everyday life. The extended family carried out a wide variety of social functions. Migration to the city and social change in general are doing away with this unit, which is now being replaced by the nuclear family. But the nuclear family is incapable of performing the same role, and no other institution has grown up to substitute itself for the structures that once existed, and so be capable of undertaking what the extended family system once did for the family members and particularly the mother.

In this new situation, men have continued to wash their hands of any responsibility at home and to evade many of the responsibilities in society and public life, responsibilities related to the need for a new organization of social life capable of solving the problems faced by women both at work and in the home. Women continue to bear the double or even triple burden constituted by their new roles in society and at the workplace, combined with their old roles at home, towards the husband, the children and sometimes relatives such as fathers, mothers, brothers, sisters and even cousins.

Whereas society has thrown overboard certain values that were an obstacle to the participation of women in the labour force, it has continued to uphold many old values with remarkable obstinacy, and in particular those values which ensure a continued exploitation of their efforts in caring for the home, husband and children, efforts which also continue to be unpaid. It has extolled the work of women and their right to education, and torn down social walls and fences that prevented women from becoming a freely circulating part of the labour force. Nevertheless, it continues to reinforce those values that bind women to their children and husbands in servitude; it continues to sing the virtues of sweet motherhood, to maintain (as in some Islamic circles) that 'Paradise lies under the feet of mothers' and that obedience to the husband is the highest of qualities in a woman and a mark of obedience to Almighty Allah. To this very day, an Egyptian woman with work and a career, even if she be a minister, is still governed by the law of obedience consecrated in the Egyptian Marriage Code. When a woman succumbs to the innumerable burdens in her job and in the home, or is unable to give her husband and children the care that is expected of her, she is not spared. Accusations are heaped on her head, not the least of which is that, by neglecting her children and not submitting herself to the husband's will and needs, she is contributing to the dissolution of 'sacred family bonds'.

Society pays great attention to preserving 'sacred family bonds' and yet cares little about what happens in matters without which the preservation of these 'sacred bonds' becomes no more than an illusion. The man's absolute right to divorce in Arab Islamic countries, to marriage with more than one wife, and to a legalized sexual licentiousness all negate any real security and stability for children, and destroy the very essence of true family life. Society raises 'motherhood' to the heavens and yet at the same time forgets to provide the facilities and means necessary for mothers to bring up their children appropriately. A woman is rarely given enough time to nurse her child, and the periods of leave afforded to her before and after giving birth to her baby are sadly inadequate.

The insistence that society has so far displayed in preserving the formal structure of the family, while depriving it of any genuine substantive content, is related to the desire of exploiting classes and the political powers that represent them to ensure that the economic functions of the family be maintained and that the family continues to bear the burden and costs of rearing children instead of these becoming the responsibility of the social system. The woman remains a source of free labour and of numerous services that would have to be compensated and paid for if other institutional arrangements were to take over her functions in the home. To prevent people from discovering the truths that lie at the basis of this touching attachment to the family system, society has all along reinforced the links between motherly love or family love and the upkeep, nourishment and rearing of children. It is as though motherly or family affection must and can only express itself in assuming unaided responsibility for their economic needs. At the same time the inequality, injustice and poverty which characterize the lives of the vast majority of people in Arab countries deprive them of any real possibility of performing adequately the functions for which the family system was created and is still maintained. The vast majority of families cannot provide their children with the required economic means. Most mothers suffer hunger, deprivation and a state of exhaustion, which renders them unfit to nourish their babies or even look after them. Without food their breasts dry up, without the basic needs of life their affection withers. Deprived of everything, they lose their capacity to give. Withered to the core by years of labour in the fields and in the home, their youth ebbs away in a matter of years, leaving a broken body and drying soul — a useless forgotten human being whose lot is to be cast aside for a younger and more attractive woman.

A woman who is educated may find more rewarding occupations and a career. Nevertheless, in most cases, the husband will continue to dominate her, to take possession of her earnings and to threaten her with divorce whenever she tries to loosen his grip or refuses to respond to his fantasies. Patriarchal norms and values continue to reign in the home, the street, the school, the mosque and the place of work and even in the concepts and attitudes propagated through radio programmes, television, films, the theatre, newspapers and magazines.

This is the situation of most women in the Arab countries. Yet I cannot agree with those women in America and Europe who draw sharp distinctions between their own situation and that of women in the region to which I belong, and who believe that there are fundamental differences. They tend to depict our life as a continual submission to medieval systems and point vehemently to some of the rituals and traditional practices such as female circumcision. They raise a hue and cry in defence of the victims, write long articles and deliver speeches at congresses. Of course, it is good that female circumcision be denounced. But by concentrating on such manifestations there is a risk that the real issues of social and economic change may be evaded or even forgotten and that effective action may be replaced by a feeling of superior humanity, a glow of satisfaction that may blind the mind and feelings to the concrete everyday struggle for women's emancipation.

I am against female circumcision and other similar retrograde and cruel practices. I was the first Arab woman to denounce it publicly and to write about it in my book *Woman and Sex*. I linked it to the other aspects of female oppression. But I disagree with those women in America and Europe who concentrate on issues such as female circumcision and depict them as proof of the unusual and barbaric oppression to which women are exposed only in African or Arab countries. I oppose all attempts to deal with such problems in isolation, or to sever their links with the general economic and social pressures to which women everywhere are exposed, and with the oppression which is the daily bread fed to the female sex in developed and developing countries, in both of which a patriarchal class system still prevails.

Women in Europe and America may not be exposed to surgical removal of the clitoris. Nevertheless, they are victims of cultural and psychological clitoridectomy. 'Lift the chains off my body, put the chains on my mind.' Sigmund Freud was perhaps the most famous of all those men who taught psychological and physiological circumcision of women when he formulated his theory on the psychic nature of women, described the clitoris as a male organ, and sexual activity related to the clitoris as an infantile phase, and when he maintained that maturity and mental health in a woman required that sexual activity related to the clitoris cease and be transferred to the vagina.

No doubt the physical ablation of the clitoris appears a much more savage and cruel procedure than its psychological removal. Nevertheless, the consequences can be exactly the same, since the end result is the abolition of its functions so that its presence or absence amount to the same thing. Psychological surgery might even be more malicious and harmful because it tends to produce the illusion of being complete, whereas in actual fact the body may have lost an essential organ, like a child born an idiot yet provided with brain substance. It can create the illusion of being free, whereas in actual fact freedom has been lost.

To live in an illusion, not to know the truth, is the most dangerous of all things for a human being, woman or man, because it deprives people of their most important weapon in the struggle for freedom, emancipation, and control of their lives and future. To be conscious that you are still a slave still living under oppression is the first step on the road to emancipation.

We the women in Arab countries realize that we are still slaves, still oppressed, not because we belong to the East, not because we are Arab, or members of Islamic societies, but as a result of the patriarchal class system that has dominated the world for thousands of years.

To rid ourselves of this system is the only way to become free. Freedom for women will never be achieved unless they unite into an organized political force powerful enough and conscious enough and dynamic enough to truly represent half of society. To my mind the real reason why women have been unable to complete their emancipation, even in the socialist countries, is that they have failed to constitute themselves into a political force powerful, conscious and dynamic enough to impose their rights.

More and more women are being drawn into the struggle for social transformation in the Arab countries. Many of them, however, still believe that the cause of women's liberation is purely a woman's problem, or a particular social change related to the family, to the husband, or to children, a problem which is completely separate and distinct, unrelated to the major political issues in society, or to the struggle for socialism, freedom and democracy.

However, the experience and mistakes of the past have contributed towards a growing maturity among the women and men who are playing a leading role in progressive social movements and parties. Many of them are realizing more clearly the need to bridge the gap between political and civil life, between the general issues of society and the personal problems and needs related to each individual, between the broad functioning of government in society and the daily participation of people in the solution of their own problems and the running of their own affairs. They feel the need for a modern theory of social transformation that links thought to action, intellect to feelings and emotion, and that is able to build up a new and higher relationship between women and men in their struggle for a better world.

This new concept of society, and of the processes related to its transformation, must be able to concretize the relationship between the general oppression of both men and women, and the specific forms of oppression to which women alone are exposed for no other reason than that they are women. In other words, there is an urgent and vital need to visualize the links between the political, economic and social remoulding of society, and the cultural, moral, psychological, sexual and affective remoulding of the human being, and to blaze the trails along which this process must advance.

The creation of a woman's movement in each Arab country, capable of mobilizing the women in every home, village, town or city, of drawing into its ranks the illiterate peasant woman, the female factory worker, the educated professional woman, will mean that the Arab movement for democracy, progress and socialism is capable of reaching every woman, and is attaining the stage where it is a real mass movement and not just the instrument of a specific class.

It is Arab women alone who can formulate the theory, the ideas, and the modes of struggle needed to liberate themselves from all oppression. It is their efforts alone that can create a new Arab woman, alive with her own originality, capable of choosing what is most genuine and valuable in her cultural tradition, as well as assimilating the progress of science and modern thought. Conscious Arab women who no longer live under the illusion that freedom will come as a gift from the heavens, or be bestowed upon them by the chivalry of men, but understand that the road to freedom is long and arduous, and that the price to pay is heavy. Such women alone are those that will lead others to total emancipation. Such Arab women will not hesitate because they know that, if the price to pay for freedom is heavy, the price of slavery is even heavier.

ع Preface to the English edition of *The Hidden Face of Eve: Women in the Arab World*, which was first published in Arabic in 1977; the English edition was translated by Sherif Hetata and published by Zed Books in 1980.

5

Women, Creativity and Dissidence

WHY the conference?

In May 2005 approximately two hundred men and women from four continents participated in a conference entitled Women, Creativity, and Dissidence that I convened in Cairo, Egypt, under the aegis of the Arab Women Solidarity Association (AWSA). One would not need to look far to find reasons for the necessity of such a global gathering at this juncture in transnational and global relations. Grave concerns about the deepening inequalities within, between and among nations and the dissatisfaction, disaffection and conflicts they provoke give pertinence and urgency to gatherings such as the Cairo conference.

In this age of rapid information access and unprecedented global plunder and greed, women, men and children all over the world are suffering from the effects of increasing economic exploitation; erosion of social and democratic rights; discrimination based on class, race, gender, colour and religion; and efforts by the media to misinform the public by mystifying and distorting current realities and future possibilities.

The Cairo conference reflected the growing solidarity among women and between women and men by bringing together female and male activists, academicians, creative artists, researchers, cultural workers and theorists. It highlighted the need to break down the barriers among women, between men and women, between academics and activists, and between groups working for peace, human rights, civil liberties and the protection of the environment if we wish to be part of the growing world movement against global violence and a global market that undermines human potential and saps material and spiritual resources.

Peoples of the Arab world, Africa, Asia and Latin America are overburdened by conflicts, violence and famine; increasing poverty generated by the greed and lack of corporate responsibility among Western multinationals; and the unbridled militarism and neocolonial assault of the current neoconservative United States administration and the right-wing apparatus of the European Union in the name of democracy, human rights and women's rights — particularly in the so-called war on terror waged in Iraq and Afghanistan and the continued Israeli occupation of Palestine.

To forcefully confront and successfully defeat this global assault on humanity, it has become necessary now more than ever before to build a united superpower of men, women and children of the world. In the midst of our rich diversity we need unity to discover and reinforce what is common to us all — our basic humanity and our longing for justice, democracy and peace despite differences of nationality, class, race, colour, ethnicity, gender or religion. We need to believe in our creativity in order to cherish and nurture this longing in all fields of human endeavour — the sciences, arts and humanities, politics, economics, culture and social change. We need to encourage dissidence and rebellion against injustice, oppression and all forms of discrimination.

Linking women, creativity and dissidence

Creativity and dissidence will continue to be linked as long as we live in a world built not on justice and real freedom but on force, false democracy, coercion, obedience and submission to the oppressor, false consciousness and fragmented knowledge, and the utilization of religion to play politics and reinforce a free market. Creativity flourishes when the mind and the imagination are freed from the chains of taboos and traditions, from the false consciousness and knowledge generated by the media and educational systems, and from the commercialization of values and morals.

The three words *creativity*, *dissidence* and *women*, especially when linked, are bound to cause fear and anxiety in most men, and some women, not only in our countries but also in other parts of the world; fear and anxiety have become more pervasive and intense since the 1980s with the emergence of corporate capitalist globalization accompanied by religious fundamentalist crusades sweeping through many parts of the world, thanks to Islam, Judaism, Christianity, Hinduism and Buddhism.

Ever since the days of the slave system and the birth of patriarchy and class, these three words were linked to the Devil, the first rebel in history, the only angel who questioned what the other angels feared to question and the only one who tried to see things from a different perspective. There is a close relationship among creativity, knowledge and awareness of what goes on around us. Creativity gives birth to new knowledge, to a new consciousness. It is a rebellion against ignorance, submission and injustice. When women rebel against ignorance, submission and injustice they instil fear and anxiety in those who rule over them.

Woman was the first in history to be creative, to be seduced by the tree of knowledge, by the new and the unknown. And gathered here at this conference we are the daughters and sons of Eve, the first rebel, and perhaps of the Devil too. We are following their path, for they were the first to show the way; they were trailblazers in dissident acts and creativity. Both were eternally cursed, banished and made to suffer because they sought to discover and to know. So it is understandable if these three words — *women, creativity* and *dissidence* — arouse waves of anger, anxiety and fear.

Women constitute more than one-half of humanity. They are the poorest and the most oppressed and exploited, especially when class, colour, race and religion intersect. Women are the people who suffer the most from neocolonialism and patriarchal structures; they are the people who need solidarity the most in the struggle for their rights. Religious fundamentalist movements — whether Islamic,

Judaic, Christian, Hindu or Buddhist — are often fuelled by their opposition to global corporate capitalism in the confusion of our age. Women are the first victims of the rigidity and patriarchal violence of fundamentalism. To fight against neocolonialism and fundamentalist movements, women must join hands, think and act together, and network. To mitigate or overcome their differences, women need awareness, a true consciousness, creativity and inventiveness.

It is not surprising that a global political, economic and social system built on power and force rather than equality and justice should have recourse to the age-old heavenly, sacred authority of religion to assert itself by launching an offensive against the growing resistance of women and men of conscience who are using their creativity to build a new world. It is also understandable that the women and men slaves of this age should in turn seek to transform religion into an ideological weapon in their struggle to be freed from the injustices imposed by those who hold power in the state, society and family.

There is an enduring struggle between the rulers and the ruled, between the patriarchal masters and the slaves, between the oppressed women and men and the corporate capitalist bosses trying to enforce their neoliberal doctrines. But in the process they end up marginalizing vast populations and creating a breeding ground for fundamentalist religious movements that will ultimately be used as a pretext for war. The situation is complicated by the exigencies of an information age.

Our postmodern age is characterized by the dominance of information technology and science. Information technology has become even more dangerous than the military weapons that are now highly dependent on this technology. The destruction of the mind, of its creativity and the nurturing of false consciousness built on scattered, delinked information, has become more lethal than destruction by war. The creation of a false consciousness among women makes them more amenable to submission and enslavement, more prone to become the tools of propagating male desire, obedient victims of male violence, and domesticated to work in the home where they are needed or toil where needed outside the home, all in the name of culture, tradition, nation, religion or divine law. When women submit, they cease to rebel against patriarchal domination and fundamentalist teachings, and they lose their ability to question, think independently and be creative. Sometimes they internalize submission so much that they take pleasure in it and may go as far as engaging in self-immolation.

It was reported a few days preceding this conference that in Cairo two young women in their early twenties, wearing the niqab that covered their entire body except their eyes, attempted to attack a bus of tourists with two outdated guns; and, having failed, one of them shot the other and then committed suicide. They were obeying the orders of their men as ordained by the religious precepts with which they had been indoctrinated, and in so doing these two young women became their own enemy.

How does a woman become her own enemy? She can do so by accepting to become a consumerist sex object, ready and eager to dress and undress for men, submit to religious precepts that are against the true spirit of religion, imprison herself in the home or wear a black tent in the humid heat of summer. When a woman is her own enemy, what can we do? This is one of the greatest obstacles that feminist movements face.

In Arab countries, conservative interpretations of religion and a cultural indoctrination in patriarchal contexts account for female subordination to men. This is not because Islam as a religion is more backward than Judaism or Christianity. Our societies have not been able to develop, to modernize economically and socially, because we were colonized for long periods of time. Our industry and agriculture have both regressed and we are exposed to market consumerism, on the one hand, and religious fundamentalism, on the other hand, after successive governments, allied first with the British and now with the Americans, have connived to liquidate progressive, democratic and left-wing movements in our countries.

Expanding the understanding of creativity

Sometimes there is the tendency to limit creativity to literature and the arts. But, in reality, creativity can be exercised in all areas of life and work, including economics, politics, culture, religion, social development, the sciences and the arts. With the global changes affecting human society, women in Arab countries and other parts of the world have exhibited an amazing degree of creativity by adapting their struggles within the family, at work and in society to these changes through innovative ideas and practices within their movements. They have broken through many of the boundaries and limitations that held them back in the past. Feminist movements have abandoned their exclusionary practices directed against men, and little by little men are changing some of their prejudices against women. Women have played an important role in the struggle against war, in movements against corporate capitalist globalization, and are increasingly visible in cultural activities and the professions. Their contributions to literature, philosophy, democratization, social movements and community development are often remarkable. Their contribution to religious interpretation and thinking, once the prerogative of men, has also been remarkable. Women have linked religion to its historical context and concentrated on the humanistic aspects of religious texts in the Qur'an, Bible and New Testament in an attempt to emphasize the areas that support justice and freedom for women and men.

Every creative contribution to human thinking leads to a struggle between the new and the old, between the oppressors and those who are seeking freedom, between the exploited and the exploiters, between the irrational and the rational. When what is new prevails, additional problems surface and newly formulated questions arise. Controversy and struggle are inevitable and necessary, especially during periods of rapid change, and they should be welcomed as positive, provided they are nonviolent, use democratic means and avoid bloodshed.

The fragmentation that has affected the feminist movement and reduced the size and effectiveness of many of its constituent organizations might conceal the fact that women's resistance to patriarchy and male domination has grown in scope and variety.

So far as religion goes, women have broken down barriers in theory and practice. They are increasingly occupying positions of authority in the churches and playing the role of imam or leading Muslim congregations in prayer. Women are also playing more visible and significant roles in politics — voting in elections, running for office, and occupying important political positions. Recently in Egypt, I presented myself as a candidate for the presidency. Not surprisingly, the first time that a woman took the audacious step to run for president in Egypt generated a lot of debate in print and electronic media in Egypt and other Arab countries.

During my run for the presidency, a controversy erupted in Egypt over the question of a woman aspiring to be president. The religious authorities had different opinions on this issue. The Sheikh of Al Azhar, Dr Mohammed Sayed Tantawi, declared that in Islam a woman can become president, whereas the Mufti, Dr Ali Goma'a, said that Islam is categorically against a woman becoming the president of the country. When asked why this was so, he replied, 'Because of her physiology and her monthly periods.' Perhaps His Excellency the Mufti does not know that in my village and in the other villages of Egypt, women often work in the fields from dawn to dusk despite their monthly periods. Peasant women sometimes give birth in the field and without any assistance, cut the umbilical cord, bury the placenta, wrap the baby in a basket, and place it on their head and walk home.

However, this does not mean that it is enough for a woman to hold a high office in order to advance the cause of women and their resistance against male domination. Women at different levels can sometimes reinforce male domination by the ideas they propagate and the policies they defend. For example, women such as Margaret Thatcher and Condoleezza Rice, who are not much different from George W. Bush or Dick Cheney so far as world-view and policies go, are capable of wreaking the types of havoc that their militaristic male colleagues have brought to different parts of the globe. Rice speaks of women's rights in Iraq but supports the Bush administration's bombing of civilian populations, killing and maiming children and women. Margaret Thatcher ruled with an iron fist, supported Pinochet, and stood against women's rights in her country.

Creativity and dissidence serve women and their causes when they raise women's consciousness, lift the veils off their minds, and enhance their resistance against patriarchal violence and inequalities in the family in particular and society at large. Creativity channelled in such a way paves the way for change; demolishes outmoded, reactionary antidemocratic structures; and strengthens political and social movements grounded in the struggle for peace, democracy, justice and gender equality.

Nonetheless, when social structures change there is always an intervening period of chaos and confusion. Transitional periods of chaos are inevitable, but we should learn how to live and deal with them, how to allay the anxiety, fear and insecurity that they often engender among men and women. Creative women know how to live with chaos because they understand that every creation is an inspiration that surges up out of chaos. Dissidence and chaos that disturb the status quo are sometimes linked to madness in the minds of many women and men, who fear anything that upsets the false stability with which they surround themselves. Creative women throughout history were often considered to be mad. Dissident women in the Middle Ages were burned as witches. I remember that as a young girl when I first held a pen to write and expressed my desire to be a writer my peers in medical college, even my girlfriends, said that I was mad. When I ran for president, an important member of the People's Assembly (the party of the ruling government) said that I was a mad woman. He insulted male candidates from the opposition by accusing them of being corrupt, dishonest or opportunistic, but the only candidate he described as mad was me, a woman.

The theory of chaos has become a part of world science. The minds of women and men have started to assimilate the idea of chaos as being the other side of order, like night is the other side to day, death a corollary to life, and madness an integral part of reason.

Old forms, new questions: resistance and change

The marriage law in Egypt has remained rigidly patriarchal. It permits the father to shirk his responsibilities. The patriarchal family law remains a cornerstone for the maintenance of the class patriarchal system; hence the ferocious attempt by Islamic political movements and most men to use tradition, custom and prevailing culture to mould the consciousness of men and women in society. Women continue to be scapegoats, despite the continued resistance and efforts of Egyptian women that have led to slight improvements such as the right of a woman to ask for divorce by going to court; but this costs money, and efforts are only possible in the cases of women who are relatively well off. In contrast, men can still marry more than one wife if they wish, and over 2 per cent of men continue to do so, especially when they grow old and want a younger woman to reinforce their waning powers, or they divorce and remarry, leaving the older wife and her children to fight for alimony in the courts.

Another recent controversy in Egypt revolves around the right of women to carry out the functions of an imam and lead the faithful in prayer. The majority of men and a number of women do not support the idea of a woman becoming an imam. Among these women is Dr Soad Saleh, dean of the School of Islamic Studies at the University of Al Azhar. She has maintained that in Islam there are strict conditions that have to be applied to those who become imams, namely maturity of mind and body, but above all they have to be masculine. Therefore a woman cannot become an imam, because she could potentially corrupt the rows of men praying behind her when she kneels down and prostrates in prayer.

The same reasoning is advanced by those who insist that women must wear the veil to avoid tempting men with their exposed hair and faces. In the reasoning of those who argue for the seclusion of women and their exclusion from performing various functions in the public sphere is the assumption that men are weak, cannot control their desires, and are liable to be sexually aroused at all times.

Despite all these difficulties, women are resisting and bringing about change in different parts of the world. During a recent trip to Algeria, I attended a conference about the new family law promulgated as a result of the continuous efforts that women's groups and associations have made in that country. Despite the vociferous campaign the Islamic political movements have launched, an Algerian man can no longer marry more than one wife or divorce without permission from the court, and he cannot prevent his daughter from marrying the partner of her choice. A woman also cannot divorce without going to court. Additionally, the head of the family is no longer necessarily a man. This responsibility can be taken over by other members of the family, by the mother or an older son or daughter if one of them is more capable of assuming the role.

These changes are extremely important because they signify a radical democratic change within the family. Democracy is a process that begins at birth and continues until the end of life. It is not just about voting in elections. Algerian women have waged continuous battles against colonialism, taken to the streets to demonstrate against the fundamentalist movement, and often sacrificed their lives in these struggles to gain more rights. Creativity, change and progress can never be achieved without paying a price; the process requires courage, a lot of courage.

Towards a new identity built on human solidarity

Despite all the difficulties that women in particular and democratic movements in general face, the world is witnessing a new creative solidarity of peoples, a solidarity seeking common goals in the richness of diversity. It is a solidarity rooted in the rejection of all forms of discrimination based on class, gender, race, colour or religion.

This world movement of peoples, of women and men against global market exploitation and those against war and violence and injustices and oppression, owes a great deal to the feminist movement and to the efforts of women who have unmasked the contradictions of the class patriarchal system; linked the personal and familial with the political; evolved new forms of democratic organization; abolished the separation between reason and emotion; and questioned the separation between the local and global, form and content, sciences and the arts, politics and social change, subject and object, spirit and body, the individual and the collective, and the self and the other, as well as between philosophical thought and theorizing, on the one hand, and the creativity of the body in dance and rhythm, in song and music, painting and sculpture, on the other hand.

Gender consciousness has brought in its wake the wave that sweeps through all boundaries and separations. It has brought erosion into science; demonstrated that creative writing, music and dance express thought and feeling in action; and narrowed the gap between theory and practice. The feminist movement has opened up to all movements the wish to build another world, to preserve the environment against the encroachments of science and technology.

This new identity, this human solidarity, this free flow of minds and bodies is exemplified in this conference that has brought together a Swedish dancer, a Hindu thinker, an Arab professor, a Nigerian poet, and researchers from Egypt, Syria and Palestine. Here we all meet in the struggle against gender discrimination, imperialism and war, and male domination and the false consciousness that make women and men accept the unacceptable. And because we are many and from diverse, rich cultures and histories, and are made powerful by our common quest for peace, justice and democracy, we are unbeatable, even though the path before us is long and arduous.

We women and men at this conference are united in our opposition to the antagonisms between East and West, between South and North, and among whites, coloureds and blacks that we have inherited from colonial history. We reject the idea that there is no meeting ground for women and men, that God created some to be rich and others to be poor, and that all this is in the natural order of things. We believe that change is the essence of life, that our creativity and social action will re-create our world. We believe that creativity can break down all sorts of barriers — between the sciences and the arts and humanities, between politics and economics, time and space, mind and body, town and gown, and theory and practice. Writing is a weapon in the fight for justice, real democracy and peace, which are built on human rights not force.

At this conference we insist on the wholeness of women — body, spirit and mind. We reject the idea that women are nothing but bodies made to be dressed or undressed, painted or veiled, to suit the sexual appetites and desires of men in the name of consumerism or the will of God. We are aware that some women have participated and continue to participate in perpetrating and perpetuating patriarchal and neocolonialist violence within and between nations.

Numerous conference presentations on the treatment of detainees and prisoners in Guantènamo and Abu Ghraib argue that the most dangerous form of terrorism is state terrorism, which uses military means to subjugate people, decimate the population, and occupy and plunder their lands. We believe that violence inside and outside the home — violence against women by men and the violence against women or men by women — is the product of male dominance and war. We also believe that it is the right of the people to resist violence and the invasion and occupation of their lands.

Women and men gathered in this conference believe that in all cultures and in all religions God should be a symbol of justice, freedom, peace, love, art and beauty, creativity and rebellion against injustice and all forms of discrimination. We must struggle against all forces that seek to create a false consciousness and against the maintenance of male domination as natural or God-ordained, as the road to happiness and success in the free market of pleasure and sex. We must cooperate with all progressive democratic social forces and above all promote solidarity among women who everyday and all over the world are proving their courage and resilience in the struggle against war and for peace, against oppression and for freedom, and against patriarchal culture, and for a new culture built on equality and respect for human- and womankind.

๛ First published as 'The Seventh International AWSA Conference' in *Meridians: Feminism, Race, Transnationalism* 6(2), 2006.

6

Women and the Poor:
The Challenge of Global Justice

WHY DO WE HAVE inequality and poverty in the world? I notice that some people still use the phrase 'Third World' to name us, to name the people who live in Africa, Asia and South America. This term is no longer used by many people, including myself, because we live in one world (not three) and we are dominated or governed by one global system which is now called the New World Order. However, we know that in fact it is an old world order which uses new methods of exploitation and domination, both economic and intellectual. Language and the media have become more efficient at obscuring the real aims of those international institutions or groups that speak about peace, development, justice, equality, human rights and democracy, but whose agreements and decisions lead to the opposite — that is, to war, poverty, inequality and dictatorship.

While I was writing this, I came across a recent issue of the magazine *International Viewpoint*. On its back cover I read a letter written by the secretary general of Oxfam in Belgium in which he explains why he resigned from the NGO World Bank Group.[1]

> The remedies provided by the World Bank for development are poisoned remedies that accelerate the process [of poverty, hunger and unemployment]. For my soul and conscience I am obliged

to tell you 'enough'. You have stolen the correct discourse of the
NGOs on development, eco-development, poverty and people's
participation. At the same time your policies of structural adjustment and your actions accelerate social dumping in the South by
obliging it to enter defenceless into the World Market.... Africa
is dying, but the World Bank is enriching itself. Asia and Eastern
Europe are being robbed of all their riches, and the World Bank
supports the initiatives of the IMF, and GATT, that authorize this
pillage, which is both intellectual and material. Latin America,
like other continents, watches in horror as its children serve as a
reserve army of labour and, worse, a reserve of organs for the new
transplantation market in North America.

These are the words of an expert who worked very close to the
international institutions that speak about development, peace, social
justice, democracy, human rights, and decide what should be done.
These international institutions are often considered to be economic
or social only. In fact, they are political as well, and the international
military machine supports them.

We all know that the United States of America is the most
powerful country in military terms in the world. In 1993 the financial editor of the *Chicago Tribune* proposed that the USA should
become a mercenary state using its monopoly power in the 'security
market' to maintain its control over the world economic system,
selling 'protection' to other wealthy powers that would pay a 'war
premium'.

How can we speak about real development in Africa, Asia or
South America without knowing the real reasons for poverty and
maldevelopment, and for the increasing gap between the rich and
the poor not only at the international and regional levels but also
within each country, at the national level? We have to make a correct
diagnosis of the problem if we wish to have the right remedies. We
cannot speak about global injustice without speaking about inequality between countries, inequality between classes in each country,
and inequalities are linked together in the patriarchal capitalist
system that governs the world today.

What is development?

Countries in our region and in the South generally are subjected to what is called 'development'. Development is not something we choose. It is dictated to us through local governments dominated by the international institutions such as the World Bank, the International Monetary Fund (IMF) and the General Agreement on Tariffs and Trade (GATT). The result of development carried out in line with the policies of these institutions continues to be increasing poverty, and an increasing flow of money and riches from South to North. From 1984 to 1990 the application of structural adjustment policies (SAPs) in the South led to the transfer of $178 billion from the South to the commercial banks in the North.

Development is just another word for neocolonialism. We need to be very careful when we use the word *development*. The word *aid* is just as deceiving: we know that money and riches flow from the South to the North, not in the opposite direction. A very small portion of what was taken from us comes back to us under the term 'aid'. This creates the false idea that we receive aid from the North.

In this way, we are robbed not only of our material resources, but also of our human dignity. Human dignity is based on being independent and self-reliant, on producing what we eat rather than living on aid coming from the exterior. Aid is a myth that should be demystified. Many countries in the South have started to raise the slogan 'Fair trade not aid'. What the South needs in order to fight against poverty is a *new international economic order* based on justice, and on fair trade laws between countries, not *aid* or charity. Charity and injustice are two faces of the same coin. If we have real equality between people and between countries, there will be nothing called charity or aid.

Countries in the South plead for justice, equality and democracy in the global society; their plea is for a *new world order based on justice*. The title New World Order has been taken from the South by the powerful military machine in the North to continue the now undivided rule of the neocolonial order following the end of the

Cold War. This New World Order was inaugurated by launching the Gulf War. The media and the international information order concealed the real economic reasons behind the Gulf War (oil) behind a false morality built on phrases such as 'human rights', 'democracy', 'liberation of Kuwait', and so on.

This was repeated with the war in Somalia. All wars in human history have been concealed behind humane or religious camouflage. If we reread the Old Testament we discover how the war to invade the land of Canaan was considered a holy war ordered by Jehovah (God).

Today we live in a world dominated by a unipolar power, by one superpower which is the USA. The USA dominates the United Nations (UN), the World Bank, the IMF, GATT, SAPs and so on. Through these international agreements and institutions the North is strengthening its grip on the world economy. The USA and powerful European countries in the North have become a de facto board of management for the world economy, protecting their interests and imposing their will on the South.

The problems facing the South are rooted in the North — problems like increasing poverty, low commodity prices, the huge debt burden, and unequal trade agreements. The trend to privatization and deregulation forced on the South has coincided with a huge and rapid increase in the profits of transnational corporations (TNCs). It is known that 90 per cent of TNCs are based in the North. They control 70 per cent of world trade. Five hundred of these corporations have almost complete control of the world economy. The South is forced to open up the agricultural sector to the TNCs, endangering its ability to feed itself.

Many fertile agricultural countries in the South, such as Egypt, where the valley of the Nile is cultivated with three crops a year, are unable to feed themselves. In Egypt we import 90 per cent of our food.[2] The export of cotton from Egypt has diminished to one-tenth of what it was in 1984, and the import of cotton has tripled.

The average monthly wage of the Egyptian worker in 1994 is 300 Egyptian pounds, whereas his foreign colleague in Egypt is paid 4,000 pounds per month. Some 40 per cent of the population in Egypt lives below the poverty line. That is, their annual income is less than $386. The World Bank and the IMF help the TNCs to relocate their units of production to the countries of the South where social costs are low. Here labour laws are not applied or do not exist, social and health insurance is lacking, labour unions are weak and dominated by their governments, collective agreements between trade unions or workers and their employers often do not exist, and legislation is enacted to favour the employers. Governments are dominated by TNCs, women and children can be used as labour at lower wages especially in the informal sector, and the pollution of the environment is uncontrolled since the technologies used are under almost no constraints.

What is a good government in the South?

The result of this international economic and international information order is constant pressure on economies to be more competitive. The aim is more and more profit with lower and low costs. The aim cannot be achieved except through growing pressure on governments in the South to cut spending and diminish social costs — especially those related to subsidies that reduce the prices of essential foods, and to health and educational services, energy, and so on. In 1977 there were widespread demonstrations in Egypt, mainly composed of the poor, women and youths. These demonstrations erupted as a result of the government's decision to raise the prices of most essential foods. The decision came after continuous pressure from the World Bank.

A good government is now defined as the government that accepts the conditions of the World Bank and submits the nation's economy to the interests of TNCs and other international groups. A good government is a government that accepts what is called aid in order to achieve what is called development.

In Egypt two words, *aid* and *development*, have resulted in increased poverty and increased deprivation. Between 1975 (when American aid began) and 1986, Egypt imported commodities and services from the USA to a total of $30 billion. During the same period, Egypt exported to the USA total commodities worth only $5 billion.[3] This shows the real aim of this aid, namely to enrich the capitalist US economy and not to help Egypt advance on the road to development.

Religion, the poor and women

In this world economic order, the indispensable sacrifices of structural adjustment are required for the globalization of the economy and of markets. They are the indispensable 'desert crossing' en route to the Eden of development (to use the words of the World Bank). This fatalistic, almost metaphysical, conception of necessity has recourse to religion. Religion is the ideology used by the rich to exploit the poor in the South. The majority of the poor in the world are women, youth and children. These days a new term, 'the feminization of poverty', is often mentioned. It means that more women are becoming poor. According to UN figures, the number of rural women living in absolute poverty rose over the 1970s and 1980s by about 50 per cent (from an estimated 370 million to 565 million), and women (who are half the world's population) work two-thirds of the total labour hours worked, earn one-tenth of total world income, and own one-hundredth of world possessions.

Gender, or women's oppression, is inseparable from class, race and religious oppression. The patriarchal class system propagates the idea that the oppression of women and the poor is a divine law and is not man-made:

> The rich man in his castle
> the poor man at his gate.
> God made them high or lowly,
> and ordained their estate.

We all know that in all religions women have an inferior position relative to men. This is especially true for the monotheistic religions. Adam is superior to Eve, and in almost all religions women should be governed by men. In human history, to exploit women and the poor was not possible without the use of religion. Slavery was considered to be a divine law by prominent philosophers in the past and even in our own day.

Now we are faced by a resurgence of religious so-called fundamentalism. Some people think it is only Islamic. This is not true. Religious fundamentalism is an international phenomenon. The international patriarchal class system is encouraging the revival of religion all over the world. Christian fundamentalism was encouraged in the USA by Reagan and Bush. They also used, and often encouraged, Islamic fundamentalism in our region, the so-called Middle East, in order to fight against the Soviet Union and communism. In Egypt it was Sadat who encouraged religious fundamentalism to neutralize the socialist, the progressive liberal and the Nasserite political currents in the country. In Algeria, it was the state (under Chadli) that encouraged the religious groups to grow in power.

The term often used to describe this phenomenon is 'state fundamentalism'. State political power and religious political power are two faces of the same coin. They feed each other. Sometimes they clash and fight each other in their struggle to dominate the state. This is what is now happening under Mubarak. In fact, they are old friends and new enemies. Sadat was killed by the fundamentalists after he had encouraged them to grow. The son killed the father. This is an oft-repeated story with which we are familiar in history. Wherever there is a religious revival, women are among the first victims. All fundamentalist groups, whether Christian, Jewish or Islamic, are antagonistic to women's liberation and women's rights. The backlash against women's rights is thus also a universal phenomenon, and is not restricted to our region.

Women and population control

The capitalist patriarchal system (reframed as the New World Order) has developed population-control policies to facilitate more exploitation of the poor and women in the so-called Third World. It is no surprise that population-control institutions (such as the Population Council, the UN International Planned Parenthood Federation

(IPPF), the multinational pharmaceuticals corporations, USAid) work in collaboration with the neocolonial global institutions such as the World Bank and the IMF. Population-control policies are a new biological war against women and the poor whose aim is to keep the economic and intellectual resources of the world under the control of minority power structures in the North and their collaborators in the South.

To hide their anti-women, anti-poor policies, population controllers have stolen the language of the women's liberation movements. Phrases such as 'women's needs', 'free choice', 'reproductive rights', 'empowerment of women' and 'family planning' are used to elaborate strategies against women and the poor. In the North, 20 per cent of the world's people consume 80 per cent of global resources. Instead of working towards global justice or a more egalitarian distribution of wealth and power, the multinational corporations work to eliminate the poor people in the so-called Third World. Women are rushed to consume unsafe contraceptive methods such as the injectable contraceptive Depo-Provera, and the contraceptive implant Norplant. The basic needs of women — such as food, education, health, employment, social, economic and political participation, and a life free of violence (whether inflicted from inside the family or by the state) — are neglected.

Population-control programmes started in the 1950s under the banner of 'poverty eradication'. The results have been the eradication of the poor, not poverty. Poverty is increasing year after year. More and more people in our countries are killed by hunger, more than those killed by war. Population-control programmes nowadays are working under new titles, such as 'to curb environmental destruction', 'to ensure sustainable growth', and so on. But none of this is happening. The reality is that women in the South are subjected to a range of coercive technologies and drugs, which have often destroyed their health and lives. People in the South are looked upon not as people but as demographic variables or population indices.

Yet people in the South are not really poor. Our continents are rich but our riches are robbed by continuous pillage by colonial and neocolonial powers.

The New Economic World Order and the media have consistently equated poverty in the South with population growth. This is another myth which hides the real causes of economic and political crisis in our countries. After the oil crises, credit-based development was forced on the South. It resulted in the debt crisis and increasing poverty and unemployment.

Commodification and trafficking of women (in the South and in the North as well) are increasing. Women are looked upon as bodies to be exploited and used to produce more profit. They must be veiled, covered physically according to the religious fundamentalists, but should be undressed according to the postmodern capitalists, or made to buy make-up and body conditioners. Sex is a commodity, a thriving industry. Sex shops and pornography, the commerce of sex, spread like wildfire.

Veiling the mind

The mass media and the international information order are working together with the international economic order to veil the minds of billions of people living on our planet. The new technology of communications transmits lies and myths all over the world in a matter of minutes or seconds.

The new international order is working to foster *globalization* or *global multinational capitalism* (the postmodern stage of capitalist development). The globalization of the economy requires the globalization of information, mass media and culture. This requires the breaking down of national and regional barriers to permit the free flow of capital, commodities, labour and information. Global capitalism requires global flexibility to enable the so-called free market (freedom of the powerful to dominate the weak). Despite the competitive struggles between the different powerful groups in the North and between the TNCs, a global market requires the establishment of a market of consumers who develop similar needs, similar interests, similar desires, and similar habits of living: that is, similar patterns of consumption. These patterns of consumption are constituted by a similar outlook on life, similar values and ideas.

This is a postmodern culture which is similar in many ways across the globe, irrespective of regional or national location.

The beauty mentality and its material products such as make-up, perfumes, earrings, fashion, and so forth are sold globally by global media (television, radio, newspaper, magazines, movies, videos, songs, music). The aim is to create a conception of beauty that becomes part of the culture and has its set of values, feelings and desires which are absorbed by the conscious and the subconscious mind. The cultural unconscious and the political unconscious are not separate from the conscious. The relation between culture, politics and economics is very important; this is true not only of the economic and political processes within which the cultural takes form, but also of the psychological processes that engage in its production and reception. I remember a French woman who came to me in 1993 and criticized Muslim women for wearing the veil. This French woman had a thick coating of make-up on her face, but she was completely unaware that this also was a veil. The French woman's veil was considered by the global media as modern and beautiful, but the other veil was considered backward and ugly; yet the two veils were almost the same since they both hid the real face of the woman.

Unveiling the mind

When we started the Arab Women's Solidarity Association in 1982 we had two major objectives: the unveiling of the mind, and political power through unity and solidarity. We faced strong opposition from local Arab governments (who work with the international capitalist powers) and from fanatical religious groups and from a variety of political parties. But we continued to resist. We had to fight at different levels and on different fronts, to link the psychological with the economic, the political with the historical, the cultural with the religious, and the sexual with the social.

To unveil the mind necessitated exposing the contradictions of the New World Order (both economic and cultural). This order encourages globalization and unification when these serve its economic interests, but fights against globalization or unification between people if they resist its policies. To unveil the mind we had to expose the link between religion and politics, between capitalism and religious fundamentalism.

The globalization needed by the international capitalist system leads people in different countries or cultures to resist homogenization resulting from the global culture, or so-called universal values. It is a self-defence mechanism. It is an attempt to hold on to an authentic identity, or authentic culture or heritage, and these are some of the factors in the growth of religious fundamentalism, racism and ethnic struggles. It is a protest movement (especially among the youth), but very often takes on reactionary, retrograde, anti-women and anti-progressive characteristics, leading to division and discord; it thus serves the purpose of capitalist globalization because it divides the people who are resisting it.

How to empower resistance

We need unity and solidarity between men and women who resist this global injustice at the local level as well as at the international level. But we need a movement that is progressive, not backward, which seeks unity in diversity, by breaking down barriers built on discrimination (by gender, class, race, religion…), and by discovering what we have in common as human beings with common interests that may express themselves differently. People can unite and cooperate if they struggle for greater equality and against all forms of discrimination. This requires establishing a network step by step from the local up to the global level to face the international capitalist network. We can use modern technology such as videos, cassettes, public radio, television and so on, and begin with local grassroots networks to create our own mass media. For example, we all know the role the cassette played in the Iranian Revolution. Many of the religious fundamentalist groups in Algeria, Egypt and other parts of the world are using the cassette, transmitters, cell phones, and so forth to reach masses of people.

Women and the poor in the South have to cooperate with the progressive forces in the North who are fighting the same battle, but resistance starts at home. We can only change the international order by each one of us, step by step, changing the system in which we live.

Without genuine democracy this movement cannot succeed. Democracy as practised in the North under the patriarchal class system is just a set of institutions such as a parliament or a congress. It is a limited, formal and false democracy which excludes the majority of women and the poor from elections and other means of expression. We need real democracy. This real democracy starts at the personal level, at home, in the family. If we have men or husbands who are dictators in the family, how can we have democracy in the state, since it is based on the family unit? Democracy is day-to-day practice and should be rooted in childhood, in the psyche, in beliefs, ethics, attitudes, and private as well as public life.

It is necessary to undo the separation between the private and the public because in this separation lies the oppression of women and the poor. We need a new family, a new educational system at home and at primary, secondary and university levels. We have to work together at home and locally, nationally, regionally and globally to restore our dignity, to satisfy our physical and mental needs, to achieve self-reliance and the right to choose our own way towards economic and intellectual progress.

Notes

1. Pierre Galland, 'World Bank: "Criminal"', *International Viewpoint*, April 1994.
2. *Al-Arabi* (Cairo), 4 April 1994, p. 4.
3. Interview with Mahmoud Wahba, president of Egypt American Businessmen, *El-Shaab* (Cairo), 26 April 1994, p. 4.

๛ Keynote address to the Global '94 Congress, Tampere, Finland, 3–7 July 1994; published in *The Nawal El Saadawi Reader* by Zed Books in 1997.

7

God Above,
Husband Below

WHEN I WAS A CHILD I did not know whether my grandmother was laughing or crying. She was probably laughing, for after she had wiped the tears away her eyes shone with a sudden light, and she would begin to laugh again, almost choking as she held the black shawl over her nose and her mouth and muttered 'Allah, let it lead to something good', only to resume her laughing until the tears welled up in her eyes once more.[1]

So I learnt from her that Al-Saadawi was the name of my great grandfather who came from Abyssinia and that Habash was the name of my grandfather whose son Al-Sayed became my father. In the official register, the names of those three men were inscribed with my name so that it became Nawal Al-Sayed Habash El-Saadawi. Somehow the name Habash disappeared on my birth certificate and my identity card and I completely forgot that it had even been a part of it, only to reappear in the files of the Ministry of Interior and of the prison authorities. I discovered this in 1981, when I had already reached my fifties. In that year I became number 1,536 on a list of people arrested by President Sadat. The authorities put me in the Women's Prison located near Al-Kanatir Al-Khaireya, about ten miles north of Cairo, near a barrage on the Nile. The officer in charge asked me my full name. I did not mention Habash. He pulled out an ancient register, flipped through the heavy yellowing pages and extracted the name Habash, followed by Al-Saadawi, a man whom I had never known, as though he were digging out two bodies one after the other from their graves. Ever since I was born the name of that unknown Al-Saadawi has been carried by my body, inscribed on my school books, my school certificates, my certificates of merit, printed on my articles in newspapers and magazines, on the covers of my novels and books written with my ink, my sweat, my tears, my blood in the stifling heat of summer days and the freezing winter nights, day after day, night after night, for more than fifty years.

On my desk lies a white envelope with my name written on it: 'Dr El-Saadawi, Visiting Professor, Duke University.' The name *Duke* rings strange in my ears like that of Al-Saadawi. Who was Duke? A millionaire from North Carolina. Just before dying, he suddenly discovered he could not take his money with him to the grave, so he thought why not leave his name on a wall, or at the bottom of a statue? Why not pay whatever sum of money was required to ensure that his name would not be buried forever with him?

But my mother's name was buried forever. She owned nothing, had no money. According to divine and to human law, her children, including me, were her husband's property. So, I never carried the name of my mother. Her name was buried with her body and disappeared from history.

Ever since I took hold of a pen in my fingers, I have fought against history, struggled against the falsifications in official registers. I wish I could efface my grandfather Al-Saadawi from my name and replace it with my mother's name, Zaynab.[2] It was she who taught me the letters of the alphabet: *alif, beh, teh, geem, dal,* all the way to *heh, wow, lamalif, yeh.* She used to press her hand on mine and make me write the four Arabic letters of my name. I could hear her voice, like the song of birds, sing out 'Nawal, Nawal.'

I hear her voice call out to me. I slip my hand out of my father's fingers, and run towards her. She carries me up in her arms, and holds me to her breast. The smell of her body is in my nose as though it were the smell of my own body. The sun is shining in the sky over Durham. It is a blue, blue sky. They call it Carolina blue.

It is like the blue of the sky in my village, Kafr Talha, in the delta of the Nile. The air in Durham in this month of October smells like the autumn air in Cairo. The past is one with the present, fuses into one long moment, which started the day when I was born a child crawling, and then walking, on the earth. My body remembers the smell of dust, the touch of the earth under my feet, the glare of the sun hurting my eyes. The plane has carried me thousands of miles across the Atlantic Ocean to the small city of Durham, and the years, more than half a century of years, have flown by. Yet the same smell is in my nose, and the same glare makes me close my eyes, and my mother's voice calling out to me, 'Nawal, Nawal', invades me with the rays of the sun through every pore. I surrender to this invasion by her voice, by her smell, by the dazzling light. I let them carry me back, once more a child darting like a butterfly through the open spaces of green under the blue sky. The sun drops gently down to the horizon, the sky throbs with red and orange colours, changing from moment to moment, the red and orange colours give way to a grey line of clouds, and the air on my bare arms and legs becomes colder and colder. But the earth still carries on it the imprint of my feet. I shiver with cold as the night envelops me. My body feels tired, but I can still feel the warmth of the earth under my feet, so I close my eyes, lie down to rest on it, sink into a deep sleep, wake up, see the stars shining in the sky above me, hear the voice of Sittil Hajja still telling me the story of her wedding night, the 'night of entering the bride', how the blood gushed out between her thighs after the *daya* pushed her long sharp finger through her virginity, how the she-ass carried her from her father's home to her husband's house. All the way the blood kept flowing down from her over the saddle, the drums beating behind her as she went along. In the bridegroom's house she lay on a mat, shrinking into the new *gallabeya* embroidered with coloured threads and spots of blood. The bridegroom called out to her in a loud, rough voice: 'Get up girl and prepare supper.' She was slow in getting up, so the blows of his long thin cane rained down on her, the same cane with which he used to guide his donkey, and he shouted at her, 'Get up, girl, may your day of reckoning rise on you at once.'

This was the custom in the village. Every husband had to beat his bride on the wedding night before he did anything else. She had to try the taste of his stick before she could sample the taste of his food so that she would know that Allah was above, and her husband below, and she should be ready for a beating if she did not do as she was told.

On the night of her wedding Sittil Hajja was only ten years old. She had not yet had her period. Habash bore down on her as she stuffed her *tarha*³ into her mouth to stifle the screams. A bride should not scream or else she would be stung by a cane, or by the neighbour's tongues, and neither she nor her father would be able to face the village.

After several years, three or four according to Sittil Hajja, her belly rose up in a first pregnancy and my father was born. She took care to make sure that the male organ was there between his thighs before letting out a resounding 'yoo-yoo'. She fought against the fever that seized hold of her and overcame it, thanks to her great joy at having given birth to a male child. After the blood ceased to flow, she performed her ablutions, and then knelt in prayer to Allah for not having let her down by giving her a girl.

Sittil Hajja lived with Habash for eighteen long years before he died. She did not have a brass bed with posts, only a mat laid over the dusty ground. She gave birth to fifteen children on this mat: four boys and eleven girls. Three of the boys died, leaving only my father. Six of the girls died, leaving my five aunts Fatma, Baheya, Roukaya, Zaynab, and the youngest Nefissa, who was still suckling at her mother's breast when her father Habash died at the age of thirty-eight. He died of bilharziasis, bleeding in his urine, like his father, like the peasants in the village had always done, throughout the ages, since the times of the pharaohs and the slaves of Egypt. The disease was a calamity sent by God, as Sittil Hajja said, but biggest of all calamities were the eleven girls born to her, of whom to her misfortune only six had died, leaving five to live on. She would clench her five fingers into a fist, as though waving it in the face of an enemy, or of Satan and say, 'Five girls. A catastrophe of girls!'

When the eleventh girl was born it had been too much for Habash. He died of grief, so they carried him away to the cemetery in a wooden box called a *taboot,* like a coffin. Sittil Hajja did not shed a tear for him. She waited until his body was buried under the earth, rose to her feet, heated a big tin full of water, performed her ablutions and knelt in thanks to Allah for ridding her of her husband. She had become a widow at the age of twenty-eight. She tied a black kerchief around her head, and swore that until the day she died she would let no man come near her again. Since her wedding night, she had hated all men, or since even before that, four years prior to her wedding night, when she was still a child only six years old and the *daya* Um Mahmoud came to their home.

The image of Sittil Hajja fades from my mind but her voice continues to reach my ears, as though rising from the depth of the earth:

I had just started to walk, go to the fields, and play with the children when that unnameable woman Um Mahmoud, that *daya*, that brazen daughter of a whore, came to the house, got hold of me, and tied me up like a chicken with the help of four other women. She said, 'Now listen to me you girl, Mabrouka, I am going to cut off your *zambour,*[4] so that you will be pure and clean on your wedding night, and your husband won't run away from you in disgust, and you won't run after men.' Then she got hold of a razor, whetted it so sharp on a stone that it cut through me like a flame. I said to myself, it's all over with you Mabrouka, this is the end. I lay on the mat, the blood gushing out of me like a tap. My mother recited the Fatiha three times for my soul as though I would die any minute. But after a few days God gave me a helping hand and I got up full of life as the Devil. You see, daughter of my son, girls have seven lives, like cats. But boys are not like girls. They have airy souls that fly away easily, and people give them the evil eye, and hang a charm around their necks. So every night I burned incense around him and recited incantations and the verse of Yaseen.[5] Poor thing, this child, the apple of my eye was so skinny and ate so little, not like those greedy girls. I used to hide food for him in a hole inside the

wall, bring him milk straight from the tit of the buffalo, and fill a
plate with cream for him. At dawn, before the sun came out, I woke
up the girls and we went off to the fields with the animals, laboured
there until sunset and came back carrying sacks on our backs. On
Saturdays, I rode to the market carrying whatever I could sell,
and I went on putting one piastre on top of the other until by the
end of the year I had three pounds, each one big enough to knock
the other down. I hid them between my breasts and when my
son Al-Sayed came home, I said to him, son, pride of my womb,
apple of my eye, here are three whole pounds, go buy a train ticket
from Benha[6] to Cairo, pay the fees of the school and the cost of
the books, and the rent of a room in the Citadel[7] and, pride of my
womb, buy yourself a pair of new shoes instead of the old ragged
pair you're wearing. Yes, there could be nothing less for your father
than for him to wear a new pair of shoes, walk with his head high,
and enter Al-Azhar and Dar Al-Oloum.[8] No way but for him to
go to the best school in Misr[9] and become the biggest head in the
whole country. Yes, there was no way but for him to get out of the
muck, never to be a peasant like his father, and die of bilharziasis,[10]
to live, and learn and become educated and become Sayed Effendi,
yes, no less than Sayed Effendi, and even Sayed Bey like Shoukry
Bey.[11] Why not? Was the belly that gave birth to Shoukry Bey any
different from your woman's belly, Mabrouka?[12] I swore an oath,
I swore by Allah and the Prophet Muhammad, by Sayedna Al-
Hussein and by El-Imam Al-Shafei[13] and Sittina Zaynab and Sittina
Mariam.[14] I said your son, Mabrouka, daughter of the woman
from Gaza that you are, your son is destined to marry one of the
daughters of Shoukry Bey, and you're not going to die, yes you will
not die before you dance at your son's wedding on the night when
he will enter into one of the daughters of those beys or pashas[15] of
Egypt. Why not? The bellies that gave birth to the beys and the
pashas are not different from your belly, Mabrouka.

The voice of Sittil Hajja echoes in my ears despite the passing of the
years. I see her tall figure, her head upright as she walks through the
village, treading firmly on the ground with her feet clad in *balghas*,[16]

watch her knock with the flat of her sunburnt hand on the door of the Omda's[17] house and shout, 'Come out, Omda, and speak to me. I am Mabrouka, the daughter of the woman from Gaza and my head can reach as high as the head of any man in this village.'

Notes

1. Accustomed to tragedy in their lives, village people are afraid to laugh, as though God may punish them for laughing, as though they have no right to laugh, so that when they do, they pray to God that it might bring something good and not evil to them.
2. *Zaynab*: wife of the Prophet Muhammad.
3. *Tarha*: shawl, usually black in colour.
4. *Zambour*: Arabic slang for clitoris.
5. *Yaseen*: a verse of the Qur'an recited to keep evil spirits away.
6. *Benha*: a provincial capital about forty miles north of Cairo.
7. *Citadel*: a district of CMO near the religious institution of Al-Azhar. The Citadel itself is a fortress palace built on a hill by Salah Al-Dine Al-Ayoubi.
8. *Dar Al-Oloum*: the higher institute for study of the Arabic language, from which graduated the teachers greatly esteemed when the national movement for independence was growing.
9. *Misr:* Egypt, but here it meant Cairo.
10. *Bilharziasis*: a worm which lives in the intestinal or urinary tract vessels and causes bleeding, among other symptoms. Very common in Egypt at that time, especially among the rural population.
11. *Bey*: a title given by the king to notables.
12. *Mabrouka*: Sittil Hajja's first name.
13. *Al-Hussein and Al-Shafei*: holy men (saints).
14. *Mariam*: the Virgin Mary.
15. *Pashas:* A higher title given to members of the upper ruling class by the king.
16. *Balghas*: Pointed leather slippers open at the back, which it was the custom for villagers, especially men, to wear at the time.
17. The village headman was very powerful at one time.

𝕫❧   First published as chapter 3 of *A Daughter of Isis: An Autobiography of Nawal El Saadawi,* first published in Arabic in 1995; translated by Sherif Hetata, it was published by Zed Books in 1999.

8

The House of Desolation

I SPENT A WHOLE YEAR in this house where reigned only sadness and desolation. The nights were long, and seemed peopled with spirits and devils: the spirits of my grandfather and of my dead grandmother and other spirits too. But the spirits of the dead did not frighten me as much as those of the living. Could Uncle Yehia's body shrink enough to let him slip under the closed door into my room?

Tante Fahima hated Uncle Yehia. She said he was stupid, had failed to finish school and had become just a 'repairer of clocks'. In my dreams the black cat changed into an evil spirit but Uncle Yehia seemed even more stupid than the black cat. He tiptoed into the room passing underneath the bottom of the closed door, crept up to the pillow on which rested Tante Fahima's head, slipped his hand under it and took the key of the door. In the dream I say to myself, 'How stupid. Why did he take the key if he can manage to get in without it?'

I never told my dreams to Tante Fahima. She would not stand my talking to her about nonsense like that. All she expected me to talk about was school, and my lessons. But Tante Ni'mat adored nonsense, adored these silly stories. They whiled away her empty hours. For her there was no better way of killing time. Her whole life was made up of empty time which she filled by talking about anything and nothing. She squatted on a carpet placed in the sunshine, with a cushion under her. At her side she placed a tray on which there was a small methylated-spirits wick burner, which she lit under a small pot of Turkish coffee. When it was ready she poured it out and started to take one slow sip after another from the small painted coffee cup, all the while sucking in what remained on her lips, and telling stories which went back as far as the day she was born. When she had finished with the various stages of the past, she went on to the future, turned the coffee cup upside down on the saucer to empty it of its remaining contents, lifted it close up to her eyes and began to read what she could see of her future in the form of black twisted lines made by the coffee dregs.

Once she was over with the future, she went back to remembering the past, to the story of her bridegroom, Muhammad Al-Shami, and their wedding night, pouting her lips to say 'Nothing, nothing at all happened on that night', then to her recollections of her father Al-Marhoum. She would ask God to forgive him his sins, especially the biggest sin of all, that of having taken her out of school at a young age to marry her off, heave a deep sigh and say, 'May God forgive him and soften the stone that lies under his head.'

Tante Ni'mat was closer to me than Tante Fahima. Out of her escaped moments of tenderness. At night, when I remembered the sadness in her voice, tears sprang to my eyes. The big house was full of sadness, a sadness which transferred itself to me like a contagion, and which I breathed in with the air respired by its inmates.

I used to see Uncle Yehia sitting in the hall, gazing at nothing, or staring at the room of his dead father, or his dead mother, smoking cigarette after cigarette until his teeth and his fingers were all yellow. Despite his habit of bursting into laughter frequently, he seemed to carry a heavy weight of sadness on his back, a sadness which had made him develop a hump, like a camel. He would walk down the railway platform, his back all hunched over, hurrying on bandy legs hidden in his baggy trousers, climb up a long thin ladder to the big clock hanging in the station, move its motionless hands, and wink at the girls standing below through the corner of one eye. He was the man who restored movement to time.

But the sadness in this house later became a source of inspiration, awakened within me a sensitivity to art, made me write. The servant girl Shalabeya is perhaps the heroine of my novel, *The Circling Song*. My uncle Yehia could be the old man in my short story 'She is Not Virgin'. My aunt Rokaya might be the woman Zakeya in my novel, *God Dies by the Nile*. Maybe Tante Fahima is the school superintendent or the headmistress, and Tante Ni'mat one of those frustrated women who are often to be found in some of my works.

The day came when I moved out of the big, sad desolate house on Zeitoun Road and became a boarder at the Helwan Secondary School for Girls. The years passed, but I never went back to visit that house. I like to recall old memories, to bring back past images, to remember places. This house was an exception. I never went back, perhaps because sadness can burn out one's heart and destroy one's memory. When I used to ask my mother why she married, she would answer with one unchanging sentence: 'To get away from the house of your grandfather Shoukry.'

This was the house of sadness where eyes turned to the colour of grey ash, where death snatched one after the other from life, where tears accumulated in a cyst somewhere in the throat, or inside the chest, where my uncle Zakareya died a young man without children, without a son or a daughter, without leaving anything behind, where Uncle Yehia died without anybody ever remembering him, where Tante Fahima lived buried in sadness with a husband who kept threatening her with divorce until the day she lay on her deathbed, where Tante Hanem passed away only to discover at the last moment that she could not take her property with her.

Was it my grandfather who caused the unhappiness which filled this house? Was it the army discipline he imposed on it? Patriarchal authority destroying those who are closest to us? The feudal class collapsing at the end of the Second World War? The patriarchal class system which rules over our world to this day? Was it a poison which runs in the blood, ran in my veins, in my arteries, a poison I used to breathe in with the air when I lived surrounded by the sadness and desolation of that house.

The last one of this family I saw was Tante Ni'mat. It was during the winter of 1959. I was in my clinic located in Giza Square. The telephone rang. A voice came to me over the wires.

—How are you, Dr Nawal, said the voice.

—Who is it? I asked.

—Don't you remember me, Warwar the slave girl?

—Tante Ni'mat! How are you Tante Ni'mat? Are you alright?

—Thanks be to Him whom alone we can thank for whatever befalls us.

—Oh my. So you still remember that, Tante Ni'mat.

—I've no one else to hold on to.

—Whom are you talking about Tante Ni'mat?

—Who else can it be besides God?

—You sound rather tired, auntie.

—I am tired, doctor, very tired.

Her voice was weak, full of that old ring of sadness, and I was hearing the hoarse breathing of a chest full of death.

She gave me her address in the district of Helmeyat Al-Zeitoun. She was living in her brother's flat, together with him and his wife and children. I entered the gloomy room they had given her next to the toilet, remembered the room in my uncle's house in Anbari. There was a 20-watt bulb hanging from a ceiling covered in black smoke. Her wedding furniture, or part of it, was piled up just anyhow, looking like a funeral pyre. In the middle was the yellow brass bed. She was lying between its bars as though crucified, her face white as the bed sheets, her eyes ash grey like the eyes of my dead grandmother, Amna. She opened her dry lips and said:

—Thank you for coming. There was always a lot of good in you, Dr Nawal.

—I'm Warwar the slave girl, Tante Ni'mat.

I heard her laugh, saw her eyes fight the darkness, saw her strain to open them, and let through the remains of an old light which had gone out years ago. She pointed to her left breast. I rested my hand on the swelling, and my body went rigid.

—It's that illness, isn't it Dr Nawal? I knew I had to die this way like my mother, and like your late mother too.

I walked out of her room. My hand felt its way to my breast. Perhaps I, too, had a malignant swelling in my left breast right over the heart. Perhaps I, too, would die within the three months I gave Tante Ni'mat to live.

I caught the train from Zeitoun station, remembered that fourteen years ago I used to take the train from the same station. Now it looked gloomy, the stairs and the walls were almost in ruins. The railway platform which in those days had seemed infinitely long had now grown so short that I walked down it from the beginning to the end in less than half a minute. I used to run along this platform panting, trying to catch the train before it left. Often I would miss it. In winter I shivered with cold, in summer poured with sweat. At times I jumped into the train after it had started moving. It was so crowded that the boys used to stand on the steps, or ride on the roof to avoid the crowding, or escape paying the price of a ticket, but sometimes the ticket collector used to climb up to them on the roof of the train, and then they would jump off onto the ground before he caught them.

One day one of the schoolboys fell onto the railway line and the train ran over both his legs. I saw him bleeding on the platform of Saray Al-Koubba station. The picture of King Farouk looked down on him, on his body cut in two lying in a pool of red blood creeping slowly over the platform which shone white like marble. A shoe had flown off the foot of his amputated leg; the other remained on the foot of the other dying leg. He could not feel anything, did not realize that he had lost his legs, smiled innocently at the people around him and asked in a childish voice, 'Where is my other shoe?'

All he could think of, all he was worrying about, was his shoe. Like me, he was in his second year in secondary school. Like me he had come from his village to go to school, and had been left by his parents to live in the huge city with relatives. My cousin Zaynab was fond of saying, *al arrayib, zarayib.*[1] Maybe like me he had a paternal or a maternal aunt who used to lay her hands on the piastres his father sent him, so he had no money to buy a train ticket, maybe he was dreaming of going to the university, of becoming a well-known scholar like Taha Hussayn.

In my sleep I saw myself lying between the rails of the Zeitoun train or of the Sayeda Zaynab tramcar. People lifted my legless trunk and laid it on a marble platform while I searched vainly for my shoe, got up and walked barefoot, then hobbled on a pair of crutches. The face of Hamida Shakankiri appeared at some distance and I watched her walking towards me on a pair of crutches. When she came near I woke up, panic-stricken, bathed in sweat.

The Zeitoun train was known for the terrible accidents which happened all the time. I do not know why but perhaps it was because it started in the very poor suburb of Matareya or of Ain Shams, ending in Koubri Al-Lemoun or Bab Al-Hadeed stations. Schoolboys and -girls lived in these two suburbs with their families or with relatives who had emigrated from the countryside. Often they were just lone migrants looking for a job or for a chance to go to school or the university. The huge city swallowed them up like an enormous drain sucking in cockroaches. A train or a tramcar could cut off one or two legs, so that individuals turned sometimes into pick-pockets or hawkers, jumping with a remaining leg on the step of a tramcar to sell razor-blades, or combs, or boxes of matches, then jumping off the other side after they had stolen someone's wallet or purse, or the sandwich that a girl was munching in the women's compartment.

In those days there were special compartments for women on trains and in tramcars. I preferred sitting in them, rather than being crowded in amongst the men, for their eyes would gaze at my breasts, or a hard finger would be dug into my flesh, or sometimes it could be that other thing they had between their thighs, becoming erect and pushing itself into some part of my body, or between my buttocks as I stood crucified between them, my hand or both hands holding on to the bar which hung from the ceiling of the tramcar, or the bus, or the train.

Sometimes I would turn round suddenly and slap one of them in the face. From where I got the courage to do this, I do not know. I was a young girl of thirteen or fourteen, almost a child, but the anger of a child is the most powerful, the most pure, and the truest of all angers. It accumulates in the body, multiplies over time, but it is like God, in that it gives birth only to itself.

I do not know how the child in me remained alive. Somehow it has escaped death. Maybe it taught itself to face death from the moment it was born and right from the start learnt not to fear it. Maybe it has built up what in our medical studies we call immunity. The body needs to be injected with germs all the time if it is to develop immunity. 'Cure me with that which is the cause of my disease.' Perhaps the saying I heard from my grandfather has some truth in it. Perhaps we need doses of death to develop immunity against it.

When I was in the second year of secondary school I was taught in a class on algebra that the negation of the negation gives us something positive, that if we add a negative sign to a negative sign it gives us a positive sign. It was the first lesson we were given in algebra and geometry, which together with arithmetic we called *riyada*. But *riyada* also meant 'exercise', in the sense of sports or gymnastics, so at first I thought that sports was what they were referring to.

I learnt to enjoy the mental exercises involved in this *riyada,* and experienced great pleasure in solving different problems in algebra. The more difficult the problem, the greater was the pleasure I experienced. Sometimes a problem would appear to me insoluble, with one difficulty coming on top of another, like a series of complicated knots. The page would be covered in brackets, and cubes, and squares, in triangles and hexagonals, so that the formula looked like a huge structure, like a pyramid rising higher and higher, and then suddenly in the middle of my confusion, in the middle of the puzzle, like a mesh out of which I could not extricate myself, and just as I was negating a negation to reach a positive proof, the whole huge structure would suddenly collapse, the knot would be undone, the problem solved and the difficult formula ended by giving me a zero. My mind kept making leaps as though I was Pythagoras in person. Logarithms became my game. I would open my exercise book in the train, or in the tramcar, and amuse myself with solving problems, almost shrieking with pleasure.

At the end of the year, after the final examinations were over, I travelled back to Menouf for the summer vacations. My certificate said that I had passed with distinction, and was accompanied by a letter from the headmistress of Al-Saneya school to the trustee of the pupil Nawal El-Sayed El-Saadawi, which read as follows: 'The pupil has been awarded top marks in algebra and geometry and thus is eligible for admission to the course line on mathematics and can be given a scholarship, and a monthly stipend. After she passes her secondary school certificate this can qualify her for admission into the teachers' institute to become a teacher of mathematics in secondary schools for girls, subject to the rules and regulations of the law which govern such matters.'

There was no boarding house in Al-Saneya School for Girls. I could not bring myself to go back to my grandfather's house and continue to be fed on sorrow. In addition, I disliked teachers profoundly, especially Tante Fahima and Nabaweya Moussa and other teachers and headmistresses of their kind. I also knew nothing about what was meant by the rules and regulations of the law. My father explained to me that the Ministry of Education needed teachers in mathematics, but that graduates from the Teachers' Institute had to continue teaching for a minimum period of four years, during which they were not allowed to marry. If the graduate at any time broke any of these rules she was required to refund the Ministry of Education for whatever had been spent on her education in the institute, as well as the stipend she had been paid during the years she had spent in it.

My father was hesitant about what was best for me to do but I very quickly took the decision to refuse, since I was not prepared to accept any conditions for the scholarship. They appeared to me as a form of servitude, as though the Ministry of Education were purchasing me at a price which was the expense of my education and then calling that a scholarship. If they thought I was an exceptional student then a free education should be my right, with no strings attached.

When I explained my decision father stood up and shook my hands warmly. 'Bravo', he said, 'you have shown that you are really a daughter of mine.' It sounded to me as though he was saying that prior to that moment he had not considered me worthy to be his daughter, or that I was able to do whatever I did only because I was a daughter of his!

When he stood up and shook hands with me his grasp around my hand was firm and strong, yet at the same time gentle and loving. I felt that he had a strength which springs from gentleness and love, for he was a very gentle father. His black eyes shone with a tear ready to drop but he swallowed it quickly. I wondered: was my father at last feeling happy with my achievements?

My brother Tala'at failed again that year, but my father was no longer terribly sad at his failure. He just closed his eyes and his thoughts seemed to wander for some time. Was I beginning to have a place in his dreams? Was he seeing in me a famous teacher? An eminent professor? A skilled doctor? Were my achievements becoming a compensation for my brother's failures? Were his dreams shifting from the boy to the girl?

Note

1. Meaning that relatives are stables full of shit.

❧ Chapter 24 of *A Daughter of Isis: An Autobiography of Nawal El Saadawi*, first published in Arabic; translated by Sherif Hetata, it was published by Zed Books in 1999.

9

The Streetwalker
and the Woman Writer

THIS IS ANOTHER PAPER which was not allowed to be presented at the Women and Creativity conference held in Cairo in October 2002. The reason for this is as follows.

On the first morning of the conference the dead body of the eminent writer A.D. Al-Masry was found on a wooden bench in the Nile Casino garden. Next to her body were found some papers written in her own hand as well as her well-known golden pen. It was therefore inferred that she died suddenly while writing the paper she intended to present at the conference. The prosecutor decided to release the street walker who, according to eyewitnesses, was sitting next to the well-known deceased on the wooden bench.

A.D. Al-Masry used to spend hours sitting on this wooden bench, trying to kill time through writing, staring at the papers for long periods and then raising her head to stare into the darkness.

On this particular October night the north air is chilly, the winds seem ready to blow and a climatic war to break out.

The dark clouds gathering in the sky intensify the darkness, the depression and the dread of wrongdoing or of anything else equally terrifying. The hissing sound of the wind merges with that of the microphones attached to tops of mosques and minarets, blaring out sounds like explosions or bullets.

The eminent writer sits with her pen poised in her hand, its golden lid gleaming in the darkness. Like other great men of letters, she is enveloped by an aura of solemnity. But, unlike them, her head is covered with a veil as white as a snow mountain while she sits silently poring over her papers and writing.

From the heart of darkness a girl emerges, walking slowly and looking completely worn out. She is slim and dressed in a tight-fitting black dress, her neck bare until the cleavage of her breasts. She stops briefly to catch her breath and turns her little head with its thick rather dishevelled black hair to look up to the sky and address God in an inaudible voice that sounds like stifled prayers.

The eminent writer looks at her for a moment and then resumes her writing, focused intently on the page. The girl walks in front of her but hardly notices her. When the girl suddenly becomes aware of her presence, she returns and sits at the other end of the wooden bench, leaving a large space between them. With some curiosity the writer raises her eyes but utters not a single word. The girl scrutinizes her with a kind of infantile inquisitiveness, staring from a distance at the letters on the page. She smiles faintly saying:

GIRL You seem quite busy with your writing ma'am.

WRITER (*in a hoarse voice*) Sorry, I'm very busy and I don't speak to streetwalkers.

GIRL (*embarrassed*) You're right, ma'am. I apologize.

The girl is about to get up and go, but the writer feels a kind of remorse or pity.

WRITER You may sit down if you wish.

GIRL I'll rest a while then be on my way.

WRITER I don't own this bench, you know, so you may sit as you please.

The girl sits down again, wiping the sweat off her face with a little white handkerchief. The writer looks at her askance as the girl looks up at the black sky, whispering to God.

GIRL You're my witness that I was not a streetwalker.

WRITER Were you then an honest girl?

GIRL (*smiling*) Thank you for the nice word although it refers to the past not the present. All my life I've never heard the word *honest*. What a lovely word!

The writer goes back to her writing. The girl looks at her as she writes. The writer seems to have difficulty writing because the pen hardly moves in her hand although it is still gleaming in the darkness.

GIRL   Would you allow me to ask you a question, ma'am?

WRITER   What kind of question? (*without lifting her face from the page*).

GIRL   Are you a writer, ma'am?

The writer raises her face and answers in a rather disconcerted voice:

WRITER   Of course! Don't you know that? Haven't you seen my picture on newspapers and television screens?

GIRL   I apologize, ma'am. I haven't got a television and I can't buy newspapers.

WRITER   One can see that.

GIRL   But I sometimes go without food in order to buy a book.

WRITER   You must have read one of my books.

GIRL   Do you have books then?

WRITER   (*enthusiastically*) Plenty of them. I even received the state award and the title of Major Writer.

GIRL   I apologize for my ignorance ma'am, but...

WRITER   But what?

GIRL   You must have a big office and a beautiful house with another office in it.

WRITER   Of course.

The girl becomes silent, hesitant, and then says with some embarrassment:

GIRL   Sorry for my inquisitiveness, but how is it that such a great writer as you sits all night here on this bench to write?

Silently, the writer goes back to her paper. The girl is also silent, her eyes wandering far. Whispering to herself, she says:

GIRL   In the distant past when I was a child, I had a little desk in my bedroom. I also had a diary I wrote in.

WRITER   (*without lifting her face from the page*) Did you write?

GIRL (*distractedly and without looking at her*) In the distant past when I was an honest girl ...

WRITER Ah, I get it.

The girl moves her head towards the writer. Her black eyes are dilated and filled with a glimmer as she asks:

GIRL What is it that you got ma'am?

WRITER The connection between writing and honour, do you get it?

GIRL I've been trying hard to get it, even though I still don't. I'm too tired to walk on. I can't even tell when the walking begins or ends. It seems as endless and everlasting as God.

WRITER (*rather upset*) May God forgive you, aren't you a believer? Don't you have faith in the One and only Being?

GIRL Sorry, ma'am, if I have hurt you. You may call me faithless, as you called me a person with no honour, but ... ah, for these hurtful words. They're more painful to the body than actual blows or kicks. These words, ma'am, are a disaster.

WRITER A disaster?

GIRL Yes, ma'am. Words are language and the only way to write, yet they are not permitted ... yes, not permitted.

The girl stops talking and becomes rather absent-minded. The great writer looks at her with a kind of interest that is markedly different from her earlier indifference:

GIRL Am I wasting your valuable time ma'am with this drivel?

WRITER Not at all ... go on ... I'm listening.

GIRL Thank you for listening. All I want to say is that writing ... ah, writing is a curious thing. Please believe me, it's not something clear that you write down on the page. This has been the case since my childhood. Nothing gave me as much comfort as writing. I loved it, ma'am, because it soothed me in its own special way. I needed it at night lying all alone, the winds howling like wolves, and sounds blaring like explosions from microphones. Nothing, nothing makes you feel equally relaxed. I walk on and on until I get exhausted, so I rest for a little while on a bench and tell myself how lucky I am because I can finally sit down, open my childhood notebook and discover the letters hiding behind the lines and the faint music of the word....

The girl stops talking, looking worn out. She wipes the sweat off her face with her little white handkerchief, catching her breath.

WRITER (*with interest*) Why did you stop? This is a lovely conversation my child.

GIRL (*smiling*) The word *child* brings back my longing for my father.

WRITER I thought that being a woman I would bring back memories of your mother.

GIRL I've never had one ma'am.

WRITER Sorry about that.

The girl falls silent for a moment, furtively swallowing her tears and adjusting the opening of her dress to cover the cleavage. Then she says:

GIRL And you ma'am, did you have a mother?

WRITER (*sorrowfully*) Yes, I had one unfortunately.

GIRL Are you married?

WRITER Yes, regrettably.

GIRL I apologize if my questions are painful.

WRITER Quite the contrary, I feel comforted talking to you.

GIRL Is your house very far?

WRITER It's quite close. Over there on the other side of this garden. Sitting here I can see it. Look, it's over there, that big white house. It's my house and I wait until dawn to go back and sleep.

In silence, the girl looks distractedly in the direction of the house, then says:

GIRL It must be really hard to wait for the dawn. The hardest thing in life is waiting. Though tiring, walking is much better than waiting. That's why I write ma'am, time goes faster when we write.

WRITER Absolutely true. But how did you realize all this at this tender age?

GIRL I had to. Three days ago I turned twenty, but I feel like I'm sixty or seventy. Every time I walk I feel that my feet are weighed down by iron chains.

WRITER And your father, where's he?

GIRL He married an honest woman with a house, just like you. The house being small, she forces him to sleep on a mat on the floor while she sleeps in bed.

WRITER Can't you sleep in your father's house instead of on this bench?

GIRL No, ma'am. I'm not even allowed to visit my father.

WRITER Don't you have any relatives? A maternal or a paternal aunt? Don't you see that you can't go on like this?

GIRL Why not ma'am? Don't you spend the night on this bench just like me?

WRITER Yes, but at dawn I go home and eat supper. Then I go noiselessly to bed so I don't wake up my husband.

GIRL You're a sensitive human being. But what does your husband do during the night? Does he write like you?

The great writer is silent and her eyes wander in the darkness. She wipes the sweat off her face with her white scarf.

WRITER If he did, it would be much easier.

GIRL My apologies. Don't go on speaking if it hurts you.

WRITER Quite the contrary, I feel a little relieved when I speak of the things I conceal from myself.

GIRL It reminds me of my childhood when I confessed to my diary the things I did not tell myself. I heard people say that my father was not an honest man and I wished to kill him to get rid of the shame, except that he gave up his honour to feed me.

WRITER All of us in one way or another put up with humiliation for a noble cause.

GIRL And what was the noble cause of your life? Writing?

WRITER Oh yes, writing my child. But what's the point of writing if it stays lying in the drawer and never sees the light? It's really hard; do you understand what I'm saying?

GIRL Yes, I do ma'am. I have a short story which did not see the light except after I offered myself to some man. All the doors were shut in my face and there was no other route. Do you say I'm not honourable?

The writer is silent for a long time, wiping her face with her white scarf and finally stammering:

WRITER No... no, I don't say this cruel word about you, because in wishing that your words should see the light you had a noble aim. This is life my child.

GIRL Are you saying that life itself is dishonourable?

WRITER Yes ... No, I don't really know the whole truth, because God alone knows ...

The great writer looks really worn out. The pen and paper fall from her hand and onto the ground. She looks with misty eyes at her watch, her fingers trembling, hardly seeing the digits on her watch.

WRITER (*exhausted*) I can't read the digits as clearly as I used to. Tell me my child what time it is. But it's awfully dark and the dawn has not come yet so that I can go home.

The girl helps the writer collect the papers dropping on the ground. The writer's panting breath shows that she is close to fainting. The girl helps her lift her swollen legs up to the bench. The writer catches her breath resting a little. The girl stares at the white house at the other side of the garden and asks in embarrassment:

GIRL Your house is close by. Should I take you to rest over there ma'am?

WRITER I don't want to go back before dawn.

GIRL (*perplexed*) Can't you go back earlier?

WRITER I can go home any time. But I prefer to stay here until the house is empty and my husband has gone to bed, do you get it?

GIRL I'm trying very hard to get it ma'am. It reminds me of my childhood when I preferred not to go home until it was completely empty and my father had gone to sleep. You must have known sorrow like me.

WRITER Sorrow? Yes, perhaps there is a connection between sorrow and writing. But I've resisted sorrow until I conquered it.

GIRL You should be happy then.

The writer closes her eyes as though slipping into a coma or sleep, her voice whispering:

WRITER I thank God for everything. He will make it up for me in the afterlife. I never harboured any evil against a single human being, not even that flirtatious young woman who drove my husband insane even though he is past seventy. He gave her the house I spent all my life's savings to get. Like you she is twenty and was once a streetwalker. Now she has the title of the honourable wife of the minister.

GIRL Should I call a doctor for you, ma'am?

WRITER (*in panic*) No, no, no, I don't want anybody to see me here.

The following morning the death of the great writer, A.D. Al-Masry, wife of the Honourable Minister of Publishing and Printing Affairs, was all over the news. A great funeral was arranged at the famous mosque at Al-Tahrir Square. Eminent personalities including ministers, ambassadors and dignitaries attended the impressive ceremony, wearing their dark glasses and black ties. They spoke softly about the latest news: the impending war, money market prices and published books available on the market.

On the wooden bench at night sat the street walker. She was the only one crying, but...

᠌ 'The Streetwalker and the Woman Writer', first published in Arabic, was translated by Amira Nowaira and published in *Breaking Barriers*, Cairo, October 2000.

10

Muslim Women in the Market

'MUSLIM WOMEN in the Market' is a misleading title because it gives the impression that it is only Muslim women who are in the marketplace. I would ask: What about Christian or Jewish women? And what about Muslim men or Judeo-Christian men and others? I cannot speak about Islam or any religion without comparing it with other religions. I cannot speak about Muslim women in isolation from the rest of the world.

A postmodern Christian and Muslim feminist

A British feminist visited me in Cairo in 1982. She was writing a book about Muslim feminists in the Middle East. I told her that I am not a Muslim feminist; rather I live in Egypt, North Africa and not the Middle East. Then I asked her where she lived. To which she responded, 'London — England is my country.' I asked, 'So you are from the Middle West?' She laughed. It was funny to abolish the name England and replace it with the Middle West instead, but to abolish Egypt and refer to the Middle East was not a joke. It was and is a serious reality.

Then she asked, if I am not a Muslim feminist, how I would describe myself. To which I replied by asking her please to describe herself first. She told me she was a Christian feminist who holds a different interpretation of the Bible. 'Eve was not a sinner and Christ was a Black lesbian woman', she explained. So, I wanted to know why she called herself a Christian. She explained that it was only a matter of culture: 'I mean my cultural identity, my authentic identity.'

More than twenty years passed and I was walking into the Guezira Club in Cairo when a veiled woman stopped me. I did not recognize her. She was the Christian feminist, converted to Islam after marrying an Egyptian doctor.

She said she had chosen Islam and the veil of her own free will and added, 'I am a Muslim feminist and the veil is part of my Islamic identity. Did you read my new book about Muslim feminists in which I...' I interrupted and admitted that I had not. 'Oh', she began, 'I have to send you a copy. It was featured on the best sellers list of the *New York Times*. It was reviewed by a feminist Muslim celebrity in USA. It was discussed on CNN and the BBC ... I believe in free choice, in diversity, pluralism and multiculturalism. Are you against free choice?' I laughed and told her, 'Yes, I am against free will and the free market too!'

The same day in the Guezira Club I met a young Egyptian woman. She wore full postmodern make-up: eyelashes, kohl, mascara, seductive look and all. Her head was covered with a silk Islamic veil. The upper part of her belly was uncovered above the tight American jeans.

She is another type of Muslim woman. She obeys her God by wearing the veil and shops at the free market and selects what she likes. Free choice... laissez-faire.

Books by Muslim feminists

Books on Islam by Muslim feminists have become a profitable commodity in the publishing market and big media. Covers of books with veiled women are now very attractive to consumers and bring in more money.

I never wanted a veiled woman on the cover of my books. I never used 'Islam' or 'Islamic women' in the title of any of my books, but publishers do what they want without your knowledge. I was never consulted about the cover of my books. Publishers change the titles of your books without consulting with you, and they omit parts or alter the arrangement of chapters as they want.

To guard against this, you have to stop your creative work and devote your time to fighting publishers or taking them to court. Agents and lawyers can devour your time and money with little result. The free market has its visible and invisible powers that can lead you to stop writing altogether. But we have to fight back and learn how to enforce our rights as writers, whether we are Muslims or non-Muslims.

In Germany the publisher of my novel *Woman at Point Zero* changed my original title into a very bad title from an aesthetic point of view. The publisher changed the title to *I Spit on You*. Is this an appropriate title for a book? I asked the publisher. He told me that in Germany it is a good title. It sells well. The culture in Germany likes aggressive titles, and the free market likes violence. Similarly, the American publisher (in Boston) omitted my introduction to *The Hidden Face of Eve* without my knowledge. When I asked her why, she said it was too polemical — which means political — and publishers (even radical feminist publishers) do not want to take risks or lose money.

The original title of *The Hidden Face of Eve* in Arabic translates as *The Naked Face of Arab Women*. This title was changed by publishers and featured a veiled woman on the cover. All my publishers in different countries are small and radical, feminist or socialist, but most of them compromise to survive in the so-called free market, which amounts to the freedom of the powerful to exploit the weaker. Dissident writers from different fields and countries cannot be in the mainstream. They are never published by big publishers and they are always ignored by big media. They cannot be part of the free market. They cannot receive big global or national prizes, nor big reviews, nor big money or positions. This is just part of the price they pay to speak their mind.

Big media stars

If you watch television in Egypt today you will see veiled Muslim feminists, who are professors of Islam at Al Azhar University or other institutions. They appear in programmes and discussions about Islam and women. They compete with the male professors of Islam or religious sheikhs. They say that Islam offers women all their rights. They try to reinterpret verses of the Qur'an and sayings by the prophet Muhammad. Some of their veils are very fashionable and are surrounded by pearls. They wear make-up and red lips and kohl and all. They have soft, feminine, seductive voices and looks. They are the model of ideal Muslim women. They are successful. They are good wives, good mothers, good professors, good writers, and they keep good houses, good gardens, good food, good cars, good children, good grandchildren, good cats, and good dogs. They are invited globally and locally to conferences on Islam and women. Their books on Islamic women are bestsellers. They receive state prizes from the head of state or minister of culture.

Yes, they are swimming in the mainstream like fish. On a golden chain on their chest they carry the name of Allah and the name of the husband, or fiancé, or boyfriend. I heard one of them say on the television that God in the Qur'an gives the right to the husband to beat his wife if she disobeys him, on the condition that this beating does not send her to hospital and that the wound will heal with no scar or just a little scar. She said also that God allowed men to have multiple wives but not more than four at one time.

She said that the Prophet Muhammad declared that women should obey their husbands as they obey God, and if he (the Prophet) allows anybody to kneel to anybody apart from God he will allow the woman to kneel to her husband.

Another Muslim woman television star said that God created men and women different, with different roles in life. Women are for the family and children and men are for work outside the home. This woman is a university professor. She works outside her home but no one has asked her why she is working outside her home. Global

Muslim women stars appear on CNN or BBC World, or in the *New York Times*, and other large media outlets.

When you read or listen to them you discover how they use Islam in the market. They criticize Islam as if it is the only religion that is racist, terrorist, sexist, anti-democratic and anti-modernist. Listening to them, you would think that honour killing, or the killing of infidels, originated in Islam. They never compare Islam to Judaism or Christianity. They never link women's issues to global politics or economics or even to history. This is risky. They will eventually lose the admiration of Judeo-Christian religious fundamentalism, which is a growing power in the market. The Judeo-Christian religious fundamentalists support the George W. Bush administration and the war in Palestine and Iraq, among others. Many times my words have been censored or cut in such big media when I have linked women's problems to global and national issues, or compared Islam to other religions. Even in international feminist conferences I meet strong opposition or hostility from some women who call themselves Jewish or Christian feminists. I remember how they screamed while I was speaking in a conference in Montreal; some of them stood up and left the hall when I said that the veiling of women started in Judaism before Islam. The global media in Canada and the USA supported them. I have not been invited to Montreal again since then, more than twenty-five years ago. The stars in the big media market are not only these Muslim women. There are many Muslim and Judeo-Christian men stars who speak in the name of their God. Fanatical religious leaders have become stars in global and local media owned by multinationals and governments working with them *glocally* (both globally and locally).

If we follow the television or radio or read major newspapers such as the *New York Times* in the USA or *Al-Ahram* in Egypt we discover how backward religious ideas are propagated. A whole page is written every week in the daily *Al-Ahram* by an Islamic writer (called Zaghloul Al-Naggar) in which he tries to convince people that all scientific facts of our modern and postmodern era are mentioned by God in the Qur'an, from the protoplasm to the atom, to nuclear power, electronic sciences, and walking on the moon. In the *New York Times* Judeo-Christian pastor Ock Soo Park tries to convince people that it is his prayer to God (and not scientific tools or digging deep in the ground) that brought water to their retreat centre (10 September 2007). Another day I see a picture caption: 'Several hundred people gathered yesterday outside the Georgia Capitol in Atlanta in a prayer for desperately needed rain. Among the participants was Pastor Marion Croom of East Point, Georgia' (14 November 2007). This reminds me of poor peasants in Egypt two centuries ago praying that God would send the rain to irrigate their land. European colonizers laughed sarcastically at them, but today they do not laugh at those pastors who pray for rain and water. On the contrary, they publish them and encourage them *glocally*. Religious fundamentalism and neocolonialism are two faces of the same coin and they are universal under all religions and not only Islam.

Virginity and deception

The backlash against the rights of women and the poor is not specific to the Arab region or to Islamic countries. The Bush administration is supported by the Judeo-Christian coalition in the United States, which is not only against women's rights, but blames broken homes on the women's liberation movement. They support what they call 'family values' and 'virginity' for girls before marriage. They now promote purity balls, in which a double morality prevails: fathers take their daughters to these purity balls to protect their virginity or save them for marriage; churches do not hold similar events for mothers and sons.

The conception of virginity is embedded in Judaism and Christianity, and is not limited to Arab or Islamic culture. For example, the Virgin Mary is the ideal mother, and nuns were traditionally veiled. The practice of veiling women was limited in Europe to traditional Jewish and Islamic groups. In today's Europe it is increasingly common among Islamic migrant communities in the Netherlands, France, the UK, Belgium, and other countries. Sometimes it is accompanied by female genital mutilation. Both veiling and female genital mutilation are considered by the political and religious leaders of these communities integral to Islamic identity, under the guise of so-called 'cultural relativism'. This is part of the deception and brainwashing of women. It occurs in Egypt and in many other countries.

The deception of cultural relativism has been going on for three decades. Deception is a form of violence against the mind. Mutilation of the mind is no less a crime than female or male genital mutilation; it is even more dangerous. It is used to mutilate the body and the soul, to justify violence against women and the poor. In some backward opinions women's rights are considered a direct attack on God's law, moral values, and sacred words.

Mutilation of the mind

Dissident writers, women and men, are struggling against the mutilation of the mind, regardless of differences in religion or culture or the so-called 'authentic identity'. But such dissidents are few, and they are tortured, imprisoned, exiled or simply ignored. The majority of people do not understand the capitalist patriarchal world in which we live. They are deceived by the word 'democracy', and will risk their lives to defend it, even though it takes away their human rights under the slogan of protecting them.

We live in one world, not three, dominated by one system, a violent capitalist, patriarchal, military system. A superpower can kill and rob people of their natural resources under the guise of false claims: from protection in the guise of early colonial wars to democracy and women's liberation in our postmodern twenty-first century. The so-called free market is nothing but freedom of the powerful to exploit the weak. The free market has no religion; it has no god except profit. It increases its profit by any means including warfare and the war on the mind by the media, education, culture and religion. All are tools designed to create obedient servants of the system.

A large part of the profit of the free market comes from selling arms — weapons which kill individuals or lay waste to nations;

weapons of mass destruction, nuclear weapons, chemical weapons, and other postmodern killing tools.

Another source of profit is women's bodies — nakedness or veiling; cosmetics and make-up; advertisements trading in women's bodies for patriarchal sexual gratification. The eye, the gaze of the free market, is mainly on women, like the gaze of religious fundamentalist men. If there were no war and no women both patriarchy and the free market would collapse: that is, the God of the free market and the God of the religious fundamentalist groups. They are twins. They serve each other in spite of superficial differences and temporary conflicts, when their economic interests clash.

To keep the free market alive and flourishing military wars will go on under any name. The name of God is the best name to be used, or His Word. Under the notion of His 'Promised Land' in the Old Testament, how many hundreds of thousands have been killed to date in Palestine? The free market produces weapons of mass destruction in order to eradicate weapons of mass destruction. This is not a joke, but a reality. The Iraq War has killed thousands every year to date, on the basis of a big lie: weapons of mass destruction in the country. Not a word about the oil there.

Fighting the infidel

The Afghanistan war from the 1980s until today has been fought on the basis of another big lie: fighting the infidels, the non-believers, the Communists of the Soviet Union, a war between God and the Devil for the sake of the free market. An army of young believers was trained in military fighting. Their minds were veiled with religious teaching and blind faith.

I met many young Egyptian fighters in Afghanistan who used to come and visit their families in Cairo during vacations. Most of them were university graduates with no jobs, with no hope except to die in the holy war and go to paradise as martyrs. The Egyptian authorities, an ally of the American authorities, encouraged those young unemployed men to kill the infidel. Thousands of young men were recruited. The streets of Cairo suddenly were filled with young men with fierce military looks and long thick black beards covering their faces. Veiled women started to appear in the streets alone or with those bearded men.

The Medical Syndicate on Kasr El Ainy Street in Cairo was suddenly invaded by young doctors wearing *gallabeyas*, beards, carrying beads in one hand and the Qur'an in the other. I remember that on one occasion I was prevented from entering the main hall of the Medical Syndicate.

I was supposed to attend a conference as a medical doctor, but the bearded men at the door ordered me to go to a small balcony, where women should sit away from men. I made a big fuss at the door, pushing my way against the bearded men to the main hall. I stood up and declared my objection to their robbing me of my medical profession and considering me a female that should cover her *shameful* face. I objected to the transformation of our Medical Syndicate into an Islamic association, the neglect our medical problems in favour of sending new recruits to fight a religious war in Afghanistan or in Bosnia or somewhere else. I saw veiled women doctors sitting in their secluded balcony, some of them covering their whole face except for an eye or two. Islam was used to fight Communism. Now, after the collapse of Communism Islam has become the new enemy. The capitalist patriarchal system cannot live without an enemy, as God cannot live without Satan.

How to be in the market

If you write against Islam your book will be a hot commodity, especially if you give it the title *Women and Islam*. If you show that Islam is against democracy, against women, along with terrorism, dictatorship, honour killing, female and male genital mutilation, killing the infidel and so on, you will be paid well — especially if you prove that tyranny or masculine violence is due to Muslim DNA or a gene. Then you will be in the mainstream in the heart of the market.

You should not support the Palestinian or the Iraqi resistance movements against foreign invasion, lest you be accused of being anti-Semitic or anti-American or supporting suicide bombers. You should not compare Islam with Judaism or Christianity, or show their similarities in relation to women's oppression or racism or terrorism, or reveal the operations of double moral standards. You should avoid historical facts, ignoring that terrorism, racism, the veiling of women, honour killing, female and male genital mutilation, religious wars, struggles over power, land, trade and money all existed long before Islam arrived. You should not write in your mother tongue, especially if it is Arabic; you should write in English or French or German if you want to be in the global market. Do not write about powerful women who resist oppression with all their might, women who can kill or die fighting, lest you be accused of being violent, aggressive or non-feminine. Many of the heroines in my novels were killers: Firdaus in *Woman at Point Zero*, Zakeya in *God Dies by the Nile*, Bint Allah in *The Fall of the Imam*. I have been accused of being aggressive, violent, and even a suicide bomber!

The pleasure of creativity

If you are creative and dissident you should ignore the free market. You should seek small publishers looking for genuine, truthful creative works. They pay very small advances and their publicity is limited, but sooner or later you will reach your audience. It is a long hard struggle against the market, but we have to do it or we will lose our integrity, and hence our creativity.

Creativity needs courage, not only to face the global or local publishing market but also your own society, the power system of your own religion, class, gender, race or country.

Creativity means self-criticism as well as criticizing the other. Critical thinking and writing are necessary for improving the self and the other. Creativity abolishes the line between the self and the other.

Some authors, especially Muslim women writers, are afraid of self-criticism, or of touching the taboos, lest they are accused of writing for the West, or showing our dirty linen to our enemies. But they end up losing their creativity and their truthfulness. Creative writers should express their ideas freely. They should be ready to pay the price for being free, self-confident, critical of any system, religion or country, including their own. All dirty linen should be exposed to be cleansed in fresh air. We should do our own washing. We should cure our own defects, and not expect others to do this work for us. From my medical and surgical experience I believe that we cannot cure an abscess without opening it, to get rid of the pus. In every society, in every culture, in every religion, there are both harmful and useful, negative and positive, values and rules. We should encourage the positive and eradicate the negative.

I do not believe in what is called religious identity, in a pure Muslim or Christian or Jewish identity, or indeed in any other. We are all mixed blood — and the more mixed the better. Pure identity means racism. From my experience, as a writer from Egypt, who started writing more than half a century ago, the pleasure of creativity and truthfulness is much greater than anything the market can give, much more important than money or sex or fame. The pleasure of creativity can erase all your pains and sufferings, can make you a very happy person in spite of everything, including threats, torture, prison, exile and death.

April 2008

11

Bodour

I saw her photograph on the Internet. Bodour's face was all lit up with hopes for the future, a face like mine when I was her age.

More than sixty years ago, I still recall, four sturdy women with fists like iron grabbed me by the arms and legs. They tied me up like a chicken which is being prepared for slaughter, then with a rusting blade proceeded to cut off the wicked, offending organ growing naturally between my thighs. Behind them stood my mother giving me a bitter smile; she knew they were cutting off a piece of my flesh as they had cut off a piece of hers when she was a little girl. She knew that she had never known happiness or pleasure. She had married and given birth to nine boys and girls without experiencing a single tremor of pleasure, while her husband revelled in it, trembling all over with ecstasy. She envied him, and deep down cursed her mother, father, and their two families for conspiring together in order to deprive her of joy.

The men preaching on radio and at mosques, as well as male and female doctors of the preachers' camp who had placed veils over their minds, told her that happiness was not connected with this cursed sinful piece of flesh. They assured her that her happiness actually meant getting rid of it and devoting her life entirely to the service of her husband and children, to prayers and fasting, and to visiting the Prophet's grave before her death.

My mother died in the prime of life, but before her death she said to me, 'Forgive me, daughter, for having done to you what they did to me without really understanding. I've lived my life in fear and ignorance, and today I die of the same fear and ignorance.'

My mother's words were the light that unveiled the truth for me and I stopped cursing my mother, father, mosque preachers, or doctors, either male or female.

Instead, I directed the anger inside me towards the outside. I channelled my energy into writing a new work to expose the hypocrisy of preachers and the backwardness of inherited practices. I produced a book that detailed the harmful effect of circumcision and revealed its medical and social consequences.

This was in the middle of the last century. As soon as my book was out, policemen were dispatched everywhere to collect the confiscated book from bookshops. It was said that the book was inspired by Satan, and that satanic glands were responsible for producing thoughts that went contrary to religion and morality. The health minister, living in fear and ignorance like other medical doctors, issued a decree to destroy the book and punish the writer by firing her and defaming her in the newspapers and media, because she had deviated from proper medical practices and the noble teachings of religion.

I have lived long enough, however, to read now that the minister of health has issued a decree banning female circumcision. But the most amazing thing for me was the Egyptian Mufti's declaration that female circumcision is against Islam. Earlier Muftis and Grand Azhar Sheikhs had announced that renouncing the practice would be sinful and an incitement to degeneration.

Did Bodour have to die so that some light might infiltrate through the dark brain cells? Did you have to pay with your own precious life so that medical doctors would learn self-evident truths? Did your young innocent blood have to be spilt so that the men of religion would understand that true religion does not cut off pieces of children's flesh to safeguard innocence and virtue?

Moral behaviour is the result of training and precept, and cannot be enforced by a blade carving off a body organ. How many children have bled to death at the hands of the rural barber or the urban doctor? But the death of boys is never publicized and therefore never reaches the media the way Bodour's case did. Are you waiting for a boy to die like Bodour so that you would ban male circumcision?

Years ago, I sent a letter to the minister of health, the Medical Union and conscientious people in the country, wherein I stated that male circumcision is physically, psychologically and socially harmful. I explained all this in a book published a few years ago.

Other books have also been published to expose the harmful effects of circumcision on boys and girls alike. But nobody pays any attention. Instead, accusations are levelled at those who oppose such practices. They are accused of apostasy and of being enemies to Islam, although circumcision is not mentioned either in the Qur'an or in the Bible. Only one verse in the Torah makes it obligatory for the males of the children of Israel to be circumcised in return for the promised land of Canaan. Today, no reasonable person in the whole world circumcises his/her children, male or female.

Even the children of Israel who believe in the Torah have discontinued these harmful practices in spite of the text. This is because they are guided by their reason and proper logic, giving more consideration to human health and well-being than to the text.

We have a venerable Islamic school of thought upholding the view that if the text runs contrary to human good, the latter should take precedence, in view of the fact that the text is permanent while what constitutes human good is subject to change.

The children of Israel have adopted the brilliant idea proposed by this creative Islamic school, while most of the Muslims in our country know nothing about it. They still follow the late Sheikh Al-Shaarawi, may God have mercy on him, who said that cutting off a woman's clitoris was a religious duty so that she would not become sexually aroused if she went on camelback. I remember having written an article in *Al-Musawar* magazine, wherein I responded to this warped kind of logic by suggesting that the male sexual organ also comes into friction with the back of the camel. Would his eminence recommend cutting it off? I also told him that riding on camelback had disappeared with the invention of the bicycle, the car and the aeroplane.

I also said that sexual arousal stems from the mind up in the head and not from the organ that lies under the pelvis. I said a great deal. The late Sheikh Al-Shaarawi accused me of being a collaborator with the Devil, and of working for Satan, while his eminence worked for God.

From this great distance, Bodour, from beyond the seas and oceans, I tell you: you could have turned into a great writer, musician, space scientist, or researcher in the chronic physical and psychological diseases plaguing our country.

Yes, Bodour, they took hold of you, tied you up as they would a chicken and slaughtered you. You were offered on the altar of their superstitions and ignorance, out of their fear of the little piece of flesh in your body that threatens their ill-founded dominance resulting from age-long misconceptions.

I ask Bodour's family to let their daughter's spilt blood turn into an inspiration enlightening people's minds. They should never resort to silence or forgetfulness, under any temptations or threats. They should raise their voices sky high in order to make of Bodour's case a national issue which is no less important than the question of national liberation. A nation without reason is bound to vanish into oblivion, and a land without humanity is bound to be swept away with the wind.

🙚 'Bodour', inspired by an Egyptian girl who died in a clinic at the hands of a woman doctor, was first published in Arabic in *Almasry–Alyoum* newspaper, and translated by Amira Nowaira, Cairo, 28 June 2007.

12

Writing and Freedom

FROM THE MOMENT the world of writing opened itself before me, I started to follow a route that was drastically different from the one preordained for me before birth. The history of enslavement dating back to pharaonic times had not only laid out the path I should follow from cradle to grave, but had also created the authorities to make sure that I did. It thus provided the authority of the father and husband in the small family, the authority of the state, the legal system, social institutions, the authority of religion and Shari'a, and finally the authority of international legitimacy.

These authorities took the shape of a pyramid. At the top, you would find what we today call the New World Order, the *New York Times* and CNN, while at the bottom there would be the local governments, local television, prisons, censorship and literary criticism.

As a child I discovered that writing was the only means by which I could breathe. But the government, the patriarchal and religious authorities, the propaganda in the media, as well as the teachings of the Faculty of Medicine (which I joined to please my father), all said to me, 'There is no connection between writing and the act of breathing in a woman.' My experience in life, however, has confirmed the very close connection between writing and the entry of air into my lungs. These hierarchical authorities joined forces and, like an iron fist, pushed me into the conjugal bed, under the illusion of love and the 'scientific' ideas, derived from Freud, that women must create babies and not ideas. At one stage of my life I produced babies and more than once in my life I was married to the brim. Yet, instead of feeling the air enter my lungs, I felt suffocated.

The more a woman dedicates herself to the institution of marriage, the more suffocated she is bound to feel. I looked up the word 'dedication' in the inherited dictionary of enslavement, and I found it connected with the devotion of slaves to their masters. It's a term that implies the act of getting lost in others, of self-denial and self-sacrifice, terms that come under the category of death or of self-destruction.

But creativity and writing are quite the opposite. They involve keeping the self alive, rather than destroying it. They mean the realization of self and not its denial.

And thus I discovered the contradiction between marital devotion and self-fulfilment in a woman's life, since marriage dictates that a woman's identity dissolve into that of her husband or into those of her children (after all, the children are the rightful property of the husband and his name is written on them). Thus the man of letters is blessed with a wife who cooks his food, washes his trousers, and offers him tea, while he sits to write down the story of his love for another woman. On the other hand, the woman of letters is blessed with a husband who turns her life into misery and scolds her all the time for having neglected to cook, wash, or sweep the floors, or for having allowed the children to scream out loud while he slept. The creative man has a wife who delights in his success and feels happier as he becomes more successful. The creative woman has a husband who gets depressed when she succeeds, and gets increasingly more depressed as she becomes more successful.

If the creative woman has the courage to suppress part of her brain, she may save herself from the depression of husbands, and may be able to avoid losing herself in the sacred women's kingdom inside the house. She will be able then to go out on the streets, demonstrating along with others and shouting 'God... nation... and king' (or whoever occupies the position of a king). But she may also find herself required to identify completely with the king or the president. If she is not willing to do that, a huge wooden gate will open up before her, leading her into prison.

While in prison in 1981, I tried day and night to discover the crime I had committed, never having been affiliated to any political party, never having committed adultery, never having carried an illegitimate child, and never having insulted anyone. After eighty days and nights in my cell, I discovered that my only crime was having been unable to lose myself in the self of the president. In ancient Egypt, the pharaoh considered himself divine, and all other selves were required to dissolve completely into his. Losing oneself has been the virtue most highly appreciated from the days of the pharaohs until now. But dissolving is the opposite of creativity. Writing means expressing my self. It means that my self will not dissolve in any other self, be it my husband, God or the president.

Writing means surviving and denying death. If it had not been for writing, all prophets, gods and pharaohs would have disappeared forever. If it had not been for the discovery of printing, we would not have known anything about those who had died. But for the Torah, the Bible and the Qur'an, we would not have Moses, Jesus or Muhammad.

Writing has the power to give life to the dead. This is why writing has become the only way I can survive. I often wonder how people who do not write manage to survive or endure life. My mother died leaving not a trace. I am one of the nine children she had given birth to. None of us carried her name. My father also died, leaving behind no mark except for his name in mine, written on my books. With the translation of my books into several languages, my father's name has become known, while my mother's has disappeared forever.

On the other hand, I feel better off than the English writer Virginia Woolf, who took on her husband's name and was known by it. A woman should use her own name on her works and not that of her father or husband. If I had to choose between my father's name and my husband's, I would certainly prefer my father's, since it is at least permanent. The husband's name may change with a change of circumstances. This is particularly true in our country. When a husband happens to fall in love with another woman, all he need do is open his mouth and utter the words 'You're divorced', three times, upon which his wife packs her bags and leaves. In the eyes of the law and Shari'a, she has become a divorced woman.

I consider myself lucky that I have never taken the name of any husband and never signed my books except with my father's name and that of my paternal grandfather, El Saadawi — the name of a man who is a total stranger to me, since he died before I was born. He died of bilharzia, poverty and enslavement, the triple chronic disease afflicting our peasants from the days of the pharaohs until the present. There are times when my name is shortened to my grandfather's name, El Saadawi. This is how this strange man gets his name imprinted on me and on the covers of my books.

Nothing consoles me more than the thought that at least on doomsday, I will be able to shed that strange name and carry my mother's. When I was a little girl, my father once told me that on doomsday people would be called by their mothers' names. I asked him why this was so, and he said that maternity was certain. So I asked, 'Is paternity not certain, then?' I saw the pupil of his eye quiver slightly, and a long silence followed. He gave my mother a look wavering between doubt and certainty.

My mother knew no man other than my father. How could she have, if she never left the house or, more precisely, never left the kitchen? After giving birth to her ninth child, she became pregnant with the tenth. She had an abortion.

One day while she slept, she dreamt of my father with another woman. Her grief made the milk freeze in her breast, forming a cancerous tumour. She died very young. My maternal grandmother used to sing to herself in the bathroom a song that went: 'Trusting a man is like trusting that water would stay in a sieve.' She used to pour water over the sieve and watch it disappear to the last drop. She would smack her lips in distress. When her husband came home late at night, she would smell the other woman in his underwear. In the morning, he would lecture her on the love of the homeland.

After the death of my grandfather, I became very sceptical of any man who chanted the song of patriotism. If he moved from the love of the motherland to the love of the peasants or labourers, my suspicions increased. If he went beyond that and held a rosary in his hand, my scepticism was confirmed beyond doubt.

Whenever I met a man who was full of religious words and clichés, and who held the rosary in his hand, I would immediately smell a rat. If this man happened to be the head of the state, the problem moved from the domain of the personal to the public. And if he happened to be my husband, the disaster would still be unmitigated, because I would then have to choose between writing and living in the Garden of Eden.

I have always chosen writing, Eden being rather out of reach, and its delights designed for the gratification of men. Prominent among these delights is the presence of fair young virgins. But I am a woman of dark skin. I have long lost my virginity and am at the moment in the menopausal phase (to use the language of the system). In paradise, a woman like me will have none other than her husband. What a disaster! To have my husband chasing me in life and after death!

That is why I have always chosen writing. I came to realize, even as a child, that I was not going to have the same fate as my mother, my grandmother or, for that matter, any other woman. Why I had this conviction is not totally clear to me. One reason may have been that I saw my father's great admiration for the Prophet, and I wanted to get my father's admiration. One day I dreamt I became a prophet and my father looked at me admiringly. When, in the morning, I told my grandmother about that dream, she just hit her chest in disbelief. She heated some water for me to cleanse myself of the guilt. A woman could never be a prophet, she told me.

That day I took up my pen and jotted down angry words on the page. My brother, who failed his exams every year, could become a prophet, while I, who succeeded every year, could not. My anger was directed at a power I did not know. My grandmother said it was God who preferred my brother, though he failed his exams every year.

There is certainly a connection between creativity and anger. The little girl is taught to conceal her anger and draw an angelic smile on her face. But no connection exists between angels and creativity. That is why in Arabic we have the expressions 'the demon of poetry' and 'the demon of art'.

I began to voice my anger against all authorities from the bottom up, starting with the authority of my father. My father, noticing a frown rather than a smile on my face, told me that frowning made girls lose their femininity. So I had to choose between femininity and writing. I chose writing.

In the dead of the night, I hugged my anger the way the woman carrying an illegitimate child hugged her secret. I told my mother that if a woman did not become angry at injustice, she would not be human. She told me that being human was better than being a woman. My grandmother raised her hand to her chin and said defiantly, 'I bet you won't find anyone to marry you. Obeying your father is obeying God.'

In obedience to my father, I joined the Faculty of Medicine and put on the angelic white coat. For years I lived with the stool and urine of patients, the rules of the Ministry of Health and the guidelines of the general director and the minister. When my father died, I was free of my promise and started to live to please no one but myself.

Creativity only begins when man is free from the wish to please others.

After my father's death, I discovered that there were other authorities trying to dominate my life. But I promised myself that no one would have domination over me, and that I would write what my own mind dictated.

So the policemen knocked on my door, broke it open, and dragged me to prison under the pretence of safeguarding my life. I walked into prison as if into a dream. The trance was not unlike the one I had when, under the illusion of love and the marriage bond, I walked back into my second marriage.

The authority of the state and the authority of the husband constitute one iron chain, whose arch enemy is writing. My husband used to fly into a mad rage whenever he saw me with pen and paper in hand.

The jailer came every day into my cell, turned it upside down, removed the tiles under the toilet, dug deep into the floor and wall, and screamed out: 'If I found pen or paper, it would be far worse for you than if I had found a gun.'

After the death of the president, I walked out of jail and into a prison-like existence. My name moved from the blacklist to the grey list, the only difference between the two being the colour of the paper. I saw people's faces, pale and sallow. Nobody believed anybody, and everyone accused everyone else. Accusations flew downwards and upwards, from the tip of the pyramid where international legitimacy resides to the bottom, to local governments, patriarchal and legislative authorities, to religious institutions, cultural institutions, the media, the press, the intellectuals, the writers and the literary critics.

Everything seemed to be receding. Even the loaf of bread, like justice, was in short supply. I realized that writing was the substitute for justice, and justice was beauty and love.

—Writing is the vain attempt to find love.
—Writing is the vain attempt to defy death.
—Both love and death are ephemeral.
—Nothing remains but the letters on the page.
—Nothing remains of gods and prophets except the books.

Without the presence of creative art to create hope from nothingness, there would be pure despair all around us. Creativity is like a spot of light in pitch darkness. It is the presence of the ray of light in the midst of this massive despair that makes our suffering in writing worthwhile.

We pay an exorbitant price for being creative, a price that may be as high as death. If the creative artist happens to be a woman, the price she pays is doubled, tripled, or even quadrupled, according to circumstances.

In addition to losing Eden, I have also lost in my life what my grandmother used to call 'the shade of a man', the shade provided by a man being, as the saying goes, 'better than the shade of a wall'. Personally, I have always preferred the shade of the wall to that of a man who became depressed because of my creativity. This was how I lost my reputation on both the personal and public levels.

The men who tried to flirt with me and found me unyielding called me a woman without femininity and a man-hater. The men who worked for God, for the nation, and for the oil kings said that I worked for the Devil and that I was advocating permissiveness and sexual freedom. The men who loved peasants and workers said that I loved women better than peasants or workers and that I believed more in sexual freedom than in class struggle; I was therefore the ally of imperialism and Zionism. The men who loved the nation for its own sake and did not savour any talk of class struggle said I was the ally of international communism because the word *class* is sometimes used in my writings.

My doctor colleagues, men and women alike (who hated any talk about politics and loved nothing better than their patients), thought I was an utter failure, having achieved none of the five goals of the profession: a clinic, a car, a house, a farm, and a bride (or bridegroom).

As for my literary colleagues of both sexes, who love to be in the limelight of the camera, the newspapers or the state prizes, and who consider that one can criticize anything or anyone under the sun except God and the head of state, they believe I have failed in my literary career because I live away from the limelight and in the area of the grey or black lists.

More than ten years ago, in 1980, one of my books fell by chance into the hands of a small publisher living in South Africa. Although he was white, he fought alongside the black Africans against the racist regime of apartheid. He was harassed and was in danger of getting killed in Johannesburg, but he managed to escape to London and started a small publishing business. This was the first book of mine to be translated into a foreign language. With it, I stepped out of local bounds, to an English readership and then to different languages.

From 1980 until now, in 1992, sixteen of my works, including novels, short stories and scientific studies, have been published. My books are now read everywhere in the world. This is how I escaped local confines.

In 1987, after the publication of my novel *The Fall of the Imam* in Arabic, the telephone rang at home. The voice of an official from the Ministry of the Interior told me that I was going to be put under constant guard.

—What for? I asked in surprise.

—To guard your life, he said.

—My life? I asked.

—Yes. Your life is under threat.

—Who's threatening it? I asked.

—This is all the information I have. We'll send the guards in an hour, he said.

—I don't want any guards, I told him, as long as you withhold information from me.

—We'll send you the guards all the same, with or without your consent, he said.

—Will you protect my life against my wishes? I asked.

—Yes, he said, your life is not yours. It belongs to the state.

The guards came to my house and stayed there for two years. Then they disappeared. Until this day I have no idea why they came in the first place, or why they left later. But I came to understand that my life was not mine.

In 1990 a journalist came along with the copy of an Arabic magazine published in London. In it was a list of 'the dead' (or those who ought to be dead). I read my name on that list, together with the names of several literary figures, writers and poets.

—Who drew up this list? I asked.

—The oil kings, was the answer.

At night, while lying in bed, I saw a small butterfly, almost spiderlike, being attracted by the light of the lamp. When it came too close, it got scorched by the heat and so withdrew a little. This movement was repeated several times until finally it burnt and fell down dead.

I wondered during my sleep about this irrational attraction to the light and the flame. In the morning, opening the magazine, I realized the connection between the oil kings and international legitimacy.

In the magazine was written that the oil kings had paid the Western alliance the cost of the Gulf War.

For the first time in history the slaves are paying their masters the cost of their own enslavement.

Things being what they are, isn't the connection between creativity and death more reasonable than the attraction between the butterflies and the light? And since creativity was up against all the pyramidal authorities, both internally and externally, isn't it logical, then, that the creative artist is threatened with imprisonment or death? All the more so if that artist happens to be a woman?

From the dawn of the history of enslavement and the rise of the patriarchal class system, there has always been a conflict between creativity and authority. This is why restrictions are imposed on free expression. Every creative artist, male or female, has a personal way of surmounting these limitations. But simple, clear and direct writing remains the most dangerous, since it conveys its message directly to thousands or millions who may be incapable of deciphering the more intricate literary discourse.

But the creative idea imposes its own method of expression. In some of my works, symbolism and suggestiveness gain ground over directness. At times I leave meanings to be read between the lines. At others I leave spaces or even ellipsis marks. I may let out an unuttered sigh that ends up in silence or a full stop. The creative reader has the task of reading the unwritten script within the written book.

When I am overwhelmed by mad courage, I write without caution. But what I write no one will dare publish. I put these in a blue file on which is written, 'To be published posthumously.' These are the writings I manage to produce away from the inner censor. This censor may hide behind a military outfit and may carry in his hand the sceptre of kings or presidents.

At other times, he may wear the body of my grandfather, who died before I was born. Or he may take off this body, disappearing without a trace except for a small, delicate cane, like the one that the teacher of religious instruction at my primary school used to carry in his hand.

The censor is ever present, always looking at you as though through a spy-hole. There is always a price to pay for creativity, a price that may be life itself.

But for me, this is a small price to pay, because I would rather lose life than lose myself. Without this self, creativity can never be.

3❧   'My Experience with Writing and Freedom', written in 1992 and first published in Arabic in *Fusul* magazine, was translated by Amira Nowaira for this volume.

13

The Three Universal Taboos:
Sex, Religion and Politics

THE OPPRESSION OF WOMEN and poor classes constitutes an integral part of the capitalist patriarchal system preponderant in most of the world, West and East, North and South, Jewish, Christian, Islamic and Hindu. Gender, class and race discrimination are born of developments in history that made one class rule over another, one race dominate over another, and men rule over women, in the state and in the family unit, which constitute the core of patriarchal class relations. But there are still many writers who close their eyes to these historical facts, for political–economic–colonial reasons. They depict the three taboos related to 'sex, religion and politics' as stemming from Islam or Arab mentality. They reduce crimes against women and poor men, dictatorship, fanaticism and obscurantism, to religious, cultural and identity factors. For these thinkers there is no link between sexual and class oppression; there is no link between global politics, national politics and family politics; there is no link between the American military invasion of Iraq and oil domination and exploitation; there is no link between money and sex; there is no link between the material and spiritual, or between the body, the mind and the spirit.

These dichotomies are prevalent in the present day and are inherited from the slave system which arose thousands of years ago. They serve to veil the mind, to deceive women and men, by hiding material–physical exploitation under false spiritual–religious happiness, or by turning the social system (made by ruling classes) into divine law.

We need to study history and the divine books (the three mono-theistic books) to understand why female genital mutilation (FGM) and male genital mutilation (MGM) arose in history, and to know that FGM is not mentioned in any of these books. MGM is men-tioned in the Old Testament (but there is nothing about MGM in the Qur'an or the New Testament). In the Old Testament there is the following verse:

> And I will give unto thee, and to the seed after thee, the land wherein thou art a stranger, all the land of Canaan, for an ever-lasting possession, and I will be their God....
>
> This is my covenant, which ye shall keep, between me and you and they seed after thee, every man child among you shall be circumcised....
>
> He that is born in my house, and he that is bought with thy money, must needs be circumcised, and my covenant shall be in your flesh for an everlasting covenant. And the uncircumcised man child whose flesh of his foreskin is not circumcised, that soul shall be cut off from his people, he hath broken my covenant. (Genesis 17:8–14)

As a medical doctor I have known the physical, mental and social problems of both MGM and FGM. It is common sense that a child (male or female) should not be cut into by knife under any religious or cultural or identity slogans. Never in my life did I perform this operation for a female or male child. I have felt it is a crime against children (eight days for the male child and 6 years for the female child).

FGM: this crime was done to me when I was 6 years old. I wrote about it in Arabic in my book under the title *The Naked Face of Arab Women* (1972), which was published in English in 1980 under the title *The Hidden Face of Eve*. The publisher changed the title; I do not know why, maybe to link it somehow with the veiling of women, or with Islam, though I never linked FGM to Islam, or any religion or culture.

FGM is inherited from the slave system, or the class patriarchal system. It is part of the patriarchal package which includes:

1. Cutting the sexual organs of the female child, especially the clitoris, to guarantee their virginity before marriage and their fidelity after marriage.
2. Veiling of women, isolating them at home under the authority of their men, forcing them to work (at home or outside the home) with no payment, to guarantee their economic dependence on their men, and therefore their submission to any type of oppression.
3. Severe punishment of women who do not obey their men. Obedience of the father and husband is inseparable from obedience to God. Punishment is by death for a woman who betrays her husband, but a man has the right to betray his wife (since God gave him the right to divorce and to practise polygamy).
4. Fatherhood should be known; therefore virginity and monogamy should be enforced on women by physical, mental, religious, moral, social, legal, political and economic means. FGM is one of the means to diminish women's sexual (and also political and social) ability and mobility, so that her husband will be sure of his fatherhood, sure that his children are his (and not another man's), sure that his children inherit his land and money and carry his name, and his father's name. Patriarchy is based on the name of the father.

From my experience as a medical doctor and a psychiatrist I learned that FGM has nothing to do with the morality of women; it does not make them more likely to be monogamous or more faithful to their husbands. On the contrary, cutting the clitoris increases women's sexual desires. Why?

1. Because the brain is the main site of sexual desires.
2. Because circumcised women have difficulty in reaching sexual satisfaction with their husbands, and they look for this satisfaction outside marriage.

Freedom and responsibility towards the self and others should not be separable. Free uncircumcised women can be more responsible towards their families if they combine freedom with responsibility. Circumcised women can be less responsible if they are oppressed or veiled (physically or mentally). Veiling of the mind is inseparable from veiling of the body, since the body and the mind are inseparable. Veiling of women became a divine code. If you criticize the veil in Egypt today you expose yourself to danger and harsh criticism (as happened to the minister of culture some weeks ago).

In Egypt some religious Islamic scholars believe that FGM is a divine order, or at least a Sunni order according to Hadith by Prophet Muhammad, but other Islamic scholars believe that FGM and the veil have nothing to do with Islam. Most Islamic and Arab countries know nothing about FGM — for example, Syria, Iraq, Lebanon, Tunisia, Libya, Morocco and Saudi Arabia. (Only Egypt, Sudan, Somalia and Yemen practise FGM.) Islam replaced communism (after the fall of the Berlin Wall) as the Devil, or the Enemy of the Neocolonial Imperialist American Empire. FGM and the veil, and oppression of women in general, became linked to Islam only (along with terrorism, backwardness, underdevelopment, dictatorship, barbarism, inability to modernize, etc.). Some people think that FGM is an ancient Egyptian or African tradition, but it is a universal slave tradition and is not related to a certain race, colour, country or continent.

Veiling, virginity and the name of the mother

The backlash against the rights of women and the poor is universal, and not specific to our Arab region or to Islamic countries. Honour crimes are related to virginity and are not limited to Arab or Islamic culture. The conception of virginity is also embedded in Judaism and Christianity — for example, the Virgin Mary is the ideal mother, and nuns are veiled. Traditions, sacred or not, reflect systems of power in the state and in the family. They change with time and place. They are not fixed or immutable or eternal. They are selectively picked up by political groups to preserve the patriarchal capitalist structures globally and locally. When women fight for their human rights under any capitalist–patriarchal system, they are labelled traitors to their religion, their country, their culture, their authentic identity, their morality, and their chastity. But we have to go on fighting; we should not be intimidated. We should organize globally and locally.

Global struggle is the solution and freedom has a high price, but the price of slavery is greater so it is better to pay the price and be free than to pay and be a slave. There must be combined efforts to mobilize men, women, youth and children so that they become organized and constitute a political and social power, capable of changing the existing patriarchal–class values and laws. This needs real democracy. This needs freedom to organize and criticize. This needs a collective struggle against state dictatorship, against family dictatorship, and against false consciousness created by governmental media and the educational system. If the state itself is based on patriarchy, class and religion, how can it fight oppression which is a product of patriarchy, class and religion?

We now have a backlash against the rights of women and the poor. The effect of globalization and American neocolonialism is increasing in Egypt, causing more and more poverty (40 per cent of Egyptians live below the poverty line), increasing rates of unemployment, deterioration of health services, education and media, and the dominance of backward fundamentalist religious political groups.

On 28 January 2007, I was interrogated in court by the general prosecutor. A trial was filed against me and my daughter, Dr Mona Helmy, who is a writer and a poet, accusing us of apostasy. Why? Because she wrote an article in a weekly (*Roza El-Youssef*, 21 March 2006) demanding that the name of the mother should be respected and not ignored and saying that she will include both her mother's and her father's names when she signs her articles and books. My crime is my writings and my struggle against the patriarchal language in religion and politics when I say that God is neither male nor female, that God is a symbol of justice, freedom and love, as my peasant grandmother said to me more than sixty-five years ago. God is a symbol of justice and not a book that comes out of the printing machine. There is no peace globally, nationally or in the family without justice. There is no freedom or real democracy without justice.

The conflict between the two conceptions of God

On 27 February 2007, Al-Azhar (the highest Islamic institution in Egypt and in the whole Islamic world) accused me of apostasy and heresy because of my play published in Arabic in Cairo (January 2007) under the title *God Resigns at the Summit Meeting*. The play exposes the contradictions and the patriarchal, class and race discriminations embedded in the three monotheistic books: the Old Testament, the New Testament and the Qur'an. It shows how these books are political, dealing with power, money and sex. Double morality prevails in the three books: inferiority of women relative to men, dictatorship, racism, war, and killing the heretic or infidel. Most governments in the world use these divine books to oppress their people. Religion is a servant to the political system. It is used by powerful groups to justify injustice as a divine order. God resigns in the play when faced by his contradictions and injustices.

With the revival of religious fundamentalist movements all over the world, oppression of women and the poor has increased. Creative thinking is condemned, because it unveils the mind and exposes paradoxes related to politics, religion and sex. Walking in the streets of Cairo and Brussels during February 2007, I met young women who cover their heads with a veil and uncover the upper part of their abdomen while wearing tight jeans. Women are the most visible victims of religious and political contradictions, of being veiled under religious pressures, and of being naked under the consumerism of globalization and the so-called free market, which is the freedom of the powerful to exploit the weak.

Egypt, winter 2007

14

Breeding Terror, *or*
An Uncivilized Clash of Civilizations

IN MONTCLAIR and in New York, which is only a short distance
from where I live, it is a beautiful, sunny day. It reminds me of the
autumn sun, back home in Egypt. But when I look at the sky there is
that empty space left by the twin towers of the World Trade Center,
a void which clutches at the heart with a dark foreboding. On the
front page of the *New York Times* I read an announcement today
concerning the agreement reached which will give the American
military 'flexibility' in operating from bases in the former Soviet
republic of Uzbekistan in return for assurances that the security of
Uzbekistan will be protected by the United States.

The word 'protection' echoes in my mind, evoking memories. It
was used by the British colonialists in 1882 to invade and occupy
Egypt. In 1991 George Bush senior visited Egypt to convince
Mubarak that Egypt needed 'protection' against the satanic Saddam
Hussein. In return for this 'protection' and for a reduction in the
Egyptian foreign military debt owed to the United States, soldiers
recruited from the poor of the villages were sent off to participate in
Operation Desert Storm launched against Iraq, in which a quarter
of a million people were pounded to death by bombs in a few
weeks in order to ensure that oil, and the Middle East, remain
under American control. The thirty allied countries in the Gulf
War declared that their aim was to 'liberate Kuwait', and badges

were distributed with these two words written in blue on a golden background. I used to see them shining on the lapels of some of the intellectuals whom I met.

I came to New York and New Jersey a few days before the terrorist attack on the World Trade Center and the building of the Pentagon. I did not watch on the television screen as the buildings burned and collapsed. I did not see the planes crashed into them, did not follow the tragedy being broadcast in detail hour after hour. I do not want to watch any more tragedies. Living in the Middle East, as it is called, I have seen enough of them, seen enough buildings collapse, enough people killed or maimed for life, enough massacres in Palestine, in Iraq, in Algeria, in the Sudan, in Somalia, in Iran, and even in Egypt.

I believe in peace. I hate war. I hate to see people killed, to see women and children die under bombs, whether in Egypt, or in Japan, or in the United States. I was surprised when journalists asked me whether I had felt pain for the thousands of civilians who had been killed in the 11 September terrorist attack. To me it was a strange question. For how can one not feel pain at knowing that thousands of innocent people were killed like that? But what was even stranger to me was the fact that no journalist had ever asked me whether I had felt pain when hundreds of thousands of Iraqis were being killed, or when half a million Iraqi children had died of malnutrition and disease because of the economic embargo, or when young Palestinians were being massacred every day by Israeli soldiers because they need a land on which to live. Could it be that there is a hierarchy of human life, that human life is valued according to its position in the hierarchy of money and nuclear power?

Unveiling the mind

Many professors in academia are fond of the term 'postcolonial', and it has become fashionable to say that we are living in the postcolonial era. But since I live in the so-called Middle East I know that it is a word which speaks a partial truth in order to hide a more important truth, to hide the fact that we live in a new or neocolonial era where colonialism is transnational, led by the United States, and has taken on other more sophisticated economic, military, technological and cultural forms. Global neocolonial powers, like the previous colonial ones, cannot continue to rule the world, to exercise their control over people unless they are able to divide them, or to throw fuel on whatever divisions already exist. Religion, patriotism, racism and other absolute, infinite, enduring, eternal values are used every day and often very effectively to divide people. The history of religions, nationalism and patriotism is linked to rivers of blood.

After the 11 September terrorist attack the Pope, clothed in his divine robes, went on a tour to Kazakhstan, Armenia, and other former Soviet republics situated to the north of Afghanistan. He went there in the name of God just before Bush declared his 'War on Terror'. Once again we are facing the fundamentalist, absolutist dichotomy of God versus the Devil, and of good versus evil, used to mystify people, to confuse them, to veil their minds. The language George W. Bush uses is no different from that of the Pope, or that of bin Laden. All three speak in the name of God against the enemy, against the Devil. The church and the mosque are not just spiritual bodies with a spiritual agenda, but also geopolitical, economic and even military bodies, but their agendas here are clothed in spiritual robes.

The multitudes of flags, the myriad signs and badges and shirts which say 'God Bless America', the chorus of patriotic slogans chanted in America today cloud the thinking of people and shift their attention away from the pressing economic and social problems which face them and the rest of the world. The massive mobilization of the American war machine is too great to be directed only against bin Laden and the Taliban, or against other terrorist groups dispersed in different countries of the world. It is meant to be used against all those who oppose the policies of the United States, primarily in the Arab region but also in the rest of the world, including the United States itself. It is being directed to deprive the American people of their freedom and their human rights. Bush has declared that he will take all the measures necessary to defend the 'security' of the United States against the 'enemies who hate American democracy and the American way of life', and these measures include a whole range of incursions on individual and community freedom. This war on terror is being used to halt the rising wave of opposition to unbridled transnational exploitation of nature, human resources and human life.

In the global patriarchal capitalist system war has been and remains the economic stimulus required to stave off recession and protect accumulation and profits. But I wonder how many bombs will be needed, and how many innocent people must die, in order to ensure that the Dow Jones and the Nasdaq will begin to climb once more.

Two faces of the same coin

With the collapse of the Soviet Union and the end of the Cold War the military–industrial complex in the United States was eager to find a new enemy so that it could maintain an economy largely built on war and the sale of arms. The Muslims and Arabs were quickly made to assume that role. The way was paved by some of the things that they did, by the corruption of rulers and their narrow interests. Marx was replaced by the Prophet Muhammad and Huntington became the theoretician of a new war. Social and economic struggles, according to him, would be replaced by the 'Clash of Civilizations'. The Christian civilization of the United States had to face enemies, and these enemies were mainly the Muslims (Arabs) and the Confucians (Chinese). This meant that the war machine of the United States was to be maintained and developed further to meet the threat coming from the Muslim world.

Throughout the period of the Cold War the Muslim fundamentalist movements had remained closely allied to the United States. In Egypt the Muslim Brothers, founded in 1928, were supported by the British and the king against the national movement, and later against Nasser. After that the United States and Sadat encouraged and supported them and some of their more radical offshoots to counterbalance opposition against opening the door to American economic and political control of Egyptian affairs. In Indonesia the United

States supported the right-wing Shariat-il-Islam against Sukarno as part of the preparations for a military coup which ended in the massacre of half a million members of the Indonesian Communist Party. In Pakistan it supported the Jama'at-e Islami against Benazir Bhutto. Later, in collaboration with Saudi Arabia and Pakistan (Inter-Services Intelligence) the CIA helped Osama bin Laden to recruit and train a guerrilla force of 30,000 militants and to build up the Taliban, which grew up in the Madrasat (Islamic Schools) founded by the Islamic fundamentalist movements in Pakistan close to the borders with Afghanistan. These operations cost the United States $3 billion.

Wahabism, the state religion in Saudi Arabia since 1932, is one of the most virulent and ultra-puritanical sects of Islam. It is opposed to any form of modernization and has exported itself to many parts of the world with the support of the United States and the wide use of Saudi petrodollars. It has funded fundamentalism all over the Muslim world, including in Afghanistan and Pakistan. The United States founded its strategies in the Middle East mainly on two fundamentalist states, one of them Muslim (Saudi Arabia) and the other Jewish (Israel).

But now the former allies have become enemies, or at least have entered into a conflict. Bush and bin Laden both use the 'clash of civilizations' as a cover and have launched a religious war which is fraught with untold dangers. While the killing goes on, the ideologists of global American capitalism are busy propagating their theories about the clash of cultures, identities, and other such things. According to them money, arms, opium and oil have nothing to do with what is going on. The other day while on the Internet I spotted a colour photograph of Bush. He was wearing a big brown and white turban and his beard had grown. He looked very much like bin Laden except that he had a fair complexion and a rosy tint on his cheeks. This photograph was certainly meant to illustrate what I am saying. They are two faces of the same coin. Together they are helping to maintain a system which dehumanizes thousands of millions of people all over the world, involves them in conflicts which prevent them from working together to face the problems on our earth.

Fighting for peace

Throughout my life I have fought against violence and racism, and for peace. Throughout my life I have suffered as a woman from religious fundamentalism of all kinds. After the defeat of the Soviet Union in Afghanistan at the hands of the Muslim mujahideen, the Afghan Arabs of bin Laden, as they are often called, transferred their operations to other parts of the world, and especially to the Arab region. They too have started to operate globally but in dispersed clusters. In 1991 my name figured on a fundamentalist death list and I was obliged to leave Egypt and live in exile for five years. From March to July 2001 I faced another fundamentalist threat. I had given an interview to a weekly in Egypt in which I said that the veiling of women was not Islamic in origin and dated much further back to Judaism, and that the kissing of the Black Stone during the pilgrimage was a vestige of pagan pre-Islamic practices. Both of these are historically recorded facts, but a lawyer named El-Wahsh, which means the beast or monster, filed a case against me in front of a religious Personal Law court demanding that I be separated from my husband on a charge of apostasy. He considered himself as a representative of God and of the nation of Islam and had risen in defence of their rights according to an old, obscure Islamic law called Hisba. I and my husband Sherif Hetata, to whom I have been married for thirty-seven years, publicly declared that we had no intention either of separating or of leaving the country even if the court issued a judgment of divorce. With the help of a wide solidarity campaign in Egypt, the Arab countries and abroad, as well as legal support from a group of lawyers, after five months we won the case.

I was brought up to believe in the basic human principles of the three monotheistic religions. But religions, like any other ideologies or beliefs, have negative as well as positive aspects and must be examined with a critical mind. Faith can lead to a blind belief; can lead people to kill others who do not believe in the same God or the same prophet or the same way of seeing things. The wars waged by Bush the father or Bush the son are not very different from those of Saddam Hussein and bin Laden. All of them claim higher, eternal principles with strongly religious overtones; all of them lead to the killing of innocent people; and none of them solves any of our problems or helps to make the world a better place. State terrorism is the elder brother of individual terrorism except that it claims the legitimacy of laws upheld by a powerful few.

The world will change when people are able to globalize from below in the struggle for peace against racism and war, in the struggle for justice against all forms of discrimination, when people cooperate together against those who divide and use attractive words to conceal what they are really doing — words like *security*, or *patriotism*, or *civilization*. We must struggle for what we have in common, for our humanity. We must fight to unveil our minds. These days people in the United States are being terrorized by another threat, that of anthrax, of a biological war. An American woman friend of mine phoned up to warn me against opening any mail coming from Egypt or any other Muslim country. I explained to her that the employee of NBC in question had been infected by a letter that had been mailed to her from New Jersey. 'My God', she exclaimed, 'then it's right here at home.' Fear is the greatest of our enemies. It can make us panic, make us blind, force us to forgo the little but important freedom that we enjoy, make us accept almost anything in the name of security or of the war against terrorism. Fear can help Big Brother drive us with a big stick into an Orwellian world.

Monclair, New Jersey, 13 October 2001

15

Remapping the World

When we say 'remapping the world', what do we mean? Who is remapping the world? And remapping it to what? In whose interests? Those superpowers who own God, absolute truths, nuclear weapons, money and media? Or the millions of women, men and children who demonstrate on the streets against those powers and their super God, super military, religious, economic, information weapons?

The history of this world is written, shaped, mapped and remapped by the brutal ruling groups who win the wars, who colonize, recolonize and neocolonize under such beautiful words as *democracy*, *civilization*, *modernism* and *humanitarianism*.

We live in a jungle where you can invade another country and kill its peoples then nobody punishes you or considers you a war criminal, but because you are the president of the United States of America, or the leader of one of its intimate allies such as Israel or Britain.

In the opera programme you introduce the evening as follows:

1989. A crucial year in world history. Europe saw the fall of a wall. In China a tank stopped for a man. In the United States Bush senior became president. The end of the Cold War heralded a new era. States disappeared, new areas of conflict arose. What impact have these crucial changes had on identity, language and literature?

When I read these words I felt I do not relate to these very important crucial changes; they may be relevant to an American or European writer, or to a writer from China, but not for me, a writer from Egypt or from Africa, or from what they call the Middle East. Middle to whom? We were given the map and the name of the Middle East by the old British colonizers. Egypt was Middle East relative to London; India was the Far East relative to the same British rulers. This false colonial language is in use today, under the neocolonizers. But the old map is changing according to the shifting interests of different dominating groups or countries.

On the old map there was a country called Palestine. Now it is called Israel. The Palestinian nation was killed; those who survived the massacres after 1948 became refugees, immigrants, dispersed all over the world. The Palestinian Holocaust and sufferings are ignored by those who write history and map or remap the world. History glorifies the Jewish Holocaust and suffering at the hands of the Nazis. History is not real history. The history of our world has been ignoring the struggles of the colonized people (not only the Palestinians) since the beginning of the slave patriarchal class system, some thousand years ago.

You consider the year 1989 crucial in world history because Europe saw the fall of a wall. The history of Europe is equated with the history of the world. A wall fell in Berlin, but what about other walls erected to enslave and colonize other nations? What about the wall in our region? For example, the wall separating the Palestinian people from their land and homes? The erection of such walls is not a crucial event to be remembered by world history, because some people do not count; they do not own nuclear weapons or big money. One American or Israeli soldier is more valuable than thousands of Iraqi or Palestinian or Afghani or African people.

Israel is the only country that possesses nuclear weapons in our region; it could eradicate nations such as Palestine, Iraq, Syria and others that do not equally possess nuclear arms. The president of the USA, Barack Obama, has declared in his speeches that the USA and Israel are one country; he ignores the fact that Israel is a colonial project working for the interests of neocolonial powers in the USA and Europe and is established on Palestinian blood and land.

You say that in China a tank stopped for a man, and this is considered a crucial world event. But what about other crucial events in our region where tanks are killing people every day? Is the life of one man in China more important than the lives of thousands in our countries, of the so-called Third World? Third relative to whom? Can we call a war criminal a member of the First World?

In the US and European academy many people say we are living in the postcolonial era. This language does not reflect our reality: we live in the neocolonial, not the postcolonial, era. How can colonial and neocolonial languages distort our vision in addition to distorting the reality of the world? This is my question.

But your question is: what are the crucial changes in our world that have impact on identity, language and literature?

My reply is: this depends on where you are in the world, what you believe and what you mean by identity. *Identity* is a dangerous word, like *religion*, because it divides people according to nationality, religion, class, race, colour, gender, and other false distinctions imposed on us from when we are born. 'Divide and rule' is the basic principle of colonialism and exploitation. You cannot dominate people except by dividing them. *Identity* and *religion* are postmodern words, repeated endlessly over the last three decades to divide us, to invade our minds, along with our lands, our material and moral resources.

Our role as writers is to demystify these words in language and in literature. There is no pure identity. Pure identity means racism. All of us are mixed blood, mixed identities, and the more mixed we are the better, the more human, fair and just. We must celebrate our common human identity and not our inherited so-called identity differences.

18 February 2009

৯ Translated by Amira Nowaira.

16

Fear and Writing

LAST NIGHT in my dream I saw God as I used to see him when I was a little child. He was angry as usual because I was not afraid of him, though he was threatening and swearing that He will burn me in hellfire after I die. My mind since childhood has never believed or imagined that I would die, let alone live this other life after death in hell.

But people around me at home, in school, on the radio, everywhere insisted that I should fear God. When they praised anybody they used the term 'God-fearing'. I felt bad because I was not God-fearing. To feel good I have to fear nobody, including Him in the sky or anybody on earth.

I started writing when I was a child. My first letter was to God. I told Him: Dear God, if you burn people in fire, what is the difference between you and Satan the Devil?

Egypt, 1 February 2009

17

Obama's Speech in Cairo

OBAMA IS DIFFERENT as a person to G.W. Bush. Obama looks more human, but politics and economic interests have nothing to do with humanity. We live in one world ruled by the capitalist patriarchal religious system. Power dominates our whole world, not justice or freedom or peace or ethics or human values. Politics under such a system is a game based on how to use beautiful words to cover ugly actions, how to use the power of God to dominate your listeners, how to select verses from holy books to hide double standards and contradictions, how to kill people and rob their land and resources and then apologize to them with tears in your eyes. We call them in our Egyptian–Arabic language 'crocodile tears'.

In Cairo, on Thursday, 4 June 2009, Barack Obama spoke to 2,500 Egyptian men and women invited by the Egyptian and US governments. They were allowed to enter the big hall at Cairo University surrounded by 13,000 Egyptian and American policemen. We are 80 million in Egypt, so those 2,500 men and women who applauded passionately thirty times during Obama's fifty-minute speech are not the whole of Egypt. They are only the chosen people. They applauded strongly when he said that Muslim women should wear the veil if they choose to wear it. As if veiling (or nakedness) is something to be chosen! As if oppression is something to be chosen by the oppressed! It's like saying girls or boys should be circumcised if they choose to be circumcised (because they do not want to be different from others), or like saying the poor people should be poor if they choose to be poor (because of their laziness or ignorance).

I read that during the Gaza massacre the Palestinians choose to be killed (or they kill their children) so that they may appear as victims and gain sympathy from the world. I was looking at the television screen, observing how Obama talks with his hands, eyes and lips. His lips and hands look less cruel than G.W.'s. His colour is more attractive, not black, not white, not yellow, a mixture of human blood and multiple races developed into a more sophisticated human being. Obama is a creative actor on stage, having learned his text by heart to sound as if there is no text at all. He is well-trained in being spontaneous.

Egyptians, Americans and the people of other countries, especially those chosen by governments, are not creative enough to understand this type of creativity: how some political leaders acquire what is called *charisma*. The Germans passionately applauded Hitler; the Russians loved Stalin; the Americans elected G.W. more than once; and Sadat in Egypt won all elections with no less than 95 per cent of votes. The most dangerous political leaders are the most charismatic; they make you sing: 'Killing Me Softly'. You sacrifice your blood for them.

One of the chosen Egyptian men screamed in the hall while Obama was giving his speech: 'I love you!' Obama replied: 'Thank you.' Obama praised the king of Saudi Arabia in his speech, portraying him as a hero of the dialogue between religions! This theocratic kingdom breeding extremism is democratic? A dictator ally of the USA can be transformed into a democratic hero. Saddam Hussein and bin Laden were freedom fighters at one time. Obama praised Netanyahu by saying that he is intelligent. Indeed, did not describe any Arab ruler as intelligent, including Mubarak sitting next to him. He did not mention the name of Mubarak in his whole speech. Did he want to distance himself as a person from himself as the American president? Did he want to expose or hide his double personality? But he is sophisticated and understands what is called in psychology 'the philosophy of the present moment, how to leave yourself to the moment but not leave the moment to itself'.

Obama's body language looks natural; he bounds up the plane steps with his hands near his chest, jumping with his body, like a happy schoolboy going to meet his girlfriend. This is not the American president but Barack Hussein Obama. I saw his speech on television and read it twice more to grasp or detect some improvement in US policy. Using beautiful words selected from the three holy books, he sounded like the Pope giving his speech in Jordan some months ago, praising the three religions. He artfully used his middle name, Hussein, to speak to Muslims, but he knows also when to hide it as a deformed organ.

Muslims listening to Obama applauded passionately when he read verses from the Qur'an. They did not notice the mistake in his understanding of Surat Al-Isra. It does not say that the three prophets Moses, Christ, and Muhammad prayed together Lilat Al-Isra. Egyptian Copts applauded when he spoke about minority rights in Egypt. Israel applauded when he confirmed that the USA and Israel are tied eternally by culture (not mutual interests) and when his voice cracked with emotion when he spoke about the Holocaust, 6 million Jews burned in Germany, their eternal sufferings, and their right to have a homeland.

Obama did not say that this homeland should have been in Germany, the country that burned them, or in Europe or in the USA, or in some other place where there is no people to be killed and robbed of their homes and land by military force. He did not ask Israel to stop its military violence against Palestinian children. He only asked the Palestinians to stop their violence against Israeli children. He did not mention the number of Palestinians killed and tortured by Israel in the last sixty years. He did not ask Israel to respect previous UN resolutions; he rather asked Israel to stop building new settlements. What about the old settlements that expelled thousands of Palestinians from their homes? What about settlements to be built under so-called 'natural growth'? He asked Palestinians to forget the past and look forward. Likewise, some days ago in his country he asked people to forget the crimes of torture, to forget the past and look forward.

But what is the function of the law if it is not to be used to investigate and punish criminals who killed or tortured? Obama shifted smoothly from ethics to politics and interests as if there was no contradiction. He said the USA has no interest in Iraq's resources. He ignored or forgot the Iraq Oil Law forced on the Iraqi government (which commits the country's oil to the monopoly of American companies for thirty years). He mentioned the danger of Iran owning nuclear power; he did not mention the danger of the nuclear military power of Israel. The real goal of Obama's speech was to mobilize the Muslim countries against Islamic extremists, to open the markets of Islamic countries to American goods under the so-called development and partnership, to guarantee Saudi and Gulf oil and other American interests in the so-called Middle East.

Egyptian people suffered because of Obama's visit to Cairo. Thousands of students did not attend their schools or universities and delayed their exams. They were closed by the government for security reasons during Obama's visit. Michelle Obama did not accompany her husband to Egypt and stayed in the USA to be with their two daughters during school exams. Many streets in Cairo were closed by the police and many people could not go to work, losing an estimated $20 million. The Egyptian government spent $500 million on the security of Obama, deployed 10,000 policemen and hundreds of police cars. Egyptian people were ordered to stay at home and not to open their windows in all areas visited by Obama, including the Pyramid region, Giza, Ain Shams, Helwan, Cairo University, certain ministries, Al Kalaa, Sultan Mosque, Kasr Al Kobbaa, and all streets leading to these areas and more.

Normal life in Cairo stopped. Streets were empty; people were prisoners in their homes. Nobody was allowed near Cairo University while Obama was delivering his speech, except for thirteen American men and women who were allowed to make a show of demonstration at the university gate, shouting slogans asking Obama to visit Gaza. Those thirteen Americans were allowed by the police to demonstrate. They, then, are the opposition, the dissidents, in democratic Egypt, while the real Egyptian dissidents are either in prison or outside Egypt. But politics is a game to be played by all parties. Only thirty minutes after Obama's plane took off, the poor Egyptian workers were in the streets were removing the artificial flowers and trees planted everywhere to welcome the demi-god of the world.

5 June 2009

Fiction and Poetry

18

Death of an Ex-Minister

The death of His Excellency the ex-Minister

PUT YOUR HAND on my head, Mother, and stroke my hair and neck and chest gently, just as you used to when I was a child, for you're the only one I have left and your face is the only one in the whole world that I see or want to see in these final moments. How I used to want you to scold me for not having visited you for five years. But you were not the only one I neglected. I neglected the whole world, including myself, my house, my wife, and my friends. Golf, which was my hobby, I haven't played once during these past five years. Even my little daughter, whom I loved so much, I haven't seen. My own face, Mother, I haven't seen my own face. As I used to rush out of the house, I'd take a quick look in the mirror, not to look at my face but to adjust the tie around my neck or to check that the colour of my shirt didn't clash with that of my tie. And when I did look at my face in the mirror, I still didn't see it. When I looked at the faces of people in the office or in the street through the windscreen of my car, I didn't see them. If they spoke to me, I didn't hear them, even if they spoke loudly. The loudest hooting from any car, even if it was directly behind me, I didn't hear. So often did a car catch me unawares that I stopped walking.

I was, Mother, like one who neither sees nor hears nor lives in this world. In what world was I living then? Is there any other world in which a person lives, apart from that of people, unless God has taken him? I knew, Mother, that God hadn't yet taken me because I didn't see my obituary in the newspaper. It's not possible for a man in my position to die like that, without a large and prominent obituary in the papers and a large funeral procession in which the leading statesmen walk, the head of state in their midst, and the whole world crying. The scene used to move me so much, Mother, that as I walked in such awe-inspiring funeral processions I wished that it was I in the box. But since I don't remember ever being inside that box and since I always used to walk along behind it, it follows that I am alive.

But I didn't live in the world in which you people live. I wasn't concerned with the matters that concern you, but with more important issues. My concerns were limitless and were more than my mind and body could bear. Sometimes my body would seize up and stop moving, even though my mind would continue. At other times, it was my mind, which would seize up until it stopped thinking, while my body kept on moving and coming and going. It would go to the office and attend meetings and head conferences and receive official guests at the airport and attend receptions and travel abroad on official missions. When I saw my body, Mother, moving like this of its own accord, without my mind, I was amazed and even scared, especially if I was in an important meeting which demanded my concentration and attention. And the only really important meeting was one in which I was a subordinate…

From the time I became a government employee, I hated being subordinate. I got used to repressing my feelings of hatred before my superiors and would give vent to them only in my office with my subordinates or at home with my wife, just like I saw Father do with you, Mother. I was unable to express my hatred before my superior, even if he was an ordinary employee, like a head of department or a managing director. And what if my superior was not simply an employee, any employee of state, but the head of the whole state? What's that you say, Mother? Yes, my dear. I used to sit in my chair before him, my mind and body tense, senses alert and wide awake, fearful that he'd suddenly ask me a question to which I wouldn't know the answer, that if I knew the answer it wouldn't be the right one and that if it were the right one it wouldn't be the required one.

What's that you say, my dear? Yes, Mother. That's the ABC of politics which we learn in the first lesson. The right answer isn't always the required answer, but the required answer is always the right one. Men like us must always be alert, in mind and body, to distinguish the right truth from the wrong truth — and that's a tough job, Mother, tougher than any other in life. I had to sit in meetings, alert in both mind and body. I'd sit in my chair, my left hand lying in my lap, my right hand holding a pen poised above a sheet of paper, ready and prepared to pick up a gesture, any gesture, be it a nod of the head, a movement of hand or finger, or a bottom lip tightening ever so slightly or a small contraction of a muscle around the mouth or nose or eye. I had to distinguish the movement of the right eye from that of the left. If I saw a movement the moment it happened or even before it happened, I had to interpret it quickly in my mind. My mind had to be even quicker than me and interpret it before I did. My eyes had to be quicker than my mind and had to see a movement even before it took place. My ears had to be fast and hear a sound even before it was made.

What's that you say, Mother? Yes, my dear. During these important meetings I relied on my five senses. My mind and body were transformed, as I sat in my chair, into a mass of hypersensitive nerves, as if naked radar wires wrapped around each other were making my head and arms and chest and stomach work. I was so sensitive, Mother, that I would feel my stomach tremble as if it contained an electrical circuit, especially when I stood next to or near him. I'd feel the fingers of my right hand tremble, even though I'd clasp them with my left hand, with both the right and the left pressed against my chest or stomach. My legs would also be pressed together, whether I was sitting or standing. That's how I was, Mother, when I was with him. My body was unable to adopt any other position. When the light fell on my face and the lens was focused on my body to photograph me for the people, I tried to release my right hand from the left and lift it off my chest or stomach but I couldn't. I'd find them heavy, as though paralysed. What's that you say, Mother? Yes, my dear. That was the picture I saw of myself in the newspapers and I was ashamed. I tried to hide the paper from my family, especially from my young daughter, who, with her little fingers, pointed to my face amongst the others in the paper and said to her mother, 'Isn't that Father, Mama?' And she, with the pride of wives of great men, replied, 'Yes, that's your father, my darling. Look how great he is, standing there with the president of state!'

My wife's voice rang in my ears and I realized it wasn't her real voice, that beneath the voice there was another that she had been hiding since time began and would continue to hide for all eternity, from the time we married until our death, hiding her real self and my real self in a deep and remote recess inside her. I sometimes felt it beneath my hand like a chronic and hardened swelling which would not dissolve.

What's that you say, Mother? No, my dear. I was ashamed only in front of my little daughter, for even though her eyes are those of a child, perhaps for that very reason, they can always see through me and expose my real self which no one on this earth, not even I myself, can uncover. Do you remember, Mother, you always used to tell me that the veil was transparent for a child? I didn't believe you at the time, but I've realized since that sometimes, when my little daughter looked me in the face with those wide and steady eyes of hers, I felt frightened. At times I thought that this strong and steady look was not that of a child, especially not of a girl, or more exactly, a natural girl. The look of a natural girl, or even of a natural boy, ought to be less penetrating, less steady, and less impudent, especially when directed at a larger and older person in authority. And what if this person is the father, master of the family and its provider, who works and who spends and whose right it is to be respected and obeyed by all the members of his family, big or small, especially the young ones?

What's that you say, Mother? Yes. That's exactly what you used to tell me when I was a child. It has always stayed in my mind, to the extent that I used to tell it to my wife and repeat it to my daughter, and I'd even say it to those employees under my leadership or authority. I felt pleased with myself saying it, like a child pleasing its mother. I even felt admiration for myself, to the point of vanity, when I saw the admiration in the eyes of the employees around me, and I grew more confident that what I was saying was absolute truth for all eternity and that whoever said anything different was mistaken or blasphemous.

What's that, Mother? Yes, my dear. All my life, from the time I was a junior employee until I became minister, I could not befriend any employee who contradicted me. And that's why, Mother, I couldn't stand that woman, why I couldn't bear to remain sitting in my chair, keeping my normal composure, as dignified as any other minister in the presence of his employees. I could only bear it, Mother, by jumping to my feet and shouting with anger unusual for me, losing my dignity and my nerve saying nothing meaningful, unlike what I was used to saying. I don't know, Mother, why I couldn't bear it, nor how I deviated from my usual calm and dignity. I wasn't angry with her for expressing an opinion different from mine, or because she was a junior employee whose view differed from that of a minister, or because she was a woman holding her own opinion before a man, or because she called me 'Sir' whereas all the other employees addressed me as 'Your Excellency the Minister'. But I was angry, Mother, because when she talked to me she raised her eyes to mine in a way I'd never seen before. Such a gaze, such a strong and steady look, is daring in itself, even impudent, when it comes from a man. So what if it comes from an employee, from a woman? I was angry not *because* she did it, but because I didn't know *how* she did it, how she dared do it.

What's that? Yes, Mother. I wanted to understand how that woman did it. The desire to know took hold of me to the point of anger, anger with myself for not knowing and because I wasn't capable of knowing. Anger overcame me to the point that, the following day, I issued her with an order to come to my office. I left her standing before me whilst I sat and made her feel that she didn't exist. And I kept her standing whilst I sat talking on the telephone, laughing with the person who was speaking to me. The strange thing was she remained standing. She just didn't hear my voice nor did she look at me, but gazed at a picture hanging on the wall. I thought she'd look at me when I'd finished on the phone but she kept staring at that picture on the wall as though I didn't exist. I tried to study her features before she moved and saw me, but she turned her head and her strong, steady eyes fixed themselves on mine. I jumped, as though all my clothes had dropped off me all of a sudden. I felt ashamed; it reminded me in a flash of my little daughter's eyes. In one moment, the shame turned to anger and in another fleeting moment, the anger turned into the desire to shame her as she had shamed me. I found myself, shouting in her face, in an unusually loud voice, 'How dare you? Who do you think you are? Don't you know that whoever you are, you're nothing but a junior employee and I am a minister and that no matter how far up the ladder you go, in the end you're a woman whose place is in bed underneath a man?'

What's that you say, Mother? Yes. Any woman hearing such words from any man would have died of shame, or would at least have fainted, especially if the man saying such things were not just any man but her superior in the government who is not merely a manager or head of department, but a minister in person. And she didn't hear those words being said in an empty or closed room, but in my office, full of men, all of them senior employees. Yes, Mother, any woman in her place would surely have died of shame. I wanted to kill her by any means, even by shame. But the strange thing was, Mother, that nothing could kill this woman. She wasn't overcome by shame, didn't even lower her eyes, didn't blink an eyelid. Perhaps, Mother, you can imagine how much anger any man in my place, in my position, of my status and manliness and pride in my own eyes and in those of the employees in my ministry, would feel? And also because, Mother, I had never in all my life seen an employee raise his eyes to those of his superior, certainly never a woman raise hers to those of a man, not to her brother or father or superior, not even to her son. And what if that man were more important than her father or superior or any other man in his own and other people's opinion and in his self-respect and in people's respect for him?

Each time I remembered, Mother, how much respect I had for my masculinity and the respect people had for my position, my anger grew more intense. How could this woman do what she did? My anger, Mother, may have cooled a bit if I'd seen her blink, just once, or if her eyelids had trembled for just one second. But, Mother, she stood before me, her eyes raised to mine, as though I were not her boss and she not my subordinate, as though I were not a minister and she not a junior employee, as though I were not a man and she not a woman, as though I were not myself and she not herself. My anger grew each time I felt that I wasn't myself, that she wasn't herself. I asked myself who she was to make me feel that I was not myself. Or perhaps it was that I got angrier each time I remembered that I was indeed myself, with all the status, authority, masculinity and self-respect that is mine. I was absolutely sure, Mother, that I was myself, with all that meant. But, Mother, and this is what drove me crazy, at the same time I felt equally sure that I was not myself, that I would never be the same again. Maybe, Mother, you can appreciate my situation and can forgive me for hating this woman so much that the following day my temperature rose to 40°C and I had to stay at home with my head burning under an ice-pack. And, Mother, my temperature did not go down until after I'd issued all the ministerial decisions in my power to break that woman and utterly destroy her.

What's that? No, not at all, Mother. I wasn't able to destroy her. She remained in existence that woman. I happened to overhear some people say that she still existed. I didn't exactly overhear it, for I used to snoop around for information about her, fearful that someone would notice me hoping to hear bad news or that she'd been destroyed in an accident. But no, Mother, that woman remained in existence. Not only did she remain as alive as any other woman but, Mother, I happened to see her once and she hadn't changed in the slightest. Her eyes were still raised and her eyelids did not tremble, even though, Mother, for all that, she was a woman like any other. I wasn't angry because she was a woman and I had never seen a woman do what she did. I wasn't angry because she was an employee and I had never seen an employee do what she did. No, what angered me and made me crazy was that I was incapable of destroying her by any decision or any authority and that she remained in existence. Her existence drove me mad, made me lose my dignity, my mind. I wanted to retrieve myself and my composure. But, Mother, she remained in existence and her existence began to threaten my own.

What's that? Yes, Mother. I don't know how I got into such a state. How could a junior employee, in the fifth or sixth grade, threaten the existence of any great man such as myself in a ministerial position? But I was really angry, angrier than I'd ever been in my life. I wasn't angry because I couldn't destroy her, with all the power at my disposal, nor because she did something no one else had done. No, what really angered me, Mother, was that she had done something I myself had never done. I have never, in all my life, been able to raise my eyes to those of any one of my superiors, even if he were a junior employee with only slight power over me. My anger grew, Mother, each time I tried to understand why I was incapable of doing that while she could, even though I'm a man and she's a woman, just like any other woman!

What's that? Yes, Mother. She was like any other woman. Like you, Mother, yes, like you. But I've never seen you, Mother, raise your eyes to anyone the way that woman did to me. Maybe if I'd seen you do it just once, I'd have been able to stand that employee. If you'd raised your eyes once to Father's, maybe I too would have been able to raise my eyes to his. Maybe I'd have been able to raise my eyes to those of any man in a position of authority. But, Mother, I've never see you do it. If you'd done it only once, it may have been possible for me to do it too because I did everything like you. Because, Mother, you were my sole example when I was a child and I used to imitate you, to imitate your every movement. I learned how to speak by moving my lips as you moved yours. I learned to walk by moving my legs as you moved your legs. I learned everything from you, Mother. So why didn't you raise your eyes to Father's so that I could have learned how to do it? Maybe if you'd done it just once, I'd have been able, as a child, to overcome my fear of him just once. And maybe, as an employee, I'd have been able to overcome my fear of any person in a position of authority.

What's that, Mother? No, my dear. I'm not blaming you. All I ask is that you stroke my head and neck and chest with your tender hand as you used to when I was a child, for you're the only one to whom I can open my heart, and to whom I can reveal my real tragedy. And the real tragedy is not that I lost my position as minister, but *how* I lost it. Perhaps the tragedy would have been somewhat lessened if I'd lost it for a serious or important or even plausible reason. The tragedy, Mother, is that the reason was not plausible and nobody can understand or believe it. Perhaps I did not know, Mother, that the reason was implausible until the day I opened the morning paper and did not find my name included amongst those of the new ministry. I suddenly felt absolutely sunk, as if my very name had fallen from my body. Every day, as I searched the papers for my name and did not find it, my feeling that I'd become a nameless body was confirmed. The telephone, Mother, which used to ring each day and at each moment, calling my name, fell silent, deaf, inarticulate, as if it too were bringing me down, bringing down my name. Such a bitter feeling of downfall, Mother, I've never experienced in all my life.

What's that, Mother? Yes, my dear, I didn't know the taste of that which I'd lost until that moment. And I fear, Mother, that that's the way of all life. We don't know the taste until after we've lost it. That in itself, Mother, is a catastrophe, because time passes and the opportunity may be lost forever. That was how it was as I sat by the silent telephone, waiting, scared that one of my family would notice me sitting and waiting. Then I'd act as if I wasn't waiting, even though I was. If only the phone had rung, just once, in any way, made any sound, man or woman, relative or stranger, big or small, human or animal, any voice, even the braying of a donkey. If only the phone had rung, just one time, and called my name.

What's that, Mother? No, my dear. The catastrophe was not that the telephone did not ring, nor that I wanted it to ring. The tragedy, Mother, was that I discovered that the ringing of the telephone, which I'd always said I hated, I didn't hate at all, but loved. The sound of the bell used to send a quiver of delight through my body which, had I only known it at the time, no power on earth could have taken from me. That delight, Mother, was greater than the delight of sex and the delight of love and the delight of food and of everything in the world. It was an unearthly, inhuman delight, unknown to human instincts, an instinct without feeling and non-instinctual, an instinct which annihilated feeling, annihilated instincts. It alone remained strong, gigantic, tremendous, capable of annihilating anything in the world, wiping out tiredness, the pressure of work, wiping out dignity, insults, making my body capable of movement and activity even as I slept, making my mind work even in my dreams, making me stand on my feet in the airport under the rays of the sun after non-stop effort, features relaxed to welcome some official guest making me sit with back and neck tensed up at some meeting or some reception, making me ready, at any moment of the day or night to adopt the official position of legs pressed together and hands clasped over the chest or stomach. Yes, Mother. This gigantic delight was capable of wiping out tiredness or effort, was even capable of wiping itself out, and myself with it if it so desired.

What's that, Mother? Yes, my dear. I lost all this delight for the sake of some insignificant thing. And what is not insignificant compared to such delight? But, to tell the truth, Mother, that thing was not insignificant. It was not something simple, ordinary. No, it was not simple and not ordinary. It was the most serious thing that ever happened to me, the most serious thing I could ever face. Like death, Mother. Sometimes I used to believe I could face even death itself. But at the time I did not know what was happening to me. I sat in my chair as usual, alert in mind and body, my nerves and senses awake. My mind and body had turned into that nervous radar mass, naked and sensitive to any gesture or movement. I sat in my chair as normal, certain that I was normal, whilst with equal certainty I knew that I was not normal and that, despite the fact that I was extremely alert, I was incapable of being alert and that, for the first time in my life, I was incapable of focusing my mind or of controlling it. My mind had begun to think by itself without me and was preoccupied with something with which I did not want to be preoccupied. That in itself would be a catastrophe if it happened to any employee in a meeting. So what about me, a minister, in this only meeting of importance, in which I was turned into a subordinate? The catastrophe, Mother, was not that my mind was out of my control, for had it been so in order to think of something important, like the annual report which I was to present or the new budget for which I was to ask, then maybe I'd have felt a little relaxed and comforted. But the catastrophe was that my mind did not think of anything important, but of something insignificant, the most insignificant thing that the mind of a man in a position such as mine, and particularly at such a meeting, could be occupied with.

What's that you say, Mother? No, my dear. I wasn't thinking about anyone. I was thinking about myself. I wanted to work out how to sit in my chair as normal, despite the fact that I wasn't normal. I wanted to work out whether it was me sitting in my chair or some other person and which of them was me. The problem, Mother, was not that I couldn't work it out, but rather that I knew that the reason for this catastrophe was none other than that junior employee. I curse the day I set eyes on her, for since then my mind has not stopped thinking about her. Perhaps I'd have found a little peace or comfort if what engrossed me was that she was a woman or a female. After all, I am a man and any man, no matter what his position, can still sometimes be engrossed in a woman. But the tragedy, Mother, was that at the time she didn't preoccupy me as a woman or a female because, in my view, she wasn't female at all. She was perhaps the only woman I've ever met in my life whom I did not feel for a second was a female. But what occupied and dominated my mind to the extent of stripping me of my willpower was that, although she was a female and although she was a junior employee, the most junior official who could enter a minister's office, she had managed to do something out of the ordinary, breaking every convention with which we are brought up from the time we're born, all the values we have known since the time we found ourselves alive and became human. The tragedy, Mother, was not that she did that and not that she did what no one else had done or what I myself had not done, but that from the time she'd done it, I was no longer myself. Whoever it was sitting in my chair was not me, but another person whom I hardly knew. I didn't even know which of the two was me. That, Mother, was the precise question which dominated my mind and body and all my senses at that meeting.

I tried so hard, Mother, to fight it. I mustered all my strength to resist it, to drive it from my mind, so that my left hand moved of its own accord as though to drive it out of my head. My right hand was, as usual, holding a pen over a piece of paper, poised and ready for any sign or sound. My left hand should have remained lying in my lap as normal, but it did not lie there. Whoever saw it move the way it did must have thought I was brushing away an obstinate fly from my face, but, since the meeting hall was clean and completely free of flies, the cleanest hall in the whole country and the last hall on earth that a fly could enter, the movement of my left hand must have appeared abnormal. And since it was abnormal, it began to attract attention. I used to hate, Mother, to draw attention to myself at such important meetings, and always preferred to remain sitting in my chair completely unobtrusive or unnoticed until the meeting was over and I had not had to face any questions.

What's that, Mother? No, my dear. I wasn't frightened of questions and I wasn't afraid of not knowing the right answer, since the right answer was common knowledge and easy, easier than any other answer, easier than any math problem I had to solve as a pupil, as easy as the simplest step in a multiplication table, two times two equals four. The difficulty, Mother, was that I wasn't scared of *not* giving the right answer but of *giving* the right answer.

What's that, my dear? Yes, Mother. That was the real catastrophe that happened that day. I don't know how it happened and I don't know if it was me who said it or the other person occupying my chair. I was still sitting in my chair, like I told you, and it seems that the repeated movement of my left hand had attracted attention because, suddenly he turned his eyes towards me reminding me in a flash of my father's eyes when I was a child. As his eyes turned towards me I tried to shrink back slightly or to move forward, just as I used to do as a pupil sitting in class, and hoped that his eyes would fall on the one sitting in front of me or behind me, and not on me. But that day I didn't move in my chair. Maybe I didn't notice the movement of his eyes at the right time, before they turned in my direction. Or perhaps I wasn't in full possession of my faculties at that moment. Or perhaps I was sick with fever and my temperature had risen. Or perhaps there was some other reason. The important thing, Mother, was that I didn't move in my chair and the full weight of his eyes fell on me, like the fall of death. When he asked me the question, my mouth opened of its own accord, involuntarily, as if it were the mouth of another person, an unthinking person quick to answer without much thought or great effort. And since it was an answer without much thought or great effort, it was the easy answer, the easiest and simplest of answers. It was, Mother, the obvious answer.

What's that, my dear? No, Mother. The obvious answer was not the right answer. The right answer is not the required answer. That, Mother, is the ABC of politics, as I told you at the start. It's the first lesson we learn in politics. How did I come to forget it, Mother? I don't know. But I did forget it at that moment. How it grieved me, Mother, to forget it. And my grief was so very, very strong that all feelings of grief disappeared, so much so that my feelings of relief were almost akin to joy. I felt, Mother, that a heavy burden had been lying on my chest and stomach, heavier than my two paralysed hands clasped over my chest and stomach, heavier even than my body sitting paralysed in my chair, heavier even than the chair and the earth beneath it, as if the earth itself were weighing on me.

What's that, Mother? Yes, my dear. I relaxed and what relaxation! How I feel this relaxation in these final moments as I leave the world and everything in it. But the catastrophe, Mother, is that despite this relaxation and although I'm leaving this world, I still put the telephone beside my head and I'm still waiting for it to ring, just once. To hear the bell, just once. To hear a voice, any voice, say in my ear: 'Your Excellency, the Minister'. How I'd love to hear it, Mother, one time, only one time before I die.

The veil

All of a sudden I awake to find myself sitting, a bottle of wine in front of me of which only a little remains, and an ashtray full of cigarette ends of a strange kind I think I have not seen before, until I remember that they are the new brand I began smoking three or four years ago.

I look up from the ashtray to see a man I've never seen before. He is naked, apart from a silken robe which is open to reveal hairy chest and thighs. Between the chest and thighs are a pair of close-fitting striped underpants. I raise my surprised eyes to his face. Only now do I realize that I've seen him before. My eyes rest on his for a moment and I smile a strange, automatic smile, as fleeting as a flash of light or an electric current, leaving behind no trace other than a curious kind of perplexity like the eternal confusion of a person in search of God or happiness. Why is there such confusion in the world and in my body at this particular moment, even though each day my eyes meet hundreds or thousands of eyes and the world and my body remain as they are? But it is soon over. The world and my body return to normal and life continues as usual. It is three or four years since I saw him for the first time and I'd almost forgotten him in the tumult of work and home and people.

My eyes fall onto his naked body and hairy thighs once more. The expression on my face as I look at his body is not the same as when I look into his eyes, for my problem is that what I feel inside shows instantly on my face. His eyes are the only part of his body with which I have real contact. They dispel strangeness and ugliness and make my relationship with him real in the midst of numerous unreal ones. Three years, maybe four, and every time I run into him in a street or office or corridor, I stop for a moment in surprise and confusion. Then I continue on my way, knowing that whilst this relationship is very strange, it is at the same time familiar and accepted, among numerous unfamiliar and unaccepted relationships.

When we began meeting regularly or semi-regularly, my relationship with him did not extend to parts of his body other than his eyes.

For long hours we would sit and talk, my eyes never leaving his. It was a sort of meeting of minds, and gratifying, but the gratification was somehow lacking. What did it lack?

I asked myself whether it was the body's desire for contact with another body? And why not? In the final analysis, isn't he a man and I a woman? The idea strikes me as new, even strange, and a frightening curiosity takes hold of me. I wonder what the meeting of my body with his could be like. A violent desire to find out can sometimes be more violent than the desire for love and can, at times, draw me into loveless contacts simply in order to satisfy that curiosity. And every time that happens, I experience a repulsion, certain in my mind that my body repulses the body of a man except in one situation — that of love.

I understand the cause of this repulsion. It's an inexplicable repulsion linked not to the body but to history. To the extent that man worships his masculinity, so woman repulses him. A woman's repulsion is the other face of the worship of the male deity. No power on earth can rid woman of her repulsion other than the victory of love over the male deity. Then history will go back six thousand years to when the deity was female. Will love be victorious? Is the relationship between us love? I do not know. I have no proof. Can love be proved? Is it the desire which rises to the surface of my crowded life, to look into his eyes? Like a person who, from time to time, goes to a holy water spring to kneel down and pray and then goes home? I do not kneel down and neither do I pray. I recognize no deity other than my mind inside my head. What is it that draws me to his eyes?

Is love simply a fairy tale, like the stories of Adam and Eve or Cinderella or Hassan the Wise? All the fairy tales came to an end and the veil fell from each of them. Many veils fell from my mind as I grew up. Each time a veil fell, I would cry all night in sadness for the beautiful illusion which was lost. But in the morning, I'd see my eyes shining, washed by tears as the dew washes the blossom, the jasmine and the rose. I would leave the mirror, trample the fallen veil underfoot and stamp on it with a new-found strength, with more strength than I'd had the previous day.

He has filled the tenth or twentieth glass. My hand trembles a little as I hold it, but the deity inside my head is as steady and immobile as the Sphinx. My eyes are still on his and do not leave them, even though I realize, somehow, that he is no longer wearing the silken robe nor even the tight striped underpants.

I notice that his body is white, blushed with red, revealing strength, youthfulness, cleanliness and good eating. My eyes must still have been staring into his, for in another moment, I realize that he has taken my head in his hand and moved it so that my eyes fall on to his body.

I look at him steadily and once again see the strength and youthfulness and cleanliness and good eating. I almost tell him what it is I see.

But I look up and my eyes meet his. I do not know whether it is he who looks surprised or whether the surprise is in my own eyes. I tell myself that the situation calls for surprise, for it is nearly three in the morning. The glass is empty. There is no one in the house and the world outside is silent, dark, dead, fallen into oblivion. What is happening between my body and his?

When I next turn towards him, he is sitting, dressed in the robe with the belt carefully tied around his waist, hiding his chest and thighs. I no longer see anything of him other than his head and eyes and feet inside a pair of light house shoes. From the side, his face looks tired, as though he's suddenly grown old and weary. His features hang loose, like a child needing to sleep after staying up late. I put out my hand, like a mother does to stroke the face of a child, and place a tender motherly kiss on his forehead.

In the street I lift my burning face to the cold and humid dawn breeze. Mysterious feelings of joy mingle with strange feelings of sadness. I put my head on my pillow, my eyes open, filled with tears. My mind had got the better of the wine until I put my head on the pillow, but then the wine took over and sadness replaced joy.

When I open my eyes the following day, the effect of the wine has gone and the veil has lifted from my eyes. I look in the mirror at my shining eyes washed with tears. I am about to walk away from the mirror, like every other time, to trample on the fallen veil at my feet and stamp on it with new-found strength. But this time I do not leave my place. I bend down, pick up the veil from the ground and replace it once again on my face.

The greatest crime

I swear to you, whoever reads my story, that I was more innocent than you imagine, more innocent, perhaps, than many of you. I became certain of my innocence after I died (I am dead now and so I can express myself without fear of you). I was as innocent as a young child — which means (if you have a good memory) that I was not innocent at all, at least not in your view. And yet I did and still do consider myself as innocent as a young child. Not one of you remembers what went on in your head when you were a child and I too was like you when I was on earth. We forget our childhood when we grow up and we forget our dreams when we awake from sleep. Such forgetfulness is sure proof that in our childhood we did things that embarrass us when we are adults and that in our dreams we did things that embarrass us when we awake.

But I am no longer like you. The experience of death has given me an inhuman courage and I no longer need to section off the phases of my life, nor to erect a thick wall to separate one from the other. I was able to acquire such a view of the disjointed and fragmented phases of your lives only after I left the earth. The spectacle of your lives before my eyes surprised me. It is really a very strange spectacle resembling, to a large extent, the body of a person from which the head is cut and the legs amputated and of which only the torso remains. It is also a frightening spectacle, reminding me of a train accident I witnessed as a young child. To this day I have not forgotten the sight of the body which had been taken out from under the wheels, without a head and without legs.

I have never forgotten that spectacle. Although, in fact, I did forget it. It is, perhaps, almost the only spectacle in my life which I did completely forget. It was so ugly that I totally forgot it. And it was so ugly that it remains in my memory and I have never forgotten it. That is what happens to you too; you forget and do not forget. And that's the cause of your suffering on earth.

But in any case, I no longer fear this spectacle and have acquired a strange courage. I can stare at it for a whole second. My courage has grown so much that I can even look into my father's face for a whole minute. My father's face was like the face of all fathers. And the faces of all fathers appear to me now like those cardboard masks which we used to buy on holidays. The eyes were not eyes but two large holes.

When I looked into them, I saw nothing. The nose was a protruding piece of cardboard and had two openings which were nothing but holes. Beneath the nose was a long black moustache and it was this moustache which used to make us laugh a lot when we were children. Each of us would take turns at wearing this mask which we'd bought for a penny and we'd try to frighten each other with that long black moustache.

I used to think that the reason I didn't love my father was because of his prickly black moustache. But now, when I stare at his face for the first time, I realize that I didn't love him because of his eyes. When I looked into his eyes, I understood immediately that it was he who killed my mother. When I was a child, I loved my mother. You do not understand what it means for a child to love its mother either, because you were never children (forgetfulness can make something that happened seem as though it had never happened). I loved my mother so much that I am incapable of describing her now, just as I was always incapable of describing her in the past. I used to imagine that I would be able to describe her once I was no longer on earth, now that everything earthly is over. But my love for my mother is not over. Only the unreal things are over while real things never end. My love for my mother was so real that I used to think that my mother was me. This was not just a belief but a feeling verging on certainty. Her body and mine were one. That bonding between me and my mother still remains as it was when I was a child, for real things stay with us. Wherever we may be, whether we rise or fall in life, they remain as attached to us as our own bodies. And my love for my mother was real as my own body. I was a small child and everything appears unreal in the eyes of a small child, as if in a dream. People are like ghosts or angels, a train runs on phantom rails and its whistle has a ring of magic, the sea is bottomless, the sky limitless, the street endless, and the dark night frightening as death.

I used to be frightened of two things: darkness and death. I'd slip out of my small bed in the middle of the night and creep into my mother's bed. I'd bury myself into her warm body and cling to her as hard as I could. I'd curl up to make my body smaller and try to shrink to the size of a foetus which could return to its mother's womb. My whole body shook with this fervent desire and trembled as in fever. I thought nothing could save me from imminent death in the darkness other than disappearing inside that warm and tender womb which would enclose me alone.

Anyone seeing me at that moment, curled up like a foetus, would have understood that this desire was real and that it was violent, that it was not so much a desire to escape death but rather to get close to my mother, so close as to stick to her, to merge my body in hers so that she and I could become one. I loved her so much that the obliteration of my body in hers was not obliteration, was not death, was not painful, was not frightening, but was the peak of my life, the climax of my pleasure, was security and total comfort.

In that state, I was not aware of anything. Everything around me had grown as warm as my mother's breasts and as silent as the inside of a womb. The world and everything in it — sea, sky, houses, trees, trains and rails — all vanished. All noise disappeared. I no longer had ears or eyes or lips but only the senses of an unborn baby, feeling nothing but warmth, smelling nothing but milk.

In such a state, I was oblivious of the presence of my father who lay beside my mother with his huge body, his long black moustache trembling with the movement of his upper lip, his lower lip drooping under the pressure of a loud snore, a long thread of white spittle drooling slowly from the corner of his mouth and over his chin. Despite his deep sleep, from which it appeared to me at the time he would never awake, he opened his eyes. And although I could not see him (because I was curled up like a foetus), I noticed the look which flashed across his eyes and immediately vanished. At that time, I didn't know whether it had disappeared of its own accord or whether he had made it disappear, but I now know that it was he who did it. Despite the dark which immersed the bedroom and although I was unable to raise my eyes to his, that look was powerful enough to penetrate my skull like an arrow. Despite the pain of that penetration, despite the fear of it, despite the pitch dark, and although it disappeared in a flash and there returned to his eyes the look of a loving father, despite all that, I knew the form of that look. It was the look of a man expressing hatred.

My father was a civilized man and like all civilized men of our time, who can control and hide their real feelings and display other feelings to show how they've progressed, like all of them, my father was able to hide his real desire to grasp my neck with his large fat fingers and fling me far away. His hand did in fact move towards me, but he resisted the movement so that it moved like the hand of a civilized father, patting his son on the shoulder. With a slow, quiet movement, he separated my body from the body of my mother and I found myself on the cold edge of the bed whilst he occupied my warm place.

It was wintertime and the night was cold. The woollen blanket reached only to the edge of the bed so that it covered just half my body and my back stayed bare. Then my father moved in his sleep and pulled the blanket towards himself so that I was completely uncovered. I shivered from the cold and my mother opened her eyes. In fact, I had not yet shivered, but she opened her eyes at the slightest movement. It may only have been the movement of the cover sliding off my back or a small muscle in my body contracting because of the cold. The movement may have happened or may have been about to happen. Even before the muscle contracted, she would suddenly open her eyes from the deepest sleep. Even before she opened her eyes, even before she awoke completely, she would reach out and cover me.

I used to be amazed and wonder at that secret, the secret of that strange telepathic power of her sleeping body to respond to the feelings of my body, despite the great distance between us, which was occupied by the vast body of my father. My amazement grew when I heard my father accuse her of being a heavy sleeper. Once I heard him arguing with her because he had been ringing the bell for a long time before she awoke and opened the door. My father also accused her of not hearing well. Once he hit her (when she was feeding me on her lap) because he had been calling her to bring him his supper and she had not heard. Once I heard him tell her that her heart was cold and unfeeling. That day I saw my mother crying alone in the kitchen and timidly I went up to her and with half-formed words (I hadn't yet perfected the art of speech) I whispered in her ear, 'You have more feelings than Daddy, Mama.' Her eyes widened as she looked at me, surprised that such a small child could understand such a large truth. She enfolded me in her arms, whispering 'My darling.'

My father was standing at the door of the kitchen and saw me in her arms. That same fleeting look passed across his eyes. It appeared and immediately disappeared, penetrating my skull and making me quake violently with the sort of trembling that afflicts the body of a person face to face with death.

If he had done what a natural person does when he hates, if he had grabbed my neck with his large fingers, I would have relaxed and would have understood that he was behaving naturally towards me. Natural behaviour, however harsh, is always relaxing and reassuring. But my father was never reassuring. I was frightened of him, frightened of any movement he made. A quiet or gentle movement terrified me more than a violent or harsh movement. And whenever I was near him and saw his hand move, even if he was not going to do anything other than pat my shoulder or brush a fly from his face or scratch his ear, it made me jump and a concealed shudder would run over my body.

I didn't know why I was unable to sit close to my father so that there was no distance between us. There always had to be a distance. Under no circumstances could I get so close to my father to touch him, unlike my mother. When she sat next to me I would cling to her. It was not normal clinging, but an urgent and violent desire to eliminate the distance between us, so that my body and hers would become one.

No one other than myself knew of this desire. I used to hide it, just like I hid my real feeling. When I sat in class and the teacher told me to repeat after him the sentence, 'I love my father as I love my mother', I repeated it without protest: 'I love my father as I love my mother.' When I learned to write, the teacher told me to write my name, so I wrote 'Samir'. He then told me to write my full name, so I wrote 'Samir Aziza'. The teacher looked at my exercise book, angrily crossed out the name 'Aziza' with his red pen and said, 'Write your father's name!' I was surprised and opened my mouth to protest, but the teacher was big and I was small, so I meekly wrote 'Sami Adam'. The following day the teacher chose me to repeat after him, 'I love my father as I love my mother', and then the whole class chanted, 'I love my father as I love my mother.' The teacher told us to write it five times in our exercise books. The next day we wrote it once more and repeated it aloud several times. For homework too we had to write it five times and repeat it to ourselves ten times, then twenty times, until I found myself repeating it in my sleep: 'I love my father as I love my mother... I love my father as I love my mother...'

Once, my father heard me repeating it and he smiled. His smile was strange. The structure of his face was not made for smiling. His forehead was prominent and wide and permanently fixed in a natural frown which did not disappear even when he slept. The bones of his face were thickset, the jaws as large and wide as those of a camel or horse. He could not disguise those jawbones, however much his lips separated to express a smile. I shuddered, the way I always did whenever I saw something unnatural. I had never seen a camel or a horse smile. 'Why don't horses or camels smile?' I asked my teacher at school. He replied, 'Only human beings can smile, Samir.'

My father did not know what was going on in my head. Some strange power enabled me to hide my real feelings. I raised my voice when I read the lesson from my exercise book: 'I love my father as I love my mother... I love my father as I love my mother...' I knew that I was lying, and because I knew that I was lying I was frightened that my father would find out. In order to deceive my father, I began to raise my voice louder and repeated, 'I love my father as I love my mother.' Each time I raised my voice, my fear grew that the lie would show. So I raised my voice more and more to hide the lie, and each time I did so, the lie showed more and each time my fear grew. It went on like that until I found myself screaming like someone crying out for help: 'I love my father as I love my mother!... I love my father as I love my mother!'

My father never discovered the truth. When he saw the tears running down my cheeks, he approached me. But, as usual, I stepped back. As he came nearer, I took another step back. He came nearer. I stepped back. He raised his hand a little. I think that he was going to pat me on the shoulder but it seemed to me then that his hand would fall on my face with a heavy slap. I jumped back to protect myself. My father stopped for a moment his eyes wide in surprise, looking and staring at me, as if wondering what the reason was. It was not the natural wonderment of a person who is ignorant of the reason. It was unnatural, the reason known, and not only known but positively tangible and felt by all the feelings and senses in the body.

At such moments a person becomes nervous. A person is not by nature inclined to such definite feelings but rather to doubt. However, nothing is as unbearable in life as doubt and that's the cause of your suffering on earth, for you live in both certainty and doubt.

But at that time I was a small child and was not able to rid him of either doubt or certainty. I had done everything in my power to memorize my lesson and repeat it aloud and had done everything in my power to make my voice sound real when I read it.

And my voice really did sound real. I couldn't do more than I had done. But my father remained standing before me. I did not see him because my head was bowed and my eyes were on the ground. I never dared to lift my head and look into his eyes. I knew that the moment my eyes met his, he would find out the fearful truth. And the fearful truth was that doubt would become certainty or that certainty would become doubt. But, although my head was bowed, I could feel that look penetrating my head, piercing through it and pressing my back against the wall. That certainty would become doubt.

And so I stayed, standing before him, unable to retreat backwards, separated from him by only one step. I knew that in a moment the distance between us would disappear and that I would become one with the wall. I pressed my back to the wall with all my strength but the wall was as solid as rock.

At that moment my mother appeared, as though she'd suddenly materialized from out of the ground. I don't know how she appeared or from where, because that day she hadn't been at home but was spending the night at my aunt's. I don't know exactly what happened to me when I saw her. Of its own accord, my body leapt towards her, with urgency and violence, the urgency of escaping from death and the violence of clinging on to life. My body, at that time, acted naturally when it clung and stuck to her. It clung on so strongly that my body became one with hers.

When I think of that day, I tell myself that I wish I hadn't done what I did. I wish my back had stayed against that wall forever. Or that I had become one with the wall. But I didn't know what was going to happen. The tragedy is that a person does not know what is going to happen the next moment, let alone the next day. This ignorance is like blindness, and in fact really is blindness. I can see you now, walking before me without eyes. Your eyes are not eyes but holes through which the air passes, like the eyes of those cardboard masks I used to buy on holidays.

I still remember that day and have never forgotten it, like the spectacle of that headless and legless body which I have never forgotten. My memory has retained everything that happened that day, even though it is very far away and despite all the years that have passed, so many years that I cannot count them. I had only learned numbers up to ten, counting on my fingers, for the teacher had not yet taught us more than that. But despite the long years I still remember everything, no matter how insignificant, every movement, no matter how simple it seemed. But none of my father's movements was simple, however simple they appeared. I could pick up that rapid fleeting look in his eyes. I saw the black of his eyes fix on my mother. I was still in her arms, hiding my head against her chest. I no longer saw my father's face, but I felt my mother's arms around me holding on to me with all her might, enclosing me in her body, folding around me and surrounding me, clasping me as though she wanted, were she able, to take me inside herself, even into the womb itself.

At that point, my father could no longer maintain his unreal face. With a rapid movement he raised his hand and I saw his face with its large wide jaws like that of a wild hyena. For the first time, the face of my father before me became natural. I was no longer afraid as I had been earlier. I don't know how my courage returned, but I said to him, whispering at first, 'I don't love you.' As he momentarily froze before me, I picked up more courage and raised my voice louder and said to him, 'I don't love you.' When I heard my own voice clearly in my ears and was sure it was mine, I became increasingly courageous and said, 'I don't love you.' I continued like that until I found myself screaming in one long continuous and endless cry, 'I don't love you!'

He leapt at me like a rapacious tiger. But my mother was faster than he. In the twinkling of an eye, my mother's ample body was between him and me. I didn't see her face because I was standing behind her, but I knew from the way the muscles of her back were contracted and the way she was standing that she was like a tigress preparing to pounce. I don't know exactly what happened next. Voices stopped being human and everything changed in a moment. Even the seconds were no longer seconds, since time had changed and was no longer time. I was incapable of understanding anything around me, even myself and the reality of my existence, whether I was alive or dead. It seemed to me that I died and awoke, died and awoke, ten times, one hundred times, a thousand times, endlessly, as if my body had fallen into a bottomless abyss spinning terrifyingly fast, faster than the spin of the earth on its axis.

Suddenly the movement of the earth beneath my feet stopped and time stopped with it. Everything stopped and froze. I opened my eyes to see my mother's body on the ground. I thought that she was sleeping, as she usually slept on the ground in the summer. Timidly, I went up to her and whispered in her ear, 'Mama'. But she didn't answer. I was surprised, for she used to awaken at the slightest sound, would awaken even before a sound was made, before a word had come from my lips, would open her eyes and awake.

Even before she opened her eyes, I would feel her body move. Before my lips moved, before I had said a word, before I myself heard it she would have heard it.

Although I somehow realized that there was no way she could hear me, I kept whispering in her ear. When my father came with my uncles and carried her away from me and the house was without her, I was surprised. It was not the usual surprise which adults experience, but the surprise of a child, a strange surprise, when all things appear unreal, as though what had happened had not happened, a dream like reality, reality like a dream. My father moved to another house and took me with him. Days and years passed. I grew up, grew old and died. And yet I still imagined that what happened had not happened.

It is only now, after leaving the earth, that I am able to see the earth clearly. And I see you clearly too. Only now do I understand the greatest crime which has been committed in secret and which no one knows about. The first crime in the life of humanity was not that Cain slaughtered Abel but that Adam killed my mother. He killed her because I loved her and did not love him. And I wish he had realized that I could have loved him had he loved me. But my father was incapable of loving. Even though I was a child, I understood that he did not love me. And he did not love my mother. He loved only to satisfy himself.

Masculine confession

Pour me another glass of wine, with a lot of ice. Let me talk and don't interrupt me. From time to time you can stroke my head or neck or chest or any part of my body you like, only don't stop me talking, because I came to you tonight to confess things I can't confess to anyone else, not even to God's agents on earth.

Actually, I don't believe in such agents and I dislike any intermediaries between myself and God. That doesn't mean that I'm proud or arrogant or that I deal haughtily with people. Quite the opposite. I'm humble and compassionate, and I am concerned for all people and for myself as one of them.

My self-concern is limitless, because I love myself. Yes, I confess to you that my only true love is my love of myself. I fell in love with myself the moment my mother gave birth to me. Her eyes shone the moment my mother gave birth to me. Her eyes shone as she said to my father: It's a boy! I loved my masculinity and from the start I realized it was the reason for my being privileged. I always had to prove its existence, declare it, show it to people to make it clear and visible and so firm that it was not open to doubt.

One day, when I was young, I was standing in the street beside my father, when suddenly a big fat foot trod on my toes. I screamed 'Ow' in pain. My father looked at me angrily and said harshly: A man never says 'Ow'. Since that day, I have never said 'Ow'. I would hold back the pain and the tears when I was hurt or someone hit me and would brace the muscles of my back and neck and tell myself: I'm a man.

Once, when the doctor was digging his sharp scalpel into the sole of my foot to remove a splinter of glass, I felt my flesh tear and the blood flow. I was drowning in a sea of sweat from so much pain, but I didn't say 'Ow'. That night, when everybody was asleep, I found myself crying in my sleep, softly murmuring 'Ow, ow' until the morning.

When I awoke, I braced my back and neck muscles, put on my masculinity and wore it proudly, telling myself: I'm a man. What did you say, my dear? My feet and fingers are as soft as yours? That's true. I belong to the leisured class, the bourgeoisie, in other words. I only use my fingers to hold a glass of wine or to sign my name on some papers in the office or to wave to friends. My friends are many, as you know, and I love them all, just as I love all people. In other words, I love nobody. That doesn't mean that I hate them. It's just that I'm always self-concerned, always absorbed in loving myself. I'm ready at any time to defend myself, by any means, even by committing murder.

Don't look at me like that, as though I'm the only criminal on earth. Crime in the lives of us men is a matter of necessity. It's the only possible way for a man to prove he's a man. But since crime calls for bravery or authority, I'm unable to be a criminal. All I have

are daydreams in which I imagine myself a bold hero, separating
heads from bodies with a rapid blow of my sword. We men have
great admiration for murderers. A man cannot admire another man
without hating him. That's the reason I feel so ill at ease when I'm
amongst important men in authority. And that's why I run away
from the company of reputable men and why I feel at ease in the
company of disreputable men. But in general, I prefer the company
of women. For with a woman, no matter how important she is, one
privilege remains mine — my masculinity. What did you say? Please
don't interrupt me. Pour me another glass of wine, with a lot of ice,
and let me unburden the crimes which weigh on my heart.

I'm not lying to you. All my crimes are human because they have
one aim — to prove that I'm a man. No man can prove his masculinity except by beating other men. So I could not avoid entering into
the eternal conflict, the conflict with all other men. In conference
rooms or in bedrooms, the conflict is one and the same. Since in
conference rooms I lack courage and authority, there's nothing left
for me other than bedrooms. Don't call me a wolf or a womanizer.
No, I'm a married man. I love my wife like I love my mother, with
the same sort of spiritual, holy love. In other words, a love in which
I take everything and to which I give nothing. That's ideal love. My
wife is the only person (and before her it was my mother) with whom
I can get angry and at whom I can rage freely. The reason's well
known. She can't return my anger in the same way. We men can't
show our anger with those who can be angry with us. I am never
angry with my boss, but I get angry quickly with my mother. And
with my wife I get angry and rage freely, as I do with my children.
All of them I provide for and feed and if they got angry with me,
they wouldn't find anyone to replace me.

That's what marriage is for. How else would it be possible for a
man to give vent to his anger if it weren't for marriage? The poorest
man from the lowest social class goes home to his wife, in the end, in
order to be angry and to feel that he's a man. What did you say, my
dear? That's why you refused to get married? You're an intelligent
woman. I don't think it's only your intelligence that draws me to
your bed, you above all other women. So why is it to you especially

that I confess, like a man does to his god? Why do I creep from my wife's bed every night to come to you? I'm not lying to you. It's not love, because, as I said, I fell in love with myself from the start and that's the beginning and end of it.

The reason, my dear, is that you're the only person with whom I don't have to prove myself a man. That wasn't clear to me in the beginning. I used to ask myself: what ties me to this woman, why do I need her so much? I discovered the reason that night. Do you remember? It was the night I came to you after my shattering defeat to my rival in the election and the violent argument I had with my wife when I found her naked in my friend's arms. I came to you and cried in your arms, and as I cried I felt as though the tears had been bottled up inside me, like steam under pressure, ever since the time my father told me off when I was a child and had said: 'A man never says "Ow".' That night I saw my tears flow like a river and heard my voice shout 'Ow' over and over again. When I came to, I found my head at your feet, kneeling at your altar like a person kneels in a house of worship. What did you say, my dear? You saw the first real smile on my face? I told you it was the happiest night of my life? It's true. For the first time in my life, I discovered how stupid I'd been. When I was a boy, I almost lost an eye in a fight to prove myself a man. In my teens, I nearly lost my life on a number of occasions because of my perpetual readiness to compete. As an adult, I almost lost my mental faculties because of my defeat and then my wife's betrayal. But everything changed that night. The false mask which we call masculinity fell away and I began to see my real self. For the first time, I discovered that I did not have to prove to myself or to others that I was a man. What does 'man' mean, after all? This discovery was the happiest moment in my life. I was so happy, I began to smother you with kisses, to kiss your feet and rub my nose in them and cry. I found that the taste of my tears and my lowly position at your feet was sweet. What did you say? I confessed my love to you that night? Yes, my dear, I told you that I loved you. But I admit that as soon as I left your place and went back home and then to my office, I felt ashamed of myself. I was ashamed when I realized how I'd revealed to you a hidden part of myself, the feminine part, the part which all men hide as an imperfection. I was so ashamed that I decided never to see you again. But I returned to you the following night and the next night and every night, without a break. I know that I am bound to you by the force of my desire not to be a man but to be myself, as I am. But I'm also bound to this false masculine world. I put on the mask and take my place in the ranks. I play my part. I deliver blows whenever the other cannot hit me and I receive blows from those above me without responding. I suppress my anger until I get home to my wife and I hold back the tears until I come to you. It's a fair division, my dear. Men like us need at least two women. A woman with whom he can get angry and a woman with whom he can cry. What did you say, my dear? Yes, my wife loves me. She betrayed me because she loves me so much. I wasn't sure of that, but now I'm convinced of it. I am devoted to my wife and desire her more and more. Yes, I desire her more, my dear, because through her I have discovered something new that I couldn't have discovered by myself. I discovered that I'm not the only man on earth. I confess to you that I feel very comforted by this discovery. It's the comfort of surrendering to a fact to which I was unable to surrender before. If men experienced such comfort just once, they'd encourage their wives to betray them as quickly as possible. How many years I lost without this comfort, my dear.

What did you say? I'm very late? Yes, yes. But I'm luckier than others. Some men die believing they're the only one on earth.

What did you say? Women know this from the start? Yes, my dear. Women are smarter than men. A woman always knows that she's not the only woman on earth. Pour me another glass, with a lot of ice. Let me die in your arms and don't interrupt me.

A modern love letter

I am writing this letter to you, my friend, so that you may perhaps understand me or that I may perhaps understand myself. The attempt may come to nothing, for who is able to understand himself or the other? Who is able to break the shell? Just as attempting to break it merely confirms that it is not broken, so attempting to understand only increases the feeling of not understanding. And yet I try. I realize for certain that the attempt is futile but that does not stop me trying, just as I do not give up living my life, knowing that death is inevitable. I am writing this letter to you, my friend, so that you may perhaps understand me or that I may perhaps understand myself. The attempt may come to nothing, for who is able to understand himself or the other? Who is able to break the shell? Just as attempting to break it merely confirms that it is not broken, so attempting to understand only increases the feeling of not understanding. And yet I try. I realize for certain that the attempt is futile but that does not stop me trying, just as I do not give up living my life, knowing that death is inevitable.

You may or may not be surprised that I call this a love letter, since in our relationship we have never mentioned the word *love*. We may have used other words, like *affection* or *friendship* or *esteem*. But these words are meaningless, imprecise. What is the meaning of the word *affection* which we once used to describe our relationship? It doesn't mean a thing. It means neither love nor lack of love, but is a halfway feeling between love and no love, a halfway position between something and nothing, when a person loves and doesn't love, is angry and is not angry, hates and doesn't hate, speaks and doesn't speak, and always holds the rope in the centre. It is that fluid moderate position in everything which psychologists praise and to which they give the name mental health. Such health, in their view, consists of moderation in all things — in intelligence, in enthusiasm, in love, in hate, in ambition, in honesty.

And because honesty knows no moderation, so a person must lie to a certain extent to win the stamp of mental health from psychologists. And since love, like honesty, knows no moderation, so the word *affection* means nothing in a relationship.

What is the relationship between us? How did it develop? Did it have a starting point? Did it, in other words, begin at the first meeting or at the last meeting or in the middle? I try now to gather the threads of my memory, to recall when the first meeting was, how your features appeared to me. The attempt seems to me now to be impossible, like trying to remember the first time I saw my face in the mirror. Or my mother's face. Or that of my father. There are some features which, the moment we set eyes on them, appear as though we have known them all along, as though they were part of us or within us and not external to us. Do you remember the first time you saw me? When was it? In your office? In my office? In your house? In my house? In a field or at one of those gatherings where intellectuals always meet? Those faces tense when both smiling and frowning, cheeks distended both in speech and in silence, stomach muscles slack when inhaling and exhaling, glances always fixed upwards, whatever that upwards is, red or green, valuable or cheap.

When I look into your eyes, I do not feel that you belong to this class. I see a different expression in your eyes which makes things different, less contradictory. Your smile is a smile, your frown a frown. Your features move with the muscles of your face in a spontaneous natural movement. I neither see it nor feel it and yet I know it exists, like the movement of time or of the earth or of an aeroplane which, although I do not feel it when I am inside it, I know to be there.

Sometimes that expression appears when I am sleeping or walking in the street or sitting or driving my car or engrossed in work. It remains before me, strangely compelling, taking me out of the state I was in, willing me to look at it, to understand the reason for its urgency. I push it away gently at first, then forcefully, then harshly, then with an anger resembling madness.

Once it pestered me with such insistence that I asked myself whether it was really a feeling of loneliness. My office is crowded, my house is crowded, Cairo is crowded. But, as in all such large cities, we live with crowdedness and loneliness at one and the same time. Between one person and another, despite close bodily contact, there is a thick wall which gets higher as people rise up the social ladder. And at night, when the city is immersed in sleep, I look around me like an orphan. I open my address book and flick through the names and telephone numbers, many numbers and many names, all set out in alphabetical order. And yet there is no one who can dispel the loneliness. This sprawling city stretched out before me is devoid of men. And yet it is crammed with males, not one of whom can meet a woman alone without thinking of jumping on her. Life in our world is made for men and nothing in it can amuse a woman other than that sort of amusement which neither amuses nor gratifies me and which only shows life in its ugliness and man in his baseness.

From time to time my phone rings and from time to time I accept some man's invitation out of my desire to find out the truth and to learn about life and people. It is also an attempt to dispel loneliness. I realize the impossibility of living inside myself, of remaining without others. If I wrote for myself alone, I would choke on my words. If I spoke to myself alone, my voice would fail. If I looked at my own face all the time, I would lose my mind.

And yet I always run from others. I love to disappear far away from them but I do so in order to remain in their thoughts. It is distance for the sake of closeness, separation for the sake of contact. And that's my dilemma. I want to be a separate entity and at the same time I want to be an inseparable part of others. This contradiction tears me apart, splitting me in two, one part inside myself far from others, the other part outside myself in the heart of others. One part is quiet and immobile and observes the movement of the other. Is it I who observe the other or is it the other that observes me? Which of us is motionless in time and place and which of us moves within time and on earth?

I am preoccupied with the answer to these questions, whilst the man who has invited me sits silently before me, looking at me now and again to catch some movement or a glance from me which could encourage him to invite me to bed. When he finds nothing, he is surprised. He may wonder if I am affected by twentieth-century complexes or if I am like a cave woman and still like rape and pain.

I cannot deny that the idea of rape, like the idea of suicide, holds some attraction for me and has been with me since time immemorial, no matter how I wrestle with its vestiges or seeds. But I do not commit suicide and nobody can rape me. No matter how difficult my life becomes, however much I suffocate, I do not commit suicide.

However much a man desires me, he cannot overpower me. It is not, as you once told me, that I kill or castrate men, but I am always able to stare a man in the eyes and can always see the muscle around his mouth or his fingers quiver. It may only be quick and last no longer than a moment or two, but it is always enough for me to see it and to bend his will to mine. His muscular power, even the power of all the men in the world, is incapable of making the muscles of my hand yield under his.

You told me once that I was a strong woman. The truth is that I'm not always strong. Sometimes I let my hand yield. Sometimes I feel as lost as a tiny speck in the grip of a wild surge or in the grasp of some vast creature as predatory as fate and I feel unable to do anything of my own will or choice, incapable of holding on to truth and reality. You once asked me about my dreams. In truth, most of the time I live in my dreams for I can choose and change them, whereas it is reality which changes me without my choosing. I no longer see reality as real unless it is rooted in my dreams. I admit to you that my unconscious is stronger than my conscious mind and most of the time I obey it.

I saw you in one of my dreams. You were sitting with me somewhere far from the world, a place enclosing us alone, something that has never happened in reality. I was sitting beside you. Deep inside me there was a violent movement, stillness and quiet on the surface. I had a feeling of some sort of sad and mysterious happiness, a silent pulse in the body, an intense elation and a desire so strong it went beyond desire. I don't know what it was exactly that I wanted. That your eyes should remain on mine forever? That you should raise your arms and encircle me and hide me inside yourself forever? I awoke from sleep but you remained where you were beside me. I closed my eyes to rid myself of you, but you stayed, near to me, almost but not quite touching me, almost but not quite leaving me. Why? Why didn't you leave me? Is there something obligatory between us? Does anyone obligate you? Does anyone obligate me? I know there is no one, no one at all. And yet I cannot say that I go to you from choice or will or that our relationship is not as vital to me as the air that enters and leaves my chest or the blood that flows in my veins.

This involuntary side of my relationship with you arouses rebellion in me, for I value my freedom. That's why I rebel against you. At times I tell you I won't see you again. Or I try to pile up your mistakes or slips of the tongue and may accuse you of things of which I accuse other men. But it is always a failed revolution, at times resembling my revolution against myself, at times making me want to throw my body from the window and rid myself of it forever. The result is always the same. My body remains attached to me and you remain in your place before my eyes, near to me, almost but not quite touching me. Why? Why do you never touch me? Are you simply a ghost? Do you exist in reality?

Sometimes, when you used to see me to the door, I would feel as though you briefly touched my hand or put your arm around my waist, a light rapid touch which no sooner happened than was gone. It may not even have been a touch since there was always a distance between your hand and my body, a hair's breadth, but always enough to separate us and for my moment of certainty to vanish. Again I ask myself whether it was real or a dream? Why does this distance always remain? Is it my fear of you? Is it your fear of me? Is there really anything to fear?

Once I wanted to dispel the dream, to reach out and touch certainty. I invited you to my house. Do you remember the date? In your voice I heard an unusual tremor of surprise or hesitation or fear or uncertainty. You did not come. I did not ask you why. I knew that, like me, you always want to waver between certainty and doubt.

Is there anything to dispel doubt? Is there proof of anything? There is nothing definite between me and you that I can cling to, no appropriate word, no language, no movement, no touch, nothing at all between us to confirm anything. But there is one thing of which I'm sure (and which also cannot be proved), and that is that you feel towards me what I feel for you, to the same extent, in the same way and at the same time. Am I mistaken? I may or may not be.

That's how I am, my friend. I draw near to you and then draw back. I appear and disappear. I step forward and then I retreat. I decide on confrontation and then I run away. Day after day, month after month, twenty months or more. You once told me that our lives are passing, that a day that has gone will not return, that I'm wasting my life searching for the impossible or the absolute, that no one except God can satisfy me. One day I was hiding my eyes behind a pair of large sunglasses and you asked me to take them off, which I did. When you looked into my eyes, I nearly confessed to you that you are the only certainty and truth in my life. But the telephone or the doorbell rang or something happened or perhaps one of your children appeared or maybe you looked away or moved your head or arm. It seems to me that you glanced at the clock, deliberately or not. It lasted no longer than a second but it was enough to tear the fine silken hair on which was balanced the feeling of certainty.

You told me once that I run away from life, that I am incapable of loving, that I suffer from the sickness of the age, that I need pills or medicine or something of the sort. I was surprised and not surprised, sad for myself and not sad. I was on the verge of feeling ill and of swallowing the pills of the twentieth century. You asked me more than once why I did not take pills, like all intellectuals. But, my friend, I do not belong to this age, neither am I one of those intellectuals. I don't read the newspapers as they do. My eyes close in spite of themselves when they look at the papers and my ears shut when they hear the news being read. When I walk in the street I do not see faces and I appear to people to be blind and deaf. But, my friend, I am neither blind nor deaf. I see every face that passes in front of me and I read every letter written on the face of the earth and I hear every sound, even the patter of an ant or the beat of an orphan heart in the breast of a child. Do you think I'm talking nonsense? Do you really think I don't see? I saw you once when I was walking along Tahrir Street. Your car was moving fast, like all the other cars. Your face was tired, like all the other faces and your eyes were sad, like all other eyes. It was very crowded, bodies crammed together, vehicles crammed together. The air was stagnant and sticky. Everyone was panting in a sea of sweat, practically suffocating, shouting for help, begging to be saved. But nobody saw anyone else. Nobody heard anyone else. Nobody saved anyone else.

Despite the speed of your car, I managed to study your face for a brief moment. Your features were not your features, your eyes not your eyes. I wondered whether it was you or not. I quickly turned around. Your car had almost vanished in the crowd but I managed to catch the number. I stood still for a moment, wondering where you had come from and where you were going and why you were going so fast. I knew that you were coming from your office and were on your way home or going to an appointment with someone big or small, someone sick or well. I knew all that and yet I stood looking around in surprise as though I knew nothing.

Then I continued on my way again, my head and heart heavy with a cold creeping depression and a question with no answer: Why all this? What's it all for? Is it the pursuit of money? Or the attempt to gain power? Or is it the search for fame? But you have a great deal of all these things. What is it then? Can it be love? But does love make a face tired and the eyes sad?

I felt I hated this city, those faces, those eyes, the hands of the clock, everything. The hatred was so intense that I tried to close my eyes and ears and all the pores of my body. I had a violent desire to run as fast as possible and get away from everything, a violent desire to separate myself from the world, to the point of dying.

But one thing I did not want — to lose your face in the crowd, that in time you should vanish from before my eyes. You know, my friend, that I don't want anything from you. I eat and drink and sleep and have sex and drive a car like yours. But I don't want to lose you in this crowd. Life without you is like a silent black-and-white movie. But with you, everything changes. Colours return and all things are luminous.

At this moment I wish that I could hold your hand in mine, that my whole life would become delicate tender fingers to touch your face, that my whole body would split into millions of tiny fingers to wipe the tiredness from your eyes. After all this, can you still accuse me of being incapable of loving? Can you again tell me that I don't understand, that I don't have natural intelligence? Can you now understand me a little? And do I understand you a little? I hope so. It must be so!

In camera

The first thing she felt was a blinding light. She saw nothing. The light was painful, even though her eyes were still shut. The cold air hit her face and bare neck, crept down to her chest and stomach and then fell lower to the weeping wound, where it turned into a sharp blow. She put one hand over her eyes to protect them from the light, whilst with the other she covered her neck, clenching her thighs against the sudden pain. Her lips too were clenched tight against a pain the like of which her body had never known, like the sting of a needle in her eyes and breasts and armpits and lower abdomen. From sleeping so long while standing and standing so long while sleeping, she no longer knew what position her body was in, whether vertical or horizontal, dangling in the air by her feet or standing on her head in water.

The moment they sat her down and she felt the seat on which she was sitting with the palms of her hands, the muscles of her face relaxed and resumed their human form. A shudder of sudden and intense pleasure shook her from inside when her body took up a sitting position on the wooden seat and her lips curled into a feeble smile as she said to herself: Now I know what pleasure it is to sit!

The light was still strong and her eyes still could not see, but her eyes were beginning to catch the sound of voices and murmurings. She lifted her hand off her eyes and gradually began to open them. Blurred human silhouettes moved before her on some elevated construction. She suddenly felt frightened, for human forms frightened her more than any others. Those long, rapid and agile bodies, legs inside trousers and feet inside shoes. Everything had been done in the dark with the utmost speed and agility. She could not cry or scream. Her tongue, her eyes, her mouth, her nose, all the parts of her body were constrained. Her body was no longer hers but was like that of a small calf struck by the heels of boots. A rough stick entered between her thighs to tear at her insides. Then she was kicked into a dark corner where she remained curled up until the following day. By the third day, she still had not returned to normal but remained like a small animal incapable of uttering the simple words: My God! She said to herself: Do animals, like humans, know of the existence of something called God?

Her eyes began to make out bodies sitting on that elevated place, above each head a body, smooth heads without hair, in the light as red as monkeys' rumps. They must all be males, for however old a woman grew, her head could never look like a monkey's rump. She strained to see more clearly. In the centre was a fat man wearing something like a black robe, his mouth open; in his hand something like a hammer. It reminded her of the village magician, when her eyes and those of all the other children had been mesmerized by the hand which turned a stick into a snake or into fire. The hammer squirmed in his hand like a viper and in her ears a sharp voice resounded: The Court! To herself she said: He must be the judge. It was the first time in her life she'd seen a judge or been inside a court. She'd heard the word *court* for the first time as a child. She'd heard her aunt tell her mother: The judge did not believe me and told me to strip so he could see where I'd been beaten. I told him that I would not strip in front of a strange man, so he rejected my claim and ordered me to return to my husband. Her aunt had cried and at that time she had not understood why the judge had told her aunt to strip. I wonder if the judge will ask me to strip and what he will say when he sees that wound, she said to herself.

Gradually, her eyes were growing used to the light. She began to see the judge's face more clearly. His face was as red as his head, his eyes as round and bulging as a frog's, moving slowly here and there, his nose as curved as a hawk's beak, beneath it a yellow moustache as thick as a bundle of dry grass, which quivered above the opening of a mouth as taut as wire and permanently gaping like a mousetrap.

She did not understand why his mouth stayed open. Was he talking all the time or breathing through it? His shiny bald head moved continually with a nodding movement. It moved upwards a little and then backwards, entering into something pointed; then it moved downwards and forwards, so that his chin entered his neck opening. She could not yet see what was behind him, but when he raised his head and moved it backwards, she saw it enter something pointed which looked like the cap of a shoe. She focused her vision and saw that it really was a shoe, drawn on the wall above the judge's head. Above the shoe she saw taut legs inside a pair of trousers of expensive leather or leopardskin or snakeskin and a jacket, also taut, over a pair of shoulders. Above the shoulders appeared the face she'd seen thousands of times in the papers, eyes staring into space filled with more stupidity than simplicity, the nose as straight as though evened out by a hammer, the mouth pursed to betray that artificial sincerity which all rulers and kings master when they sit before a camera. Although his mouth was pinched in arrogance and sincerity, his cheeks were slack, beneath them a cynical and comical smile containing chronic corruption and childish petulance.

She had been a child in primary school the first time she saw a picture of the king. The face was fleshy, the eyes narrow, the lips thin and clenched in impudent arrogance. She recalled her father's voice saying he was decadent and adulterous. But they were all the same. When they stood in front of a camera, they thought they were God.

Although she could still feel her body sitting on the wooden seat, she began to have doubts. How could they allow her to sit all this time? Sitting like this was so very relaxing. She could sit, leaving her body in a sitting position, and enjoy that astounding ability which humans have. For the first time she understood that the human body differed from that of an animal in one important way — sitting. No animal could sit the way she could. If it did, what would it do with its four legs? She remembered a scene that had made her laugh as a child, of a calf which had tried to sit on its backside and had ended up on its back. Her lips curled in a futile attempt to open her mouth and say something or smile. But her mouth remained stuck, like a horizontal line splitting the lower part of her face into two. Could she open her mouth a little to spit? But her throat, her mouth, her neck, her chest, everything, was dry, all except for that gaping wound between her thighs.

She pressed her legs together tighter to close off the wound and the pain and to enjoy the pleasure of sitting on a seat. She could have stayed in that position forever, or until she died, had she not suddenly heard a voice calling her name: Leila Al Fargani.

Her numbed senses awoke and her ears pricked up to the sound of that strange name: Leila Al Fargani. As though it wasn't her name. She hadn't heard it for ages. It was the name of a young woman named Leila, a young woman who had worn young woman's clothes, had seen the sun and walked on two feet like other human beings. She had been that woman a very long time ago, but since then she hadn't worn a young woman's clothes nor seen the sun nor walked on two feet. For a long time she'd been a small animal inside a dark and remote cave and when they addressed her, they only used animal names.

Her eyes were still trying to see clearly. The judge's head had grown clearer and moved more, but it was still either inside the cap of the shoe whenever he raised it or was inside his collar whenever he lowered it. The picture hanging behind him had also become clearer. The shiny pointed shoes, the suit as tight as a horseman's, the face held taut on the outside by artificial muscles full of composure and stupidity, on the inside depraved and contentious.

The power of her sight was no longer as it had been, but she could still see ugliness clearly. She saw the deformed face and remembered her father's words: They only reach the seat of power, my girl, when they are morally deformed and internally corrupt.

And what inner corruption! She had seen their real corruption for herself. She wished at that moment they would give her pen and paper so that she could draw that corruption. But would her fingers still be capable of holding a pen or of moving it across a piece of paper? Would she still have at least two fingers which could hold a pen? What could she do if they cut off one of those two fingers? Could she hold a pen with one finger? Could a person walk on one leg? It was one of those questions her father used to repeat. But she hated the questions of the impotent and said to herself: I will split the finger and press the pen into it, just as Isis split the leg of Osiris. She remembered that old story, still saw the split leg pouring with blood. What a long nightmare she was living! How she wanted her mother's hand to shake her so she could open her eyes and wake up. She used to be so happy when, as a child, she opened her eyes and realized that the monster which had tried to rip her body to pieces was nothing but a dream, or a nightmare as her mother used to call it. Each time she had opened her eyes, she was very happy to discover that the monster had vanished, that it was only a dream. But now she opened her eyes and the monster did not go away. She opened her eyes and the monster stayed on her body. Her terror was so great that she closed her eyes again to sleep, to make believe that it was a nightmare. But she opened her eyes and knew it was no dream. And she remembered everything.

The first thing she remembered was her mother's scream in the silence of the night. She was sleeping in her mother's arms, like a child of six even though she was an adult and in her twenties. But her mother had said: You'll sleep in my arms so that even if they come in the middle of the night, I will know it and I'll hold on to you with all my might and if they take you they'll have to take me as well.

Nothing was as painful to her as seeing her mother's face move further and further away until it disappeared. Her face, her eyes, her hair were so pale. She would rather have died than see her mother's face so haggard. To herself she said: Can you forgive me, Mother, for causing you so much pain? Her mother always used to say to her: What's politics got to do with you? You're not a man. Girls of your age think only about marriage. She hadn't replied when her mother had said: Politics is a dirty game which only ineffectual men play.

The voices had now become clearer. The picture also looked clearer, even though the fog was still thick. Was it winter and the hall roofless, or was it summer and they were smoking in a windowless room? She could see another man sitting not far from the judge. His head, like the judge's, was smooth and red but, unlike the judge's, it was not completely under the shoe. He was sitting to one side and above his head hung another picture in which there was something like a flag or a small multicoloured banner. And for the first time, her ears made out some intelligible sentences:

Imagine, ladies and gentlemen. This student, who is not yet twenty years old, refers to Him, whom God protects to lead this noble nation all his life, as 'stupid'.

The word *stupid* fell like a stone in a sea of awesome silence, making a sound like the crash of a rock in water or the blow of a hand against something solid, like a slap or the clap of one hand against another.

Was someone clapping? She pricked up her ears to catch the sound. Was it applause? Or a burst of laughter, like a cackle? Then that terrifying silence pervaded the courtroom once again, a long silence in which she could hear the beating of her heart. The sound of laughter or of applause echoed in her ears. She asked herself who could be applauding at so serious a moment as when the mighty one was being described as stupid, and aloud too.

Her body was still stuck to the wooden seat, clinging on to it, frightened it would suddenly be taken away. The wound in her lower abdomen was still weeping. But she was able to move her head and half opened her eyes to search for the source of that applause. Suddenly she discovered that the hall was full of heads crammed together in rows, all of them undoubtedly human. Some of the heads appeared to have a lot of hair, as if they were those of women or girls. Some of them were small, as if those of children. One head seemed to be like that of her younger sister. Her body trembled for a moment on the seat as her eyes searched around. Had she come alone or with her father and mother? Were they looking at her now? How did she look? Could they recognize her face or her body?

She turned her head to look. Although her vision had grown weak, she could just make out her mother. She could pick out her mother's face from among thousands of faces even with her eyes closed. Could her mother really be here in the hall? Her heartbeats grew audible and anxiety grew inside her. Anxiety often gripped her and she felt that something terrible had happened to her mother. One night, fear had overcome her when she was curled up like a small animal and she'd told herself: She must have died and I will not see her when I get out. But the following day, she had seen her mother when she came to visit. She'd come, safe and sound. She was happy and said: Don't die, Mother, before I get out and can make up for all the pain I've caused you.

The sound was now clear in her ears. It wasn't just one clap but a whole series of them. The heads in the hall were moving here and there. The judge was still sitting, his smooth head beneath the shoe. The hammer in his hand was moving impatiently, banging rapidly on the wooden table. But the clapping did not stop. The judge rose to his feet so that his head was in the centre of the stomach in the picture. His lower lip trembled as he shouted out words of rebuke, which she couldn't hear in all the uproar.

Then silence descended for a period. She was still trying to see, her hands by her side holding on to the seat, clinging on to it, pressing it as if she wanted to confirm that it was really beneath her or that she was really sitting on it. She knew she was awake and not asleep with her eyes closed. Before, when she opened her eyes, the monster would disappear and she'd be happy that it was only a dream. But now she was no longer capable of being happy and had become frightened of opening her eyes.

The noise in the hall had died down and the heads moved as they had done before. All except one head. It was neither smooth nor red. It was covered in a thick mop of white hair and was fixed and immobile. The eyes also did not move and were open, dry and fixed on that small body piled on top of the wooden seat. Her hands were clasped over her chest, her heart under her hand beating fast, her breath panting as if she were running to the end of the track and could no longer breathe. Her voice broke as she said to herself: My God! Her eyes turn in my direction but she doesn't see me. What have they done to her eyes? Or is she fighting sleep? God of Heaven and Earth, how could you let them do all that? How, my daughter, did you stand so much pain? How did I stand it together with you? I always felt that you, my daughter, were capable of anything, of moving mountains or of crumbling rocks, even though your body is small and weak like mine. But when your tiny feet used to kick the walls of my stomach, I'd say to myself: God, what strength and power there is inside my body? Your movements were strong while you were still a foetus and shook me from inside, like a volcano shakes the earth. And yet I knew that you were as small as I was, your bones as delicate as your father's, as tall and slim as your grandmother, your feet as large as the feet of prophets. When I gave birth to you, your grandmother pursed her lips in sorrow and said: A girl and ugly too! A double catastrophe! I tensed my stomach muscles to close off my womb to the pain and the blood and, breathing with difficulty, for your birth had been hard and I suffered as though I'd given birth to a mountain, I said to her: She's more precious to me than the whole world! I held you to my breast and slept deeply. Can I, my daughter, again enjoy another moment of deep sleep whilst you are inside me or at least near to me so that I can reach out to touch you? Or whilst you are in your room next to mine so that I can tiptoe in to see you whilst you sleep? The blanket always used to fall off you as you slept, so I'd lift it and cover you. Anxiety would wake me every night and make me creep into your room. What was that anxiety and at what moment did it happen? Was it the moment the cover fell off your body? I could always feel you, even if you had gone away and were out of my sight. Even if they were to bury you under the earth or build a solid wall of mud or iron around you, I would still feel a draught of air on your body as though it were on mine. I sometimes wonder whether I ever really gave birth to you or if you are still inside me. How else could I feel the air when it touches you and hunger when it grips you. Your pain is mine, like fire burning in my breast and stomach. God of Heaven and Earth, how did your body and mine stand it? But I couldn't have stood it were it not for the joy of you being my daughter, of having given birth to you. And you can raise your head high above the mountains of filth. For three thousand and twenty-five hours (I've counted them one by one), they left you with the vomit and pus and the weeping wound in your stomach. I remember the look in your eyes when you told me, the bars between us: If only the weeping were red blood. But it's not red. It's white and has the smell of death. What was it I said to you that day? I don't know, but I said something. I said that the smell becomes normal when we get used to it and live with it every day. I could not look into your emaciated face, but I heard you say: It's not a smell, mother, like other smells which enter through the nose or mouth. It's more like liquid air or steam turned to viscid water or molten lead flowing into every opening of the body. I don't know, mother, if it is burning hot or icy cold. I clasped my hands to my breast, then grasped your slender hand through the bars, saying: When heat becomes like cold, my daughter, then everything is bearable. But as soon as I left you, I felt my heart swell and swell until it filled my chest and pressed on my lungs so I could no longer breathe. I felt I was choking and tilted my head skywards to force air into my lungs. But the sky that day was void of air and the sun over my head was molten lead like the fire of hell. The eyes of the guards stung me and their uncouth voices piled up inside me. If the earth had transformed into the face of one of them, I'd have spat and spat and spat on it until my throat and chest dried up. Yes, my daughter, brace the muscles of your back and raise your head and turn it in my direction, for I'm sitting near you. You may have heard them when they applauded you. Did you hear them? I saw you move your head towards us. Did you see us? Me and your father and little sister? We all applauded with them. Did you see us?

Her eyes were still trying to penetrate the thick fog. The judge was still standing, his head smooth and red, his lower lip trembling with rapid words. To his right and to his left, she saw smooth red heads begin to move away from that elevated table. The judge's head and the others vanished, although the picture on the wall remained where it was. The face and the eyes were the same as they had been, but now one eye appeared to her to be smaller, as though half-closed or winking at her, that common gesture that a man makes to a woman when he wants to flirt with her. Her body trembled in surprise. Was it possible that he was winking at her? Was it possible for his eyes in the picture to move? Could objects move? Or was she sick and hallucinating? She felt the seat under her palm and raised her hand to touch her body. A fierce heat emanated from it, like a searing flame, a fire within her chest. She wanted to open her mouth and say: Please, a glass of water. But her lips were

stuck together, a horizontal line as taut as wire. Her eyes too were
stuck on the picture, while the eye in the picture continued to wink
at her. Why was it winking at her? Was it flirting with her? She had
only discovered that winking was a form of greeting when, two years
previously, she'd seen a file of foreign tourists walking in the street.
She'd been on her way to the university. Whenever she looked at
the faces of one of the men or women, an eye would suddenly wink
at her strangely. She had been shocked and hadn't understood how
a woman could flirt with her in such a way. Only later had she
understood that it was an American form of greeting.

The podium was still empty, without the judge and the smooth
heads around him. Silence prevailed. The heads in the hall were
still close together in rows and her eyes still roamed in search of
a mop of white hair, a pair of black eyes which she could see with
eyes closed. But there were so many heads close together she could
only see a mound of black and white, circles or squares or oblongs.
Her nose began to move as if she were sniffing, for she knew her
mother's smell and could distinguish it from thousands of others.
It was the smell of milk when she was a child at the breast or the
smell of the morning when it rises or the night when it sleeps or the
rain on wet earth or the sun above the bed or hot soup in a bowl.
She said to herself: Is it possible that you're not here, Mother? And
Father, have you come?

The fog before her eyes was still thick. Her head continued to
move in the direction of the rows of crammed heads. The black
and white circles were interlocked in tireless movement. Only one
circle of black hair was immobile above a wide brown forehead, two
firm eyes in a pale slender face and a small body piled onto a chair
behind bars. His large gaunt hands gripped his knees, pressing
on them from the pain. But the moment he heard the applause, he
took his hands off his knees and brought them together to clap. His
hands did not return to his knees, the pain in his legs no longer
tangible. His heart beat loudly in time to his clapping, which shook
his slender body on the seat. His eyes began to scour the faces and
eyes, and his lips parted a little as though he were about to shout:
I'm her father; I'm Al Fargani who fathered her and whose name

she bears. My God, how all the pain in my body vanished in one go with the burst of applause. What if I were to stand up now and reveal my identity to them? This moment is unique and I must not lose it. Men like us live and die for one moment such as this, for others to recognize us, to applaud us, for us to become heroes with eyes looking at us and fingers pointing at us. I have suffered the pain and torture with her, day after day, hour after hour, and now I have the right to enjoy some of the reward and share in her heroism.

He shifted his body slightly on his seat as if he were about to stand up. But he remained seated, though his head still moved. His eyes glanced from face to face, as if he wanted someone to recognize him. The angry voice of the judge and the sharp rapid blows of his hammer on the table broke into the applause. Presently the judge and those with him withdrew to the conference chambers. Silence again descended on the hall, a long and awesome silence, during which some faint whispers reached his ears: They'll cook up the case in the conference chamber… That's common practice… Justice and law don't exist here… In a while they'll declare the public hearing closed… She must be a heroine to have stayed alive until now… Imagine that young girl who is sitting in the dock causing the government so much alarm… Do you know how they tortured her? Ten men raped her, one after the other. They trampled on her honour and on her father's honour. Her poor father! Do you know him! They say he's ill in bed. Maybe he can't face people after his honour was violated!

At that moment he raised his hands to cover his ears so as not to hear, to press on his head so that it sunk into his chest, pushing it more and more to merge his body into the seat or underneath it or under the ground. He wanted to vanish so that no one would see or know him. His name was not Al Fargani, not Assharqawi, not Azziftawi, not anything. He had neither name nor existence. What is left of a man whose honour is violated? He had told her bitterly: Politics, my girl, is not for women and girls. But she had not listened to him. If she had been a man, he would not be suffering now the way he was. None of those dogs would have been able to violate his honour and dignity. Death was preferable for him and for her now.

Silence still reigned over the hall. The judge and his entourage
had not yet reappeared. Her eyes kept trying to see, searching out
one face amongst the faces, for eyes she recognized, for a mop of
white hair the colour of children's milk. But all she could see were
black and white circles and squares intermingled and constantly
moving. Is it possible you're not here, Mother? Is Father still ill?
Her nose too continued to move here and there, searching for a
familiar smell, the smell of a warm breast full of milk, the smell
of the sun and of drizzle on grass. But her nose was unable to
pick up the smell. All it could pick up was the smell of her body
crumpled on the seat and the weeping wound between her thighs.
It was a smell of pus and blood and the putrid stench of the breath
and sweat of ten men, the marks of whose nails were still on her
body, with their uncouth voices, their saliva and the sound of
their snorting. One of them, lying on top of her, had said: This
is the way we torture you women — by depriving you of the most
valuable thing you possess. Her body under him was as cold as a
corpse but she had managed to open her mouth and say to him:
You fool! The most valuable thing I possess is not between my
legs. You're all stupid. And the most stupid among you is the one
who leads you.

She craned her neck to raise her head and penetrate the fog with
her weak eyes. The many heads were still crammed together and
her eyes still strained. If only she could have seen her mother for
a moment, or her father or little sister, she would have told them
something strange. She would have told them that they had stopped
using that method of torture when they discovered that it didn't
torture her. They began to search for other methods.

In the conference chamber next to the hall, the judge and his
aides were meeting, deliberating the case. What should they do
now that the public had applauded the accused? The judge began
to face accusations in his turn:

—We're not accusing you, Your Honour, but you did embarrass
us all. As the saying goes: 'The road to hell is paved with good
intentions!' You did what you thought was right, but you only
managed to make things worse. How could you say, Your Honour,

about Him, whom God protect to lead this noble nation all his life, that he is stupid?

—God forbid, sir! I didn't say that, I said that she said he was stupid.

—Don't you know the saying, 'What the ear doesn't hear, the heart doesn't grieve over'? You declared in public that he's stupid.

—I didn't say it, sir. I merely repeated what the accused said to make the accusation stick. That's precisely what my job is.

—Yes, that's your job, Your Honour. We know that. But you should have been smarter and wiser than that.

—I don't understand.

—Didn't you hear how the people applauded her?

—Is that my fault?

—Don't you know why they applauded?

—No, I don't.

—Because you said in public what is said in private and it was more like confirming a fact than proving an accusation.

—What else could I have done, sir?

—You could have said that she cursed the mighty one without saying exactly what she said.

—And if I'd been asked what kind of curse it was?

—Nobody would have asked you. And besides, you volunteered the answer before anyone asked, as though you'd seized the opportunity to say aloud and in her words, what you yourself wanted to say or perhaps what you do say to yourself in secret.

—Me? How can you accuse me in this way? I was simply performing my duty as I should. Nobody can accuse me of anything. Perhaps I was foolish, but you cannot accuse me of bad faith.

—But foolishness can sometimes be worse than bad faith. You must know that foolishness is the worst label you can stick on a man. And as far as he's concerned, better that he be a swindler, a liar, a miser, a trickster, even a thief or a traitor, rather than foolish. Foolishness means that he doesn't think, that he's mindless, that he's an animal. That's the worst thing you can call an ordinary man. And all the more so if he's a ruler. You don't know rulers, Your Honour, but I know them well. Each of them fancies his brain to be better than any other man's. And it's not just a matter of fantasy, but of blind belief, like the belief in God. For the sake of this illusion, he can kill thousands.

—I didn't know that, sir. How can I get out of this predicament?

—I don't know why you began with the description 'stupid', Your Honour. If you'd read everything she said, you'd have found that she used other less ugly terms to describe him.

—Such as what, sir? Please, use your experience to help me choose some of them. I don't want to leave here accused, after coming in this morning to raise an accusation.

—Such descriptions cannot be voiced in public. The session must be closed. Even a less ugly description will find an echo in the heart of the people if openly declared. That's what closed sessions are for, Your Honour. Many matters escape you and it seems you have little experience in law.

A few minutes later, utter silence descended on the hall. The courtroom was completely emptied. As for her, they took her back to where she'd been before.

A private letter to an artist friend

Since you opened your heart to me and reproached me sternly yet gently, the gentleness making me cry more than the sternness, since you did that, I now have the right to reproach you, as one artist to another, as a woman to a man between whom the feeling of closeness is firm and deep-rooted and as translucent as pure air. But although we feel it to be deep and almost filling us, we are incapable of holding on to it in a moment of reality. And it seems that this is the only characteristic of feelings of closeness, that in so far as they are real they seem to us like a dream.

Since you did that, allow me to reproach you. I have never reproached anyone before. I never reproached my father or my mother for bringing me into this world without consulting me; neither will I reproach God for taking me without my volition. No, I reproach no one, neither man nor woman nor God, neither in love nor in hatred. And how much more harm I've suffered through love than through hatred!

But you have become one of those rare and exceptional people in my life. And when I pick up my pen, what I write is not for people in general to read but rather for one particular person, for him alone to read, separate from all the rest.

At times, even if I try, I find myself unable to write deep and very personal things for myself, as though there were some deep-seated wound, some bottomless well into which I have fallen. And I feel the pain in my skull reach to the very core. Is it my destiny to be something other than what destiny decreed for me? Not to be female (in the accepted sense of the word) and not to be a doctor (according to my degree from medical school)? Or is it really my destiny to be a person before being a female, an artist before being a doctor?

Ever since I was born I have felt my struggle to be with destiny itself, although another side of me realizes that destiny is with me, that it is destiny that wants me to be an artist and a person. What, then, is that other force that wants me to be a female and a doctor? Is there any destiny other than the destiny we know?

All my life I have been torn between two destinies, like a piece of meat held between predatory jaws. I try to run away and sometimes I believe I have managed to escape, that I am spared. I take a deep breath and pick up a pen to pour myself onto paper, truthfully, as naturally as death, as simply as a spontaneous smile on the face of a child. And, with the naivety of a child, I believe I have done nothing worthwhile. Even as the words on the page seem to me inadequate, less and weaker than myself, the world around me quakes in fear, as though honesty were no longer a word but a beast of prey, as though truth had become like death or worse.

And is there anything worse than death? Or perhaps it is our lives which, at times, become worse than death. I used to ask myself this question, but I don't know if there is an answer, in life or in death. Most of the time, I don't know the difference between living and dying. At times my life seems to me like death, whilst at others death suddenly appears to me to be the only hope for living.

A deep pain reaches deeper than any knife can. I look around me, searching for others like me who carry knives in their bodies, looking for another person who can tell me, 'Yes, you're in the right and the world is in the wrong. You tell the truth and the world tells lies.'

But such people are very rare, as rare as a truthful word lost between heaven and earth like a drop of water lost in the sea, like an honest heartbeat lost inside the breast and which not one of us can find even if we wanted to. How often, amongst the millions of heartbeats, is there a real one? Every minute the heart beats about seventy times, four thousand times an hour, three million times a month. How many times does the heart beat in a lifetime? Do any of us recognize a true heartbeat amongst the millions? And even if we did recognize it, could we grasp it, if we wanted to?

Contrary to what they taught me, I realized that the sum of my life did not amount to the number of years between the date of my birth and my death. I realized for certain that there is a heartbeat other than that of the heart and that the sum total of my whole life may be the one true heartbeat I manage to grasp amongst the millions of untrue ones, or a spontaneous truthful word which I manage to capture on a page amongst the millions of unspontaneous words.

I realized this truth for certain. I realized it with my mind and body, with both together, and with all my senses. And yet, how often did this extraordinary certainty turn, at times, into extraordinary doubt, which itself became certainty and whilst anything else became doubt. At such times I feel as if I have been slaughtered, physically and mentally, that I am in the wrong and that it is the world which is right. I may see myself walking in the street or driving my car, but I know for certain that I have been slaughtered, that the body which is moving is not my real body, that the murderers have hidden my body in a hole in the ground. And I see my unreal body move before me. It may shake hands with people. It may smile. It may pretend and tell the world it is right and I am wrong....

How did I pull my slaughtered body from out of the ground? How did I force my semi-paralysed hand to hold a pen? I don't know, but at any given moment, when I may be sitting or standing or driving, alone or with other people, I see my body rise of its own accord and find myself standing when I was sitting, or sitting when I was standing, or running away from people when I was with them or running towards people when I was alone.

With a shudder of fear, like one coming face to face with death, I discover to my great surprise that my body is really trembling, that my voice trembles. But it lasts only for a fleeting moment, like a single cry which I may hurl in the face of a speaker to silence him or in the face of a silent person to make him speak.

In one such moment, the speaker was an important man, my supervisor in my medical work. He was one of those men of whom the world is full: a doctor who measures his medical achievements by the area of land he owns in this world; a man like the males of the world, who know women only as females. He wanted to treat me like he treats the rest of the world, but I refused. Refusal for me was easy and natural, since I am a person by nature and not a female. And I am by nature an artist and not a doctor. Refusal for me is as easy and natural as the air I breathe. But for him, refusal was hard, harder than death.

It has always puzzled me why men are unable to cope with refusal, especially the refusal of a woman. I see the face of one of them, from which the blood ebbs away until it becomes as white as death. Does this refusal expose his real face to himself, so that he realizes for the first time that it is a dead face? Or that he is refused within himself as well and is suddenly unable to cope with both refusals together?

In an authoritarian tone he told me that no employee ever argued with him, that no woman had ever defied him before. He opened the drawer of his luxurious desk and took out certificates testifying to his superiority and heroism and his victory medals. The walls of his room were plastered with golden frames containing certificates from Egypt and abroad. The blood returned to his face and it was no longer white. His head was held high above a short neck bound by a large necktie (in the American fashion) and his chest was puffed out by tense back muscles which he held with difficulty and effort as if he were unable to convince his own body muscles of his numerous external achievements, as if internally he were defeated by a failure of which no one knew.

Perhaps he saw or felt that I was the only one who witnessed his failure. And because I was a woman, his failure was compounded. His pleasure turned to anger, his approval to disapproval. The desire to nominate me for promotion and to raise me up to seventh heaven turned into the desire to bury me in the heart of the earth and to close the hole with sealing wax.

It was not the first time I'd witnessed a man's failure. There are many men but the number of failures is greater, and in the end I was only one woman. But despite being a woman, despite being only one woman, I had realized that amongst the multitude of men there was at least one who was not defeated. I realized that with every step I took, with every movement or turn I made, be it merely a momentary head movement walking down some street or other, whether consciously or unconsciously, willingly or unwillingly, with mind or body or both together, I realized that I was searching for that man. I also realized that he was not the only man, that there were maybe two or three or four, maybe no more than could be counted on the fingers of one hand, but they were there, albeit rare, and as long as they were there, I had to search for them.

I noticed you once, when I was walking at my normal fast pace. I was angry with that supervisor and when I'm angry I begin to walk faster. Anger shows me heading for a new battle. I must not waste time along the way; each second of my life becomes valuable and the feeling of time passing becomes so oppressive that I must run, scared that death will catch up with me before I can enter into combat, as though it is the last battle of my life and after it I will die. But since I am basically dead, I'm not afraid of death. And because I don't fear death, people are afraid of me. That is the only reason that I come out alive from every battle and remain on earth.

That day you asked me about my anger, so I told you. I hadn't told anyone before and didn't know what to say. Even if I had known, I wouldn't have been able to speak, for there was nobody to hear me or to believe me had I spoken. And what could I have said? That the whole world was in the wrong and I alone was in the right? That the world was mad and I alone was sane? That since the time I was born I have felt letters coursing through my veins like the circulation of blood? That when I hold a pen, the whole world disappears along with the pleasures of food and love and sex and death? That I vanish into a sentence like one lost to love or death? And yet, despite all that, I realize that I'm not lost to anything. Can I say that art was my choice and will but that I am female by chance? That since childhood I have rejected my femininity because it was not me, not of my making, but rather that of a world full of masculinity but void of men? Can I say that I tackle my life with little intellect but with a lot of love? That I do not praise the intellect, despite my medical diplomas, since it's the world around us which moulds our intellects? And because the world is false, it has made our intellects false. In our revolution against the world, we must revolt against our own intellects. Can I say all this? And if I were to say it, would anyone believe me?

That day you told me you believed me, I was so surprised that I couldn't believe it. I sat transfixed in my chair before you. I wanted to stay a while but I got up and left. I don't remember why I left. Maybe someone came in; maybe the phone or doorbell rang. What matters is that I left and that we've met only rarely since that day. Sometimes I catch sight of you walking fast in the street, while I too am walking fast. Sometimes I notice something you've written and I stop and remember. Or sometimes I notice your face in a sea of faces and I look up and wave to you from afar if you've seen me. If you don't see me, I turn around and walk away quickly. And despite my rapid steps, I used to feel as though something of you was with me forever. I ask myself whether you too feel that I gave you something of myself in a moment which has passed and which I cannot retrieve. Sometimes I'd get into my car to come to you but I'd stop myself and wonder what I'd say to you. Whether you remembered what happened between us. Whether something really happened for you to remember.

I don't know if something happened. If it did, what was it? Was it something that the memory can hold on to as proof? Something which could justify my going to you, were I to go? One reason I could put into words were you to ask me why I'd come?

How many years passed without my going to you? I don't know.

I don't measure time in terms of years. My whole life, in my view, may not be equal to one moment which I feel with my mind and body and with all my reserve energy. I have always realized that the senses I have are not all I have, that under the surface is a pulse other than that of the heart, another mind under the mind, another body under the body. Is there another whole woman inside? And which of them is me? Which is real and which unreal? I have always felt that there is only a hair's breadth between the real and unreal and I continually try to cross it to reach the unknown. Both the known and the unknown I feel like fear inside my body. Medicine and surgery have broken the fear of the body, in my view, and art the fear of the unknown. I allowed myself to talk about all the parts of the body like poets talk of the beating of the heart. And I always ask myself why the beat of the heart is the only one permitted.

How many years passed without me coming to you? I don't remember. But I do remember that once, on the spur of the moment, in one of those leaps when I cross that hair's breadth between the known and unknown, between certainty and doubt, when I realize that the world is in the wrong and I am in the right and I break out of my life like one possessed by the sudden desire for death, or I break out of my death in the sudden hope for life — in one of those moments I reached for the telephone and called your number. A man's voice replied and said that you weren't there, so I left my name and number and said I was waiting for your reply.

How many years did I wait? I don't remember and did not try to remember. I grew sad and the sadness erased my memory so that I no longer remembered. Each time I did remember, I grew sadder and forgot until I was sad no longer and no longer forgot. And on the occasions when I almost did remember, I did not know exactly what there was to remember. Nothing had happened between us that the memory could hold on to and there was no proof, no reason, no justification which I could speak of, had someone asked me.

Once I noticed you from afar and I stopped and moved in your direction. But then I turned around and walked away quickly, asking myself if it was love or not. Have things got so complicated? To the extent of being unable to distinguish love from lack of love, to see white from black? Like a blind person, I stood still for a moment to hold my head in my hands and close my eyes or open them. I asked myself if the world had stolen the sight from my eyes, if the world had fragmented the nerves of the eye and heart.

I realized that the world had fragmented everything, fragmented humanity into master and slave, fragmented the individual into mind and body, the body into reputable and disreputable parts. I realized that the world had fragmented everything, apart from myself. Had fragmented men, women, children, rulers and ruled. There is nothing separating political fragmentation from sexual fragmentation. The truthful artist falls with his truthfulness into the game of politics and drowns with his art in the snares of sex. Both politics and sex are the adversaries of art and of humanity. But the artist who, through his art, is committed to the ranks of the ruled in any name or land; who, through his humanity, rejects the body of the rulers in any shape or form; who, by his view, is attracted to sex under the illusion of any love; who is committed to the world with everything in it and on it, while knowing for certain that the world will fragment him, is just as certain that he will never be fragmented.

How many years passed without me going to you? Once I happened to open a newspaper, even though I never look at papers in a world in which pens and bodies tell lies. But that morning, for some reason, I picked up a paper. Perhaps I intended to line a kitchen shelf with it, but I noticed your face and read your careful black words. The printed letters looked almost like your handwriting. The truthfulness of the words on the page had a movement which resembled the movement of your eyes when they look at me. Did you see me in front of you as you wrote? But you haven't seen me for many a long year and no memory, however powerful, can retain something that happened many years ago, let alone something that did not happen.

When the phone rang, I believed it came from anywhere in the world but your office. When I came to you, I thought we would exchange some commonplace words, like those accepted courtesies between acquaintances and friends. But your words were not commonplace and your reproach was not commonplace. Inasmuch as I was surprised, I was not surprised. Inasmuch as I was hurt, I was not hurt. I told you that I had tried once to contact you but had got no reply. You did not believe me and told me that if I'd wanted to come, I would have come. I insisted that I had tried, but you did not believe me and told me that had I really wanted to get in touch with you, nothing could have prevented our meeting. You were very harsh in not believing me. The more your harshness hurt me, the more surprised I was. Perhaps you saw the surprise in my eyes resembling tears. I was so surprised I almost did cry. After all these years, can the memory retain something that did not happen? Or, if it did happen, was it only for a brief moment like a flash of light which appears and then vanishes, like the heartbeat which beats once, then falls into oblivion amongst the millions of others?

When you took my hand in yours to say goodbye I knew you would kiss me and that your kiss on my face would be tender and delicate, almost translucent, like the kiss of a child kissing another, innocent and yet not innocent, like all instinctive feelings.

You gave me your phone number on a scrap of paper and I promised you I'd phone. I was sincere in my promise but as soon as I went out into the crowded street, everything seemed to me like a dream or an illusion. The reproach seemed to be something normal which can happen between any two friends meeting after a long separation. The kiss also seemed normal between friends or colleagues. And, walking at my rapid pace, I realized I would continue walking at my usual speed until I died walking, that many more long years would pass before I could distinguish the real from the unreal, that I was incapable of defying death, unable to cross that hair's breadth between doubt and certainty. Am I in the right and the world in the wrong? Or am I in the wrong and the world right? If you did not believe me that time, I reproach you. If you did believe me, my reproach of you is all the stronger.

🙚   *Death of an Ex-Minister* was first published in Arabic in 1980, and translated by Shirley Eber in 1987.

19

My Ideal Mother

WHY WAS I filled with this strange sense of tranquillity? I had the sensation preceding loss of consciousness when one has received a sudden blow to the head. I switched off the light and lay down in bed. I tried to close my eyes, sliding almost into unconsciousness. How often have I imagined the moment when fantasies would become real and concrete, and are not just abstractions that my mind would dismiss as though they had never happened?

Yesterday I celebrated my fiftieth birthday all by myself. Fifty! How strangely the figure rings in my ears! A woman should never turn fifty before becoming a grandmother, before marrying and producing children and grandchildren, and before going on pilgrimage to repent of her sins and coming back home with the newly acquired title of *Hajjah*.

I never married and never produced any offspring. Neither have I ever gone on pilgrimage or been called *Hajjah*. On the streets, whenever someone called me *Hajjah*, I would correct the mistake angrily saying, 'I am not a *Hajjah*.' At the club, whenever somebody called me 'Madam' I would correct the mistake with equal vehemence saying, 'Don't you Madam me!' He might ask me with the insolence reserved for women of fifty, 'So how should we call you, then, Madam?' My answer would be equally angry, 'I am Miss Attorney.'

Everything in my life seems strange because I'm a woman who was never preoccupied with men. I was never busy thinking of sex, lust or marriage. I've lived my life as a pure and chaste woman. I've turned fifty without seeing my body sag or wrinkles appear on my face. My stomach is flat and when I walk my steps are vigorous and energetic. My eyes are filled with lustre and joy. I am a woman who, in spite of being fifty, still looks as young as a woman of thirty, perhaps even of twenty. I am a woman whose heart had never been broken by a man, a woman who tried through her work as an attorney to bring about justice, a woman who had an office on a small street off Tahrir Square. My help was sought by women who had been abused, beaten up, deserted, divorced and deceived, and by women looking for justice. But justice had no eyes and like a blind creature it lived in total darkness.

I was a child of six when my father got married to another woman without my mother's knowledge. He asked me not to tell her the fact. My mother, however, had taught me to always be truthful. So I told her everything. My father beat me up badly and divorced my mother to punish me. This is how I came to live with her without any family or income. My mother had left both her family and her work to marry him. Although she had a university degree, she lost her job and could not go back to it after her divorce. She worked as a cleaner because there was a surplus of people with university degrees, so they were forced to take up cleaning jobs and spend their lives in an unclean environment. But my mother had just one worry: to offer her daughter a clean existence. It did not matter if she became tarnished in the process. Stains, after all, would be easy to wash clean.

Many men proposed marriage to my mother, but she turned them all down without even batting an eyelid. The condition of the marriage was to give me up, because a husband cannot bear to have anyone share his wife with him, even her own child. She put me though school and university. We lived in a neighbourhood of decent families, where fathers took charge of the expenses. My mother lied to people and told them that my father was providing for us. My father, she told them, was a man of integrity who never divorced her to marry somebody else without her knowledge. She let it be known that she was a government employee with a monthly salary like other employees. The truth was that she was an employee, but at the lowest level of the workers' echelon, working twice as long as the employees in the mid-ranks but receiving half their pay.

My mother came back late at night and went out again at dawn while I slept in bed. She prepared food and put it on the table: the cup of warm milk with honey and the pie piping hot from the oven, which I used to sink my teeth into and cry as though I was biting into my mother's worn-out flesh. I did not know how I could repay her for all she did, although she has never asked for any repayment. She was as happy when I succeeded each year as if it was her own success. When one of the professors proposed marriage to me, her face was all lit up. 'My dear child', she said to me, 'get married and be happy.' 'But how can I possibly do that Mum?' I asked, 'How can I leave you when you have refused to marry for my sake? How can I possibly leave you? Who will look after you through the nights when you fall ill? How often have you stayed next to my bed when I was sick? How can I leave you to live with some man?' 'You will have love, my child, and marriage', she said, 'you will have a family. When I die, you will be alone.' 'At forty Mum, you are still young and we will go on living together until an unselfish man comes along and accepts to have you live with us.' 'Men with positions don't accept to have their mothers-in-law with them. Get married my child, and don't think of me.' 'But how can I do that?' I asked, 'How can I forget about you when all you thought of was me? Where is the justice or the logic here, Mum?' 'My dear girl', said my mother, 'life is illogical and unfair, why else did your father behave the way he did? And neither is he the only man to do so; there are countless others who behave in exactly the same way.' 'This is unfair, Mum. I will stay with you and live for you as you have done for me.' 'My child', my mother said, 'a mother gives her life to her children, but they are not required to give theirs to her.' 'I can't accept that, Mum', I said. 'I believe in justice and in God who is just, and will never give up the idea for the sake of any man.'

This happened when I was still a law student. Other men proposed marriage to me, but as soon as I mentioned my mother, they simply vanished. I realized that love was an illusion, marriage was an illusion, and family was also an illusion. Nothing was real except a man's selfishness. I learnt this truth at the age of six when my father left us to marry another woman. I opened my eyes one morning to find my father gone. He vanished from our life like a fantasy and took with him marriage, love, family and fatherhood. All these disappeared like phantoms in one fleeting moment. In such situations, a woman would find herself all alone, with nothing to provide her with a clean existence except an unclean job.

My mother came home one night all tired and drenched in sweat and tears. She had been laid off together with a number of women cleaners. With the increase in lavish government spending on parties, decorations for victory celebrations and on trips abroad by high-ranking officials, the budget could no longer pay for the wages of the employees of the lower echelons. I was still a university student when we unexpectedly lost our income. I heard my mother crying in the dead of the night. One night, she cried producing a strange sound almost like that of a wounded animal. I tiptoed out of bed and saw her in the bare lounge lying underneath a huge male shape who was pressing down on her worn-out body with a strange kind of violence as though she was a floor mop. In the morning she handed me the ten-pound note to pay the last instalment of the college fees.

The note was tattered, unclean and smelling of sweat, exhaustion and old stains of blood. I concealed it by wrapping it in a clean piece of paper from my lecture copybook. I did not touch it with my hand as though it was contaminated, fearing it might give me some kind of skin disease. I hid it in my leather bag in the middle of copybooks and got rid of it at the Student Affairs' office. I deposited it into the hands of the employee as payment for the fees. I felt a strange kind of shame filling me, akin to the loss of consciousness one suffers from after one has been hit on the head. I walked with my women colleagues through the college garden with my head bent and completely speechless. I told myself that I would keep the secret so deep in my soul that nobody, not even a genie, would be able to find it. How often had I thought of such a moment ever since I heard my mother's sobs at night! I was determined to face that particular moment when it came. But here it was, taking me completely by surprise. I was sure my mother was an honest woman, more honest than any other woman in the whole world. Ever since my father left us, I have never felt the extent of her honesty as I do now. I stifled the voice inside me which wanted to say out loud that my mother was one of the most honest women of the world, a woman on a par with the Virgin Mary. I raised my hand to my mouth to stop the words coming out. My women colleagues were far too preoccupied with their own stories of love, men and marriage to worry about me. Their eyes sparkled with joy and hope. I almost said to them that it was an illusion, nothing more nor less. But my voice was choked. I withdrew from their company and disappeared in the restroom. I went home early and kept my silence. I knew I would wake up in the middle of the night as I often did when I was hiding something inside me. My heart beat out of fear of such a moment. I slept in fits and starts, was visited by terrifying dreams, and woke up to find it five minutes to midnight according to my wristwatch. I lay on my back and closed my eyes. I heard the horn of a car on the street and a sudden braking and a thumping sound. I shivered in bed. Could it be my mother? I tiptoed barefoot into her room, but her bed was as empty as though she had gone forever. My heart sank in my chest, and the question I did not want to ask myself floated on the surface of my consciousness. If it was my mother, what would I do? I heard my heart beats but I stopped myself thinking. One question kept pestering me. I tried to breathe regularly and counted on my fingers, one, two, three, as though something was bound to happen before I got to ten. I fell into the coma of sleep. I heard the strange sound, the sobbing of the wounded animal. I got out of bed, tiptoeing barefoot. I saw him in the bare lounge. It was my father with his huge body, his bulky nape of the neck and his frizzy black hair. He was lying on top of a girl who was not my mother, pressing hard on her worn-out body with a bizarre kind of violence as though she was a floor mop. I held up the knife I got from the kitchen as high as I could, and brought it down on my father's neck. I woke up from the dream all soaking in my sweat. My hands were clean of any blood. How often had I seen this dream since my childhood? I've been seeing it time and again, a hundred times almost, since he left us.

I slipped under the covers, shuddering as though I was in the grip of fever. I fell into the oblivion of sleep then woke up at one o'clock in the morning. I remembered a movie I had seen a month earlier. The son lived with his mother because his father had divorced her to marry another woman. His mother worked as a cleaner to pay for his education, food, clothes, and a new pair of shoes instead of the old worn ones. She refused to marry and dedicated her life to him, suffering humiliation and indignity to provide him with a life of dignity. All this was for nothing. He held up a knife and killed her when he caught her with a man.

I disappeared under the covers as though suffering from a bout of fever. I shut my eyes and tried to refrain from thinking. I counted on my fingers, one, two, three, as though something was going to happen before I got to ten, as though my mind would disintegrate and get blown into smithereens over the pillow. The knife in the son's hand seemed to carve off my flesh. Spots of blood covered the sheet. Did I commit a crime while sleeping?

My teeth clattered and my heartbeat accelerated. I could not tell whether I was the murderer or the victim. I sobbed soundlessly in the stillness of the night. I needed the sympathy or pity of some human being. Nobody, however, could help me out of this quandary. Nobody could share the pain I felt in my bones.

I heard the sound of the key turning in the door. I was all ears listening to the sounds of barefoot steps on the floor of the lounge. Did my mother take off her shoes to drown her presence in the silence? I hid my head under the covers. Now I was in the same position as the son. I heard the suppressed sobs of the wounded animal and the thud of the two bodies crashing against the floor. I could not distinguish the man's voice from my mother's. I tried to stop my mind filled with people's talk. I tried to cancel the present moment and replace it with another which was free of shame. The word *shame* pierced my ears like a blazing hot rod.

Pain! Pain seeped through my brain, taking it apart then taking it apart yet again, until it was transformed into a different brain, a clearer brain, a clean nascent brain. I fell asleep at dawn then woke up. I heard my mother's voice calling me to drink my morning milk. It was the first day of spring, Mothers' Day. Now I was at the moment of truth. I got up and went to the bathroom. I looked into the mirror. The two eyes filled with sunlight looked at me.

ह▪ Translated by Amira Nowaira, Cairo, 1999.

20

A Paper that was Never Presented
for Publication

This paper may never see the light,
because the subject oversteps all the red lines.
So I resorted to symbolism and imagination,
to fool the authorities and the powers that be.
And because I was unexpectedly dispatched to the other world
I could not attend the conference.
Would women ever become free
if they continued to wait,
squatting like hens,
with the doors all shut,
and the police everywhere?
They are incapable of protesting,
and she always arrives late,
and sits like a goddess on the throne,
peering down at them from the high podium,
her eyes lethargic,
noticing their vulgar make-up
and their plain faces.
An eloquent speech was composed for her
about the great achievements made
for the liberation of women.
Amazement appears on the faces of the audience

and roads are emptied of people.
Everybody goes home,
feeling down in the dumps,
because the conference has come to an end
without producing a single result,
without liberating a single woman.

Write my daughter so that you may live

Writing was forbidden
to both women and slaves,
because their destiny was to die,
and because immortality was reserved
for male gods alone.
In my childhood I used to be afraid,
so terrified that I obeyed
the commands of God, and King,
the commands of nation, father and mother.
My mother always came last,
even though she was the only one I saw,
the first face I got to know,
and the first voice I heard.
Though first, she was pushed to be last.
She wrote in secret and hid her words underground.
Like me she was afraid, and so she died.
But before breathing her last, she said to me,
'Don't follow in my footsteps, child.
Write... write so that you may live.'

In the autumn of 1981, a sense of gloom filled the women prisoners
in my cell. Death was the ghost that haunted our existence. Without
much ado, the poem sprang up like a giant inside me, resisting
despair, challenging death. I heard my angry voice saying, 'We won't
die, and if we did, we wouldn't die silently. We won't proceed in
the dark without creating a fuss. We have to get angry, stamping
forcefully on the ground and shaking the heavens. We won't die

without having broken the iron fence. Should we then die, we would not die in silence.'

Memoirs from the Women's Prison 1981

In my secret diary in 1947 while I was still a boarding pupil at Helwan Secondary School, this poem was written in black ink, but it is permanently engraved in my mind and on paper:

> Every night before I descend into sleep, I say to myself
> the morning will definitely come and I won't die,
>   and even if I did,
> nothing would hurt me after death:
> failing my exams, being beaten
> on the knuckles with the ruler,
> feeling the bitter cold, the scorching sun, or the fires of hell,
>   all cannot touch me.
> There was nobody in the dorm to ask except my friend.
>   So I asked her, 'Do we die?
> Does it hurt to die? Where are we?'
> Now here in the morgue, in the land of no place and no time,
> love does not exist except after we burn up in the blaze
> and turn to ashes, like the sands of the Helwan desert.
> It's, my friend, as though we had perished before our time.
> I've seen this scene in my dream, and I knew we were
>   proceeding
> to some unfamiliar place. Shall I turn out tomorrow to be
>   the person I want?
> A poet, a revolutionary, or even a sinner?
> Shall I see my name on a banned book? Shall I reach the sky
> with my pen and make the rain obey my command?
> Shall I make the day, the poetry, and the prose
> flow from my sinfulness? Let God burn me in hell
> and let the earth drink my blood, but I shall not die.

Helwan Secondary School 1947

☙ Translated by Amira Nowaira, October 2002.

21

Sixteen Short Poems

There is a man

There is a man for whom the women clamour.
Designated a great writer, thinker or whatever,
he writes a daily column in a major paper.
His image appears within a picture frame,
smiling, sometimes sulking,
with his full face or profile.
By soaring high he reaches rock bottom,
killing the victim among us and rewarding the criminal,
trailing after emperors like an ostrich
or a meek lamb,
and carving in history his name as well as his father's
        and grandfather's.
One day he told me 'I love you',
So I said, 'Show me what you have.'
But he had nothing,
except for what lay between his thighs.

Cairo 1975

A half-man

My friend is married to a man married also to another.
He divides his life fairly and squarely between them,
one half for my friend and the second half for the other woman.
A married man once came to me and said 'I love you.'
I asked him what he wanted.
He said a lawful wife in accordance with God's precepts.
I said being a whole woman I could not accept half a man.
He went livid and accused me of heresy.
Pointing his gun at my head, he said,
'Death to the woman who does not know God.'
So I pointed my gun at his head saying,
'Death to the half men.'
So he retracted and went back to his wife.

Those who saw God

A ruler once said that he saw God.
His rival retorted saying,
'I saw God before you did.'
Another rival over power said,
'But I saw Him before either of you.'
So they all fought together,
each saying that he had seen God before the other impostor.
I said they were all impostors who have not seen God any of them.
They asked, 'Hasn't anybody really seen God?'
I said, 'I saw God in my childhood, my mother saw Him in her
        youth and my grandmother saw Him in her advanced years.'
They said, 'Your words are heresy. God does not appear
    to women.'

Cairo 1977

Rewarding the culprit
and twice punishing the victim

He desired a young woman who was not easy to get.
With a head on her shoulders, she was much prouder of it
than any other part of her body.
He followed her on her way back from school
and kidnapped her with two others.
In a deserted house they raped her, one after the other.
Then they dumped her on the street.
A court sentenced all three of them to death.
One of them, however, proposed to marry her.
So the victim was punished twice and the criminal was rewarded.
All three were released without bail,
in accordance with article 291 of the current law.

Cairo 1998

An interim husband

Like other husbands with a fiery temper
he flung the divorce statement at his wife thoughtlessly.
Whenever his boss rebuked him,
he would yell at the top of his voice, 'You're divorced, divorced,
        divorced.'
So his wife, according to the law, was duly divorced.
Then he would take her back as soon as his rage subsided
or when his boss smiled at him.
One time he wanted to take her back, but the legislator would not
        accept,
'No, brother, you can't take her back before she weds another man.
It's your punishment
for flying into a temper.'
So the woman asked, 'Why should I sleep with a man I don't
        want?
This is punishment for me and not for my husband.'
But the legislator did not hear what the woman said.

Cairo 1976

A different woman

I am a completely feminine woman.
I don't submit to the law of obedience,
I don't pluck my eyebrows,
And neither do I apply kohl to my eyes
Or sway on my high heels.
I honour my promises without fail.
With the first morning ray
I drink my coffee,
I write my poem.
I walk through the city before sunset,
carrying my candle,
looking for a single person capable of keeping promises,
a person who comes precisely on time
and never lags behind as other people do.
A person who does not stand idly by,
or lower his head
before the president.

Cairo 1983

Thieves of honour

The thieves of honour are men who speak about nothing else
except honour.
They have sex within marriage as outside it,
pretending to be honourable.
They cheat on their wives with the wives of other men,
with mistresses, black slaves and servants,
with white foreigners and secretaries,
then claim that they are honourable men
who have loyalty to the nation.
They are never punished
because they have the law,
Shari'a and the constitution
on their side.

Cairo 1990

In full view of everyone

I had a daughter called Courage.
I left her ill in Baghdad,
trembling in the winter cold,
without food, medicine or cover.
I opened the newspaper yesterday
and saw the depraved American
accusing her of disobeying
international legitimacy, UN resolutions,
Security Council, and the inspection committee.
She was hit by a cruise missile
in full view of all
who anxiously followed the scene.
Our Arab rulers
secretly meet the great powers
and receive aid
like beggars.
And I am chained to my bed,
disarmed and my mouth muzzled.
My daughter Courage is dying
in full view of everyone.

Cairo 1991

Arab rulers

I feel ashamed when I see them meekly sitting
in front of their superiors abroad,
like virgins smiling timidly and demurely.
They listen and obey, and never raise their voices
when they speak,
and never cross their legs
when they sit.
They place their crossed arms over their hearts
when they stand.
But once they're home, they turn into tigers,

their voices blaring through microphones and amplifiers.
They sit with their legs arrogantly crossed,
The soles of their shoes almost piercing the eyes of those sitting
to their left or right.
Each one of them carries the title of 'servant of the people'
although he is nothing but
their gladiator.

Cairo 1993

Arab rulers once again

They are men who are dressed to kill, brought together only by
    the American president,
only the American president.
He sets them off one against the other.
They engage in wars against each other
and against their people
in the name of international legitimacy or democracy.
He pays them to topple one another,
and implicates them in his plans under the illusion of aid.
They compete to please him and starve their nation,
terrorizing both men and women.
They come to grief only too late.
So they hold a meeting called
the Arab summit,
then they go back home
and the story starts all over again.

Cairo 1999

They said you were shame personified

Oh mother, you gave birth to us, and spent your whole life
nurturing us, all gratis.
Please be merciful to us because we gave up on you,
because we could not face the merciless patriarchal authority,
the more merciless power of the state,

and successive family men.
They have wiped out your name from our memory,
hoping we would forget you forever
and feel no pride in you
or in carrying your name.
They said you were shame incarnate
and should be hidden away from view.
They said you were a woman and should have no voice.
Even though you are the source of existence,
this vast universe has become too small to keep you, mother.
Take us to your warm tender bosom,
to the first sip of water and the first morsel of bread,
to your first word of love and justice.
All words have now turned into knives assassinating us
        one after the other.

Cairo 1984

The sin suspended in history

My mother wrote my name in my birth certificate as
Eve.
Eve means life which engenders everything.
Virtue, honour and good all come from Eve
because Eve was the first to savour the taste of knowledge,
while Adam skulked behind,
tasting knowledge after her
and in compliance with her insistence and encouragement.
Without Eve there would be no humanity
and no knowledge.
Why then did Adam receive God's words
in the singular and not the dual form that includes Eve as well?

Cairo 1991

Inspired by the verdict pronounced by an Al-Azhar sheikh legitimizing the restoration of the hymen

I would not restore my virginity.
In fact as in dreams I've lost it.
From my memory I've removed it.
I began to smile back at the sunshine every morning,
write a poem to share with others,
or play a tune as birds sing their songs.
But they came to ask me:
Where is your virginity?
I said I lost it in my childhood.
They said they would restore it to me with the surgeon's scalpel.
I said, 'My dear sirs, I would not have it restored.
I leave you the freedom
to restore your own virginity if you wish.'

Cairo 1999

Daughter of Egyptian Isis

My mother gave birth to me and left me a child
under the mercy of the state.
My father hated the king and the English
while his friends and colleagues demonstrated
against the regime.
So I had a windowless prison
and lived in a home with a man who was my jailor.
I had a dream that got snatched by a vulture,
a mind of my own and a star in the sky
which was mine,
and a tree I embraced in the prison yard.
I learnt to break rules and traditions,
and to improvise a new script,
for I am a woman from Egypt.

Cairo 1988

My grandmother

In my childhood I had a grandmother
Who told me my first stories of love.
Opening the door at dawn and going on to the fields,
she received the dew on her bare face.
She planted, watered and returned home with her produce,
her gown smelling of cotton buds,
and orange, fig and mulberry flowers.
At sunrise the smell of her bread would rise high
and at sunset her chicken soup would nourish me.
I buried my head in my chest and slept,
fearing no conquerors or tyrants,
trampling on the king's picture
and chanting against the British.

Cairo 1992

My mother

Who fostered the hostility between us?
Who made me look up to the sky
but never see you?
And read history
but never find you?
And extend my eyes to life, religion and the state
but never see your name?
Why have they crossed out your name, mother?
If I said I was your daughter, they would go mad and say:
'You're your father's daughter, carrying his name from cradle
        to grave.
Should he divorce your mother, he will be your guardian.
A woman can be the guardian of nobody
even when she becomes a minister in the government or a
        president.'

Cairo 1997

 ✺   Translated by Amira Nowaira.

22

Inspired by the Summit Meeting
with the Elite

THE SOUND OF HANDS CLAPPING rings in your ears. The dream persists in spite of the arrival of the morning light. An invitation card to the meeting arrives, its edges all decorated in gold and carrying the eternal stamp that has survived from the days of the Pharaohs. The time is ten o'clock sharp at the Great Auditorium, one whole hour and a half before the start of the event. Formal dress and tie are a must.

You wrap something like a scarf around your neck, and twist another long scarf to create the shape of a turban around your head. Your hair disappears from the eyes of all men, except his. He closes his eyes and yawns three times. He swallows the blue pill with some water and goes back to sleep, continuing his dream about the pretty secretary who punches at the computer. She looks like the fair intern of the White House.

You swallow the bitterness in your mouth. In two days you will be forty-five. The figure has an ominous ring in your ears evoking the menopause, or the age of despair. He is thirty years older than you and yet he gulps down the Viagra without any despondency or despair. He married you when you were eighteen, still dreaming of the boy your age, born with you in the same year of defeat.

By wearing the veil, you impose seclusion on yourself. Men are everywhere: on streets, and buses, and standing in neighbouring windows. In your dream, they compete for you, drawn to you by the glow in your eyes lined with kohl and by the repressed invitation on your red lips. You press the lipstick on those same lips before you leave the house. You put a dash of blusher on your cheeks and apply some shadow over your eyelids. You spray some perfume under your armpits.

You walk slowly as if you were a government minister, your hefty body swaying above your high heels. You straighten your back and neck, while on your head sits the turban, allowing nobody to glimpse even a single hair. Everything is permissible except for that little hair to appear.

You get ready for the important meeting. You wear the new suit made of English wool, its colour continental blue and with a pattern of red flowers. It caught your eye walking down Regent Street in London while you were attending a conference on religions two years ago. You keep it hanging in your cupboard, wrapped in transparent nylon, and take it out into the light only on special occasions. On your chest you place the golden brooch with the diamond stone. You fix the pearls around your turban and a few pieces of jewellery around your neck and wrist.

You come down the marble stairs of the new villa. You hear the sound of your pointed heels as they click against the floor. You look at your gold watch a little nervously. You are worried about arriving late. Inside your bag, which you hold under your armpit, you feel the presence of the invitation card, carrying your full name, your official title in the ministry, and your eminent position in both elected and appointed chambers.

The driver opens the door of your long black car for you. The windows are tightly closed, allowing no noise or dust, their dark tint concealing the inside while the outside is clear to your eyes. Like ministers, ambassadors, kings and presidents who use the same huge cars, you experience the voyeuristic pleasure of seeing without being seen.

From behind the dark glass you see ghosts walking in fog; their faces are pale and livid or fat and flabby, and their eyes are half-shut in a coma-like trance. The high walls are covered with ads showing naked women sitting on top of cars, with guns in their hands and a Dunhill cigarette between their lips.

Since you got married you have become indifferent to everything: sex, love stories and eating popcorn in movie theatres. You have become so indifferent that you stopped even talking. Nothing is left of life's pleasures except food and compulsive shopping. But the pleasures of the afterlife are certainly more lasting. In the dream you see the palace in paradise, the silver cups carried by little boys. You are attracted to the boy your age whose phantom roams around your bed all night long. You try to chase the phantom away by reading the Surat of the Throne in the Qur'an. It can chase away all the spirits and *jinnis*, but not this boy.

Your car stops at the security check. It is protected by guards, government spies, and men who look from behind their black glasses. You stand in a long line with three hundred others. You are amazed at the number of those invited. You had thought that the select few were few in number. But they turned out to be quite a lot, each one of them carrying the title of great thinker. They arrive two hours before the appointment wearing imported, well-ironed woollen suits. It is clear that the muscles of their legs wobble underneath their tailored trousers. Around their necks is tied the well-knotted tie. Their hair is dyed pitch black, and their sunken eyes and swollen eyelids tell their real age. Their noses shine with the ecstasy of the Viagra, and they walk slowly and languidly. At the door they shove and push like school children wanting to enter first.

The door is as narrow as a prison gate, not allowing anyone to enter with his head held high. It allows no more than one person at a time and sideways. You stand at the end of the line. You have imagined that you would be first, but it turns out you have come last. The select few always arrive before you wherever you go. They manage to sniff the odour of authority well ahead of you, a gift that has been inherited from the days of serfdom and confirmed by the male genome map.

Your head bends low on entering and your body twists and turns. You swallow the humiliation with your bitter saliva. Nothing consoles you except the fact that you are not alone in this. If the affliction is general, you will be exempted from blame. In the line ahead are all the faces you see on newspapers, screens, and magazine and book covers.

The ritual of admission is long and tedious because of the congestion, the broken electronic eye and the insistence of the security to strip you of your clothes in spite of the fact that you do not take them off. After the inspection, you enter the great hall where a picture the size of the globe hangs near the ceiling, secured by nails that are as steadfast as the national principles. With a pair of dark glasses on the eyes, he hides behind a pillar of smoke like a god.

All the front rows are reserved. Their seats are made of red velvet and have golden edges. Stuck on the back of each seat is a piece of paper on which is written the name and the title. Seating is arranged according to rank. First come the ministers, ambassadors, advisers, the clergy, the police and the media, followed by the singers, broadcasters, musicians, some scientists and astrologers, psychiatrists and soothsayers. At last come the literary people, the novelists, both realists and dreamers. No one can play truant. If one happened to be undergoing a heart operation in the hospital, one would soon come out of anaesthesia and arrive two hours before the time, wearing a formal suit and a tie, with the jacket all buttoned up. One would sit with the rest folding arms and legs, feet imprisoned in a shiny shoe crossed underneath the chair and getting swollen from prolonged sitting. One would sit one hour after another without going out to the toilet because all the doors are closed, allowing nobody in or out.

Then the high-pitched shout is heard. All jump to their feet clapping. You find yourself clapping vigorously with the right hand against the left nonstop. The beats within your chest become irregular. Your chest rises and falls imperceptibly. Minutes pass but the clapping does not stop. Magic hands open a secret door in the wall. All eyes are riveted on the open door, mesmerized. Then the procession slowly files in. The guards come in first in civilian clothes. The door stays open without any one appearing. Silence reigns for a few moments as if death has overtaken the whole place.

Then the sparkling mass appears. The flashes, lenses and cameras all light up. You cannot see the face even if you stretch your neck as far as you can. The silvery lights melt in the texture of the ironed suit. The shoulders are padded and the broad chest looks like a shield.

The cheering continues during your sleep and does not stop even in the morning. You do not know whether this is the truth or a dream. You sit and clap with the others, the hands all raised up. Nobody excepted. As you clap you feel humiliated, but swallow your humiliation with your bitter saliva. Nothing consoles you except the fact that everybody else is clapping. If the epidemic is general, you are not to blame. Your eyes inspect the hall looking for one person who is not clapping. You see him sitting at the other end of the last row, the boy your age who was born with you in the same year of defeat. He keeps his hands resting at his sides, not raising them high. He is the only one not clapping.

2🌑 Translated by Amira Nowaira, Cairo, 1998.

23

The Impact of Fanatic Religious Thought:
A Story of a Young Egyptian Muslim Woman

AN EGYPTIAN man had been very strict with his daughter, only permitting her to work outside the home on condition that she be completely isolated from men. She found that 'ideal' job. Many months later, in the spring of 1988, this same man brought his daughter to my office to see me in my capacity as a psychiatrist. The following is based on the young woman's true story. Egyptian television wanted to produce a film based on this story — on condition that the protagonist not be a veiled woman, as she was in real life.

A few days ago a young woman came to me. She told me her story and asked me to write a prescription. I didn't prescribe any medication. I don't believe that pills can cure this young woman. The problem seems to be psychological and social. This is why I would like the readers to consider this case.

Last year the young woman began staring into space at night without sleeping. When she goes off to sleep she sees a flood inundating the land and the Prophet Noah embarking on his ship and leaving her behind. She finds herself in life after death, walking on a narrow path with the inferno lying below her. Her feet are bleeding and her body, off balance, is about to fall. She opens her eyes and finds herself asleep in bed under the blankets drowning in her own sweat. She reads the opening sura of the Qur'an and thanks God that she hasn't died yet and has a chance to repent. She goes to the bathroom and washes five times. She dresses herself in a long, loose robe and wraps her head with a thick cloth. After she prays she sits with God's book in her lap, reading and asking God for forgiveness for her grave sin. There is nothing in her life except that sin.

Since she was born she has gone to bed hearing the voice of her father reciting the Qur'an. Since infancy her face has not been seen by a stranger. During her student years she never talked to anyone. After graduation she went to work in a place where there was no one other than herself — a storeroom in the basement of a small museum never visited by anyone. There she would sit at her desk with a register in front of her recording the number of mummies that came in to be stored or registering the ones already there. She would dust the mummies with a small yellow cloth. She would count them and record them in the register. She would close the register and put it in a drawer. Then she would open up God's book and read until the time the employees leave work. Carrying her handbag she would walk for an hour and a half to her home. She would cover the distance with a steady, controlled pace, no movement of her body discernible under her thick robe.

Her head, wrapped in the black cloth, she kept inclined towards the ground. In the heat and cold she walked the distance twice a day, back and forth. She did not ride the bus so that no one would brush against her from behind. She did not take a taxi alone with an unknown driver. At home she washed off the dust from the road, performing her ablutions and praying before she ate. After she ate she would go to sleep with God's book under her pillow. She would wake at the sound of her father's voice calling her to fix his food. After he eats he prays and asks God to protect his daughter from the Devil. If it were not for the forty-seven pounds every month he would not have let her leave the house. He is an old man without an income and she has no husband to support her. Nobody approached her for marriage except the son of his sister, who is penniless and unemployed. If God had sent her a husband in sound financial condition she would not have left the house.

In her room she would pace up and down in prayer. She did not ask God to send her a husband. Since childhood she has dismissed the idea of marriage. Her mother died haemorrhaging when her husband hit her after she had gone to bed. Death was inevitable, but she wanted to die in a different way, not by being beaten. There was no man in her life. She knew nothing about the other sex. If she heard music or singing coming from the neighbours' houses she would plug her ears with her fingers and shut the windows and doors tight.

One day last April she was sitting as usual at her desk. She had finished counting the mummies and statues when she discovered a statue that was not there the day before. She looked back over the entries in the register, closed it and put it back in the drawer. She opened God's book and started to read without a sound, her head bowed. While she was reading, her eyes peered through the two narrow holes of the black cloth and moved around the mummies and statues.

They became fixed on the face of that statue. The features were carved in a strange way. The strangest of all were the eyes. They were looking at her with a movement in the pupils that she had never seen before in any other statue. She asked God's forgiveness. She asked God to protect her from the Devil. She bowed her head to continue reading but her eyes moved involuntarily towards the statue, which was smaller than the other statues. The dust covered it as if it had been neglected for years in the storeroom. She removed the dust from the statue, putting it near the window. She returned to reading God's book but her eyes peered through the two small holes, attracted by the face of the statue and its eyes with their strange movement. The eyes were slanted slightly upwards like Ancient Egyptians' eyes. She held the statue in her hand covered with a black glove and started looking for a symbol or letters that might reveal the name of the person or the time he lived. There was nothing. She put the statue back and returned to her seat behind the desk. Her eyes settled on the lines in God's book. But the question turned around in her head: has anybody else before her seen this movement in the eyes of the statue?

No other person worked in the museum except the old woman who was the manager. She would come down to her from time to time inspecting the entries in the inventory and passing her eyes over the statues one after the other; she might stop at one that would draw her attention. That day her eyes passed over the small statue without being attracted by anything. The young woman was puzzled. Why hadn't the director seen the movement in the eyes of the statue that she saw? The same question nagged her every day.

Now, as soon as she enters the office and sits down, her eyes settle on the face of the statue. The movement in his eyes is still there. Now it becomes a movement especially for her. He looks nowhere with these eyes except at her. Since she saw the statue for the first time she has never stopped looking at it. If she turns her head away or leaves the office his eyes are always in front of her, continually looking at her with the same expression, as if he were alive now, not seven thousand years ago. In his gaze there is no arrogance of the Pharaoh gods nor humility of the slaves. What is in it? She does not know. Every day she is overcome by her desire to know. This grows day after day into a sinful desire. Whenever she sits at her desk she looks around her, afraid that the director might suddenly appear and catch her while she is looking into the statue's eyes. The thing she fears most is that an order will be issued to transfer him to another storeroom. When she goes to bed she is unable to sleep. What happens if she returns to her office in the morning and does not see him? Since finding him she has started to walk to her office with a faster pace, and when she opens the door and enters, her eyes peer through the two holes looking for his face among the faces of the other statues. When she sees the movement in his eyes her closed lips part with a faint sigh beneath the black cloth.

One day she entered her office and she did not find him. She searched all over the storeroom but he wasn't there. She looked in every corner, below the legs of the large statues, on the floor where hundreds of small statues were lying. He wasn't there. She returned to her desk to sit down. She couldn't write anything in the register and she couldn't read a single line in God's book. Her head was bent and her heart was heavy: Where did he go? His place next to the window is vacant. The whole universe is empty. There is nothing in her whole life. Nothing at all. Her hand under the black glove is cold and the blood in her veins stops moving. All around her she sees nothing but death in the shape of stone statues. Sitting at her desk she herself is also dying.

She lifts her eyes with an abrupt movement, in the same way that air rushes out of the chest before the last breath, and sees him hiding behind the windowpane. The director, if she had appeared at this moment, would not have understood what has happened. The young woman's outside appearance is the same. She is sitting in her chair behind her desk with the register in front of her. Her head is bent and nothing in her moves except the black pupils visible through the two holes and the hot blood rushing in the veins under her skin.

Before leaving that day she hid him in her handbag to take him home with her. In the morning she brought him back to his place. The director did not notice his absence and reappearance. At home her father did not notice that the statue was inside her wardrobe. At night after her father sleeps she takes him out of the wardrobe and places him in front of her and does not stop looking at his face. She sleeps with her eyes fixed on his eyes. In her dream she sees him standing while a flood inundates the earth. She sees him standing in front of her in flesh and blood. And the flood inundating the land and the Prophet Noah climbing into his ark and leaving without him. Could it be that he is the son of the Prophet Noah who did not get into the ark and was drowned? Could it be that he is a sinner who followed the Devil and not a believer who followed God? And, more important, is it possible for him to come back to life after dying seven thousand years ago?

In the morning when she opens her eyes, the question spins in her head. She walks down the street to her office with her head bent, afraid to raise her eyes. Afraid she will see him in front of her in flesh and blood the same way she saw him in her dream. Through the two small holes in the black cloth her eyes start to move, to rise slowly, glancing cautiously in the faces of the passers-by. Perhaps among these human beings there is a face that resembles his? Or eyes with the same look?

Two months pass and she does not stop this thinking. Her eyes do not stop stealing a glance at the faces of people on the street as she moves back and forth between home and office. Sixty days pass and among the faces she does not see a single one that looks like his or among the eyes any that have his look. She sleeps restlessly and while she sleeps the dream recurs. She sees the earth inundated in a sea of water and herself standing at the entrance to the city, and suddenly she sees him in front of her. Now he does not notice her presence. He walks calmly forward, then turns around and looks at her. In his eyes is the same look, which never changes. The water covers him from all sides. He keeps looking at her until he disappears under the water. His eyes are the last to disappear.

In the morning she opens her eyes with the roaring of the water still in her ears. The voices screaming for help are muffled by the sound of the crashing waters. In the moment between sleep and wakefulness the dream seems to be the destruction of her town seven thousand years ago which she has seen with her own eyes. He was drowned seven thousand years ago among those God took in the flood. She continues lying on her bed. It is late for getting to the office. She rises, her body heavy, and in the mirror she sees her eyes red and full of tears. With a touch of her finger she recognizes real tears. She knows she was weeping over his drowning. What made her weep most was that he was not a follower of God.

She recognizes clearly that he was a follower of the Devil. No matter, tears continue to gush from her eyes as she stands in front of the mirror. It is as if he has died at that very moment, not seven thousand years ago.

On her way to the office that morning as she stopped at an intersection, she lifted her eyes to look at the traffic light when suddenly she saw him among the people crossing the street. She recognized him immediately. The face was his face — the Ancient Egyptian features. The eyes were his eyes. In them there was the movement and the look. Involuntarily her body lunged towards him. She was about to grab him by the hand but she stopped at the last moment. Her closed lips parted under the black cloth crying, 'You?'

The street was crowded with people rushing along their way. They stopped, amazed at the scene. They saw her rushing towards him, and him fleeing from her. It is not normal for a young woman, walking in the street, to rush in this way towards a man she does not know. And she is not just any young woman. She is a creature of whose being nothing is visible except through two small holes in a black cloth. She is rushing towards him and he is escaping from her with fast steps. The scene appears to the onlookers both strange and amusing.

Their laughter rang in her ears and she shrank under her thick clothing. She continued to shrink all day long sitting at her desk with the register in front of her. Her head was bent. Only her eyes moved towards the window where he stood in his place. His face was the same, and his eyes had the same movement and a look more human than the eyes of the people in the street even though he died seven thousand years ago with those who drowned in the flood. She wept for his death. Every human being dies but the stone statue lives seven thousand years. Is the stone more permanent than humans?

The question turns around in her head without an answer. Now she has a friend made of stone. She feels his presence more than the presence of any human being with a body. The word 'body' escapes from between her closed lips without a sound. The word in itself produces a shiver in her own body. She doesn't know exactly where the shiver is. Through the two holes, from under the thick cloth, her eyes steal a look at her body. In her chest there is a heart that beats. In her head there are veins through which blood flows hot as air. Her mind understands that her friend is nothing but a statue of stone. But she sees in his eyes the look of one about to speak.

Is it possible he will speak? And in what language? In Arabic or Ancient Egyptian? Is it fantasy or reality? And if it is fantasy where does it come from? Does her imagination mix with the blood in her veins and head? The question turns in her head with the movement of blood like a whirlpool in the sea. And the water drowns her like a flood and he is standing in front of her and in his eyes there is a human look. Deep inside herself she is sure he is a human being — more human than all the people in the universe. He cannot be an

evil person. She can swear in full consciousness that he is a follower
of God and not of the Devil.

She was fully conscious. If anyone saw her they would have no
doubt about this. Her father sees her the same way he sees her
every day: full of modesty, totally covered, going to her office and
returning home on time. The director of the museum sees her
sitting conscientiously with the register in front of her, and when
she finishes the inventory there is nothing in front of her except the
Book of God. On the road she walks in her measured step with her
head lowered.

One day while she was walking she turned her eyes and through
the two holes saw him step out of the door of a house and cross the
street with calm steps, mindless of the screaming horns. She saw
him. The same person. She could not mistake him after all these
days.

Her feet were nailed to the ground. Her hand inside the black
glove was raised over her heart. He was standing in the middle of
the street. Around him the cars were rushing like the flood. She
thought he would fall and be drowned among the wheels but he
did not fall. He continued walking in his calm pace towards Nile
Street. Her body rushed after him.

She recognizes that he is a phantom and not a reality. But she
sees him with her eyes. So long as she sees him with her eyes she
doesn't care whether he is a phantom. Her feet walk behind him.
In her ears she hears the sound of his shoes on the pavement. He
is only a few steps ahead of her. If she speaks to him it is possible
he will hear her.

She does not know what to call him. He doesn't have a name.
Her sealed lips under the thick cloth part with a sound: 'You.' She
sees him turn around and look at her, face to face. She recognizes
that it is him.

The eyes are his eyes and the expression is his expression. She
hears him say, 'Who are you?' His surprise silences her. She stands
nailed to the street. He spoke in Arabic not ancient Egyptian. She
thought he knew her as she knows him. How is it that she knows
him all this time and he asks, 'Who are you?' She stands looking

at him, without moving. Then she directs her eyes towards the ground. Her head remains lowered for a long time as she shrinks in shame inside herself. After all this he asks her who she is. Her mind does not believe it. She lifts her eyes once more to be sure of what is happening but he has turned around and gone his own way, disappearing among the people.

The second day on the way to her office her head is lowered as usual but her eyes are moving like two bees behind the two holes looking at the faces of the people. Her mind says to her that he is no longer living, that he lived seven thousand years ago, but her eyes never stop searching. Her mind tells her he exists. She has seen him. So long as he exists she can see him again. She is overtaken by the wish to see him in any shape. Let him be made of flesh and blood or of spirit without body. What is important is that she sees him. What is the difference whether he is a spirit or a body so long as she is able to see him?

She waited in the same place where she had met him yesterday.

When he appeared in the street, fully conscious she lunged towards him. It was him, with his face and eyes and human expression. Nothing had changed except that a black moustache had grown over his upper lip. Her closed lips part underneath the thick cloth emitting a word without a sound: 'Male!' Never before in her whole life could she utter that word. She thought, he was simply a human being without sex but this moustache means that he is... Her feet remained nailed to the ground, her hand inside the black glove was raised up to cover the two small holes in the thick cloth.

When she lifted her hand from her eyes the street was still crowded, but he was no longer standing in front of her. She was still standing modestly, completely conscious. Hanging from her shoulder, secure in the cavity between her arm and chest, was her leather handbag. It pressed through the thick cloth next to her left breast. She felt the touch as if it were electricity. Her mind recognized that it was only a leather handbag with nothing inside it except her purse and the small statue of stone. But the touch continued to run from her left breast like electricity.

She went home that day without her handbag. Without opening it she threw it in a large dump. She even left her purse inside. She imagined that if she opened it she would see him. She had become afraid of seeing him. She did not know why she was afraid. But she started to shake with fear. The fear accompanied her all the way home. She lay down on her bed. She realized that the handbag was no longer with her. She thought that the fear would leave her but until morning the fear never left her. On the second day the fear continued to accompany her in the street, in the office, in the house, everywhere. It accompanied her like the trembling of a feverish person. One night her father heard her moaning in a low voice. Her body shook with the trembling like a person racked with malaria. Her father took her to a doctor. She took medicine for thirty days but the fever remained. At night her father heard her speaking to somebody as she said her prayers. He thought she was speaking to God, asking his forgiveness. But her voice became louder and her words became clearer. She was not talking to God. She was cursing the Devil in words that could never come from the lips of a pure young woman. He believed that she had committed a sin that she was keeping to herself, not daring to reveal it to anyone. He took her to a holy man to whom people repent their sins. But after her repentance her fever continued. And once more the pills the doctor prescribed failed. When the director of the museum visited her she said the young woman was not suffering from malaria but from a psychological condition. That is how she came to me.

❧ Paper presented to the Second International Conference of the Arab Women's Solidarity Association, 'Contemporary Arab Thought and Women', 3–5 November 1988; translation from the Arabic by Ali Badran and Margot Badran, published in *Noon* 3, November 1989, in *Index on Censorship Newsletter*, 15 February 1989, and *The Nawal El Saadawi Reader*, Zed Books, 1997.

PART THREE

Drama

24

Twelve Women in a Cell

THERE I WAS with eleven other prisoners, because Sadat had decided to put a stop to the opposition and silence all those whose voices didn't agree with his own. I remember on the day of my arrival, 6 September 1981, one of those Muslim sisters called out, on seeing me: 'Nawal El Saadawi, you deserve to be hanged for your writing.' However, several days later, this woman had become a friend. Reaching an understanding of each other, which seemed impossible at the outset, became more of a reality day by day.

Characters

SALMA Abou Khalil, young uneducated girl from the streets
ALIA Ibrahim Chawky, young woman, a freethinker, divorcée
SAMIRA el Fichawy, elderly teacher and fundamentalist Muslim
BASSIMA Charafel Din, elderly teacher and progressive Muslim
AZZA Mortada, slim, pretty, around 40, researcher, Westernised
LABIBA Tewfik, clerical worker, non-political, unhappily married
MADIHA Abdel Azim, atheist
NAGAT Soleiman, young Christian girl
HADIA Marzouk, unveiled Muslim
ETEDAL El Cheikh, high-school student and devout Muslim
NEFFISSA El Charkawy, university student and government spy

RACHIDA Zakaria, pregnant, devout Muslim
WARDEN, Fahima
ZOUBA the prostitute
ZEINAB the criminal
SABAH the beggar
POLICEMAN
GOVERNOR
INSPECTOR
RUBBISH COLLECTOR

Act One

Darkness, silence, an empty stage. The portrait of a man is hanging in a huge golden frame decked with a string of fairy lights. The facial features are stern, the eyes piercing; the smile is broad and sardonic. A faint spot of light signals the dawn. Birds sing. All is calm. SABAH *enters limping. She is wearing a threadbare djellaba; her hair dishevelled. Her face is stained with dark blotches, mud and tar. She sits on the ground to rummage through a pile of rubbish, singing sadly.*

SABAH (*sings*) Sad times these,
Bending double those who once lived well,
Giving myrrh to him to drink at his ease,
And the son-of-a-bitch ruling as he pleases,
Patience. Wisdom.
The pretender's unmasked.
A real charmer but his heart's full of smoke.
Patience… patience…
Everything in its time.
(SABAH *gets up, moves bent over and limping. She continues her lament in the same sad tone.*)

SABAH   Honest people thrown in the mud,
The son-of-a-bitch ruling as he pleases.
(*A* POLICEMAN *suddenly appears, seizes her violently by the neck.*)

POLICEMAN Come here you, beggar, daughter of a beggar. You've
    been told a thousand times that begging's against the law.
    And the law's what counts. Here's for you. (*He gives her a
    beating.*) What do you mean, eh? Take that and that.
    (*He continues to hit her.*)

SABAH (*moans*) Sing for the daughter. What does the bastard
    care?

POLICEMAN What daughter? What bastard? Move on.

SABAH They're going to take her in again. Whenever they see her
    they lock her up. They've got nothing else to do.
    (*The* POLICEMAN *pulls* SABAH *off. Sound of boots and police
    siren. Lights fade. The sound of a large key turning three times
    in a lock. A metal door opens and clanks shut.*)

SABAH Nothing else to do....
    (*A faint light. We find* SABAH *next to a small barred door in
    the prison's outer yard. The door leads to an inner yard and
    a second barred cell.* SABAH *puts her hand through the bars
    and tries to grab a tuft of watercress but she cannot reach it.
    The prison walls are very high, topped with barbed wire. The
    sound of a curlew singing —* SABAH *looks up.*)

SABAH (*Sings*) Patience... patience... Everything in its own good
    time.
    (*A* RUBBISH COLLECTOR *enters and sweeps up, leaving some of
    the rubbish behind.*)

RUBBISH COLLECTOR: Clear off, you're a gonner if the Warden sees
    you.

SABAH Where will she go?... She has nowhere to go?

RUBBISH COLLECTOR What? Nowhere to go? Aren't there enough
    rooms for you here?

SABAH There's nowhere for her: not inside or outside.

RUBBISH COLLECTOR There's plenty of room, why are you sitting
    there?

SABAH This is her place.

RUBBISH COLLECTOR Used to be for the likes of you, now it's for
    them, the politicals.

SABAH It's her place, it's her cress, they've taken it.

(*The* RUBBISH COLLECTOR *shoves her with his broom. She goes out singing. The dawn fades up and we see the beggars' cell. It is divided by a clothes line. Suitcases and boxes, a gas stove, a rubbish bin, beds and mattresses on the floor. To the right sit the veiled politicals, an old cloth spread as a prayer mat on the floor.* SAMIRA *kneels praying, face to the wall. Behind her kneel* RACHIDA, NEFFISSA *and* ETEDAL, *praying.* HADIA, *unveiled and with her hair loose, sits reading the Qur'an.* SALMA *stands on guard at the gate, watching the yard. To the left* BASSIMA *and* AZZA *lie on the beds.* MADIHA *and* NAGAT *make tea and* LABIBA *sits alone, head in hands*)

(*The prison* WARDEN *enters hurriedly.*)

SALMA   (*Rushing back.*) The warden!

(*The veiled women stop praying.* LABIBA *calmly crosses her arms.* MADIHA *and* NAGAT *hide the stove in a box.* BASSIMA *stands and lights a cigarette and* AZZA *puts rollers in her hair.*)

WARDEN   The Governor and the Inspector are coming today. There might be a search: I'll let you know. The police inspector has been in this morning. No hassle. I don't want them finding anything or they'll be down on me — and you. Won't they Madame Bassima?

BASSIMA   Of course, of course, God willing, there'll be no problems.

WARDEN   Get rid of that mirror.

SALMA   (*naively*) Why?

WARDEN   A woman died last year.

SALMA   Why?

RACHIDA   (*Gives* SALMA *a nudge.*) Don't you know why people kill themselves in prison, idiot?

(WARDEN *continues to search.*)

WARDEN   No money, no newspapers, no radio, no paper and no pen — with politicals — worse than a gun.

SALMA   I haven't got one. Don't know how to read or write.

(*The* WARDEN *goes to inspect the bathroom.*)

BASSIMA   (*worried*) If you've got something — hide it.

LABIBA (*angry*) Inspections, searches, haven't they anything better to do than give us this shit?

(*The* WARDEN *comes back.*)

WARDEN The washroom's filthy and the yard has to be swept and watered — I've been here for twenty years and I'm not lowering my standards now, am I Salma?

SALMA Why me? Why don't you ask Etedal or Hadia?

HADIA You do absolutely nothing all day.

SALMA And what do you do?

HADIA I read the Qur'an.

SALMA So it's work to read the Qur'an, is it?

SAMIRA What are you saying? May God forgive you. To read the words of God is the finest work there is.

WARDEN But if you're all reading the Qur'an, who's going to clean the washroom?

SAMIRA Some people do nothing, they don't read the Qur'an or pray — Let them clean the washroom.

(BASSIMA *lights a cigarette.*)

BASSIMA (*ironic*) Look Madame Fahima, I'm far too old to clean the floor. I never cleaned it at home, so why should I start here?

AZZA It's unthinkable one of us should have to do it.

LABIBA I have three domestics at home, Madame Fahima.

WARDEN I didn't mean... I know you're all educated and come from good families.

SALMA Does that mean I'm not from a good family?

WARDEN You're still young, my little Salma, you can't compare yourself to them.

SAMIRA Salma is the same as the rest of us and perhaps even better than some. At least she covers her head and respects God.

LABIBA How dare you?

WARDEN Calm down, ladies. I'll find someone else.

(*The* WARDEN *exits.*)

SAMIRA (*imitates* LABIBA) 'I have three domestics, Madame Fahima!' Look at who's sticking up for the working classes.

LABIBA Look at who's got nothing to do except read the Qur'an.

SAMIRA The world passes, only God remains.

LABIBA And who's going to work to feed you? God?

RACHIDA May God forgive you.

NEFFISSA The real food is from God and the real cleanliness is from your faith and dirt comes from...

SAMIRA Sinners!

BASSIMA Calm down. We've got more important things to worry about. Like the search.

(PRISON WARDEN *enters*.)

WARDEN I've found someone, from the prostitutes' cell. She's very clean.

SAMIRA (*Sits up*.) A prostitute? That's impossible.

RACHIDA/NEFFISSA (*together*) Outrageous!

WARDEN What's wrong with prostitutes? They're the cleanest of the lot. I've seen 'em all: Criminals, drug dealers, thieves and some of them are good people; it's life that's let them down. Lots of innocent people inside, ladies. Bet you never thought you'd land up in here. (SAMIRA *shrieks*.)

ALL What is it?

SAMIRA Cockroach.

(SALMA *squashes it with her slipper*.)

WARDEN Cockroaches, beetles and lizards. You'll get them all in here if you don't clean up. I'll get Zouba, she's a good girl.

SAMIRA Why stop there? Why not a thief or a murderer?

WARDEN They're just ordinary people, they simply had a moment of anger. Feel sorry for them.

(SABAH *appears at the bars*.)

SABAH Give her a pinch of cress.

SALMA (*to the* WARDEN) Who's that?

WARDEN It's forbidden to speak to the other prisoners. Clear off.

SABAH Get your filthy face out of here. (*Pointing to her face*.) That's life.

WARDEN Dead right. Get it out of here. The governor's coming.

SABAH This is the beggar's cell. She's here because she lives here. She planted the cress.

WARDEN Salma, give her a bit of cress.

(SALMA *gives her some watercress.* SABAH *eats it.*)

WARDEN Now go and get Zouba!

(SABAH *goes off and calls out loudly.*)

SABAH Zouba! Zouba!

WARDEN I forgot to tell you, Madame Bassima, once Zouba's
cleaned up, give her a couple of cigarettes.

BASSIMA In that case, we need some more. I've only got my own
and I can't give those up.

(NEFFISSA *stands in front of the door watching the yard.*
SALMA *wanders around and stops in front of the portrait.*)

SALMA (*pointing to the portrait*) Who's that man?

WARDEN Good God. That's not a man, girl. That's the Governor,
at the top.

SALMA Top of what?

WARDEN On top, on top, on top.

(*She indicates much higher than herself.*)

SALMA As high as the sky?

WARDEN Even higher.

SALMA Higher than the sky? Higher than God?

WARDEN Heavens above! Who's higher than God? You're joking.

RACHIDA Don't be stupid, he's the one who's put you here.

SALMA (*even more naively*) Does he know me? I don't know him.
Reminds me of someone.

RACHIDA (*mocking*) Perhaps he looks like your dad?

SALMA (*hurt*) I don't remember what he looks like. All I remember
is my mum's old man — I used to call him Dada. He looked
like this one. (*Everyone laughs.*)

WARDEN I don't know why they've put you in with the politicals.

SAMIRA I'll give my right hand if she's not putting it on.

BASSIMA (*whispers to* AZZA) I can't stand being in the same cell as
them.

(NEFFISSA *screams.*)

WARDEN What's up? Another cockroach?

NEFFISSA No. A man.

(NEFFISSA *runs to put on her veil and the others do the same.*)

WARDEN My God! It's the Governor!

(*The* PRISON WARDEN *rushes to open the gate to the outer yard.
The* GOVERNOR *appears, holding his cane regally. Behind him,
the* POLICE INSPECTOR, *wearing dark glasses. The* POLICE
INSPECTOR *raises his glasses and looks at the yard.*)

INSPECTOR (*to the* WARDEN) Nobody's cleaned in here!

WARDEN Sorry Sir. Right away Sir.

(*The* GOVERNOR *looks around. The* WARDEN *tries to stop him
going into the cell.*)

WARDEN (*spluttering*) A moment, Excellency, just give them time
to cover themselves.

GOVERNOR Nonsense. Let me in.

INSPECTOR This isn't just any man. Move aside, woman.

(*The* WARDEN *steps aside; the* GOVERNOR *goes toward the cell,
then stops at the entrance, hesitates.*)

GOVERNOR (*to* WARDEN) You're a woman. You check they've
covered themselves.

(*The* WARDEN *goes into the room. The veiled women are seated
to the right.* SAMIRA *is alone reading the Qur'an.* RACHIDA
and NEFFISSA *are completely covered.* HADIA *and* ETEDAL
reveal only their eyes; even their hands are covered. SALMA
*is sitting next to them, her head veiled, wearing a djellaba.
To the left, on a bedcover, are seated* BASSIMA, AZZA, LABIBA,
MADIHA *and* NAGAT. *They are unveiled and have not covered
their hair. They wear either djellabas or dresses.* BASSIMA
smokes. The GOVERNOR *waits outside, nervously tapping his
cane.*)

INSPECTOR (*apologetically*) It's because they're...

GOVERNOR I don't understand them. How can they be political?
Overturn a government with their veils on?

(*The* WARDEN *appears behind the barred door.*)

WARDEN Ready, Sir.

(*The* GOVERNOR *enters first. He surveys the cell, closely
inspecting the walls and staring attentively at the faces. He
twiddles his cane. The women remain seated and silent,
watching the* GOVERNOR *and his retinue. They all stare at the
prisoners; the* INSPECTOR *scrutinizes each of them in turn.*)

GOVERNOR (*still whirling his cane*) I hope that you're happy
here… with us.
(*Silence.*)

WARDEN Very happy, Monsieur, very happy to see you.

GOVERNOR Silence, woman, I'm not addressing you.

INSPECTOR Silence Fahima.

GOVERNOR Anyone need anything?
(SALMA *gets up and goes to him.*)

SALMA Yes, me.

GOVERNOR Name?

SALMA Salma Abou Khalil.

GOVERNOR Well, Salma?

SALMA I want to know why I'm here.
(*The* WARDEN *turns away to hide her smile, the* INSPECTOR
twitches, looks embarrassed.)

GOVERNOR You're asking me? You don't know why you're here?

SALMA (*naively*) No, I don't know.

WARDEN It's not for him to say.

SALMA Then who'll tell me?

INSPECTOR Tomorrow. At the interview.

SALMA What interview? Tomorrow? It's always tomorrow.
(*The* WARDEN *turns her face to the wall. The* INSPECTOR
whispers to SALMA. SALMA *goes back to sit next to* HADIA *and*
ETEDAL.)

GOVERNOR Any more questions?

BASSIMA (*Gets up.*) Monsieur, none of us knows what we're
accused of or why we've been put in this beggar's cell.

INSPECTOR It's the best room in the prison. It's the only one with
a washroom.

AZZA Monsieur, conditions are appalling; no visits, no food, no
papers, no radio and all day the chimney smokes us out.

SAMIRA And all night cockroaches and bugs…

ETEDAL (*small, tearful voice*) We haven't seen our parents and
they don't even know where we are.

BASSIMA (*nervously*) Monsieur, no-one should have to put up with
this life. We're all tired. Very tired.

MADIHA (*calmly*) We haven't even been questioned or allowed to see our lawyers.

GOVERNOR Nothing to do with me. Not my department.

LABIBA Whose job is it, Monsieur?

GOVERNOR I don't know. We'll sort something out, eh?
(*He looks at the* INSPECTOR.)

INSPECTOR (*politely*) We're waiting for instructions from the top.

SALMA (*Gets up quickly and looks up.*) From the top, from the top? Up there?
(*The* WARDEN *hides her face in her hands. The* INSPECTOR *takes* SALMA *by the hand.*)

INSPECTOR Sit down next to the others, Salma.

GOVERNOR Any other questions?

ETEDAL (*feebly*) I'd like a pen and paper to write to my mother.

GOVERNOR (*hardens*) All contact with the outside world is forbidden. No letters in or out until we have orders that permit it.

WARDEN They're well aware of it, Monsieur. They're very good really. It's the best cell in the prison.

INSPECTOR Of course they're educated and respect the law.

AZZA (*whispers to* LABIBA) What law? If they kept to the law, we wouldn't be here.

LABIBA Stop or I'm going to explode.

AZZA Calm down, it's all right. Shh…
(GOVERNOR *talks to the* INSPECTOR.)

GOVERNOR The Inspector tells me the food's good here.
(*He smiles at* SALMA.) Isn't that so Salma?
(SALMA *gets up.*)

WARDEN Excellent, better than they get at home.

SALMA I'm always hungry here, two pieces of bread a day isn't enough.

GOVERNOR Why only two pieces? They should be getting three!

WARDEN It's because—

GOVERNOR No excuses. From today you must give them three.

WARDEN Yes, sir.

LABIBA (*coughing*) The chimney smokes all day, it's choking us. If we go on coughing we'll end up with pneumonia or TB.

GOVERNOR Professor Labiba perhaps you're allergic, not quite adjusted to your new life here. The air's a little different to what you're used to, that's all. If you've a complaint, we can call the specialist in to see you.

(GOVERNOR *walks round twirling his cane.*)

Everybody happy then?

(*Silence.*)

We'll take your silence as a yes, then. Always the way with women, isn't it? (*He laughs.*)

INSPECTOR Too right, too right.

GOVERNOR Since everything's in order, we can go.

INSPECTOR Sir, if you don't need me, I'll stay on. I want some information.

GOVERNOR Good. Carry on.

(GOVERNOR *exits,* WARDEN *following.* INSPECTOR *remains.*)

INSPECTOR I need some more details, ladies. Bassima Charaf El Din? (*He takes out a notebook and pen.*)

BASSIMA Yes.

INSPECTOR You're married, aren't you?

BASSIMA My husband's dead.

INSPECTOR (*coldly*) I'm sorry.

BASSIMA Don't be. It was ten years ago.

INSPECTOR You have a place in Heliopolis?

BASSIMA A four-storey house.

INSPECTOR How did you get this house?

BASSIMA Thanks to God.

INSPECTOR Surely you inherited it from your husband?

BASSIMA I've never inherited anything. I've worked for the government for thirty years.

INSPECTOR So you bought it with your savings?

BASSIMA Doesn't the government encourage savings?

LABIBA It's all she's got, that house.

(INSPECTOR *goes over to* AZZA.)

INSPECTOR Azza Mortada?

AZZA Yes.

INSPECTOR Married?

AZZA No, I'm not married.

INSPECTOR A widow perhaps, like Madame Bassima?

AZZA No.

INSPECTOR Then what are you?

AZZA Divorced.

INSPECTOR I do beg your pardon. And you have a daughter — sixteen years old?

AZZA Apparently you know everything about me.

INSPECTOR Wouldn't you be better off staying at home looking after your daughter?

AZZA I'm best left here.

INSPECTOR Welcome then.

  (INSPECTOR *goes to* RACHIDA *and* NEFFISSA.)

INSPECTOR I can't tell one from the other.

  (*To* RACHIDA) Who are you?

  (*Silence.*)

SAMIRA They can't unveil in front of a man.

INSPECTOR But you do.

SAMIRA Each sect has its own rules. As the Prophet has written.

RACHIDA, ETEDAL, HADIA, NEFFISSA (*together*) As the Prophet has written.

INSPECTOR (*to* RACHIDA) Who are you?

SAMIRA She's not allowed to speak either.

INSPECTOR But you can speak as much as you want to. Who are you anyway?

SAMIRA (*with dignity*) Professor Samira El Fichawy.

INSPECTOR (*indifferent*) Delighted. Are you married, divorced or widowed?

SAMIRA None of them. I have devoted myself to God.

INSPECTOR Spinster.

SALMA (*whispers*) What's that?

  (INSPECTOR *goes to* ETEDAL.)

INSPECTOR Name?

ETEDAL Etedal Mohamed El Cheikh.

INSPECTOR What do you do, Etedal?

ETEDAL I'm still at school.

INSPECTOR The law forbids the veil at school.

(ETEDAL *looks down and says nothing.*)

NEFFISSA We can do without school.

INSPECTOR Who said that?

(NEFFISSA *says nothing.*)

INSPECTOR Who said that?

NEFFISSA I did.

INSPECTOR Who are you?

NEFFISSA Neffissa Mohamed el Charkawy.

INSPECTOR Occupation?

NEFFISSA Student, at the University.

INSPECTOR But you no longer go to the University do you
Neffissa? You have to choose the veil or the University?
(NEFFISSA *says nothing.*) What's it to be?

NEFFISSA The veil.

SAMIRA There's no education to be had at the schools or the
universities.

INSPECTOR Really? Then where?

SAMIRA Only the Qur'an can teach us. As the Prophet has written.

MUSLIM SISTERS (*together*) As the Prophet has written.

(INSPECTOR *goes to* SALMA.)

INSPECTOR And where have you come from?

SALMA From my house.

INSPECTOR Which school do you go to?

SALMA I don't go to school.

INSPECTOR Can you read or write?

SALMA No.

INSPECTOR What does your father do?

SALMA I dunno. I've never seen him. He left.

INSPECTOR And have you got any brothers or sisters?

SALMA Lots and lots.

INSPECTOR How many?

SALMA I dunno. My dad's had a lot of kids, my mum says.

INSPECTOR You live with your mother?

SALMA (*sad*) She's got a new man and they've had so many kids,
she can't look after me.

INSPECTOR Don't you see her?

SALMA I go and see her sometimes. Or she comes to see me. She'd
come here if she knew where I was.

INSPECTOR Who do you live with?

SALMA My Granny. She's blind so she can't come unless someone
comes with her. She's probably looking for me now.
(NAGAT *cries. The* INSPECTOR *puts his notebook away.*)

LABIBA Stop it. You're driving us crazy!

INSPECTOR All right. I'm going.

AZZA You've nothing better to do than bother us, have you?

INSPECTOR You're not the only ones here, you know. I want to
see you all out of here safe and sound, believe me. (*kindly*)
Let me know if there's anything you want, ladies… Madame
Bassima?

BASSIMA (*touched*) No, thank you.
(INSPECTOR *exits. Silence.*)

SAMIRA They're all the same. Real jokers. Snakes in the grass.

BASSIMA It's true. A few minutes ago he implied I was some sort of
criminal.

AZZA He told me to stay at home and mind my daughter.

SAMIRA He called me a spinster.
(RACHIDA *takes off her veil, her long hair falls about her
shoulders.*)

RACHIDA (*Mimics* INSPECTOR.) Which one are you?

NEFFISSA (*Unveils and mimics* INSPECTOR.) The veil or the
University? What's it to be? May you burn in hell.
(SALMA *takes off her veil and imitates the* INSPECTOR'S *walk.*)

SALMA And you, where do you live? None of your business. I live
where I like. (*She bursts into laughter.*)

SAMIRA Listen, girl — we don't believe a word of it. What did he
whisper in your ear?

SALMA When?

SAMIRA Why did he take you aside? What did he say?

AZZA Go on, Salma. Tell us.

SALMA I don't know what he said, so how can I tell you?

BASSIMA You have to. The last thing we need is a spy.

SALMA What's that?

SAMIRA Someone who spies on others.

SALMA I'm not a spy. I swear it. I haven't done anything. I
haven't... I haven't...
(*She bursts into tears.*)
(*The* WARDEN *enters with* ZOUBA *the prostitute, wearing a
white low-cut djellaba. She is slim and vivacious.* ZOUBA
enters, broom in hand. The WARDEN *closes the door behind her
and speaks through the bars.*)

WARDEN Sweep the yard and water the cress, it looks half-dead.
Don't go near the politicals or speak to any of them.
Understood?

ZOUBA (*Chewing gum.*) Understood, Foufou. No worries.
(WARDEN *leaves.*)

ZOUBA (*Singing and sweeping.*)
Whoever wants to marry me,
Show me what you can do,
Don't bore me to death,
With your life history.
(RACHIDA *sees her through the bars.*)

RACHIDA Look what she's wearing. Showing off all she's got.
(NEFFISSA, HADIA *and* ETEDAL *come over to watch.* SALMA
follows them.)

ZOUBA (*sings*)
Whoever wants to many me,
Show me what you can do,
Don't bore me to death,
With your life history.

SALMA I've heard that on the radio. Who sings it?

RACHIDA We never listen to the radio.

LABIBA She might have picked up some disease.

ETEDAL Or AIDS.

SALMA What's that?

HADIA You don't want to know, Salma.

SALMA I do.

RACHIDA A whore in here!

HADIA She could lead us astray.

AZZA Can't be that difficult then.

SAMIRA (*angry*) We're too strong for that.

AZZA I wasn't thinking of you.

SAMIRA Why not? I'm as good as them.

BASSIMA Calm down. We'll ask the Warden to send us someone
   else. The prison's full of them.

RACHIDA Full of them.

NEFFISSA There must be honest prisoners, at least some with more
   self-respect than a whore.

HADIA Anything's better than a whore.

AZZA Really? You don't think stealing or murder is worse?

HADIA Selling oneself is the worst crime of all.

AZZA How can you tell which is worse?

HADIA There are major crimes and minor crimes. The sins I
   commit are small and God forgives me.

SAMIRA Nonsense. If you're a believer, any sin is a crime.

HADIA I know what I'm saying.

RACHIDA You know nothing at all, Hadia!

HADIA I know more than you.

NEFFISSA Calm down, the lot of you. And Hadia, shut up.

HADIA I can say what I think.

NEFFISSA Shut up!

HADIA Why should I?

SAMIRA We don't want to know.

HADIA Then put your fingers in your ears.

BASSIMA Come on, prostitutes and criminals, they're all as bad as
   each other.

HADIA You can't compare a thief and a murderer. God permits a
   hungry man to steal…

SAMIRA God permits us to kill the infidels. A sin of any kind is a
   crime against God.

   (ZOUBA *is heard singing and sweeping.*)

ZOUBA Oh my love, come and see,

Since you left, what's become of me.
I watch and wait
Hiding my heart—
It's tearing me apart
Crying to myself
Crying for you
Again, my love.
(RACHIDA *and* NEFFISSA *cover their ears.* SAMIRA *counts her beads and reads the Qur'an.* ZOUBA *stands at the entrance.*)

ZOUBA If you'll let me ladies, I'd like some water for the cress. (*Nobody responds.*)

AZZA Come in. The bucket's under the sink.
(ZOUBA *goes and gets the bucket, waters the cress, then comes back to wash the floor.* SAMIRA *shrieks.*)

ZOUBA What's up?

SAMIRA A cockroach.
(ZOUBA *stamps on it, carries on sweeping.*)

ZOUBA Afraid of roaches? Let's hope whoever put you in here gets what he deserves.
(*She gestures to the portrait.* ZOUBA *rolls up her sleeves and scrubs the floor.*)
(RACHIDA, NEFFISSA *and* ETEDAL *read the Qur'an.* SAMIRA *reads alone to one side.* HADIA *sits in the corner thinking. The rest talk among themselves.* HADIA *gets up, goes to the bars and starts to scream.*)

ZOUBA What is it? Another roach?

HADIA A man!
(*The women rush to put on their veils.* ZOUBA *rushes to the door.*)

ZOUBA No men in here.
(*The* INSPECTOR *and the* PRISON WARDEN *enter carrying a small case.*)

ZOUBA God it's the boss. Quick.
(*She hides in the washroom. The* WARDEN *opens the door and goes in, leaving the* INSPECTOR *in the entrance for some moments.*)

INSPECTOR Check they're decent, Fahima.

WARDEN Ladies, are you ready?

SAMIRA Yes.

WARDEN OK, monsieur.

INSPECTOR Which one is Madame Bassima?

BASSIMA Here. What is it?

INSPECTOR There's someone outside, says he's your uncle.
Brought you this.

BASSIMA Where is he?

INSPECTOR In my office.

BASSIMA Can I see him?

INSPECTOR Visits are forbidden, as you know. Do you want me to
tell him something?

BASSIMA Tell him I'm well... he's an old man, he's sick, he
musn't... (*She wipes away tears, lights a cigarette.*)

INSPECTOR Give her the case. It's been checked.

(*He exits, followed by* WARDEN; ZOUBA *comes out.* BASSIMA *sits
down and opens the case, breathes in the smell of fresh clothes
and bursts into tears.*)

BASSIMA It's the smell of home.

(ZOUBA *and* AZZA *try to console her.*)

ZOUBA You'll be free tomorrow, God willing. Home in no time.

BASSIMA My uncle's very old with a bad heart. He couldn't bear it.

AZZA He'll be all right, don't worry. I tell myself the same thing.
Don't let yourself get in a state. What can I say? I've left my
own kid on her own.

MADIHA I'll light the stove for tea. That will calm us all down.

ZOUBA (*sympathetically*) You have a daughter, like me, Madame
Azza? How old is she?

AZZA Sixteen years and all alone.

ZOUBA Lucky for her — my girl's only eleven and she's going with
a man.

AZZA What man?

ZOUBA The man who ruined my life and hers. I'd kill him if I
could.

AZZA What's he done to you?

ZOUBA He makes me work. Makes me do this, dirty work. But he's
not worth swinging for. Without my Yasmine, I'd have done
away with meself long ago. I've got her photo, look, she's
pretty; look, look...
(*She shows them all the photograph.*)

BASSIMA She is lovely.

MADIHA Like her mother.

SALMA May God keep her safe, Zouba.
(HADIA *and* ETEDAL *look at the photo, but say nothing.*
SAMIRA *looks away, embarrassed.*)

ZOUBA Don't you like it?

SAMIRA I don't want to look at pictures.

RACHIDA It's not allowed.

NEFFISSA Never go in houses with dogs or pictures.

ZOUBA Good lord... what's wrong with dogs?

SAMIRA These are God's words.

BASSIMA Don't get involved Zouba. Just carry on...

ZOUBA Learn something new every day.
(*She goes to get the bucket from the washroom.*)
(*Silence.* MADIHA *pours tea into glasses.*)

BASSIMA God knows when we'll get out of here.

LABIBA God didn't put us in here.

BASSIMA Who else can we ask for help?

AZZA There are people outside, you know. No one person can
change the law when there are fifty million who believe in it.

BASSIMA There's the one that's to blame. Up there.
(*She points to the portrait.*)

AZZA He can't break all the laws and get away with it.

BASSIMA You'd think so, but who's to stop him?

AZZA Who knows? Last night I had a bad dream. I was in our old
house at Zagazig and there was my dead father in front of me
with his hands up, like this. Then I was outside the Pyramids
near the Sphinx and she had her hand raised too. On the
stone there were hieroglyphics and people were asking me
what they meant. But I couldn't read a single word. Then I
heard Samira calling me for prayer and I woke up.

BASSIMA Samira and her friends don't go through it like we do. Day and night it's the Qur'an. Inside or out, it's the same for them. They're probably freer in here. They can meet with other people, they can talk. And the food here's probably better than they get at home.

AZZA It's true, life's so busy for us — committees, meetings, trips, conferences. I don't know how to get by without a newspaper, or the radio, or even a pen and paper.

BASSIMA Stop it. I can't go on like this.

AZZA You have to.

BASSIMA I can't.

AZZA Yes, you can. Just think how much we'll laugh when we get out of here.

BASSIMA I don't think so. That man takes everything and spares no-one.

AZZA We have to hope.

BASSIMA We have to pray.

AZZA What? Next you'll be taking the veil and when you get out of here no-one will recognize you.

(*They laugh.*)

BASSIMA Louder, louder. Samira will tell us it's a sin to laugh — a crime to be happy.

(AZZA *laughs even louder.* BASSIMA *lights a cigarette.* ZOUBA *comes out of the washroom.*)

ZOUBA Spick and span. Give us a fag, love.

(BASSIMA *gives* ZOUBA *a cigarette.*)

ZOUBA Worth a million pounds this fag. I'd give up everything for one puff.

AZZA Just one?

ZOUBA It's the only drug I need. Some of the others are at it all night.

SALMA What does that mean?

SAMIRA Quiet. I don't want to know.

ZOUBA All right. I'm going. Open up, Foufou, and let me out. It's all real spotless.

WARDEN Well done, Zouba. It's nearly four o'clock. Time to lock

up for the night. (*She lets* ZOUBA *through and shuts the door.*)
'Night ladies.

TOGETHER 'Night, Madame Fahima.

WARDEN Don't need anything?

BASSIMA Some paraffin for the stove and I'm almost out of
cigarettes.

WARDEN All right.

(*She locks up and leaves. They lie down. The* MUSLIM SISTERS
go back to reading the Qur'an. ETEDAL *stares our through the
bars.*)

LABIBA We can't sleep now!

MADIHA Let's do something.

AZZA What?

MADIHA You could talk politics, Bassima. And you could tell us
about France, Azza.

AZZA Well, I could tell you about my research...

MADIHA Great. Come and listen everyone. What's up, Nagat?

(NAGAT *sits and cries in a corner.*)

NAGAT I miss my mother.

MADIHA Come over here, with us.

(NAGAT *goes to sit with them.* ETEDAL *suddenly falls on the
floor and has a fit.*)

ETEDAL Maman! Maman!

(ETEDAL *loses consciousness.* MADIHA *tries to bring her round
with some Eau de Cologne but* SAMIRA *pushes her violently
away.*)

SAMIRA Take that away from her.

MADIHA It's only a little cologne.

SAMIRA It's got alcohol in it.

MADIHA She's not going to drink it — just smell it.

SAMIRA Doesn't matter.

LABIBA Oh, my head! It's bursting.

(*They all go back to their places wearily and lie down to go to
sleep. The light fades. Silence for some minutes.*)

SAMIRA (*cries out*) Praise be to Allah! Praise be to Allah!

LABIBA I can't stand it. I can't stand being woken up like this.

SAMIRA Prayers before bed or you'll sleep with the Devil.

LABIBA I can sleep with whomever I want to.

SAMIRA And I can pray whenever I want to.

AZZA Yes, but not so loud. We're trying to sleep.

SAMIRA You don't praise God in whispers. You use your whole voice.

AZZA You could try.

SAMIRA If you don't like it — ask for another room — how about solitary confinement?

(SAMIRA *turns to the wall and continues.*)

SAMIRA Praise be to Allah! Praise be to Allah!

(RACHIDA, NEFFISSA *and* ETEDAL *sit behind her and pray.* HADIA *prays alone in a corner.*)

RACHIDA Come and join in, Hadia.

HADIA No, I prefer it this way.

RACHIDA You can't pray alone.

HADIA Why not?

RACHIDA You can't.

SAMIRA Let her: she's a Faramawia.

HADIA I'm not. You bloody Khomeiniste.

AZZA (*to* BASSIMA) We're in a madhouse.

BASSIMA My body's numb and I can't breathe. I think I'm having an attack.

AZZA It's all those cigarettes.

BASSIMA I can hardly breathe.

AZZA You'll have to give up.

BASSIMA I couldn't cope.

AZZA You could try Valium—

BASSIMA Let me be, will you?

AZZA Let's have some tea. Labiba, tell us about your job, what you were doing.

LABIBA With this headache?

AZZA Well, tell us what your dream was.

LABIBA It's always the same nightmare.

AZZA Well, what about your bloke? He must be missing you.

LABIBA You're joking. I only stay with him for my daughter's sake.

AZZA She's grown up now. She's working: my daughter's still young, her life's ahead of her.

BASSIMA Thank God I've got no worries — no husbands, no sons and no daughters!

AZZA We're all daughters and mothers, Bassima.

(*The* MUSLIM SISTERS *finish praying and set to reading the Qur'an.* ETEDAL *goes to get tea.*)

MADIHA Better now, Etedal?

ETEDAL Yes, thanks.

MADIHA Come here a minute.

ETEDAL I'm worried about my mother. She'll die if she finds out I'm in here.

MADIHA She won't. She's all right, I'm sure. Come on, give us a smile.

AZZA You smile like an angel, Etedal. (ETEDAL *smiles.*) Tell us about your dreams.

(ETEDAL *drinks her tea.*)

ETEDAL I see my mother out shopping for my wedding dress, but whenever she goes into a shop, they say they've none left. In the end, she can't go on and so she says, 'Why? Why can't you sell me a dress for my daughter?' 'We don't have any for jailbirds', they tell her.

AZZA Why are you dreaming of that?

ETEDAL Because if they ban the veil at school, I have to stay at home and be married. A priest has asked for me.

MADIHA A priest?

ETEDAL I have to marry a man of God.

AZZA And not finish school?

ETEDAL I hate school. If I go there I'll burn in hell forever.

AZZA Forever?

ETEDAL I feel sorry for you. Why don't you pray? You'll go through agony, you know.

MADIHA I grew up in a house where no-one prayed. One side of the family were Muslim, the others Coptic.

ETEDAL Coptic? Infidels?

(NAGAT *gets upset, moves away.*)

MADIHA You've upset her.

ETEDAL I forgot she's a Christian.

LABIBA How could you forget?

ETEDAL She looks exactly the same as us.

LABIBA Well, she's not. They're not like us.

ETEDAL Sorry.

SAMIRA There's only one God, the Prophet Muhammad, the greatest of them all, has said so. Come here, Etedal, don't waste your time with them.

(ETEDAL *rejoins the others reading the Qur'an.* NAGAT *weeps and* MADIHA *goes over to sit with her.*)

MADIHA Don't listen to them, Nagat. What do they know, anyway?

NAGAT I say my prayers. I always go to church, how can they call me that?

MADIHA God alone knows who believes and who doesn't. I've never read the Qur'an. I know how to read French, English, German but not Arabic.

NAGAT Samira looks at me as though she hates me. I can't bear it. I want to ask them to move me.

MADIHA That's what they want us to do. Why do you think they've put us all together in here?

NAGAT At school I was the only one, too. 'Infidel! Infidel!' I've heard it all my life. (*She starts to cry again.*)

MADIHA Come on, let's get some fresh air.

AZZA We have to stop all this moaning. Someone please tell me something new and interesting. My brain's seized up.

BASSIMA My mind's numb — and my body. We'll never get out of here. The whole country's asleep.

AZZA People aren't mad.

BASSIMA Then, why don't they protest?

AZZA We're not forgotten. The whole world knows about us. Someone will speak up—

BASSIMA Organize a demonstration perhaps? Come off it.

AZZA We have to hope, Professor. Help each other get through this. We're not going to die in here.

LABIBA I think I'll die in here. I do.

(*She stares out. An uneasy atmosphere prevails. We hear the sounds of cries from outside.* ETEDAL, SALMA, HADIA *and* MADIHA *run towards the door and look through the bars.*)

ETEDAL God, let me out of here!

MADIHA You'll be the first to go, Etedal.

SALMA Me too. I'm getting out with her.

(SALMA *jumps about then falls down laughing.* SAMIRA *gives her a dirty look.*)

SAMIRA You're a disgrace, Salma. Why don't you cover your head in front of the door?

SALMA Nobody's out there. Not a single man. Not even Muhammad, the rubbish collector.

SAMIRA You know his name then?

SALMA Yes, Muhammad. It's the name of the Prophet, okay?

SAMIRA How do you know that? Did anyone else know his name?

(*Everyone keeps quiet.*)

RACHIDA How could we? We don't talk to men, do we?

SALMA I heard him talking to Sabah in the yard.

ETEDAL Who's Sabah?

SALMA The beggar woman. I heard them talking. What could I do? Shut my ears?

RACHIDA He could have seen you.

SALMA He had his back to me.

RACHIDA He could have turned round.

NEFFISSA They all try to look in.

SALMA Who? There are no men out there.

RACHIDA This Muhammad's a man.

SALMA He only comes once a week.

RACHIDA How do you know? Do you count the days, then?

SALMA I've seen him once in a while, that's all.

SAMIRA You'd do better to read the Qur'an than to waste time with such nonsense.

(SALMA *goes and sits next to* HADIA *and stares at the Qur'an.*)

LABIBA When will God save us from this?

BASSIMA I can't take much more.

AZZA They won't forget us. I know it.

MADIHA   We have to think of something.

LABIBA   We've nothing to read except the Qur'an.

MADIHA   Then let's read it.

BASSIMA   You can read it. I'll give it a miss.

AZZA   Then tell us, something else.

BASSIMA   I'm too tired. I want to sleep. Sleep my way through all this. (*She lies down on the mattress.*) Before they arrested me, I was in hiding for some time. You can't imagine how tired I was. All I wanted to do was find a bed and sleep.

AZZA   I thought of hiding too. But then I said, 'What have I done wrong?' Nothing. When they take everything away, what can we do? We have to speak out. Against him.

MADIHA   He wants even more than God.

LABIBA   More than God... more than God...
    (*Silence and sadness descend.*)

SAMIRA   (*Takes her rosary and prays in a low voice.*) Allah is beyond all. Allah is beyond all. Allah is beyond all.
    (*Suddenly she starts to scream — ETEDAL joins in too.*)

MADIHA   Oh! What is it now? A cockroach or a man?
    (*Lights fade.*)

Act Two

Darkness and silence. Heavy knocks on a wooden door can be heard, becoming louder until the door opens. The sound of marching boots approaching. A woman's voice screams out, 'No!' Silence returns. Cries of a new-born child are heard. The sound of boots going away. Sounds of a key turning in a lock and a metal door opening. Slow, heavy footsteps can be heard, then a metal door closes. Silence. A light fades up on the same cell. A new prisoner, ALIA, stands in front of the door. She is tall, young, with long hair and a simple white dress. She seems nervous and examines the room intently. A washing line divides the room in two. On the right side are the MUSLIM SISTERS; on the left the other prisoners are sleeping. SALMA gets up and goes over to ALIA.

SALMA Who are you?

ALIA Alia Ibrahim Chawky.

SALMA Where you from?

ALIA From home. What about you?

SALMA They took me from the street. I was going to see my
       mother.

ALIA They broke down the door. They knocked for a long time
      but I wouldn't let them in.

SALMA Why should you?

ALIA They had no orders, no warrant, nothing.

SALMA They don't tell you anything. 'Where are you going, love?'
       they said: 'Come with us, we'll take you home' they said. I
       would have yelled out if I'd known.

SAMIRA Who's that?

SALMA A new prisoner.

SAMIRA (*getting up*) Muslim or Christian?

ALIA What a question. I haven't been asked that since I was at
      school.

SAMIRA You must be a Christian.

ALIA No.

SAMIRA Then you're a Muslim? A Jew?

ALIA (*laughing*) No. No. No.

SAMIRA My God. An atheist.

LABIBA (*jumps*) What's the matter? You're not calling us to
        prayer?

AZZA What is it?

SAMIRA A new one?

AZZA (*happy*) Alia, this can't be true!
      (*They hug each other. The others wake up.*)

AZZA I'm so pleased they put you with us.

BASSIMA Pleased? How can you…

AZZA I can't lie about it. She's my friend. I wish all my friends
      were here with me.

BASSIMA How can you be so selfish?

AZZA I mean it.

ALIA I love her honesty.

SALMA I like you Alia a lot but...
       (*She whispers in* ALIA'*s ear.*)
ALIA   My father's a Muslim, his father was a Christian. My
       mother's a Muslim, her grandfather was Coptic. So what
       does that make me?
SALMA The same as your father.
ALIA   If it pleases you.
SALMA I like you, so I'm glad you're a Muslim after all.
       (SALMA *goes into the washroom.* ALIA *and* AZZA *sit.*)
ALIA   What's all this religious stuff?
AZZA   We're not in prison; we're in a madhouse.
       (ALIA *looks shocked.*)
AZZA   What have they done to you? And your little boy, where's
       he?
ALIA   He'll be six weeks old tomorrow.
AZZA   Who's looking after him?
ALIA   My neighbour's taken him until I get back.
       (AZZA *doesn't know what to say.*) What about your daughter?
AZZA   She can look after herself.
       (MADIHA *lights the stove, helped by* NAGAT. LABIBA *goes over
       to the door.* SAMIRA *and the* MUSLIM SISTERS *pray or read the
       Qur'an.* BASSIMA *opens her case, takes out soap and a towel.*)
LABIBA The Warden's here!
       (BASSIMA *quickly shuts her case. The* WARDEN *enters.*)
WARDEN The Inspector's coming in later. There may be a search.
       Make sure you hide that stove and anything else that
       shouldn't be here. I've got a migraine already.
       (*She goes out.*)
AZZA   She's the same every day. Always something wrong.
BASSIMA (*to* ALIA) You haven't brought anything with you?
ALIA   They told me I'd be gone for two hours. Then I'd be home
       again.
       (BASSIMA *puts her case in the corner, goes into the washroom
       with soap and towel.* AZZA *goes to a small bag, takes out a
       djellaba and a towel, which she tears in half.*)
AZZA   Take it. I've two of these with me. You have one. My sister

sent them, she may send me more. We're allowed clothes, but not food, and you can't eat what you get in here.

MADIHA At least there's tea. (*She gives* ALIA *a glass.*)

AZZA Tea and cigarettes... Valium, speed...

(*They laugh.*)

AZZA In the prostitutes' cell you can get anything.

ALIA Is there any water to have a wash?

BASSIMA (*Returns.*) They call that a washroom but the water's freezing.

(ALIA *takes the towel and djellaba and goes in.*)

ALIA I'm used to that. I'm just glad there's water here.

(*The prison* WARDEN *returns with the* INSPECTOR. NEFFISSA *jumps up and runs away from the door.*)

NEFFISSA There's a man coming.

(*The* MUSLIM SISTERS *put on their veils.* SALMA *too. The* WARDEN *opens the door.*)

SALMA It's only the Inspector. It's not a man, after all.

SAMIRA Of course, he's come to see you, hasn't he? To get information.

SALMA What?

SAMIRA (*sarcastic*) You don't understand anything, do you, poor girl?

(*The* INSPECTOR *puts on his dark glasses before entering.*)

WARDEN Ready, ladies? The Inspector's here.

(MADIHA *hides the stove and the tea things. The* INSPECTOR *looks around coldly, examining each of them.*)

INSPECTOR Where's Madame Alia Ibrahim Chawky?

(ALIA *comes out of the washroom, wearing the djellaba, a towel slung over her shoulder, her hair wet. She goes up to the* INSPECTOR, *stares him in the eye.*)

ALIA I'm Alia Ibrahim Chawky.

INSPECTOR (*overly polite*) Excuse me, Madame Alia. I'd like a few details from you, if I may. There are some omissions.

ALIA Really? Is that possible? With all your technology and foreign experts?

INSPECTOR You seem well up on it all.

ALIA I know what I've seen.

INSPECTOR Happy here?

ALIA (*inspecting the cell*) Absolutely. It's infinitely preferable in here, away from the newspapers and the photographs. (*She stops at the sight of the portrait on the wall.*)

ALIA Can't get away from him anywhere.

INSPECTOR Where do you live?

ALIA In the house where you arrested me.

INSPECTOR Ah, yes... um... and you're married?

ALIA No.

INSPECTOR Not married?

ALIA No.

INSPECTOR A widow?

ALIA No.

INSPECTOR Divorced?

ALIA I divorced him.

INSPECTOR Ah yes, his name?

ALIA I don't remember.

INSPECTOR But you have children?

ALIA No.

INSPECTOR But it's noted here that you have a child of only six weeks.

ALIA Since you know so much, why ask me?

INSPECTOR We need the name of the child.

ALIA What for?

INSPECTOR We just fill in these forms correctly. The name of your son is required.

ALIA He's my son. It's my business.

INSPECTOR Your attitude could get you into trouble.

ALIA Is that a threat?

INSPECTOR Nothing of the sort. I've got to get on, that's all. I've so many others.

ALIA Don't forget anyone, will you?

INSPECTOR It's not my job to say who comes or who goes — it's not my prison.

ALIA Then whose prison is it?

INSPECTOR How should I know? It belongs to God.

ALIA God has prisons, does he? I didn't know that.

SAMIRA Allah forgive you, Sir. These prisons are not God's, they
are his. (*She points to the portrait.*) They belong to injustice,
not to God. (*She falls on the floor, crying.*)
(*The* MUSLIM SISTERS *rally round her.*)

AZZA Everyday you come here and drive us mad. We've had
enough.

INSPECTOR What did I say?

RACHIDA Shame on you... shame.

INSPECTOR All I said was... everything belongs to God, even this
place we're in now.

AZZA We've had enough of your questions.

INSPECTOR I've had all I can take, too. Why can't she just give me
the name?

ALIA Why must you have it? What do you want with a newborn
child anyway? (*Silence.*)

INSPECTOR I'm sorry but I must fill out the form. I can't leave it
blank. I'd lose my job. I do what I'm told, that's all. Now,
let's finish this and I'll go. You won't see me again. (ALIA
says nothing.) It's a formality. We don't want your son. What
would we do with children? Or anyone else? I've a little boy
myself and a new baby. I haven't seen him yet. I couldn't get
home... You think I like being here all the time?

AZZA You can phone home for news. Your wife's there looking
after the children while ours are out there, somewhere, alone.

INSPECTOR It's your own fault, you women who want to work, to
be independent, to meddle in politics. Well — this is politics.
(*He gestures the cell, the portrait.*)

LABIBA I have no wish to meddle in politics; I simply work in an
office where they asked my opinion. So I gave it, that's it.
That's why I'm here.

BASSIMA We all spoke out. We tested their democracy and this is
what we got.

MADIHA This has gone on long enough. When's it going to end?

INSPECTOR (*Shrugs.*) We're still waiting for new orders.

AZZA It's not enough they've put us here? What more can they
    want?

INSPECTOR Madame Alia, you have to tell me, please. (*She
    says nothing.*) You refuse to answer. Believe me, you will,
    whatever it takes.

    (*The* INSPECTOR *goes out. The* WARDEN *returns.*)

WARDEN What was that for? You don't know him like I do.
    Yesterday he saw Zouba leave here. He had her strip, and
    then he searched her. Thank God he found nothing because
    if he did, I'd be the one he'd have for it and he won't stop
    until he gets what he wants. (*Silence.*) Tomorrow, he'll tell me
    to put you in solitary: I'll come and get you straight away. If
    he tells me to beat you — I'll beat you and if I can't get you
    to cough up, he'll send for others. (*She comes nearer.*) I'm on
    your side, but in front of them I can't be. I can't lose my job.
    Once they had me hit a poor woman, worse than Sabah, the
    beggar who hangs around here — I knew she was innocent
    and I hit her. What could I do? I hit her and I asked God to
    forgive me. I went home, sick, went to bed for a week. We're
    human beings; we care more than you do.

    (*The* WARDEN *wipes her tears, looks at the women then goes
    out, locking the door.*)

    (*Silence.* BASSIMA *smokes a cigarette.*)

BASSIMA I'm afraid for you, Alia. It's not worth it.

MADIHA Try and be flexible.

SALMA What's that?

LABIBA She's always been stubborn — makes trouble for herself
    and those around her.

NAGAT They won't hurt your son. They've already taken his
    mother from him. That's enough.

AZZA Anything's possible. You've no idea.

NAGAT What would they do to children?

AZZA When they fail with us, they start on them.

BASSIMA (*laughing*) If they fail with Alia, who will they beat?

AZZA Somebody weaker — Nagat, Etedal or Salma.

SALMA They'll beat me too, will they? I haven't done anything.

(*She hits herself on the chest. They all laugh except* SAMIRA *who carries on reading the Qur'an.*)

SAMIRA Don't worry: even if they beat everyone else they'll leave you be. They never hurt their own.

SALMA (*Does not pick up on this.*) It's not fair. My dad and my mum used to hit me — even my gran used to hit me.

(SALMA *laughs.* BASSIMA *takes food from her case.*)

MADIHA Who wants tea?

SALMA Me, me, me.

(BASSIMA *looks astonished.*)

BASSIMA You never stop.

SALMA Lots of sugar.

(SALMA *sees* BASSIMA *eating biscuits.*)

SALMA Can I have some?

(BASSIMA *gives her one: she crams it into her mouth.*)

SALMA Gimme, gimme.

(BASSIMA *gives her another one: She eats it greedily.*)

BASSIMA What an appetite!

AZZA It's her age, at sixteen you're ravenous. I hide the food to keep mine slim.

BASSIMA (*Laughing with a mouthful.*) Like her mother.

AZZA Why not? I've always been thin.

BASSIMA I couldn't care less.

(ALIA *goes to the door.*)

ALIA I need some fresh air.

AZZA I'll just take my rollers out and join you.

(AZZA *opens a box and takes out make-up, eye-liner and a mirror.*)

AZZA (*to* BASSIMA) I could write to my daughter with this — got a bit of cigarette paper?

MADIHA They let you keep it?

AZZA It's Zouba's.

LABIBA You'll catch something.

AZZA That's all I need.

LABIBA I've forgotten what my face looks like. I wouldn't let my husband near me.

AZZA I'll go for you then, he'll do just fine for me.

BASSIMA (*laughs*) Then Labiba will kill you and she'll never get out.

LABIBA I wouldn't do that. She's my friend.

AZZA What's the matter? Too ugly? Wouldn't he fancy me?

LABIBA Not at all, I think you're lovely. I didn't think of you that way.

AZZA Why not?

LABIBA My husband would go after anything — even his own mother. Now he's getting on, he's after the young ones like you.

AZZA They're all the same. Why do you think I'm divorced? Or, more to the point, I asked for one. I'm the one doing the divorcing, aren't I, Alia?

(ALIA *walks around, not listening.* AZZA *laughs and* BASSIMA *tries to hide this from* SAMIRA. *Exit* AZZA *to join* ALIA.)

BASSIMA You look very tired, Labiba.

LABIBA Very, very tired. I can't take any more. I couldn't sleep. I actually started praying last night. It's like your period, it comes and goes.

BASSIMA Mine went ages ago. What are we going to do? You'll be the first to go. You've had nothing to do with politics.

LABIBA Nothing. I don't even read the newspapers.

BASSIMA What newspapers? Come on, you have to laugh. At least you've got a family to go back to.

LABIBA Who'd miss me? We only stay together for the kid.

BASSIMA You'd do the divorcing, would you? (*Laughs, stops.*) Alia frightens me.

LABIBA She is stubborn. I've known her for twenty years.

BASSIMA She's frightened for her son.

LABIBA She's not frightened. She's never frightened.

BASSIMA What could they do to a baby?

(ZEINAB, *one of the criminals, enters haughtily, carrying a tray of cigarettes and tea. The* WARDEN *follows.*)

ALIA Some personality!

AZZA One criminal to another. She's almost running the place.

ALIA Let's go in.

(ALIA *and* AZZA *go back in.* ZEINAB *is sitting next to* BASSIMA.)

ZEINAB Is it all there?

BASSIMA Perfect.

AZZA Listen…

ZEINAB I'm a bit down today.

AZZA Why? That's not like you.

WARDEN She's had some bad news. Her daughter's real sick.

AZZA What's up?

ZEINAB I swear to God if she dies…

WARDEN Sorry, ladies. But she killed for that girl.

ZEINAB Yes. Yes. I killed the son-of-a-bitch. My father said 'If you leave him, I'll cut you up.' Seven kids I got from him, all dead, except her, the little one. Lazy bastard, slept all day, a thief like his father, stoned out of his mind. She told me what he did to her.

MADIHA Why did she do it?

WARDEN She saw him with the little one.

MADIHA With your daughter?

ZEINAB (*Looks at her hands.*) I killed him. When I saw him do it with my own eyes. (*She shuts her eyes.*) I hit him with the pickaxe, chopped him up, put him in a bag and threw him into the sea. (*She laughs.*) The fish finished him long ago. (ZEINAB *gets up suddenly.*)

AZZA Where are you going?

ZEINAB Where do you want me to go? To see my daughter. She's all I've got.

WARDEN She's not here. You can't see her. She really thinks she's going to… Where is she? In the middle of Egypt?

ZEINAB It depends on God… if He takes her, I'll cut him out too.

WARDEN Ssh, Madame Samira will kill you and cut you up if she hears you.

ZEINAB (*crying*) Who will? Nobody can kill me — it's my daughter who's sick that's killing me.

WARDEN Get up. Get up. God'll look after her. Today has been a nightmare. The Inspector's out there, looking for a cell to put the new girl in. Seen her?

ZEINAB Which one?

WARDEN The one out there with Azza. Called Alia Ibrahim
Chawky. May God protect her.

ZEINAB What's she done? Killed someone?

WARDEN She's so full of herself, that one. Even braver than you
— 'I divorced him', says she.

ZEINAB I should have done that. How many times did I dig and
plant and carry it all on my back like a slave?

WARDEN She's nobody's slave, her. These politicals are something
else.

ZEINAB They're soft, come off it.

WARDEN These are ladies, not peasants.

ZEINAB Who do you think you are? Three pips on your shoulder
and you think you're so great? Peasants are better than them
in God's eyes. (ZEINAB *sees the cress, which is dying.*)
Look at your 'ladies'. Can't even keep the cress alive. It's had
it.

(LABIBA *comes up to the* WARDEN.)

ZEINAB Is that the new one?

WARDEN No.

LABIBA (*Approaches* ZEINAB *shyly.*) I want to ask you something.

ZEINAB At your service.

LABIBA When you saw your husband... I mean to say when you
saw...

ZEINAB Him with her? It's not a secret, everybody knows.

LABIBA What did you feel?

ZEINAB Nothing. I killed him straight off.

LABIBA Ah! And your daughter?

ZEINAB I don't understand.

LABIBA Were you jealous?

ZEINAB (*tapping her chest*) Jealous of her? My daughter's my life.
I'd have killed and killed again for her.

(AZZA *and* ALIA *come out.*)

AZZA Labiba's always jealous. You know her daughter's very
pretty. She's even jealous of me and I wouldn't look at a
married man.

ZEINAB They're not worth it. What about you, beautiful?
        (*To* ALIA.)
WARDEN This is Madame Alia who's just arrived. (ZEINAB *looks at*
        ALIA *admiringly*.) Such a good person. Such a pity she'll be
        going into solitary. Aren't you scared?
ALIA No. Never have been and never will.
ZEINAB Must have nine lives, like me, eh?
WARDEN (*Cuffs her.*) Like you? She's an educated woman, Zeinab.
        I don't know what he'll do. The Inspector's gone mad.
ZEINAB What can he do to her? She's not frightened. I've been
        there and I'm still alive.
WARDEN You're used to it. They haven't got a clue.
SALMA What's so bad about solitary? I thought prison was full of
        ghosts and rats and snakes.
WARDEN Prison's no joke and I can throw you in solitary any time.
        (SALMA *makes for the* WARDEN, *who holds up her hand.*)
WARDEN Keep off! You've no right to be any closer than three
        metres. That's the rules.
SALMA How do we know the rules? We can't listen to what they
        say on the radio in here. (*Everybody laughs.*)
WARDEN What are the rules? That prison should straighten you
        out.
SALMA They want to set us right do they?
AZZA (*laughing*) And file our nails. By the way they're long, we
        don't have any scissors.
ALIA Or anything else. (*They all laugh.*)
AZZA We could sharpen them on men.
ZEINAB Not all of them.
AZZA Why not?
WARDEN Because she's in love with a guy in the men's prison.
        They write to each other and want to get married next year.
ZEINAB Why not now?
WARDEN They have to give their approval.
ZEINAB They have to stick their nose into everything. (*She stops
        laughing.*) Honestly you're all wonderful — only why did you
        let the cress die?

ALIA What?

ZEINAB I can't bear to see anything die. A dose a day's all they
need. I've made a vegetable garden in our yard.
(ZEINAB *drags* ALIA *outside.*) Come and see.

WARDEN Don't start. She can't go out there.

ALIA And what d'you use for gardening?

ZEINAB A pick-axe.

WARDEN A pick-axe!

AZZA And you took my tweezers?

ZEINAB I'll get you one. Everyone here can garden.

WARDEN They won't garden. These are ladies.

ALIA Oh no, we're not. We're going to plant things.

SALMA Me too.

WARDEN What do you know about growing things?

ALIA All my aunts are peasants. In my village I was always in the
fields with my cousins. If I hadn't gone to school I'd still be
there.

SALMA You remind me of someone — my aunt Tafida. She was
nice and she was pretty... She's not there anymore.

AZZA Where is she?

SALMA She went to Bahrain and she never came back.

ZEINAB Alia's one of us. I'm going to get her a pick-axe so she can
plant things.

ALIA And some seeds. Bring me some Molokhia seeds and some
cress and some parsley and some broad beans.

SALMA I love beans!

ZEINAB I'll steal some from the dealers. They've got everything.
Colour TV, the lot.
(*Suddenly we hear a cry from inside the cell.* RACHIDA *has
fainted. They surround her and* MADIHA *tries to revive her
with cologne, rubbing some on her skin.*)

SAMIRA Take that away.

MADIHA Call a doctor quick.

WARDEN Straight away.

SAMIRA She can't see a doctor.

WARDEN Are you going to let her die?

MADIHA Get a woman doctor.

WARDEN I'll call one. (RACHIDA *signals 'no'.*)

SAMIRA Wait, she wants to say something.

RACHIDA I don't want anybody.

WARDEN Why Rachida? Why? You're in prison my little one and you must look after yourself. We're lucky to have a woman doctor.

MADIHA This is silly Rachida, let the doctor have a look at you.

SAMIRA God will look after her.

WARDEN But the medicine could help her.

HADIA Believe in anyone else and you offend Him.

WARDEN It's a crime to call a doctor now, is it? I can't take any more of this.

(ZEINAB *returns with a pickaxe.*)

ZEINAB Here you are. Dig deep, it's hard to get anything to grow here but God's given it to us, so might as well use it.

WARDEN Better off talking to them Alia, than wasting your time digging. Talk some sense into them.

(*Exit* WARDEN *locking the gate.*)

SALMA Can I have a go?

ALIA We'll take it in turns.

SALMA This is my part of the yard.

ALIA And this is mine.

AZZA I'll do the watering.

MADIHA I'll do the planting.

(ALIA *begins digging,* SALMA *clears the stones,* LABIBA *comes out.*)

LABIBA What's all the racket?

SALMA We're going to have beans, we're going to eat beans.

(SALMA *skips around.*)

LABIBA I'm not hanging about in here till beans grow.

(*To* BASSIMA, *who's smoking.*) Can you believe it? They think they'll be here to pick them.

BASSIMA Probably longer. We'll never get out with Alia around.

(ALIA *is joking with* SALMA, AZZA, MADIHA *and* NAGAT.)

BASSIMA She's forgotten all about her son. I'd go out of my mind with worry.

LABIBA Alia's like that. She can forget anything.

BASSIMA Anything but herself. Never lasted two minutes on a committee. Too headstrong.

LABIBA Full of herself.

BASSIMA She's always got to make herself felt. Nothing but trouble. She's always banging her head against a wall like a kid. She's free to do as she likes, so long as she doesn't hurt us.

(SALMA *fills a bucket of water from the washroom and carries on watering the ground.*)

BASSIMA Look at that girl. I never know how to take her. Is she sly or just naive?

LABIBA It's a madhouse... us with them — these people who don't even believe in doctors!

(RACHIDA *has dozed off.* ETEDAL *watches the gardening.* ZEINAB *returns with seed.*)

ZEINAB I've got the seeds.

(ETEDAL *takes the bags, looks at her.*)

ETEDAL (*Touches her hair.*) Why don't you cover it?

ZEINAB What is this? You going to your own funeral?

ETEDAL I'll wear what I like.

ZEINAB Who told you to wear it? Your dad?

ETEDAL It's my decision. I'll pay the price.

ZEINAB You done something wrong?

ETEDAL It's a crime to wear the veil at school, so —

ZEINAB Going hungry is the only crime I know.

SALMA Is that the seeds?

(SALMA *takes a bag and runs off.* ALIA *digs energetically.* AZZA *collects the stones.* MADIHA *smooths the ground with her hands.*)

MADIHA The seeds need sorting.

ETEDAL I'll do it.

BASSIMA I like Neffissa. She never upsets anyone.

LABIBA Careful, she can hear us.

BASSIMA I didn't say anything wrong. Rachida's nice, too. Face of an angel. Poor thing, in her condition and suffering with it. I really feel for her. What if she has it in here?

LABIBA Let's hope we're not still here then. She's not far gone.

BASSIMA That's all we need — a baby screaming.

LABIBA Couple of days ago I was woken by a baby crying
— newborn. I don't know why, I had the strangest feeling
I'd been born here and that I was going to die here. Can you
believe I'd forgotten the world outside, as if I'd never known
it. I forgot my husband's face, my daughter's face, what our
house was like...

BASSIMA (*Smokes.*) Stop it. Don't go on like that. Let's get some
fresh air.
(*They go to the yard.* NEFFISSA *takes out a pencil and paper
from her cape and makes notes, then puts them away and
reads the Qur'an.* WARDEN *appears followed by* ZOUBA.)

WARDEN Clean the washroom and get the laundry and be quick
about it in case the Inspector comes. I'll be watching.

ZOUBA OK, Madame Foufou. (*Sees the prisoners busy gardening.*)
My, aren't we working hard! What next?

AZZA Since Alia came things have changed.

ZOUBA I've got something to tell you.
(*She takes* AZZA *into a corner and takes a piece of paper from
her blouse.* NEFFISSA *secretly watches them.*)

ZOUBA It's from your daughter.

AZZA It's not true! How'd you get it?

ZOUBA Keep your voice down. It fell out of the sky, that's how.
Read it quick in the washroom, then burn it. You must burn
it. They might search us. I'd be a gonner. Not you — me.
(AZZA *goes into the washroom.* ZOUBA *collects the laundry.*
AZZA *comes back and hugs* ZOUBA.)

AZZA Thank God, thank God. It's all alright. (*She kisses her.*) How
can I thank you?

ZOUBA A cup of tea?
(AZZA *makes tea and gives* ZOUBA *a cup.*)

AZZA Mmm. The best tea I've ever tasted.

ZOUBA Because you're happy.

AZZA And because I've been moving around and working — I've
got back some energy. I feel I can breathe again.

(ALIA *enters, sweating and goes to the washroom.*)

ALIA   I need to shower.

AZZA   The water's freezing.

ALIA   You go first. Take it slowly.

ZOUBA   Give me your clothes and I'll wash them for you.

ALIA   No. I'm used to washing my own.

ZOUBA   You don't have anyone to do it for you?

ALIA   No.

ZOUBA   I never do the washing at home. I've got a fantastic place
— all mod cons. But in here I'd do anything for a fag. I'm
addicted.

ALIA   Me too.

ZOUBA   Oh yeah? To what? Cigarettes? Drugs or something else?
(*They laugh.*) So what are you addicted to?

ALIA   To life. You can do anything if you want to.

ZOUBA   I can't give up smoking. I hate myself. I smoke to forget.

ALIA   You're a good soul, Zouba.

ZOUBA   Am I? (*She bursts into tears.*)

ALIA   See, you're crying. That's your soul. Don't fight the despair
— feel it.

ZOUBA   Feel what? I want to kill myself but I go on for my
daughter.

ALIA   I'm a mother, too. I've left my son to come here. I'm prepared
to stay and even die here. Why? Everyone says I should
be at home looking after him, everyone from the Inspector
down. What does bringing up children mean? Feeding
them, clothing them, paying their school fees? Everyone's
frightened of speaking out because of their children. And so
it goes on. I'd rather go to prison — that's worth passing on.

ZOUBA   You could die here.

ALIA   I'd die out there if I said nothing.

(AZZA *enters with wet hair.*)

AZZA   That was really good. I took my time. I went right under.
After a while I almost thought it was warm.

ZOUBA   That's why you're in here. Can't tell hot from cold. We
know we've got bodies — we sell them.

AZZA And we sell our opinions. When we refuse to, they send us
here. That's what politics is about.

ZOUBA What?

AZZA About the fact you risk getting beaten for bringing a letter.

ZOUBA The whole world's upside down. Honest people die of
hunger while thieves and liars rule the world. Some of
the girls on the game never have to come in here. Why?
— Money, that's why. And the dealers live like kings.

ALIA It's all a sham out there. In here we know what's what and
I don't feel so uneasy... there's nothing to hide. I could see
people were fed up, getting more and more worried about
the country falling apart but everyone told me: 'You're
wrong, Alia, people are perfectly happy and everyone's
better off.'

AZZA Three or four people are better off while millions go under.
(ETEDAL *enters in a rush, carrying a bucket.*)

ETEDAL I'm going to water the beans. (*She sees* ZOUBA, ALIA *and*
AZZA *drinking tea.*) Tea?

AZZA There's some in the pot. Come and sit with us.

ETEDAL I like you, you know, but... you'll suffer forever.

AZZA I like you Etedal, but you'll end up like the others with no
proper education.

ETEDAL I'll marry a good man.

ZOUBA To take charge of you.

ETEDAL Why not?

ZOUBA If he's honest, he'll be poor. If he goes off you, he'll
remarry. If he goes abroad for work, he might not come back.
If he dies, you'll end up begging.

ETEDAL Stop it. You only think of the worst.

ZOUBA Well, what if it happens? You gonna sit and wait for a
miracle?

SAMIRA That's all we need. Get out! Before you upset the lot.

SALMA What's up?
(ETEDAL *goes and fills the bucket with water.*)

SAMIRA Keep out of it, you, you little spy, I'll throw her out if I
want to.

(*All the prisoners crowd round, hearing the shouts.* ALIA *goes to* SAMIRA.)

ALIA No you won't. It's not your cell. Some of us want her to stay. (ZOUBA *rushes out to the yard,* SALMA, ETEDAL, MADIHA *and* NAGAT *go after her. They call for* ZOUBA *to come back.* AZZA *goes out too.*)

AZZA Come inside Zouba. (ZOUBA *refuses and remains sitting with her head on her knees, crying gently.*)

ALIA (*to* SAMIRA) What's more, you've no right to accuse Salma of being a spy. Who agrees? (*Silence. They all look at each other.*)

BASSIMA We've no proof, but she seems so naive...

ALIA Is that a reason to accuse her? Spies are rarely naive.

NEFFISSA She says she doesn't even know why she's here.

ALIA I don't know why I'm here. I've never joined a political party, never been on a committee — only expressed my opinions.

AZZA I don't know why I'm here.

MADIHA Neither do I.

NAGAT Neither do I.

ETEDAL Me neither.

BASSIMA Well I know why I'm here. Because I've a duty to stand up for human rights.

SAMIRA I'm here because I respect God in a world of atheists. (*They all listen intently.*)

ALIA There are twelve of us in here and half of us have no idea why we're here. So don't accuse Salma without any proof.

SAMIRA Then why did the Inspector take her aside? Whisper to her? She tells him our secrets, that's why.

ALIA He'd hardly do that, if she was really working for him.

AZZA Besides, she's as good as gold.

ETEDAL Yes, she is.

NAGAT It's true.

MADIHA She's good, despite all this.

HADIA I know her; we sleep next to each other. We talk a lot. (HADIA *takes* SALMA's *hand and sits next to her.*)

ALIA Most of us disagree with you, Professor, so you've no right to accuse her...

SAMIRA I know she's a spy and I'm never wrong. God speaks to the pure and the faithful.

ALIA God speaks to us all and you're not being fair to Salma.

SAMIRA I'm never wrong.

HADIA You are, Samira. Where's your proof?

SAMIRA God speaks to me, every day.

HADIA And God tells me every day that she's not a spy.

SAMIRA I know God. I've seen him. You haven't.

HADIA I have, too.

SAMIRA You've never seen him. You Faramawia.

HADIA You're the Khomeiniste.

(*They hear the prison* WARDEN *outside talking to* ZOUBA.)

WARDEN What are you doing here? The Inspector's on his way. Hurry up... clear off.

(ZOUBA *goes.* WARDEN *enters, worried.*)

SABAH The Inspector's coming. I've never seen him like this. He's got men coming and going, bringing things in. We're all afraid of what he'll do.

(WARDEN *looks at* ALIA.)

WARDEN Madame Alia, couldn't you just do what he asks? He'll destroy you.

ALIA My father tried it. My brother tried it. My husband tried it. They tried it at work — and now this little man wants to try it. Let him. I'm not afraid.

SALMA (*Hugs* ALIA.) I'm not afraid.

(ZOUBA *and* ZEINAB *return.*)

ZOUBA The Inspector wants to take Madame Alia.

ZEINAB We won't let him.

WARDEN What are you doing here?

(SABAH *comes back.*)

SABAH (*sings*) The girl gets thrown inside,
While the son-of-a-bitch—

WARDEN Come on, clear off, the lot of you.

ZEINAB He won't touch her. He won't dare.

(ALIA *paces up and down.* SALMA *and* ETEDAL *begin to cry. The* WARDEN *doesn't know what to do. After a moment she exits.*)

WARDEN (*mutters*) Wish he'd drop dead…

HADIA (*Raises her arms.*) May God strike him dead on his way.

SAMIRA May God take him and all men like him.

ETEDAL May God take him.

AZZA Who is he? He's a nobody. We should complain to his boss.

SALMA Yeah. Why don't we?

MADIHA We've nothing to write with.

ETEDAL I've got something.

(*She brings out a pencil and a scrap of paper from under her cape.*)

AZZA I'll write it and we'll all sign it.

SAMIRA I'm not signing anything.

AZZA Why not?

SAMIRA What's the use of complaining about one tyrant to another?

NEFFISSA That's right. They're all the same.

(*There's a din outside. The* WARDEN *returns.*)

WARDEN Get to your places, or else. Where's Neffissa?

(NEFFISSA *gets up immediately. Everyone is surprised.*)

WARDEN Come with me. The Inspector wants to see you.

NEFFISSA I've done nothing. You can't put me in there instead of—

ALIA You can't!

WARDEN Why would he do that? What have you been up to?

ALIA I won't allow you to take her in my place. Take me. I'm ready now.

WARDEN The Inspector's not ready for you. He's got other things on his mind. This place is getting jumpy since you arrived and we're all working overtime.

(*She leads* NEFFISSA *out.*)

HADIA What will they do to her?

SALMA Maybe she's got a visitor.

AZZA It's not allowed.

SALMA Please help her.

HADIA   May God have mercy —
> (*Lights fade. Only the portrait remains illuminated and seems even more menacing. A strong voice calls out: 'No mercy. Never.' The lights fade up on* HADIA *who is on her knees staring at the portrait.*)

HADIA   Who spoke? Was it you?
> (*Lights fade down on* HADIA. *The portrait remains illuminated.*)
> (*Downstage lights fade up on* NEFFISSA *standing in the* INSPECTOR'*s office next to a desk with a telephone. She raises her arms and murmurs something. The* INSPECTOR *arrives, wearing dark glasses and comes up behind* NEFFISSA, *who is busy praying.*)

INSPECTOR   Tell me what you tell God, Neffissa, and take off that veil, since we're alone.
> (NEFFISSA *removes her veil and gives her notes to the* INSPECTOR. *He reads them and puts them in his pocket.*)

INSPECTOR   This individual's wearing me out, Neffissa. What do I do with her?

NEFFISSA   Put her in solitary as soon as possible before things spread.

INSPECTOR   And what if I do? There's nothing in the rules about this. If things change and they're relaxed, then I'll be in trouble for punishing her. I've asked for a transfer back to the police. At least the rules are clear there and you know what you're doing.

NEFFISSA   Put her in solitary and get out. She's stirring things up all over the place and you're in charge.

INSPECTOR   You don't know what's happening outside. We're having a crisis. (*Gestures to the portrait.*) He thinks the world's against him.

NEFFISSA   His agents tell him who these people are, don't they?

INSPECTOR   But if it's true?

NEFFISSA   Just put her away. She's dangerous.

INSPECTOR   You're right.

NEFFISSA   I'm going back.

INSPECTOR What will you tell them?

NEFFISSA I'll say my father died.

INSPECTOR (*laughs*) Again?

NEFFISSA (*Puts on her veil.*) Why not?

>   (*Lights fade on them and come up in the cell.* ALIA *continues to pace up and down while everyone else waits. The* WARDEN *tries to get the prisoners to move away from the door. There is a silence and then we hear the sound of gunfire. Lights out on the portrait. The* WARDEN *opens the door.*)

WARDEN It's over! You're free to go! Free...

>   (ETEDAL, HADIA *and* SALMA *begin to dance around.* RACHIDA *gets up slowly and joins them.* LABIBA *kneels.*)

LABIBA Thank God!

>   (AZZA *and* ALIA *hug each other.*)

AZZA Congratulations.

ALIA To you, too.

>   (NEFFISSA *rushes out. The prisoners outside come in.*)

ALL: We're free... free!

>   (*Lights fade. Silence. Lights up on the portrait — a new picture has replaced the old one. In the cell* ALIA *remains, standing. The doors are locked.*)
>   (SABAH *is behind the door, singing.*)

SABAH (*sings*) Sad times these, bending double those
>   Who once lived well.
>   Here's the girl thrown into prison,
>   And the son-of-a-bitch ruling as he pleases.
>   The pretender's unmasked,
>   A real charmer but his heart's full of smoke.
>   Patience... patience...
>   Everything in its time.
>   (WARDEN *arrives and unlocks the door.*)

WARDEN Back again Sabah? We'll never get rid of you.

SABAH They take her and let her go. They let her go and they take her. They've nothing else to do.

WARDEN Clear off, love. The Inspector's on his way.

>   (WARDEN *goes into the cell and looks around.*)

WARDEN The Inspector's coming, hide all your things. Don't want
any trouble; I've got kids to think of.
(INSPECTOR *enters, wearing dark glasses. It's not the same
person but his gestures and movements resemble the former*
INSPECTOR.)
INSPECTOR Excuse me. I'd like a little more information. (*He
takes out pencil and paper.*) Your name Madame? (ALIA *says
nothing, stares back at him.*) I'm waiting. (ALIA *says nothing.*)
Aren't you tired of this? (ALIA *says nothing.*) Answer me.
Aren't you tired? (ALIA *says nothing.*) I'm tired. I really am.
I'm worn out but it seems you're not. What are you made of?
Tell me? What? Steel?
ALIA Yes.
INSPECTOR What are you?
ALIA Human.
(*The sound of a curlew. Black-out.*)

End

29 Translated by Marion Baraitser and Cheryl Robson, first published in
Plays by Mediterranean Women, Aurora Metro Press, 1994.

PART FOUR

Interviews

25

Feminism in Egypt:
A Conversation with Nawal El Saadawi

NAWAL EL SAADAWI is a striking example of the way the social and economic changes in Egypt in the past thirty years have altered the preoccupations of women involved in the feminist movement, and the social groups from which they come. She differs considerably in class and outlook from the first generation of Egyptian feminists at the beginning of the twentieth century. Early feminists were mostly from the urban upper class, often wives of prominent politicians. They concerned themselves first and foremost with the question of personal freedoms for women and, more generally, with the nationalist issues common also to male political activists. Efforts to help women from less privileged sectors of society emphasized charitable work, not radical change. Focus on personal liberties was understandable in a society which allowed little freedom even to the most economically privileged women. Their methods of seeking change, though, were not likely to have widespread impact in a society where the majority of the population was poor and lived not in cities, but as peasants in Egypt's overcrowded agricultural region around the Nile Delta.

Saadawi comes from a rural background. Through education she has become, by her own definition, 'a middle class or lower middle class' professional woman living in the city. Hers was probably the first generation of women for whom such a transition was at all common – and it was not made without effort and determination. The challenge was less achieving an education than making a career afterwards. The strains of working in a profession with male colleagues who are often unwilling to accept you (something certainly not unknown in Europe and the USA) are considerable. 'You have to be a genius in order to be accepted', she says. 'This is positive because you work very hard and use all your potential, but it is negative in that it causes severe psychological strain and frustration.'

The earlier feminists seldom had paid employment. For women of Saadawi's generation, their rights as working people, as well as the rights of women in the family and in marriage, have come to the fore. Saadawi seems to consider the two as linked and interacting. She is concerned with the continuing power men exercise over women, not just abuses of that power, and constantly links the workings of this patriarchal system to two other factors — class and imperialism. This approach is not universally accepted by feminists in Egypt.

Her concern over the influence of imperialism leads her to the view that imitation of Western behaviour and lifestyles — even those associated with 'liberation' in the West, especially sexual freedoms — is not the way to liberation for Middle Eastern women. She believes women should look for their identity within their own culture. Above all, she has come to the conclusion that women will not achieve anything without organizing politically, on their own initiative.

Writer and doctor

Saadawi's influence has spread well beyond the boundaries of her native Egypt. As a writer, she has been a powerful force in influencing women, particularly in the Middle East, to think about their position in society in new ways. *The Hidden Face of Eve* draws on her experience of many years as a doctor working in Egypt. The book, which highlights a variety of forms of women's oppression in Egypt, is certainly not comfortable reading.

Saadawi rose to the position of Director of Public Health, and frequently made herself unpopular with the authorities for her outspokenness, both in the course of her medical work and in her writings on women's questions. Saadawi now works in Beirut, responsible for the women's programme of the UN Economic Commission for West Asia. Previously, she spent a year in Addis Ababa in charge of the UN women's programme in Africa. She expects to leave the UN soon. She says there is 'too much bureaucracy and discrimination against women', and adds, 'they do not believe very much in creativity. They want people who just obey.'

Although she has now worked in and has experience with a wide range of Third World countries, she very much identifies with Egypt, and with the Egyptian countryside in which she was brought up. She comes from the village of Kafr Tahla, in the Delta, some forty kilometres from Cairo. She returns there three or four times a year. Part of her family still lives there. She says they put no pressure on her to return; she finds they accept her different lifestyle and 'even they are changing their customs and their value system.'

She admits that this sort of relationship between an educated woman and her family in the countryside is not very common, 'but it is happening. As educated women, we are aware that we should have organic links with our roots if we are going to make any changes. We are different from the Egyptian educated woman who is Westernized, who usually ignores where she came from or hides that she came from a village or a poor family. She tries to imitate the west and to belong to the upper class or the middle class. But I think some women in my generation in Egypt now are even proud of their origins.' She feels this is even more the case in her daughters' generation and that 'there is a sort of decolonization wave among young people.'

Despite the persistence of many forms of oppression in the rural areas, vividly described in *The Hidden Face of Eve*, Saadawi sees many economic and social changes here since she went to live in the city. Where women are concerned, there is little documentation or statistics on changes in their position as workers. 'Women working in agriculture as peasants do not receive wages, they work a piece of land for the family. They constitute the majority of women in Egypt and are employed. But, officially speaking, they are not considered part of the labour force. They are invisible in the statistics.'

Rural change

The changes which have occurred in the countryside, affecting men and women, have come about, she thinks, not so much as a result of land reforms or legislation, but primarily because of land shortage. 'Even if land reform gave a small piece of land to the family, the woman works for the husband and family in a patriarchal class system.'

'Maybe the family, instead of having nothing, has a piece of land it works together. You can say the family benefited, but the role of women did not change much. The same laws, the same customs continue — they are not paid and are still dependent on the family and husband economically.'

Changes among rural women were most marked among those who came from landless families. 'Many people, men and women, are landless and are leaving the village, taking work in industry, or educating themselves and their children so that they may have job opportunities.

'That is what happened to my family. My family was poor, and by education we acquired new status and became middle class. In the generation of my father only boys were educated — his sisters and mother were kept in the village because they still had a piece of land. Now my generation is educating both boys and girls to the same level — right up to university.' This is now common practice in Kafr Tahla, she says. In upper Egypt, land scarcity makes education even more of a pressing priority.

Attitudes to family size have also changed. Unless the family has land and needs the labour of a large number of children, the tendency is only to have three or four children, rather than eight to ten. Saadawi herself is one of nine.

Though education has certainly brought social change, particularly for women, Saadawi has little reverence for the value of the education system itself, which she regards as very narrow and not

necessarily a means of enlightenment. 'This is because of the cur-
riculum itself. Whether education is free or paid, it's the same.' She
points out that much of the present system was inherited from the
British and French. There is strong emphasis on memorization and
examinations, to create civil servants — 'not creative people who can
rebel against the system. Education is a tool of oppression also.'

Nonetheless, education and urbanization have meant that many
more women who live in towns and cities now have a university
education — 50 per cent of Egyptian university students are women
— and far larger numbers go out to work. The reason is more often
economic necessity than free choice. 'They need the jobs. Economically speaking, many women cannot afford to stay at home. That's
the big change. Those who stay at home are the upper classes only
— some 5 per cent of the population.'

Going out to work does not necessarily change a woman's home
life dramatically. Unless she has an extraordinarily enlightened
husband, often it means two jobs, housework and waged work,
but Saadawi does consider that the very fact of earning a living
gives the woman more independence. 'At least she can escape and
do something.' Saadawi refers in *The Hidden Face of Eve* to the
helplessness of economically dependent women in the face of divorce
or mistreatment, and she seems to think that the increase in working
opportunities for women may do a good deal to combat this.

Working women under Sadat

At the moment, on the employment front, the situation is increasingly difficult. Saadawi confirms Judith Gran's point (in *MERIP
Report* 58) that

> Sadat's economic policies have de-emphasized the importance
> of Egyptian technicians, professionals, and managers and have
> encouraged instead the proliferation of a whole spectrum of inter-
> mediaries and brokers between foreign capitalists, local capitalists,
> and the Egyptian government and public sector. The opportunities
> open to both men and women of the petit bourgeoisie have de-
> clined, while the economic pressures on them have intensified.

Saadawi adds that these changes have affected working women very badly 'because the public sector was diminished. This had provided a lot of work opportunities for women, and equal pay. Unemployment is increasing, and when you have a society like that with fewer jobs, who takes the jobs? The men, the breadwinners.'

She also points to the gross exploitation of child labour, with examples of girls of six and seven being employed in workshops and factories in appalling conditions. As Director of Public Health she would obviously be aware of cases like this. She maintains that in present conditions laws prohibiting child labour are 'no more than ink on paper. If the system does not maintain the laws on public health, who then can?'

On social and personal relations, particularly relating to marriage, divorce and family law, she feels similarly that legal changes alone will not alter things much. 'It's people's awareness and their political power that really protects them. With regard to marriage law, there was some marginal reform, but not in the essence — for instance, polygamy still exists; a women herself cannot divorce. There is no equal treatment in marriage and divorce law between men and women. But the Egyptian woman is having her equality by her power not by the law'. Among educated women, she maintains, 'reality is in advance of the law.' On the other hand, 'illiterate women are compelled to accept their husbands' domination'.

She contrasts the situation in Egypt with that in Tunisia, 'where there is a very advanced law on marriage and divorce but the reality of the Tunisian women is still backward.' She puts very strong emphasis on the need for women to organize themselves politically, a much stronger emphasis than was evident in *The Hidden Face of Eve*.

Women and the left

The difficulties are considerable — not least on the left, where politically active men are not necessarily willing to accept women as equals. 'Even those [men] who say they are socialist or Marxist or of the left, even if they are convinced mentally, still at a psychological level they have this schizophrenia. That's why a lot of progressive women cannot join left parties or trade unions. They feel themselves as powerless, coming at the back, and not having women's problems as a priority. I think this is everywhere, not just in Egypt, but I also think that the presence of women in large political groups, trade unions and left parties is very important. They have to work to organize themselves and be politically powerful in order to enforce what they want. Without this I don't think they can succeed.'

She admits that such a movement does not yet exist in Egypt, 'but at least women are aware of that. There are now small groups in many Arab countries convinced that they should have their own organizations, as women. These are not social or charity organizations. They are political.' These groups are mostly among professional women like herself. Although working-class women sometimes get involved in trade unions, Saadawi points out that they seldom have the time or energy for political work, whereas professional women usually do have this privilege.

Saadawi stresses the need for women to find an identity of their own — not only separate from men, but also challenging the negative view of their culture and society, which is a legacy of colonialism and imperialism. 'Now, in the West, everything relating to Muslim society is negative. But there are positive things. Studying history is important for this reason. It gives us some confidence in our roots, our civilization, and we build on this. The colonizers tended to alienate us from our past and our history and to impose only the negative part of our history.

'We have discovered that the Arab woman many years ago was very strong. We are restudying our history — of people, not of kings and governors — the history of people's participation in political power and revolution.'

Saadawi has had wide experience with women's situations in other parts of the Arab world. I asked her how she felt Palestinian women were faring in Lebanon, where she is now working. She told me that while the family unit among Palestinians, particularly in the camps, has in some ways been strengthened as a protection, 'most of the women whom I met, especially the young women, looked on the PLO, on the revolution, as their family.' More surprisingly, she cited instances where 'the father doesn't think about his daughter's honour, this traditional concept. Fathers I met even approved of their daughters attending meetings until one in the morning. Inside the camps and outside, people say "we have to do it".'

Saadawi is aware that the success of a nationalist struggle does not automatically lead to liberation for women. 'The Algerian revolution tried to get rid of the French. They needed women at that time. After they succeeded, they returned to the same patriarchal class system of oppressing women. If the Algerian women had been organized and powerful as a group nobody could have taken their rights from them.

'Nasser came in Egypt and said we will have socialism. Then he died and the whole thing collapsed. Who guarantees the rights of people — men, women, workers, poor people? It's those people, not the governments, not the leaders. This is why I am convinced that women should be politically powerful inside a revolution. Otherwise they may be used by the revolution as tools, as cheap labour, cheap fighters — to die first and be liberated last.'

On the revolution in Iran, she was cautiously optimistic. Of the leadership she said, 'I can't say it's very reactionary. Regarding political and economic aspects, it is more or less progressive. If we come to women, I think they are having problems.' She considers the law on the wearing of the chador in government offices as 'negative'. She points, however, to the imbalance in the coverage of this and related questions in the Western media. 'There are many powers working in the Middle East to safeguard oil, and they are using Islam to veil not only women but men too. It's a matter of who benefits from the veil, who benefits from the most negative parts of Islam. Who is blowing up the most reactionary parts of Islam, even in the Iranian revolution? It's the mass media in the West.'

In Iran, however, she considers that the progressive forces which do exist will win on the women's question. 'I think this is a fanaticism which will be conquered.'

๛   First published as 'Feminism in Egypt: A Conversation with Nawal Saadawi', an interview with Sarah Graham-Brown, *MERIP Report* 95, March–April 1981.

26

Fed Up with Limited Thinking

AN INTERVIEW with the Belgian philosopher Lieven De Cauter, initiator of the Brussels Tribunal on the war in Iraq, at which El Saadawi was a witness.

The novel that was stolen

DE CAUTER You live a dangerous life and your troubles never seem to stop.

EL SAADAWI On 28 January 2007, the general prosecutor interrogated me and my daughter, Mona Helmy (who is also a writer and a poet), because a fundamentalist lawyer filed a trial against us, accusing us of apostasy. Mona wrote an article in the weekly *Ros El Yousef* that children should be named after the mother and the father. This would solve the problem of 2 million illegitimate children, because now children who only carry the name of the mother are marked for life as illegitimate, they are second-rate citizens. This proposal was considered apostasy and against Islam, because there is a verse in the Qur'an that says that children should take the name of the father. I was interrogated in the same trial for defaming God, by trying to change the language of the Qur'an: that we should not call God He, but He/She.

DE CAUTER Did you actually write that?

EL SAADAWI Indeed, I had said in an interview that we should 'de-masculinate', 'de-gender' God, because he is a spirit, so he has no gender, no body, and therefore no sexual organs. God should be neutral. So this was the crime of which I was accused, so my head should be chopped off and my legs.

DE CAUTER Your legs?

EL SAADAWI There is a punishment called *El Hiraba*, which is cutting off first the left arm and the right leg, and then the right arm and the left leg. And to finish it they cut off the head. That is what the fundamentalist lawyer asked for as punishment for me.

DE CAUTER And now you face a new trial for your latest book?

EL SAADAWI The play *God Resigns at the Summit Meeting* was published recently in Cairo by Madbouli, along with all my other forty-three books, which the publisher reprinted for the book fair. The state security service went to the publisher and threatened him that if he didn't destroy the entire edition, he would face great danger. I learned from the publisher that he destroyed my play, as the police had ordered him, but the play had already been in the marketplace for a week or so. Some of my friends who read the play before the book fair advised me to leave the country immediately. They told me that nothing like that had ever been published in the history of the Arabic language. A few days ago, then, on 28 February, Al Azhar University, the highest counsel for religious affairs, condemned the play and is filing a second case against me, demanding a severe punishment.

DE CAUTER Why did you write the piece?

EL SAADAWI I actually wrote it during a stay at Duke University in 1996, but, in a sense, the play has been with me all my life. My grandmother taught me that God is justice; that God is not a book. As a child of nine, I wrote a letter to God because I felt discriminated against in relation to my brother, who could get out and play while

I had to stay in and help my mother. When I was thirteen, I wrote 'The Memoirs of the Girl Zouad' about this oppression (it was subsequently published). So, God was interfering with my life from the very beginning, with my dreams, with my emotional life, God was there between the sheets. So I wrote a play where he resigns....

DE CAUTER What is the story?

EL SAADAWI The story is that the prophets, from Ibrahim to Moses to Christ and Muhammad, are gathering in summit meeting, questioning God about the many contradictory commands in his three holy books. Quoting from the holy books, they accuse him of worshipping himself, of a personality cult. Indeed the God of monotheism is a jealous God. The gravest crime in monotheism is to worship another God. God sits on his throne and tries to answer them, and some witnesses come, like Adam and Eve, and a fictional character called Daughter of God. She is the young girl who represents the author. I called her that because we know the son of God only, but now it appears that God has a daughter as well; because, if he has a son he can have a daughter too. And there are other characters from the tradition of Islam, Judaism and Christianity, who are witnesses of the injustice of the Divine Law. Then there is a character called Iblis, the devil. He appears on the scene to tell God that he resigns. He tells God he is tired of corrupting people: 'I am tired of the job that you assigned to me. To whisper in the ears of people so they do evil.' So God is at a loss. He asks his prophets to help him appoint a new devil, for the world cannot be without a devil. Because when there is no devil, nobody needs God. Then comes a funny scene: God looks around and wants to appoint one of his prophets to the role of devil, but they all refuse. The prophets go on interrogating God but they get into quarrels among themselves. God is more and more cornered and he cannot respond any longer; it is all so contradictory what he has said, and at the end of the summit of prophets he resigns. The end goes like this: 'He, the supreme God, in a voice filled with sadness: "I am not longer interested in eternity."' Then the police come in and arrest the author of the play, the daughter of God.

DE CAUTER A beautiful name, because all of us are children of God.

EL SAADAWI Yes, but in the Old Testament God says that he has no daughter, only sons.

DE CAUTER And he is accused of sexism for that.

EL SAADAWI Of course he is accused of sexism, but also for racism, class bias; and for having ordered the killing all those who don't believe. Why do we have fundamentalism? Because in the three holy books there are fundamentalist teachings. One Arab Parisian editor told me this could be a turning point in Arab culture. People will say: before 'God resigned' and after. He hopes it will start a new enlightenment in our countries. It is a political play, because religion is a political ideology. All political regimes from the Roman Empire, all empires, including today's empire, have used religion. Bush, the leader of the American Empire, uses Christian fundamentalism and, in a sense, Islamic fundamentalism and Jewish fundamentalism. All the fundamentalists have a basis in the fundamentalist teachings in the three holy books.

DE CAUTER How does Islamic fundamentalism help the American Empire?

EL SAADAWI Ah, when I give a lecture, I make a link between global politics and local state politics, but I also link it to family politics and sexual politics... I connect George Bush's policy to female genital mutilation and the veiling of women.

DE CAUTER Are you a Freudo-Marxist?

EL SAADAWI No, I don't carry the names of other people. We have to go beyond Freud and Marx. We are beyond Freud and Marx, beyond Foucault and Derrida. We add to Freud; we add to Marx. Religious people stop with their prophet. But philosophers go beyond philosophers. I don't want to be called a Marxist. I follow my own brain. We need a new philosophy for the world ... free thinkers, people who are not afraid of dying. I am fed up with this limited thinking;

and with the state of the world and the revival of the most reactionary political and religious ideas. We still live in a jungle. Look at
the blood every day; look at the blood in Iraq; look at the blood in
Palestine, in Afghanistan. We are forced into famines in Egypt, in
Africa, because of the dictatorship, because of capitalism, because
of the American–Israeli Empire. And they follow their God, they
follow their Bible. The Judeo-Christian fundamentalist coalition is
gaining power in America.

DE CAUTER You were explaining the link between American Empire
and Islamic fundamentalism?

EL SAADAWI Take Reagan and Sadat... Reagan was a neocolonial
mind. He and George Bush, the father, were working with Sadat.
They were using the Islamic right-wing groups to do several things.
They used them to fight against communism and Nasserist groups,
against socialists, feminists, even liberal democrats. Second, they
used them to divide the country with and by religion, for you
know we have Christians in Egypt. They keep dividing people
with religion. That is what the British Empire did: they divided
people by religion. And that is what the American Empire is doing
now in Iraq: they divide the people by religion, Sunni and Shia.
Israel created Hamas, the Islamic fundamentalist group, and now
Hamas is killing the secular Fatah. In Afghanistan the American
Empire encouraged the Taliban and bin Laden himself to fight
communism. Many Egyptian young people were trained by the CIA,
mostly Somalis and Sudanese. They collected unemployed young
men; they trained them and gave them weapons to fight the Soviet
Union. They are called 'the Arab Afghans'. Usually, I say in my
lectures that George Bush and bin Laden are twins. So, now you
see the connection between Islamic fundamentalism and American
Empire.... But after the collapse of the Soviet Union, they don't
need them anymore.

DE CAUTER I am not so sure about that.

EL SAADAWI No, I mean they still need them, but in a different
way. We did a study in Egypt in an association that was closed

down by the government; it was called the Egyptian branch of the Arab Women's Solidity Association. And we found a link between the Americanization of Egypt and the Islamization of Egypt, from Sadat to the present. There are many contradictory phenomena. The veiling of women increased and genital mutilation increased. The teaching, the 'dose' of religion in schools and in the media, increased — in short, what we call the Islamization of Egypt. I can give you statistics: the rate of female genital mutilation increased, 97 per cent of girls are now circumcised. But now I come to Americanization. Under Sadat's 'open door policy' the economy of Egypt started to depend on the so-called free market and global consumerism; women are torn between models — they should be veiled according to religion and they should be half-naked according to consumerism. And, indeed, in the streets you see the girls with veils but they have jeans and naked bellies. You can see the contradiction on the bodies of women.

Their heads are veiled but their belly is naked

DE CAUTER Well, it is an essay in itself. It seems to me that after the collapse of the Soviet Union, the American Empire had a big problem: they had no enemy left. The neoconservatives saw the danger early on (as they state in their book *Present Dangers*): no good politics without a good enemy.

EL SAADAWI It is like God without the Devil! Like Iblis in my play!

DE CAUTER So, you would agree that the Americans use the wave of Islamic fundamentalism and helped create it, as you said, by supporting bin Laden and training these Arab Afghans. Now the enemy has grown up. They have the ideal enemy because now, as the Madrid and London bombings prove, it is not only an enemy without, but also an enemy within. And that is the best enemy.

EL SAADAWI Exactly. Iblis, the Devil or Satan, was the best of all angels. His name was Lucifer, the carrier of light (like Eve was the carrier of knowledge), but he became the enemy. The system of heaven correlates with the system of earth. Sadat was assassinated by the Islamic group he helped create. The bin Laden family was on good terms with the Bush family. You know that the family of Bin laden was evacuated after 9/11? I am very critical — this is important to stress — of some Muslims in the West, who are attacking only Islam, like the Somali woman who made a film on the oppression of women in Islam and who was recently deprived of her Dutch nationality ...

DE CAUTER Ayaan Hirsi Ali...

EL SAADAWI ...she was critical of Islam, as if Islam is the only religion that is against women, the only religion asking for the killing of others or cursing the others of being heretical and so on. I am critical of all monotheistic religions. They are very similar. I have spent twenty years comparing the three holy books. There are some people who exaggerate their criticism of Islam fundamentalism, to gain the approval of the West, of the American Empire, and of Israel.

DE CAUTER Indeed Hirsi Ali is now working for a neoconservative think-tank, the American Enterprise Institute...

EL SAADAWI ... and she is not alone, there are many people who play this game against Islam. And in my play you find that Muhammad is slightly more progressive than other prophets in relation to women, and indeed the Qur'an is more progressive in relation to women and the freedom of the mind than the Torah and the New Testament.

DE CAUTER But Christ defended the adulterous woman and prevented her from being stoned to death?

EL SAADAWI I know, 'he who is without sin can throw the first stone.' But the Virgin Mary shows a fixation on virginity. There is no virginity of man and this produces the double moral and political standard: chastity for women and promiscuity for men, monogamy for women and polygamy for men. It is the basis of patriarchy. Virginity is the cause of veiling, of honour crimes, of the stoning of women, and so on... Virginity is the basis of oppression of women, of double morality; it is the basis of female circumcision, of clitoridectomy. That has been the evil until the present day. And this is in the Old and New Testament.

DE CAUTER But is that not a legacy of patriarchal anthropological structures, which in a sense are transported or adopted by religions, but not invented by them? For instance in Ancient Greece women were also confined to the house...

EL SAADAWI Religions are servants of the political system and not the opposite; the economic and political system is reflected in religions. Greece had a slave system. Aristotle claimed that slavery is natural, for both women and slaves. His biological theory is that the foetus gains life from the spermatozoid of the male, and the ovum is silent; there is no life in the ovum. The woman is only the carrier of the foetus. Aristotle was propagating the inferiority of women. In Ancient Egypt it was totally different: our Goddess Nut, she was the Goddess of the Sky, of intelligence, and her husband Geb was the God of Earth and he was representing the physical, the body. With the end of the matriarchal system and beginning of the patriarchal slave system, everything was reversed. I have another play called *Isis*, about the conquering of Nut and how the male god, her husband, was elevated from the God of Earth, to be the God of the Sky ... Ikhnaton started monotheism. In his vision the universe was governed by one Sky God. This was the new God of Ikhnaton. The Pharaoh was God and monarch. And ever since monarchs have imitated God and God was an imitation of monarchs. That is the essence of all political theology. Moses lived in Egypt, he was an Egyptian (as Freud stated) and he was inspired by Ikhnaton. He quoted Ikhnaton and thus he started monotheism ... and that new God is the God of the play.

DE CAUTER ... which brings us back to your 'trip' to Brussels.

EL SAADAWI I left Egypt, because friends advised me to leave, because of both my trial and my play. I was looking for peace to try and finish a new novel. I was keen not on saving my life, but on saving my new novel. So I crossed the Mediterranean with my very precious manuscript I had worked on for two years. I took a big part of my savings because I didn't know when I would go back — if I can go back.

DE CAUTER You were a sort of refugee?

EL SAADAWI No, no, I was a novelist trying to find a safe place to finish my novel, which I thought would be my last. I carried three precious things in my handbag: my novel, my passport and my money. The manuscript was the most precious to me. And then the train robbery happened. It was as if my life ended.

DE CAUTER What happened exactly?

EL SAADAWI There were three men, one dazzled me with a light and it made a noise, as if something fell on the ground under my seat, so I bent down to look for it, and then the second man took the bag. I jumped up. There were other passengers. People were in the way. I was trying to follow the thieves on the platform. The friend who was with me stayed on the train to protect the luggage. She was afraid to lose me and so she pulled the alarm... I was mad... It was like madness. I was running behind the ghosts.... That is the way I lost my last novel. Now I am staying in Belgium and then I go to the United States because they have given me the International African Literary Award. I am going to receive it on 16 March 2007. And then I will stay in the States as a visiting professor. I am waiting for the decision of the court cases in Egypt; I am following the court via my daughter and husband. If the court condemns me, I cannot go back.

DE CAUTER And now?

EL SAADAWI I am continuing to reconstruct my novel.... It may be my last. I will sign it by the name of my mother, Nawal Zenab El Saadawi. My daughter is signing as Mona Nawal Helmy; men and women are following us. If I can reconstruct my novel, then I can die... Things are getting serious. The people around me are getting worried. I might need all the support and protection I can get. But freedom to me means responsibility. It is the responsibility of the writer to speak up. I say what I believe, even if I have to face death for it.

Brussels, 16 February 2007

27

Conversations with
Nawal El Saadawi

THIS DIALOGUE with Adele Newson-Horst took place over a six-month period, during which El Saadawi candidly answered numerous requests for information and clarification. Her wry wit, passion and sharp intellect reign in the conversations transcribed here.

NEWSON-HORST How would you describe yourself?

EL SAADAWI I am African from Egypt, not from the Middle East. The Middle East is a term used relative to London so that India becomes the Far East. I am not from the Third World. There is one world that is a racist and a capitalist-economy world. I became a feminist when I was a child and started to ask questions... to become aware that women are oppressed and feel discrimination. Feminism is very broad in the Arab world and includes issues of political, historical, cultural, personal, social and religious significance.

But, more than anything else, I am a humanist. I am a humanist and socialist and I am against classism, racism, against all kinds of discrimination, and if God is unjust, I am against him too. I cannot abide injustice. I might have been a minister or dean of a medical college, if I could accommodate injustice.

NEWSON-HORST You also object to cultural relativism and identity politics, right?

EL SAADAWI Yes, there is no pure identity but the human identity. In literature, the brain was created when the character walked out of the chorus and started to speak alone. To insist that there is an essential identity is to promulgate division.

NEWSON-HORST And that is what fundamentalism does. So, describe God to me.

EL SAADAWI God is justice. We know him by our conscience. As children, we become very small in relation to the Creator. That diminishes us. Creativity is related to knowledge. In order to be creative, we must be disobedient, like Eve. If we are afraid of the Creator, we will be reluctant to trust ourselves. If you don't feel you are a genius, you cannot create. To write you need confidence, courage, trust of self, and dissidence.

NEWSON-HORST In the play *God Resigns at the Summit Meeting*, the daughter of God challenges him. Master Radwan claims never to have heard that name and declares her name heresy. Why did you write the play?

EL SAADAWI The play, in fact, lived with me since my childhood when I heard my peasant grandmother say that God is justice and we are him by our minds. Also, my father, who graduated from Al Azhar, said the same thing. He told me that God is justice, freedom, love and beauty. He also said that God is not a book that comes out of the printing machine, that He is not the Qur'an or the Bible or any book.

NEWSON-HORST Has the play ever been produced?

EL SAADAWI *God Resigns at the Summit Meeting* and *Isis* have both been adapted to the theatre in French and will be acted in Brussels during the last week of November 2007. A Moroccan professor at Duke University summarized *God Resigns* in English, and Duke students (from the Religion Department) acted it on the University's stage in 1996. My husband, Dr Sherif Hetata, has just finished the English translation of *God Resigns*.

NEWSON-HORST There is another case pending against you and your daughter...

EL SAADAWI My daughter, Mona Helmy, was trained in environmental studies. She has her Ph.D. and is now a writer and poet. Her first collection of poems, *Traveling into the Impossible,* will appear in November 2007. She started a campaign to name children for both the maternal and paternal line. A suit filed against her is still pending. She writes an essay every Saturday in a famous weekly in Cairo called *Roza El-Youssef.* In one of her articles, written on Mother's Day (21 March 2006), she wrote that children should take the name of the mother and the father, that the name of the mother should have the same honour as the name of the father. This will solve the problem of 2 million illegitimate children living on the streets in Cairo, with no human rights (just because the father refused to give his name to the child). Mona started a very important debate in Egypt and Arab countries about this. I wrote in support of her proposal. Many people supported her, and many were against her. A case was filed against her as an apostate and enemy of Islam, and the general prosecutor in Cairo interrogated her in January 2007, but the verdict has still not been revealed.

NEWSON-HORST In your novel *The Fall of the Imam,* the Great Writer explains: 'Since the day he [the Imam] bestowed the title [of Great Writer] on me and then decorated me with the Medal of Art and Literature, I decided that it would be wrong for me not to be at his side all the time.' And, in *Reading Lolita in Tehran,* Azar Nafisi echoes your sentiment when she asserts, 'Like all other ideologues before them, the Islamic revolutionaries seemed to believe that writers were the guardians of morality. This displaced view of writers, ironically, gave them a sacred place, and at the same time, it paralysed them. The price they had to pay for their new pre-eminence was a kind of aesthetic impotence.' What do you see as the challenges facing literature and art in a religiously pluralistic environment?

EL SAADAWI The challenges facing literature and art are many, especially in countries like ours where the fundamentalist religious political groups have increasing powers. Supported by neocolonial–capitalist–patriarchal global and local authorities, those groups are threatening creative thinking. They veil the mind of men and women all over the world. They are local and global, and they create fear. Many writers have stopped writing because of this fear. Some names appear on the death lists of these religious groups, including my name.

Let me add that writers who serve the authorities like the Great Writer in my novel *The Fall of the Imam* suffer what may be called creative impotence. They lose their genuine voice and become puppets of the regime. Or they stop writing because of the fear most writers have of losing their creativity. They become rich, famous, and receive highly coveted prizes. The minority struggle to keep their creativity. They are then punished as dissidents to different degrees.

NEWSON-HORST According to your daughter, Mona Helmy, on 4 September 2007 the court in Cairo decided to combine the two cases against you. The first calls for the minister of culture to ban all your books, including the most recent play. You are accused on insulting God and the prophets. The second case calls for the minister of the interior to destroy all the books you have written, to prevent you from leaving Egypt, to arrest you the minute you arrive at the airport, and to withdraw your Egyptian nationality. The cases were then slated to be judged on 2 October 2007. They have again been postponed until 4 December. What is your reaction to this?

EL SAADAWI If there is no condemnation, I will go back home. If there is, then I will continue living outside of Egypt. It is a very unpredictable situation because the government is unpredictable. If they strike a deal with the Muslim Brotherhood, they will make me a scapegoat and punish me. I am busy now writing my new novel.

NEWSON-HORST This is the one you call the 'stolen novel', right?

EL SAADAWI It is very difficult. I wrote the novel during the last two years in Cairo. I carried it with me to West Virginia to receive a literary prize. I made other stops along the way. On a train from

Rotterdam to Brussels, my handbag was stolen. It contained my manuscript, my passport and my money. Eventually, the passport was recovered. So I am now writing a new novel. Some of the previous one is present, but I cannot totally reproduce it. It is the stolen novel and I am trying to remember it, but, of course, you can't write it again.

NEWSON-HORST What misconceptions about your work would you like to clear up?

EL SAADAWI I would like to clear up a number of misconceptions about me. First, I do not hate men. In our association, 40 per cent of the members are men who are opposed to the patriarchal capitalist system. The objection to the patriarchal capitalist system rests with its creation of a permanent underclass and inequality.

I am not against God. God (male or female) is a symbol of justice and not a printed book.

I do not write for the West. I write for people everywhere who believe in justice, freedom, love, equality, peace and creativity. But I do write in Arabic; therefore I write mainly for people in our countries.

I am a feminist writer. This is complicated because I do not support women like Condoleezza Rice, who are biologically female but adopt the patriarchal capitalist mindset. I am a humanist writer.

October 2007

🪶 First published as 'Conversations with Nawal El Saadawi', an interview with Adele Newson-Horst, in *World Literature Today* 82(1), 2008. Reprinted by permission.

Bibliography

Books by Nawal El Saadawi

Memoirs of a Woman Doctor, ed. Adele Newson-Horst, trans. Catherine Cobham, City Lights, San Francisco, 1993; first published in Arabic, 1958.

Searching, trans. Shirley Eber, Zed Books, London, 1988; first published in Arabic as *The Absent One*, 1968.

Woman at Point Zero, trans. Sherif Hetata, Zed Books, London, 1982; first published in Arabic, 1973.

God Dies by the Nile, trans. Sherif Hetata, Zed Books, London, 1984; first published in Arabic as *The Death of the Only Man on Earth*, 1976.

The Hidden Face of Eve: Women in the Arab World, trans. Sherif Hetata, Zed Books, London, 1980; first published in Arabic, 1977.

The Circling Song, trans. Marilyn Booth, Zed Books, London, 1986; first published in Arabic, 1978.

She Has No Place in Paradise, trans. Shirley Eber, Methuen, London, 1987; first published in Arabic, 1979.

Death of an Ex-Minister, trans. Shirley Eber, Methuen, London, 1987; first published in Arabic, 1980.

My Travels Around the World, trans. Shirley Eber, Methuen, London, 1991; first published in Arabic, 1982.

Memoirs from the Women's Prison, trans. Marilyn Booth, Women's Press, London, 1986; first published in Arabic, 1983.

Two Women in One, trans. Osman Nusairi and Jana Gough, Saqi Books, London, 1985; first published in Arabic, 1983.

The Well of Life, trans. Sherif Hetata, Lime Tree, London, 1993; first published in Arabic, 1984.

The Fall of the Imam, trans. Sherif Hetata, Methuen, London, 1988; first published in Arabic, 1985.

The Innocence of the Devil, trans. Sherif Hetata, Methuen, London, 1994; first published in Arabic, 1992.

Love in the Kingdom of Oil, trans. Basil Hatim and Malcolm Williams, Saqi Books, London, 2001; first published in Arabic, 1993.

A Daughter of Isis: An Autobiography of Nawal El Saadawi, trans. Sherif Hetata, Zed Books, London, 1999; first published in Arabic, 1995.

Walking Through Fire: The Life of Nawal El Saadawi, trans. Sherif Hetata, Zed Books, London, 2002; first published in Arabic, 1995.

The Dramatic Literature of Nawal El Saadawi, trans. Sherif Hetata (*God Resigns*) and Rihab Bagnole (*Isis*), Saqi Books, London, 2009; first published in Arabic, 1996 (*God Resigns*) and 1966 (*Isis*).

The Nawal El Saadawi Reader, Zed Books, London, 1997.

The Novel, trans. Omnia Amin and Rick London, Interlink Books, Northampton MA, 2009; first published in Arabic, 2004.

Published interviews

Beall, J. (1989) 'Nawal El Saadawi: Interview', *Agenda* 5, pp. 33–9.

Benn, M. (1992) 'Veils East and West: Nawal El Saadawi, the Arab World's Highly Public Dissident Feminist, Talks to Melissa Benn about Her Life as a Lone Voice', *New Statesman & Society* 223(5): 19.

Bhaduri, A. (2006) 'Interview: George Bush and Bin Laden Are Twins', *News Line*, July: 53–9.

Cohen, J. (1995) 'But Have Some Art with You: An Interview with Nawal El Saadawi', *Literature and Medicine* 14(1): 53–9, 60–71.

Desai, G., and D.C. Moore (1993) 'Feminism and an Arab Humanism: An Interview with Nawal El Saadawi and Sherif Hetata', *Sapina Bulletin* 5(1): 28–51.

Farry, M. (1990) 'In Conversation with Nawal El Saadawi', *Spare Rib* 217, October: 22–6.

Farry, M. (1991) 'Time to Come Together: In Conversation with Nawal El Saadawi', *Spare Rib* 221, March: 12–15.

Franke-Ruta, G. (2006) '*Woman at Point Zero*: Nawal El Saadawi, Egypt's Leading Feminist, Hopes to Finish What She Started before She Was Forced to Flee', *American Prospect* 17(6): 15.

Graham-Brown, S. (1981) 'Feminism in Egypt: A Conversation with Nawal Sadawi', *MERIP Reports: Middle East Research and Information Project* 95, March–April: 24–7.

Hitchcock, P., and S. Hetata (1993) 'Living the Struggle: Nawal El Saadawi Talks about Writing and Resistance', *Transition: An International Review* 61: 170–79.

Johnson, A. (1992) 'Speaking at Point Zero: Off Our Backs Talks with Nawal El-Saadawi', *Off Our Backs* 22(3): 1, 6–7.

Joseph, N. (2002) '9/11 From a Different Perspective: Interview with Nawal El Saadawi and Sherif Hetata', *Women in Action* 1: 19–21.

Lerner, G. (1992) 'Nawal el-Saadawi: To Us, Women's Liberation is the Unveiling of the Mind', *Progressive* 56(4): 32–5.

Lightfoot-Klein, H. (1994) 'The Bitter Lot of Women: An Interview with Nawal El Saadawi', *Freedom Review* 25(3): 22–7; edited version in *The Nawal El Saadawi Reader*, Zed Books, London, 1997, pp. 65–9.

Malti-Douglas, F. (1990) 'Reflections of a Feminist', in M. Badran and M. Cooke, eds, *Opening the Gates: A Century of Arab Feminist Writing*, Indiana University Press, Bloomington, pp. 394–404.

Namatalla, A. (2005) 'With a Little Common Sense', *Egypt Today: The Magazine of Egypt* 26(2), February.

Newson-Horst, A.S. (2008) 'Conversations with Nawal El Saadawi', *World Literature Today* 82(1): 55–8.

Race and Class (1980) 'Arab Women and Western Feminism: An Interview with Nawal El Saadawi', *Race and Class* 22(2), July: 175–82.

Sesay, K. (2007) 'Spotlight on Nawal el Saadawi: The Creativity of Nawal; the Dissidence of Saadawi', *SABLE Litmag for New Writing* 11: 6–21.

Shiva (1997) 'Problems Facing a Women's Movement in Islamic Countries: Interview with Nawal El Saadawi', *Avaye Zan (Women's Voice)*, November; *Iran Bulletin*, November 1977.

Shofar, A. (2005) 'Ending Subjugation: Dr Nawal El Saadawi, Activist, Scholar and Egyptian President Candidate', *Black Issues in Higher Education* 22(6), May: 34–6.

Smith, S. (2007) 'Interview with Nawal El Saadawi (Cairo, 29 January 2006)', *Feminist Review* 85(1): 59–69.

Selected criticism

Aghacy, S. (2001) 'Nawal El Saadawi: Better to Pay and Be Free than to Pay and Be Oppressed', *Al-Raida* 18–19(93–94): 2–4.

Ahmed, L. (1989) 'Arab Culture and Writing Women's Bodies', *Feminist Issues* 9(1): 41–55.

Amireh, A. (2000) 'Framing Nawal El Saadawi: Arab Feminism in a Transnational World', *Signs: Journal of Women in Culture and Society* 26(1): 215–49.

Darraj, S.M. (2003) '"We All Want the Same Things Basically"': Feminism in Arab Women's Literature', *Women and Language* 26(1): 79–82.

Darwish, A. (2001) 'A Rebel without a Pause', *Middle East* 314: 11.

Hitchcock, P. (1997) 'The Eye and the Other: The Gaze and the Look in Egyptian Feminist Fiction', in O. Nnaemeka, ed., *The Politics of Mothering*, Routledge, London.

Majaj, L.S., P.W. Sunderman and T. Saliba, eds (2002) *Intersections: Gender, National, and Community in Arab Women's Novels*, Syracuse University Press, Syracuse NY.

Malti-Douglas, F. (1995) *Men, Women, and God(s): Nawal El Saadawi and Arab Feminist Poetics*, University of California Press, Berkeley.

Mehta, B.J. (2007) 'The Works of Nawal El Saadawi', in *Rituals of Memory in Contemporary Arab Women's Writing*, Syracuse University Press, Syracuse NY, pp. 152–87.

Moghissi, H. (2000) '*A Daughter of Isis:* The Autobiography of Nawal El Saadawi', *Women's Studies International Forum* 23(2): 265–6.

Mule, K. (2006) 'Buried Genres, Blended Memories: Engendering Dissidence in Nawal el Saadawi's *Memoirs of a Woman Doctor* and Tsitsi Dangaremba's *Nervous Condition*', *Meridians* 6(2): 93–116.

Royer, D. (2001) *A Critical Study of the Works of Nawal El Saadawi: Egyptian Writer and Activist*, Edwin Mellen Press, New York.

Saiti, R. (1994) 'Paradise, Heaven, and Other Oppressive Spaces: A Critical Examination of the Life and Works of Nawal El Saadawi', *Jounal of Arabic Literature* 25(2), pp. 152–74.

Tarabishi, G. (1988) *Woman Against Her Sex: A Critique of Nawal El Saadawi*, Saqi Books, London.

Toomer, J. (1997) 'Barnard College Celebrates African Women Artists', *New York Amsterdam News* 88(44): 23–5.

Valassopolous, A. (2004) 'Words Written by a Pen Sharp as a Scalpel: Gender and Medical Practice in the Early Fiction of Nawal El Saadawi and Fatmata Conteth', *Research in African Literatures* 35(1): 87–107.

Vinson, P.H. (2009) 'Political History, Personal Memory, and Oral, Matrilineal Narratives in the Works of Nawal El Saadawi and Leila Ahmed', *National Women's Studies Association Journal* 20(1): 78–98.

Zabus, C. (2007) 'On Spurious Genesis: Nawal El Saadawi', in *Between Rites and Rights: Excision in Women's Experiential Tests and Human Contexts*, Stanford University Press, Stanford CA, pp. 96–123.

Index